Hades Gate

A
Guy Bowman
Thriller

D1519780

J.S. Maine

www.JSMaine.com

Every man thinks less of himself for not having been a soldier.
Dr. Samuel Johnson

They are, in fact, men apart – every man an emperor.
Field Marshall Montgomery, on the Parachute Regiment

Utrinque Paratus
Ready for Anything
Motto of the Parachute Regiment

Contents

1

Douma – Syria. March, 2014

Each of a million nerve endings felt pricked with red hot wire. He couldn't breathe when the voltage hit; couldn't think as he seethed in anticipation of the next mind-shredding jolt.

He forced himself to watch as her gaze drifted from his agony back toward the dial. Another jolt. Not enough to finish him off – she was too smart for that – but enough to make his hips buck, his fists bunch in their straps and his spit fizz behind swollen lips.

He guessed he was near the end now, pulse flickering, heart barely shunting blood through his fading brain. Somewhere nearby, voices and laughter were fading, too.

Time to die?

There was only her now, and this pain she brought, hour after hour. He wanted to crawl out of his skin, to peel free from this agony. No training prepared you…

Utrinque Paratus. The motto of his old regiment loomed like an only friend. *Ready for anything.* A way of thinking he wasn't willing to abandon. Not just yet.

Through stinging sweat he saw her steal a glance around the room to the men watching, betting, and jeering his torture. She leaned down, stroking his forehead with a curled finger. She was gentle in these moments, like a lover. She leaned closer, dipping her tongue between his bloodied lips, sighing, her eyes fixed on his.

'Why are you doing this?' he whispered. He heard a catch in her breathing, her lips diverting to flicker over his cheek, arriving at his ear, out of sight of their noisy audience.

'Hush…hush.'

Guy Bowman tugged upwards on the canvas restraints binding his bloodied wrists to the rusted metal frame. No, they wouldn't tear free, just as they hadn't over the last several hours. But if keeping up the struggle, buying time, was all he could do, then he'd do it.

Between her shocks and caresses he heard the distinct crump of NATO M252 mortars bursting nearby, each one landing closer.

A blast outside the door was followed by chaos as the men who'd been watching seized rifles, unsheathed knives, scrabbled over crumbled masonry and raced to an unknown fate.

He looked back to her. They were alone now. She seemed unconcerned by the blast, too immersed in her work. In him.

'So beautiful for me, like this. So beautiful. Be brave a little longer and maybe I will help you.' Again her tongue sought his and delicately lapped the cuts on his lips, savoring the blood. 'Be brave just for me. For Eva.'

And once more her hand drifted down between his bare, sweat-soaked thighs.

2

Liverpool. Truck Stop: Tues 17th Dec, 2020 – 8:05p.m. GMT

The truck stop outside Liverpool Quays was quiet. At around 8p.m. Guy Bowman wouldn't have expected it any other way. But something had disturbed him, making him shift in his truck's sleeping pod. For a few seconds he lay, eyes closed, unmoving. Should he grab some dinner and make a start on the emptying motorway? Or push back into sleep for an hour or two?

A rap on the cab's door made him sit up. He checked the truck's security screen. The night shot, ghosted with sodium flare, showed a couple of police cars, blues flashing, and three cops in hi-vis jackets positioned outside his cab. Off to the right of the screen he caught the rear end of a black SUV. A Range Rover, maybe a Jag. These days they all looked alike.

Guy caught his reflection in the truck's slab of door mirror. A wipe of black hair, serious beard shadow, and dark eyes set in lean, regular features. He didn't linger over the face; he'd been on nodding terms with it for almost thirty-five years.

Keeping the cab locked he cracked the window an inch. 'Is there a problem?'

'We're doing some checks in the area, sir. Been a lot of migrant activity and your vehicle's been selected for inspection.'

Guy glanced again to the unmarked car at the right of his screen. 'Do you have a warrant? Any ID?'

'If you'd just step down from the rig, sir. Bring your license and haulage documents please.'

Guy took another look at the screen. The second cop was standing tight to the cab's passenger door; the third lurking a few feet further back. All three were lean and rangy under their vests. Not the average overfed traffic cop. None of it felt right.

'I need you to step down from the vehicle, sir…'

Guy sucked a long breath, letting his muscles lengthen and release. If he had to fight, the lorry's cramped cab wasn't a great place to limber up. He pressed a button on the dash and the driver's door released. He climbed down.

The first cop scanned the license by torchlight. Neither of the others seemed concerned with getting the truck unlocked or inspecting the cab. Guy waited, barefoot and yawning. The cop looked up. 'Captain Scott's here. He'd like a word with you, sir.'

At the mention of Scott, Guy's stomach tightened. So the charade of a random search was over. The man addressing him was an agent; a field operative from a unit of British Intelligence, not some pie-eater from traffic control.

The agent moved off toward the nearby SUV. Guy followed. He and Scott went back a long way, after all.

Still, unannounced covert appointments with the 'Captain' could only mean bad news.

And Guy wanted none of it.

3

US Embassy. London. 8:15p.m. GMT

Lee Crane let security pull back the Embassy's heavy glass doors. Men liked opening doors for Lee. Her boss, Barbara Gifford, waived her through first.

Outside, a soft London rain greeted the women. Ahead of them embassy limos wrangled into practiced holding patterns. Barbara shivered, easing on delicate kid gloves. Lee wrapped a navy scarf around her neck, tucking it into her coat. 'It was the perfect going-away party, wasn't it?'

'I'm going to miss all this.' Barbara turned to the shiny monolith behind her. 'Had a lot of excitement over the years. Lived through interesting times.' Several floors above them a stars and stripes snapped hard in a quickening wind.

'I'll really miss you. We all will.' Lee reached into her coat pocket for her phone. 'Let me double-check your U.S. number.'

Barbara linked an arm through Lee's. 'Same here, but it's time for fresh blood. The Corps needs smart young women. I know your mother's proud of you and the work you do here.'

'Aw, shucks.'

'It's true. You're all so damn cyber-savvy. Tech's like a

second skin, a sixth sense. I'm a neanderthal by comparison – my guilty little secret.'

'Not so much of a secret, Barbara, truth be told.' Lee began digging in her handbag.

'Guess I haven't been fooling anybody, huh?' Barbara gave Lee's arm an affirming squeeze. She watched as her friend's agitation increased. 'Something wrong?'

'My new phone – I'm sure I had it when I left the party. Dammit, I'll have to go back upstairs.'

'Shall I call security, have them check for you?'

'No, I don't want to make it a big deal. It'll be in the bar, maybe the restroom.'

'Let me call your number, see if anyone picks up.'

As the call connected, Barbara handed Lee her phone.

'It's gone straight to voicemail, like it's switched off. I never do that.' Lee handed back the phone.

Glancing up into cold raindrops Barbara took her final cue. 'Well, happy hunting for that phone and remember, Bill and I will want to see you when you're back in the States. We're there for you, got it?'

'Some of your Florida sunshine would sure feel good right now.'

The women embraced, holding their hug a little longer than usual. Barbara untangled herself and strode toward the waiting Ambassador's Limo.

Lee turned back into the Embassy and began her search. She checked her office. The restroom. The bar. And three cans of trash. Every security guard she asked had the same answer: *No, ma'am, no one's handed in a phone.*

'It's an iPhone, in an Hermès leather case. You'd notice it.' Both were birthday gifts from her wife, Jennifer.

No, ma'am, 'fraid I haven't seen it…

She was going to hate telling Jen it had gone missing.

Lee reemerged into the evening chill, grateful to have an embassy car appear with suave synchronicity. Much later, when she recalled that night, Lee would be aghast at her failure to check the driver's lanyard or security tag. Distracted, she'd settled into the vehicle's warm interior. There'd been no reason not to.

No reason at all.

A hard bend in the car's progress made Lee look up. They were heading west across Hyde Park Corner, bearing into Knightsbridge. Lee leaned toward the intercom screen.

'What route are you taking?'

When her driver made no reply Lee rapped the screen. 'We should be heading along Bayswater.' She rapped harder.

No response.

'Can you hear me?'

Still silence.

She battered the glass with the heel of her hand. 'Where are you taking me?'

Instinctively she reached for her phone – and the first stab of disabling fear sliced through her. She sat upright, heart pounding, mind tumbling. The car slowed, almost stopping at a red. Lee tugged at the door handle; locked.

'For fuck's sake stop!' she screamed. Slipping off a shoe she banged the screen with a steel-tipped heel. A wasted effort; embassy cars were bullet proofed inside and out.

Sickened by her own desperation she threw herself back into the seat.

The car snuck past Harrods before creeping into a dark tree-lined street and pulling over.

Immediately the rear door opened and a bald, smartly-suited, thickset man climbed in. An equally well-dressed blonde woman entered on the opposite side.

'Do as you're told – it'll go easier for you.' The woman produced a thick zip-tie.

'Get the fuck out,' Lee screamed, pushing her toward the sealed door.

The blonde's sharp punch to her jaw spun Lee straight into the man's waiting arms. Blood bloomed over her teeth and lips, her vision tunneling, fading. She felt the edge of the zip-tie dig into her wrists. A sting in her neck. Then . . . nothing.

4

Liverpool. Truck Stop – 8:12p.m. GMT

G uy.'
   'Sir?'
'Jump in.'

Guy sank back into plump leather while the uniform closed the door.

Captain Reggie Scott looked almost unchanged in the three years since Guy had last been face-to-face with him. The night when Guy and the Intelligence Service had parted company for good. The Captain, or "Scott" as close colleagues knew him, sported the same plentiful brown hair in the same chiseled style. The astute brown eyes were undimmed, too. It was a face which physical blows had puffed and scarred, but the tissues had long-since fused into primary planes, rugged angles. His bruiser's hands emerged from what Guy hoped wasn't the same brown raincoat. A whiff of bourbon hung in the confined space of the car. Something else unchanged.

Scott was old-school, but no one had the minerals to ask *how* old. It had always struck Guy that Scott incarnated decency itself – or maybe he'd just been its guardian too long.

'Sorry to drag you out of your pit at this hour, Guy.'

Scott flashed a look over to the truck. 'Are they comfortable? I've heard some have proper bedding, coffee maker, little microwave, is that right?'

'It's okay, sir. I've slept in worse places.' Despite having left the service Guy had no qualms about using the formal term of respect due the man.

'Indeed you have.' Scott let a smile die as quickly as it was born. He pulled a small flat tin from the inside of his coat, tugged out some tobacco and began rolling a cigarette. 'The Bureau needs your help, Guy.'

Guy took a breath, ready to shut the conversation down…

'Of course you're no longer an operative and what I'm about to propose is strictly off-book, but I wouldn't be tapping you tonight without good reason.'

Guy swallowed his barely launched protest, realizing that the elaborate set-up hinted at a major op. His heart rate was picking up.

'The issue here is secrecy, which we both know has become impossible to sustain.' Scott put the roll-up to his lips, leaving it unlit. 'Hence my visit to this grubby little truck-stop in darkest Cheshire.

Guy nodded, taking a look out to the covert agents gathered around his truck. 'Still, it seems a tad theatrical. Especially as we both know I'm neither a viable nor willing agent.'

'Theatrical? You think? I prefer to see it as hiding in plain sight.'

'Searching my truck with a bunch of phony uniforms, blues and twos screaming, is a form of hiding?'

Scott didn't blink. 'Fake news, hacking, cyber crime, all these make it a reasonable tactic. Seems to me if you want privacy these days it's best to point straight at yourself, invite attention. People soon move on. Besides, it's a ploy you use yourself. Retired intelligence officer turned truck driver. Hiding in plain sight, Guy? My people tell me it's proving a success for you.'

'It's no ploy, it's my life now. I'm easy with it, not hiding or dodging any bullets. I'm afraid you and the lads from traffic control had a wasted trip.'

Scott smiled and offered Guy his tobacco tin. Guy declined. Scott lit the paper twig he'd made and pressed a button in the door panel, easing further back into his corner. An extractor fan began whirring somewhere inside the car's heavy coachwork.

'I've been thinking for a while that intelligence security, at least as it's practiced by our existing agencies, is a busted flush. When I commission operations nowadays I use a modus-operandi outside anything MI6 or the CIA would likely sanction. Theirs is a blown world, fatally compromised. When everyone uses the same methods, the same protocols, the same people, it becomes wise to do something else. Play a longer game, as it were.'

'Sir, I no longer have the need or the stomach for the work…'

'Guy, just hear me out. I'm running an operation that confronts an evil so malign it undermines what you and I consider the civilized world.'

Guy felt his stomach tighten again, his mouth drying. This

was exactly the level of field responsibility and engagement he'd tried to escape. But here in the dark cabin of the car, in what he knew would be a Faraday cage of surveillance discretion, the presence of his old Commander was playing him like a Class-A drug.

5

**Schloss Altenberg: Austria – 8:25p.m. GMT
(9:25p.m. Local time.)**

Moonlight pushing through cracked glass made Eva
Ivanka Bazarov open an eye. Through a mist of breath
the bedroom looked bruised. A scrap of net was kicking in
a draft from the window. Outside, Eva knew greasy clouds
would be shrouding frosted firs, a blue-grey mist crawling
over mud and gorse. She checked her watch then drew her
legs up in a fetal curl. She had fifteen more minutes before
the deadline expired.

On the other side of the room her young son dozed
on, his head a bushy dot above a heap of old blankets.
Eva listened to Arkady's breathing, regular but with a
bronchial whistle; a hoarfrost coating the fine bracken
of his lungs.

Swinging her legs out of bed she pulled a burner phone
and a pistol from under her pillow, slipping them into the
thigh pockets of the combat pants she'd slept in. Pulling her
tee-shirt down over her cold stomach she threw a blanket
round her shoulders and pushed her feet into matted
slippers. Eva stifled a phlegmy cough with a cupped hand
and padded over to a thick wooden door. She walked a

corridor past identical doors. The old castle's interior was chilled by the December gloom. Patches of swollen plaster oozed as she passed. She walked oblivious to the slap of her slippers over the flagstones, to whatever dread her steps might cause.

At the third door she crouched and lifted a small gate covering a spy-grill. There she was, the solitary young woman, curled in her cage. Eva took a link of keys from her trouser pocket and slipped into the cell. She unplugged one of two electric bar fires keeping the shivering bundle alive and, without speaking, relocked the cell, carrying the heater to her own room before angling it, at a safe distance, toward her sleeping son. From the mound covering him she took a short black puffa-jacket, replacing it with the blanket from her shoulders. She zipped the jacket over her tee-shirt and headed for the kitchen.

Eva sat at the computer, pulled up the Tor browser and clicked on a .onion link. In a darknet chatroom she found the message she was waiting for:

It can be done. Tonight. Three thousand US Dollars now, two thousand on delivery.

She opened a payment window and sent the currency. Five seconds later she had a confirmation. A remaining balance of four thousand dollars was all the private capital she had left in the world. The concluding payment would halve that. She clicked back into the message window and left a reply: *You're paid. Don't fail. My reach is long.* She scrambled and trashed her history cache then powered the computer down.

Heart pounding, she flicked on a kettle and shook powdered coffee into a mug, picturing the events she'd just set in motion. Crossing her arms she leaned against the battered wooden table which filled the centre of the high, square room. She looked to the gradually lightening fields beyond the schloss, down the hillside across the valley, and over the sweeping spruce-tree terrain – terrain which had always made the place so difficult to approach or attack. She splashed scalding water over the coffee, knowing how bitter the cheap brown powder would taste – as miserable as the constant cold and the stale, unseasoned food. But the wretchedness of it all steadied her. Helped her focus.

That there had ever been a time of plenty, a time of pleasure or purpose, seemed unthinkable now. She lowered her head, rubbing thin red knuckles into her eyes.

'Mamma?' Arkady's cry was weak but not troubled.

'I'm making coffee, shh. I'll come in a minute.'

'Can't you keep him quiet? He's become a real nuisance. I've told you, Eva, he needs to be sent away to be schooled. To become a man. It's past his time.'

Eva felt her soul shrivel as her brother entered the kitchen. It was the second time in recent weeks he'd threatened her with forced separation from her son. She threw an inadvertent glance back to the computer.

Ded Bazarov passed her like a wraith, gliding over the roughly tiled floor, his lean frame perfectly erect, his poise shaming his sister's mounting inner chaos.

He settled on the other side of the room by a high window, his back to her, attention directed to the grey north. Eva could picture her brother's grape-green eyes reflecting the faint starlight. How well she knew that impenetrable gaze, fringed with long soft lashes, that perfectly trimmed goatee framing his delicate jaw, those sensual, almost feminine lips. She took in the wide shoulders, skeletal under a habitual grey cashmere sweater, the diminishing swoop of his torso to an aesthete's waist – whatever else her brother did with his wealth he was no gourmand.

Then there was his silence. So imperious. So implacable.

She knew it could be deadly.

Eva crossed to an ugly nest of drives and cables splayed over the table, some hanging in loops to the floor. A widescreen monitor came to life as she stabbed in an entry code. She linked a flash drive to the computer, uploading the video footage she'd shot that evening.

'Eva.'

She startled, burning her lip on her first sip of coffee.

Her brother spoke without turning, his voice a cool monotone. 'Work on the girl first thing in the morning. She cries all the time. Get close-ups of her tears.'

6

Truck Stop. Liverpool – 8:33p.m. GMT

It's a very bad gig, I'm afraid, and it'll require very good people to sort it out. I don't have many such people anymore, that's why I'm here.'

Guy exhaled, looking back into Scott's waiting gaze.

He'd left Her Majesty's Intelligence Service convinced that doing so was a reinstatement of his autonomy and sanity. He'd opted to take a haulage job; long days and nights alone, miles of anonymous tarmac. The banality of it would melt the shadows in his psyche. And yet…

Guy sensed he'd spent the last few years only half-alive. Though he'd escaped the source of his pain he'd found no way of healing it. But here, with Scott's hint of a mission, he caught flashes of bronze and brass on his tongue as adrenalin swam through his system. A feeling of decisions being made by his deeper self, a self which thousands of hours of trucking had barely silenced, let alone repaired. His spirit was responding while his mind took a back seat. The sensation was as welcome as it was troubling.

Scott chose his moment. 'There's no question of you being formally recruited, Guy. I believe UK and NATO intelligence is completely compromised now, at every level. This operation requires work outside any established protocols; no license, no contract, except the one you'd strike with me.'

'You say the mission confronts some tangible evil?'

'Lives are at stake. Civilian lives. But the roots of the operation run deeper than we yet know. And it's urgent, a matter of days now.'

'If I agree to play how do we proceed?'

'I'd give you a full briefing this morning in a secure location a few miles from here – you can make your decision then. Bear in mind, no one else has the intelligence I'd be sharing with you. It's a dangerous gig with minimal support. I'd drop you like a stone if you were compromised and you couldn't expect any retrieval if things go wrong. The payday is a large one though, reflecting the risks.'

Guy raised a hand. 'I don't need to know the fee, sir. I'll make my decision once I've heard the details.'

'Good.' Scott pulled a hip flask from his coat and took a sip. 'It's Maker's Mark, not the smoothest bourbon in the world, but nicely astringent. I've taken to it.' He offered the flask. Guy declined. 'My lads here will look after your truck. We'll go on alone to the briefing. If you refuse the mission you'll be brought back and your keys returned. You can then get on with your chosen life.'

'My anonymous transcontinental existence?'

'Yes. And I can't say I'd blame you.'

'Okay, let's go. I'll grab my boots from the truck. And I'll take a slug of that bourbon now, sir.'

7

Foundation Offices. London – 8:40p.m. GMT

In the London offices of the Foundation For Recovery From Torture, Dr. Christine Wellesley had worked late. Now she was on her way through reception, fastening buttons on her black trench-coat as she went.

The reception was unmanned but Christine wanted to let security know she was finally leaving for the night. She checked her watch before glancing up at a bank of security screens opposite the reception's main desk. Presumably, Michael was doing his rounds, though he wasn't visible on any of the CCTVs. Instead, a slight figure Christine didn't recognize ghosted one of the basement-view screens. It was too late for any cleaner to still be working, surely?

Christine moved closer to the monitors. She saw a cleaning trolley parked askew, untended in a narrow corridor, and someone in faded overalls with a baseball cap shadowing the eyes and a hygiene mask hiding nose, lips and chin. The cleaner wasn't mopping or polishing, but opening files. Confidential files, detailing intimate accounts from the Foundation's clients.

Christine stared in horror. Yes, the intruder was clearly

rummaging through files legally accessible only to the Foundation's senior consultants and staff.

'Michael?' Christine's call up the lobby stairs went unanswered. She waited a few seconds before parting swing doors into a softly lit, lilac-painted hallway, a color chosen to promote calm among the Foundation's more traumatized clients. 'Michael?' In the loaded silence Christine checked that the thick paneled doors to the street were locked. She pressed a panic button set into an edge of the reception desk. A siren chirped as a ceiling light began to strobe.

Slinging her bag tight to her shoulder Christine headed down to the basement. The information in those vaults was politically explosive, containing accusations against governments and heads of state. As important to Christine, such testimonies had been given in good faith by frightened people who'd been guaranteed anonymity and the Foundation's protection. Christine wasn't going to allow any compromise of her patients' courage.

Clattering down the metal staircase, rounding their final curve, Christine found herself facing a slender, wiry female stuffing papers into a single, bulging folder.

'What the hell do you think you're doing? Those files are private.'

Wide eyes, almost jet black, were the only features visible between the medical mask and pulled-down cap.

'Look, no one here will hurt you. Just put the files down.'

Hesitating, the woman glanced down to the file then ripped a single sheet from it, ramming it inside the bib of her overalls. Christine sensed she wasn't dealing with a professional thief.

'I won't press charges if you just give me the page you've torn out, put down the file and leave.'

Pulling a blade from her hip pocket, the thief began to run hard for the stairs.

Above her, Christine heard Michael start a rapid descent. 'Watch out Michael, she's got a knife…' Christine swung her bag as the raised blade neared, but found herself falling backwards as the intruder shoved her savagely aside. The precious file fluttered like a bird, its sheets fanning out across the floor. Christine kicked out at the woman, tripping her, sending her headlong into the heavy cleaning cart, upsetting a pail and disgorging assorted mops. The woman cursed as she attempted to regain balance. Her knife hand flailing, the blade slashed Christine's ankle. Christine stifled a yell.

As Michael hit the bottom of the stairwell, the intruder spun away, racing along the basement corridor, smashing down the handrail on an emergency exit and leaping up several stairs to the dark, wet streets above.

'Are you ok?' Michael indicated the reddening gash on Christine's ankle, but she was already getting to her feet.

'It's only a scratch. I've got a first-aid kit upstairs in my office. Just help me grab those papers off the wet floor, quickly, before they're completely ruined. Then let's call the police.'

8

Safe House. Toxteth – 9:10p.m. GMT

A twenty-five minute drive brought Guy and Scott to the safe-house. Guy had taken no interest in the route; he figured the less he knew of the journey the better.

'Would you mind… ?' Scott passed an open palm over his face, motioning that Guy should cover his eyes as he left the car. 'It's for your safety.'

'Understood, sir.'

Guy heard footsteps approaching from his left, then a hand on his shoulder. Moving off, he caught whiffs of stale urea, petrol and hot metal. From under his palm he glimpsed slicks of water beaded green by oil droplets, some sticky tire tracks; he was in a multi-storied car park. He let himself be led up concrete steps, along a thickly carpeted corridor, until a heavy door closed somewhere behind him. He was told he could uncover his eyes.

Blinking into focus Guy discovered a soullessly modern, neat apartment. A show flat unblemished and sterile. The dry tang of newly unwrapped furniture along with the gleam of chrome fittings and glass table tops added to the neutrality. Internal doors led to bedrooms with obligatory, over-lit bathrooms. Through long net curtains he glimpsed a neon cityscape, braided by the black strip of a river.

Reggie Scott took a seat at the kitchen table, opening an attaché case and pulling out a laptop and files. Guy crossed to a brushed-steel fridge and filled a glass from its water dispenser as Scott began speaking behind him.

'This location has no prior intelligence history, nor is it traceable to any previous operatives. It was one of several options booked two hours ago through Airbnb for a single night's use by an anonymous business executive arriving from Tennessee. About as 'proofed' a location as it's now possible to get. There's been no time for anyone to infiltrate, bug or monitor it.'

'Airbnb?' Guy smiled as he sipped the bland, chilled water. 'Takes hiding in plain sight to counter intuitive levels. Nice.'

Scott nodded. 'With that knowledge are you willing to continue the briefing, here?'

Taking his glass over to the table Guy cast a further look around the room. A far cry from the breeze-block briefing holes he'd known in Vauxhall Cross or the peeling brickwork of Whitehall's warrens. 'Yes, sir.'

'You recall the phenomenon of "snuff" movies?'

'People being killed on film?'

'Indeed. The victims were usually purported to be abused and raped before being despatched for the evident enjoyment of the viewer. Long before our friends from ISIS caught the bug, of course.

'I thought all that was an urban myth?'

'The snuff phenomenon was no myth. The CIA infiltrated some Columbian gangs who'd begun making the stuff and took them down with extreme prejudice. The Feds were ruthless, and for a while word on the street was clear: *Get caught making this stuff and you're as good as dead yourself.*

'Life before the internet, eh?'

'Which brings me neatly to our purpose, Guy.'

'You're going to tell me that someone out there is making death porn?'

'Seeing people from affluent and influential families being tortured to death is proving, for some, more entertaining and rather more lucrative than the average box-set binge.'

'People are being targeted for use in these movies just because of their social status?'

'Women, mostly. Attractive, young and well-connected. The victims are being slowly, expertly, tortured to death over many hours. The price payable for access to the material is proportionate to the desirability of the victim. We've been tracking this via the darknet, only just managing to keep the details out of the public domain and the responsible press. Just. But if this becomes common knowledge there'll be hysteria. Any recriminations will be on an international scale.'

'How so?'

'These films are being made with the tacit support of various rogue states and those who fund them. The populist desire for retaliation here at home and in the States could be unstoppable. But there's been an urgent development. We'd been making solid progress in determining the identity of some key figures but in the last few weeks they've gone to ground, the chatter's dried up. We had two agents engaged who we now believe have been caught, probably executed. Our targets are now working below the darknet itself.'

Guy considered the statement. 'Below the darknet? I didn't know there was anything lower.'

'Quite. Our targets appear to be operating at a whole new level of deception and encryption; an elite niche of cyberspace we're calling Hades' Gate.'

'And the victims are all female?'

'Yes, mostly chosen for their US or UK connections, then abducted to order, sometimes from straight off the street. There are two recently missing women who we believe may be hostages.' Scott spread a series of headshots over the table. 'A nineteen year old college student, Stacey Drayton-Carter, studying at the London School of Economics. A twenty-three year old female journalist, Tyler Warren, working for Fox news in London. The LSE student is on heart medication. Her parents advise she'll deteriorate rapidly unless she gets her meds, which obviously isn't happening.'

Guy ran a hand over his drying mouth.

'We know of one target who appears to be at the heart of this, making millions. We want him, and we want his hostages freed. But he might be just the tip of the iceberg. If we move in covertly we stand a chance of exposing the whole set-up. The only way this will work is to send in one choice pair of boots on the ground.'

'Expendable boots?' Scott's silence told Guy all he needed to know. 'And you have confirming footage, sir?'

Scott nodded. 'The video is a little out of date but we recognize some of the players.'

'Why don't we have anything more recent?'

'It's beyond classified. You're going to need a strong stomach'

Guy drained his glass. 'You better show me what you have.'

9

Foundation Offices. London – 9:25p.m.

Upstairs in her office Christine Wellesley had pulled down a first aid box and wrapped a wide bandaid around her ankle. Then she'd made spread pages from the strewn file over the carpet, arranging them in numbered order. Only one sheet appeared to be missing; the one Christine had seen the thief stuff into her overalls. Studying the damp papers she realized with a jolt that these were her own notes for a patient named Guy Bowman and the missing page would contain all of his contact details.

Most of her patients at the Freedom From Torture Foundation were clinical referrals, men and women who had experienced unspeakable torments. Doctors like Christine worked to liberate them from their darkest memories, asking them in the process to relive moments of utter despair. It wasn't easy remaining a calm but involved presence when treating the effects of unfathomable depravity, of suffering no human should ever have to endure.

Christine found that her work for the Foundation brought meaning to her life. It had become her calling.

Guy Bowman had appeared at the Clinic one January morning three years ago. No appointment. No referral.

The receptionist on duty sensed his urgency and alerted Christine.

Seeing Guy's name on the damaged file brought to life again all he was, and all he'd become to her.

FFRT DOSSIER: INITIAL INTERVIEW CASE NOTES. <u>CLIENT 4538. M/31.</u>

JAN 08 2016.

Client (GB) has self-referred today. Calm but insistent on seeing DR immediately, evidencing a mounting, possibly intolerable, degree of distress. No specific trauma reported. GB appears to be in some degree of denial.

Despite his insistence on seeing someone he spent most of the session in silence, as if needing a place to simply be, to exist. Client frequently placed his head in his hands or sighed repeatedly. Eyes closed for extended periods.

Jan 15, 2016

GB appeared calm and initially communicative; chit-chat, weather, travel, etc. Then fell into silence. Asked him 'what can I do to help you

```
today?', GB's eyes closed and he
leaned forward with head in hands,
as before. Appeared to be recalling
trauma without wishing to reveal or
detail it. Session completed with
client expressing thanks.
```

Christine leaned back, feeling the fresh cut to her ankle nip under the bandage. Her fingers strayed to the back of her neck, flicking hair from her suddenly damp nape. For the first time that night she wanted fresh air.

And she knew why.

10

Cargo Hold: Mid-flight. 9:40p.m GMT

Lee came to on her back, heart pounding, drenched in sweat. She was tightly gagged with tape, she could taste and smell its plastic backing. Inches above her face was a board with a series of crudely drilled holes. A trickle of saliva caught in her parched throat; she tried to cough but began to choke. She raised her head as far as the board above her allowed and glanced down the length of her body. Pinprick light enabled her to see that her arms were kept cuffed to the inside edges of what she realized was a long crate, or coffin. She was still fully dressed, her ankles and knees tightly bound with more tape.

A tear of hot salt dripped down her cheek into her ear. She sucked a breath through her nose but it felt shallow, insubstantial. Her throat and sinus were filling with mucous and the sealed gag allowed no air past her lips. Panicking, she turned her face aside; more liquid eased into her throat. She'd have to concentrate if she was going to slow her racing heart, if she was going to survive.

She closed her eyes against the dancing light but the darkness only brought deeper isolation. She preferred to see the crate around her with its whiffs of cheap pine and pungent glue. It was a boundary she could negotiate. Instinctively she began to pull at the wrist-cuffs screwed to the crate. The strain brought cutting pain, but it felt better than passivity, than immobility.

This pain was her choice.

From within it she could believe she was fighting back.

11

Safe House. Toxteth – 9:42p.m. GMT

Scott rolled a cigarette then took out a hip-flask. Guy shook his head.

'The footage you're about to see ran on the darknet about eighteen months ago. The idea was that you'd pay to stream the broadcast live, watch the execution unfolding in real time. But the process has become more sophisticated. Certain individuals get gilt-edged invites to attend the actual event. All at a price, naturally. These are held twice a year as far as we can tell. The executions are the climax to a weekend long house-party, a sadomasochistic rite pumped to the max. Always a different location, different city, Kiev, Tunis, Madrid, for example. Once it's over those who've attended climb into their Ferrari's and Bentley's and disappear into the night, until the next time…'

Guy nodded. 'You said executions?'

'I'm afraid so, yes. Each of these events builds towards the filmed deaths of the hostages.'

'What do we know about the people who attend these gigs?'

'An especially perverse jet set. Anyone from minor members of the House of Saud to bored Russian oligarchs, sporting barons, international playboys and their assorted partners. We think it costs around half a million US dollars to attend one of these weekends.'

'And how much to link to the live stream?'

'For this particular film it was one hundred and fifty-thousand US dollars.'

'Many takers?'

'Intelligence chat estimates that, worldwide, over five hundred punters sign up for the live event.'

'So someone's making a killing, huh?'

'That joke isn't funny anymore.' Scott drew hard on his new cigarette. 'We have a single remaining lead. Our last agent had a GPS position in Austria, but his final message was aborted mid-sentence. We assume he was captured. That was last week.'

'So you think the next event will occur somewhere in Austria?'

'Given the disappearance of our agent, we think that's looking likely. We think the next event will occur in six days' time. The selected hostages may already be confined at the location.'

'So you need verification of the location and the presence of hostages? Then you'll send in an exfil team?'

Scott paused. 'If a rescue op remains the only way through, then yes. But I'm loath to involve any government or military authorities. Even putting a team on standby is risky. If you can verify the location and provide details of the layout and security, then we have a chance to raid it and close down the whole operation. With your intelligence

I can send in a small, closely vetted team at ultra-short notice.

'It's come to something when you need to have your black ops boys vetted.'

Scott didn't flinch. 'I'm not prepared to take any chances. I want these bastards brought in, I want everyone who buys or otherwise supports their material, and I want the hostages freed. Ideally we can seize their equipment and software and compromise whatever darknet protocols they've created, destroying the whole operation, root and branch.'

'Let me get this straight. You can't monitor the operation currently because they're using an internet protocol we don't have? This Hades' Gate configuration?'

'Exactly. This operation, at least as far as you're concerned, requires investigation at the target location. It's isolated and dangerous work. We don't know if they interrogated the other agent, or even if he's being held alive. Since he knew nothing about my department's involvement he can't have told them much. I believe you'd be going in with a clean slate.'

'Not quite, sir. At the very least they now know they're being tracked, if only by single operatives. That'll make them edgy.'

'It's not a straightforward situation, I know. But you don't figure on any lists of active intelligence agents, Guy, though you do have the field craft and evasion expertise to survive out there. You see now why I've come to you in the manner I have and my decision to go in with basic, non-tech soldiering. They'll never be anticipating your involvement.'

Guy said nothing.

'Shall I go on?'

Guy's nod in return was barely perceptible. He was already streaming escape and evasion techniques, the possibility of capture, and its consequences…

Scott leaned down and stabbed the laptop with a single finger before turning away to the window. He'd clearly had his fill of whatever this particular home movie contained.

Guy turned to the screen. A title appeared against a black background.

The Marsyas Project

After a few seconds the text dissolved to a brick-built cellar with two bare bulbs. The dim footage had no sound. In the centre of the cellar strapped to two wooden frames were a man and a woman. The figures were naked and inverted, heads inches from the floor. Around them stood a group of six men in combat fatigues and balaclavas. Another couple were in Taliban-style mufti, faces wrapped. All were armed, most were smoking. The bound, inverted figures seemed inert, frozen with terror. A figure stepped forward and jabbed them with a rifle barrel, making each captive flinch and buck in their bonds. Still clearly both alive.

Now one of their tormentors stepped forward and began weaving a long curved knife over and around the naked figures, the blade tracing lines and spirals millimeters above the vulnerable, twitching flesh. The knifeman, grinning with evident anticipation, then brought the blade up close to the camera, waiting for the swimming lens to focus on its serrated edge, before the screen faded, suitably enough, to black.

A new graphic showed a digital clock counting down, a date, *12/02/2016,* then a price; *$120,000.*

'Fuck her.'

The words were spoken in an eastern European accent. The voice was female. A voice he knew.

Guy's mouth went bone dry.

The same woman's voice had featured in his dreams almost every night for the last six years. A voice he'd driven thousands of midnight miles to try to silence.

Guy forced himself to refocus. The instruction had been given to a naked man. An equally naked, shivering female was on all fours in front of the noncompliant male.

'Fuck her, hard.'

But the man remained motionless, his head bowed. Even in the cellar's low wattage Guy could see his body was bruised, his thigh and shoulder glowed purple and black. His right eye socket was badly beaten, though the wound appeared congealed, the dried blood brown and crusted.

'No? You won't take the American bitch?'

A woman in black combat boots stepped from behind the lens to whisper in the naked man's ear. As she spoke she raised the tip of a baton to her captive's backside. The man jerked forward, stifling a cry between gritted teeth. She'd zapped him with a cattle prod.

As Guy watched her saunter back toward the camera, he felt as though he were falling, his heart pounding as his hands shot down to brace himself in his chair. Scott spoke from somewhere… *'very unpleasant I know; would you rather not go on?…Guy?'*

He realized he'd blacked out; a millisecond, the blink of an eye. Had Scott seen? Guy couldn't tell Scott how he knew the woman in the film.

Eva.

He'd been at her mercy once, and could never be again.

He swallowed, pulling his gaze back to the screen.

'OK, no problem for you not to fuck. But it's a big problem for the bitch.

She gave a new instruction, the tone throw-away. A moment later a lean, muscled man in a dark t-shirt stepped into the frame, his face covered with inked designs. Russian prison tattoos, Guy noted. The shot was too blurred for Guy to be sure. The man brought the crying female up from all fours into a kneeling position, and in a single movement punched her mouth, sending her backwards and sideways to the floor. His bunched fist looked larger than her face. It was clear he'd used a fraction of the force available to him.

Guy recoiled at the sudden blow to the young woman. Tattoo man brought her to her knees again, a steady stream of blood now painting her chin, dripping onto small pale breasts.

Now you gonna fuck the bitch? Eva's laughter from behind the safety of her camera made Guy burn. His heart was pounding at what he saw.

Can't fuck? Too bad.

Off-camera Eva must have given another order as the victim got a stinging slap to the same side of her face, spinning her onto her stomach. Tattoo was warming to his work and brought her swiftly back to a kneeling position. Fresh blood appeared from her nose as well as her swelling lips. He raised his hand to repeat the blow, but the naked man now spoke. *Okay. Enough! Okay.*

Good! I like to see you understanding my ways and that you want to make me happy! You are a clever soldier. But you can't fuck with that shriveled dick. The American bitch will be suffering until you are hard enough – you choose how long.

The young woman was slapped again, this time across her temple and ear. The sound of the blow was sharp, sickening. Guy heard himself gasp in rage.

Wait, leave her. I'll do it. The naked man reached down and grasped his cock. A peal of laughter from the mistress of the occasion rang out as he began frantically pumping the flaccid shaft, readying himself to enter the brutalized captive now weeping at his feet.

Guy closed the laptop and shoved his seat back from the table.

'It's not for me, sir. I'm afraid you've been wasting your time.'

Scott turned back from the netted windows. 'I see. You're quite sure? As I mentioned, the proposed fee reflects the risks. You'd never have to work again.' The Captain waited. But Guy now appeared strangely remote, almost implacable. If he'd been revolted he was giving nothing away. 'You're aware, Guy, that any current hostages are in the same plight?'

'I'm afraid I can't help them, or you, sir. I doubt if anyone can.' Guy saw what might have been anger, might have been sorrow, darken Scott's eyes.

'I know I've given you a lot to consider, and that it's difficult work. I'm going to give you a code. If you change your mind over the next few hours use it to contact me; I'll be waiting. Otherwise it will expire at 9a.m. tomorrow. I'll need till then to get flight clearances and equipment options sorted at the base. Contact the Bureau with *ea980p.'*

'You can trash the code now, sir. I won't be using it.'

Scott gave a slight shrug, his usually alert demeanor betraying more than a hint of weariness.

'Let's get you back to your truck, Mr Bowman. I'm sorry to have troubled you tonight.'

12

Foundation Offices: 9:53p.m. GMT

Waiting for the police, Christine flipped through the notes she'd written two years earlier. She recalled the assault on her senses, begun when she'd opened the door of her office to an imposing presence. Guy Bowman.

Guy's discharge papers from the Parachute Regiment detailed gunshot injuries and subsequent medical treatment. There was no reference to any post-traumatic stress, nor of his having been subjected to brutality or interrogation. On accessing his medical history Christine discovered an adolescence of rude health; a collarbone broken playing rugby at fourteen was the only significant shade in his early years.

He'd appeared to her an attractive, together male of thirty-one, dressed in jeans and a pressed tee-shirt, a nicely cut jacket of softest leather, and what she'd later learn was a signature pair of well-polished Chelsea boots.

His dark hair was short, neat through the sides, longer on top, falling from a natural parting to fringe the right brow and temple. Though clean shaven, his beard shadow was heavy. Christine's recall of her instant attraction to the man annoyed her. She was surrounded by eminent colleagues, distinguished men of all ages, and spent a great deal of time tactfully rejecting dinners and country house weekends. She'd never responded to any of them as she did to Guy.

She'd liked his lean, muscled body, still hardened by his elite military past.

But perhaps it was really Guy's unaffected intelligence, the absence of any pretension, that drew her. Or was it his reserve, that noble woundedness she found herself wanting to know, to explore...

Jan 22 2016.

The patient responded to questioning though I've chosen not to push. Today GB seemed more prepared to speak of his trauma. He reported recurring nightmares, self-imposed social isolation, self-directed anger. GB's trauma relates to a period of capture and interrogation during active service in the middle east but he was reticent to reveal details. (There is no mention of capture in his army medical file.) He was willing to speak only in generalities about his experience, although a rising tide of emotion was evident, but suppressed. Telling me this much, even after three weeks,

```
seemed to distress him despite his
desire to confront his past.
   He seemed agitated toward the end
of the session (finger-tapping;
sudden silences, resistance to
verbal prompts). Client regained
composure before leaving.
```

A pencilled squiggle in the margin of her notes shocked Christine. Embedded alongside her clinical observations was a tiny emoji of her own face with the eyes enlarged. A secret cypher, like something from a schoolgirl's diary. Christine rooted in a drawer for an eraser. Finding one, she began to rub away at the unprofessional, unsettling avatar she'd drawn.

Glancing again at the date of the entry she realized it was less than two weeks after composing that distracted doodle that she'd first slept with him.

Christine backtracked to one of the earliest pages in Guy's file. An entry from a personal journal she'd asked him to keep.

```
'I remember seeing some war footage
of a girl, a young teenager. I
now know it's famous footage…from
Vietnam. The girl's running toward
the camera with some other kids on
a rain-streaked road, she's naked.
She's been burned by Napalm. She's
crying, reaching out for help.
I remember thinking she was so
```

young and her life was hanging
by a thread. I could feel her
terror, she was a civilian and it
devastated me to see anyone paying
this price for someone else's
war. The image stayed with me for
months, I couldn't stop thinking
about it. I learned her name, Kim
Thi. She became known worldwide
as the Napalm girl. I guess that
photo was a catalyst for lots of
people, it certainly was for me. I
felt an anger I'd never experienced
before. I was determined to somehow
avenge the girl's suffering. Then
a couple of years later I saw
some newsreel of NATO troops, UN
Peacekeepers, white helmets and
all, somewhere in the Congo. They
were there to protect civilians
from the warlords and self-styled
generals who were stripping the
country, and stripping them. Rape,
torture, slavery, genocide. I
heard the reporter use the phrase
'peacekeeping troops'. I watched
the news again that night, I stayed
in just to catch that report. I
remember seeing these troops, those
distinctive helmets, handing out
food and water. They had armored
cars, flak jackets, full combat

```
kit, so it was clear that they
could fight and defend themselves
if they needed to. But they were
there to keep the peace, to protect
civilians against violence and
intimidation. That's when I knew. I
wanted to be part of something like
that, to be one of them. Not long
afterwards, during my 'A' levels,
I began to think about a life in
the army. That's when I made my
first contact with the recruitment
boards.'
```

The intercom on Christine's desk buzzed. 'Hello doctor, the police are here.'

'Thank you, Michael. Send them up.'

As she gathered the crisp pages into a pile she found herself reflecting on how Guy had disappeared from her world as quickly as he'd entered it – and even more unexpectedly.

Christine had never had sex with a patient. The thought of compromising fifteen years of medical training along with seven years of clinical practice, risking her livelihood and reputation in the process, was appalling.

And then she met Guy Bowman.

Christine checked the bandage on her throbbing ankle and reflected on what she'd read. Was it one of life's ironies that a man initially intent on keeping the peace, on rescuing those who needed help, should himself have been the victim of brutal mistreatment. Or did Guy's seemingly altruistic desire to be in a combat zone have other, less noble motives?

Her patients had sometimes found themselves face-to-face with their worst nightmares. Such confrontation might be the making of them; more frequently it broke them. All she could do then was help them sift among the shattered pieces of their lives, reshaping them into something meaningful.

A knock on her office door broke her reverie.

13

Truck Stop: Liverpool – 10:36p.m. GMT

Back in his truck Guy's world felt preternaturally silent. He put his booted feet up on the wide dashboard.

Mastering fear had been central to his training as a Para; drilled into every action. Every day in the grueling months of the regiment's 'P Company' had meant developing a new relationship with fear; confronting it was an opportunity, a trial of self-knowledge. Fear-of-fear was the real enemy. Once you'd checked out of that head space, life changed.

The squabble of nearby magpies wings beating past the cab's open window broke into his thoughts. The morning would bring nothing but terror and despair for anyone now caught up in a mess like the one Scott's footage had exposed.

He thought again of his own fear. If his training had taught him anything it was that fear never diminished if you ignored or bluffed it. He remembered the 'milling' of his P-company days; being in the ring with an opponent of roughly equivalent size and weight, having to fight with 'controlled aggression' for an unbroken minute at a time. Controlled aggression meant you had to abide by key rules: no kicking, no biting. But any sign of weakness, any unreadiness to dominate the fight would count terminally against you. Your fellow troops and your depot instructors would watch you fight; they'd know, as all men know, who was bluffing and who was truly up for the moment.

There'd been nothing in his training Guy had feared more. It wasn't the combat, the potential wounding, but the dread that his fight would be poor, unmanly. That it would not be worthy of him or his chosen regiment.

Milling showed whether you were ready to go in hand-to-hand, bayonets, knives, with as many opponents as your mission threw at you. *Utrinque Paratus.*

Nothing in Guy's childhood had prepared him for this. From adolescence he'd been an imposing and vigorous kid, ensuring few people crossed him deliberately, but he'd never known the rough and tumble of sibling fights, nor the brawling of Saturday night pubs in some derelict town out in the sticks. Many of the guys in his regiment came from tough, even brutalizing homes. They'd been using their fists pretty much all their lives. But being a Para meant more than being an unthinking brawler or killing machine; many of his comrades were bright, thoughtful, skilled in containing conflict. This had made him all the more determined to become the kind of man the regiment prided itself on producing.

In the run up to his enlistment Guy had joined a boxing gym. For eight weeks he knuckled down, sparring and training with the gym's most practiced fighters. He developed a life-affirming sense of purpose whenever the gloves went on. He learned to blink away the shock of sudden pain, to recover focus when his head was spinning from a punch.

He also learned to punch another human being with the sole intent of causing maximum damage, ensuring they couldn't get up again.

Still, on the morning of his milling bout he was saturated with fear and adrenalin; he hadn't slept, his world shrank to encompass only the form and face of Johnny 'Spider' Macduff. Johnny got his moniker from his ability to shin up a rope and leap fearlessly around the highest planking of the Para's notorious 40 foot high 'trainasium' scaffold.

Their 'mill' happened about nine weeks into the 22 week P-company assessments, when Guy and Spider were both at a new peak of physical prowess.

Guy broke Spider's nose and jaw within ten-seconds, leaving him reeling. A second flurry of body shots fractured two of Spider's ribs. The depot staff pulled Guy from the ring and called off the mill. Spider left Paratroop selection for good later the same morning.

Guy had discovered what would become his chief weapon, a key to self-knowledge: The greater the pressure, the more ruthless he could be.

14

Corpus Christi Campus. Cambridge – 11:55p.m. GMT

In her campus office Diamond Orinitri sipped freshly brewed Lapsang while flipping the pages of a classified file delivered by courier earlier that evening.

She was reading a draft thesis; *Stability Issues of Quantum Encoding in Bioengineered Materials.* As she studied the paper's functions and equations Diamond found her stomach knotting, even while the scientist in her thrilled at what she was seeing.

At 12:02a.m. she made a call. Scott picked up.

'I've got some rough notes and a take on what I think the target is doing. But the material is a few years old, things may have developed significantly from what I'm reading here.'

Scott's voice was warmly affirming in response. 'Sounds intriguing. We'll collect you at 12.30. The agreed place.'

At the deserted cab stand outside Cambridge station Diamond watched a bland Peugeot minivan pull up, all taxi-badging and smoked windows. Its side-door slid back and Diamond gripped an outstretched hand before stepping inside. The man she knew as Scott indicated a bench seat as the door behind her shut. Settling in, Diamond found herself in a windowless cube. A single roof-light burned hard yellow. She felt the vehicle slip into gear before pulling away, out through the town and into the leafy Cambridge carriageways.

'We can talk freely, the car's EMP shielded, no signals in, none out.'

Diamond pulled her notes from an attaché case, fanning some pages over her knees. 'Ded Bazarov never completed his thesis, he left the institute prematurely. But I've cross-checked some redacted links and he'd been on the DARPA radar. It's likely they were grooming him.'

'You think he got cold feet? Bailed?'

'I don't think Bazarov gets cold feet. No. It's more likely he knew he was onto something and wanted to develop it independently. But the DARPA folk wanted him on board. He had some interesting ideas.'

'Like what, exactly?'

'This particular paper is about the potential of bio-tech when linked to a quantum computer. But by this point he'd also been working on advanced AI in general.'

Scott eased back into his seat and meshed his fingers. 'I'm all ears, but be gentle with me, Ms Orinitri.' His sudden clumsiness made him wince. The young woman's loveliness had drawn words rich with an unintended, possibly compromising inference. To his relief Diamond flashed a smile, unleashing a dimple in her flawless profile. Scott tried to ignore the glimpse of perfectly aligned, almost miniature teeth. He thought of his own, soused with years of ale and scotch, and shut his smile down fast.

'These two fields – quantum computing and bio-tech – are developing at a rate which leaves even their researchers floundering. The details are fiendish but the essential principles aren't difficult to grasp.'

Scott nodded, opting not to offer any further unintended sexist lapses. He wondered how Diamond's admirers coped when confronted with her mix of beauty and genius – those sapphire eyes burning from within that flawless mocha skin. Diamond indeed... *Did a woman like this even indulge admirers? Did anyone even use the term?* He decided a lighter tone might help. 'I managed to unbox a new iPhone last week so perhaps there's hope?' He made a point of not grinning.

'Well, hope springs eternal.' Her smile appeared to indulge him.

'Returning to my point, Commander, Bazarov's work in quantum computing could move the field along at lightning speed and with unpredictable ends.'

'But I understood that quantum computing was largely theoretical?'

'That's only partly true. No large-scale programmable Q-computers actually exist. Yet. But Bazarov looks to have been on the cusp of making such power accessible.'

Scott sighed. 'I've been in the intelligence game for a lifetime and I've learned never to underestimate the human lust for power. Sadly, it still surprises me.'

'Really? That surprises you?' Diamond leaned slightly

away as she searched Scott's face. 'Jobs, Zuckerberg, Gates, Musk, Branson, Dyson? Pioneers like these always push toward a breakthrough point. Perhaps Bazarov is merely seeking his place at the top table.'

'That's a very benign assessment, Ms Orinitri, given that our target is committing heinous crimes in order to buy his place-setting.' Scott ran a hand over his face. 'You mentioned Bazarov's notes pointing to some kind of breakthrough. What did you mean?'

'A quantum computer could instantly overwrite or crack any cryptographic code. Nothing in either the public or security sector would be safe, everything would be hackable. Power stations, satellites, banking and state intelligence agencies would all be liable to manipulation or destruction.'

Scott gazed back at her. 'I've heard this before, of course. It's an ultimate armageddon scenario.'

Diamond nodded, but didn't pause. 'A quantum computer would utilize qubits, the way a digital computer uses bytes. Current research is hampered by the fact that qubits are ghosts. They hold their quantum state for tiny fractions of a second. The more qubits that get linked together, the more unstable their interactions become. Google, Microsoft, Intel and the JEDI initiative are all researching and developing hard-tech Q-platforms to gain such stability, but the error rates are high. Q-systems get jammed with their own quantum junk. Bazarov's notes hinted at plausible ways of weaving Majorana fermions to make them more stable.'

'Major who?'

'I'm sorry, of course. Theoretical building blocks of matter which are their own antiparticles.' Diamond watched Scott's face darken further with incomprehension. 'That's a key requirement for genuine qubit stability. If Bazarov can get a hundred or more qubits working in a steady, programmable state, well…the learning rates and capabilities for any attached AI program would be incalculably enhanced.'

'Go on.'

'He'd create a quantum supremacy; a genie that couldn't be outpaced, let alone put back in its bottle. The world would never be the same again.'

15

Eva watched from her window over the courtyard as a horse-box was towed in under floodlights and parked adjacent to the stable block. Two thickset men unlocked the rear of the trailer and dragged out a plain wooden box with four looping rope handles, two on either side. A steady rain was falling and the courtyard's muddied cobbles shone, greasy in the harsh light.

Occasional sounds floated up to the window as Eva pictured the woman inside the box; bound, gagged, terrified. She tugged a thin cardigan more tightly around herself as the cargo was carried out of the rain by Ded's men, before disappearing into the stable block.

Yury Rostrov – Ded's personal bodyguard – appeared from a corner of the yard, loping like a wolf over the cobbles, his starving eyes huge in his gaunt tattooed face, eager to view the new delivery. The mere sight of him brought Eva a familiar nausea.

Rostrov had been bought at no little cost from Russia's barbarous Black Dolphin prison in Ural, and was considered a one-off even by that hell-hole's Bratva. When choosing his bodyguard Bazarov had sought the hardest of the hard, and Rostrov's rep had come up repeatedly. He'd been feared even among the cannibals, pedophiles and serial-killers infesting that bleak facility. His new allegiance lay partly in his determination never to return to Black Dolphin's regime of solitary confinement and cold soup, where inmates were forbidden to sit or rest at any point in their sixteen- hour working day.

Now, for as long as he was kept busy, fed and paid, Rostrov proved manageable. Unless Ded set him on someone.

Through the window to Eva's left soared the whitewashed wall of the schloss, like a Disneyesque tower. She pictured the warmth and opulence within the dozens of rooms, the polished floors, the chandeliers, the thickly-carpeted boudoirs. So different from the bare quarters she was enduring.

'Eva.'

She heard her brother call from along the landing. He didn't shout. His tone was matter-of-fact, precise. She yearned to know that same serenity, the quiet conviction that wrapped him like a premature shroud, isolating him from the noise of the world.

'Eva, the embassy girl is here. Where are you?'

Eva stroked Arkady's hair, whispered to him to be a good boy and to wait here for her, that she wouldn't be long. The boy was coloring a picture book, seeming unconcerned at her leaving. She was glad of that. Eva slipped him a pack of biscuits to keep him further absorbed. She picked up her jacket and, locking the door behind her, headed out along the corridor. She joined Ded at the top of the wooden stairs leading down from their sleeping quarters to the stables. Hay, urine and old leather tack incensed her descent behind her tall, graceful brother. She watched his shoulder-length hair, glossy and thick like a young woman's, his lean fingers stroking the bare bannister. She shuddered.

In a stall the sealed box had been set down on a mound of hay. Beside it lay an opened crate, its lid propped at an angle. Eva knew it had contained the body of a young woman who'd died in transit, the corpse hastily buried. Eva didn't know where, and didn't want to.

A handful of Ded's men had collected around the new crate. Now, as their lord approached, each took a small step back. Ded nodded to Rostrov who produced a wide-bladed knife from his belt and began levering it under the lid of the box.

Inside, Lee Crane opened her eyes and winced against the shrieking nails and sudden intrusion of light as the lid was pried away. She was exhausted; starved, dehydrated, her hair matted with sweat, face streaked with mascara tears, limbs numbed by forced immobility. A breeze fluttered over her as the lid was finally wrenched back. The crisp night air in her crusted nostrils was like balm. A scent of hope. Blinking back the light, Lee saw a group of roughly dressed, unshaven men staring down at her. There were gross comments, laughter. One man, much cleaner and more composed than the rest, took pictures with a phone, panning the camera along the whole length of her bound body. She watched him check and review the shots, appearing satisfied. Then he knelt alongside her, bringing a knife close to her cheek, his eyes fixed on hers. Lee sensed him measuring her fear, approving it.

'Hello, Lee. Be still now.'

She flinched as he grasped her throat, securing her before sliding the blade under the duct tape wrapping her cheek, slitting the windings with a single, deft twist. Lee spasmed as his soap-scented fingers traced her upper lip, the flesh still swollen, raw from the punch she'd taken. He pulled the severed wrappings from her face, slicing away any fronds of hair trapped in the glue of the tape. He reached inside her lips and drew out a pad of soaked cloth.

Lee lay in silence feeling like a reptile spread on its morning rock. Air, sweet air. A primal instinct advised silence as the man lifted her skirt and his buddies made faces at her saturated, soiled state.

'Take her to the cage and give her food and water. She's weak. We can't lose her.' The man moved away from the edge of the crate, out of her vision. Now a woman appeared and gazed down at her, eyes calculating, estimating a later outcome.

A woman.

Lee held her gaze, imploring a connection. But like the man before her, the woman stepped back out of sight…

Eva reached the foot of the stairs in the stable when she heard the woman in the crate scream. Turning back she saw Rostrov standing over the box, mouth gaping, fingers tearing at his trouser belt as the others egged him on. She heard thuds, cries, and muffled shouts from inside the box as the pig lowered himself onto the pretty, blonde American.

Hades Gate

Eva stole a look up the stairs to her room praying her son was unaware of the agonies unfolding in the courtyard below. She turned away, following her unconcerned brother, climbing the stairs in silence.

16

Minivan. Cambridge – 12:45a.m. GMT

The minivan slowed for some overnight roadwork.

'Yes, the world would surely change forever.' The impact of Diamond's words brought a mutual silence. She shuffled her pages into a slender pile and produced three sheets. 'It gets worse. Looking at Bazarov's equations from the Bernstein Centre for Computational Neuroscience I think he's intent on linking his own brain to a quantum computer.'

'How did you get hold of those pages?'

'I have history at Bernstein, and still know people there. They forwarded copies of everything Bazarov had left in their vault.'

'How lucky for us.'

Diamond looked up, aware of an irony in his tone. 'You mean the likelihood of my doing research in the same place as Bazarov?'

'It's an interesting coincidence, surely. And coincidences are so often more than they appear.'

Diamond shook her head. 'Not in this case. There's a relatively small contingent of scientists working in this field. Besides, I think of coincidence like a spacetime wormhole, only in consciousness. Something that allows two otherwise incongruent states to align congruently, as in entanglement. It occurs all the time, but usually we're not *conscious* enough to recognize it. We're surprised by coincidence but in the quantum world it's the norm.'

'And we're just the quantum world writ large, after all?'

Diamond laughed. 'Obviously. We're living stardust, Commander.'

Scott nodded. 'Sometimes it doesn't feel that way, does it.' Another silence loomed. Scott broke it. 'Anyway, the material from the Bernstein Institute…you mentioned that neurotech could confer an almost infinite knowledge? You meant Godlike?' Scott couldn't be sure but he thought he saw Diamond flinch.

'I don't really do God. Not a concept I'm comfortable with. But certainly, Bazarov is pursuing power unlike any ever known. At DARPA they were manipulating organic enzymes with just a few digital bytes and coming up with materials that never existed before.'

'Do you mean new kinds of matter?'

'Yes, potentially.'

'All this begs a basic question: could he really get his quantum computer up and running?

'In theory. You have to understand…' Diamond stared off into space, trying to formulate her response. 'The world is experiencing a rate of change unlike anything that's gone before. In my field it's referred to as superintelligence, or Life 3.0 – the next stage of evolved intelligence. Think of the first stage as microbe to man, and the second as man to digital intelligence. The third stage transcends the plodding capability of a chess computer. It means digitally intelligent matter which autonomously modifies and refines itself. It's about smart machines designing smarter machines than themselves, ad infinitum.' Diamond looked over at Scott's thousand-yard stare, an ambiguity playing over his lips.

'Then felt I like some watcher of the skies when a new planet swims into his ken.'

Diamond exhaled a short gasp of recognition. 'Keats, very apt.'

'Oh, you know the poem?'

Without hesitating Diamond picked up the verse where Scott had left off.

'Or like stout Cortez when with eagle eyes he star'd at the Pacific – and all his men

look'd at each other with a wild surmise – silent, upon a peak in Darien.'

'Though in our case it's fairer to say we gaze on this new world while *silent, within a minivan, in Cambridgeshire.'*

Diamond's instant laughter lightened their apocalyptic mood. 'But seriously,' Diamond continued, 'the analogy with Keats' poem is perfect. Digital tech is ushering in a world where what was unthinkable yesterday feels unremarkable today. The speed and miniaturization of digital growth has been almost exponential, but it's starting to slow – we're reaching a point where we won't be able to make the chips any smaller. And if I understand this document correctly, Bazarov may be capable of jumping to a new level of qubit cellular encoding. Imagine a mind like Bazarov's manipulating the world via thought alone.'

'It's horrific.'

'In the world of AI researchers, consciousness is referred to as the 'C' word and free will as the 'F' word.'

'You mean those concepts are unsayable?'

'It's considered a layman's mistake to impute consciousness or free will to any digital intelligence. But, in my opinion, quantum computation makes that assumption less of a fallacy.'

'Why?'

'Because any such function would be operating outside known limits, outstripping an organic sentience like ours, and perhaps becoming *conscious* in a way we simply won't comprehend.' Diamond paused here as if newly reminded of the stakes. 'But, if it's any comfort, I don't think he'll be powering up his malignant genius any time soon, unless he's much further down this road than I'm calculating. He may be a wunderkind, but he'd need huge funds to make this a reality.'

Scott thought of the sums that the Hades Gate events brought in to Bazarov's coffers. Tens of millions of dollars every few months. 'Could he have built such a computer, with no one outside his select group or team knowing? Is that possible?'

'Anything's possible and *anything's* becoming more possible than *anything's* ever been. The puzzle itself is creating the puzzle.' Diamond began folding her notes back into her bag as Scott rubbed an ear lobe in mild desperation.

'Run that by me again. The puzzle...?'

'Life 3.0. You see, it's not merely Bazarov who's exploiting this potential, it's the cosmos itself. The universe has been evolving since the beginning of time. It evolved mankind and mankind developed tech. Tech evolution is still, well, evolution at work. Its roots are in the big-bang.'

Scott looked staggered at the enormity of the concept. 'I feel as though I've swallowed the red pill. Right now I need a super-intelligent cognac and a quantum English supper. I know somewhere nearby. Join me?'

'I'd prefer to get back while all this is fresh in my mind, sir, if you don't mind. I've a lot more work to do.'

'Yes, yes, Doctor Orinitri, naturally. Just as you wish.'

'Diamond is fine, really.'

17

Schloss Altenberg. Austria – 12:35a.m GMT. (1:35a.m. Local time.)

Today had been an anniversary.

Ded jabbed open a file on his desktop. News clippings, screen shots, some links now redacted and defunct.

He sipped at a Calvados, grazing the familiar headlines and paragraphs; he didn't have to read them, he knew their story by heart. He clicked through the NYT reports of atrocities in small towns among the Soviet satellite states grown lawless after the collapse of the old order.

The Calvados worked like anti-freeze on the ice crystals which thickened his blood whenever he visited this strange world; so distant, so lost. His uncle's wedding, held at the farm they'd visited each summer. He clicked again, lingering over a photo of his fifteen-year-old self, taken sometime during that same fateful year. A scholar in a dark blazer; jet hair and downy lip, a hesitancy in the dark eyes glancing sidelong at the lens. The long, straight nose, the symmetrical brows and mocha skin; a troubled meld of east and west. Next to that, a picture of Eva, ten years old. Pigtails, bathing suit, a squinty grin into sunlight. Her body the color of milk. And seeing her like this, *he sees everything again…*

They're bored with the wedding. The dancing and the gushing bonhomie embarrasses them. They slip away through split wooden fencing, taking their cake-filled bellies to the scrubland and rusting machinery in the high field.

They loll, chewing grasses, content with familiarity. The beer he's been allowed makes him drowsy, faintly irritable. He lies back, arms folded behind like a pillow. Eva's giggling and teasing reminds him he's not yet free of boyhood, though his body tells him otherwise, hourly. There's a woman at the wedding, an aunt, vivacious, distractingly pretty. He blushes when she looks at him. He aches. He can think of nothing else and closes his eyes to summon her. Eva drags a dandelion over his face.

He curses and sits up to see men arriving in an open-backed cattle truck, rifles and knives at the ready. Their vehicle, lurching across the farm's rutted entrance, is a bristling porcupine of menace. Soon shots and shouts ring out from the awning where the wedding party reels on.

He drags Eva beneath the old harvester. The hard rubber of its tire scrapes her cheek as she slithers under. They hide behind weed-clogged scythes. More screams come up from the house. More shots. Men's voices, a baby's cry, women pleading.

From the west a lowering sun illuminates people tumbling through its slanting rays, like motes. The corn in the field beyond the fallen guests glows russet and old-gold.

More screams, barked orders, shots. For the first time in his life Ded Bazarov knows terror. He could spring up, run a thousand miles an hour, but for the paralyzing horror binding his legs.

Smoke rises from lacy curtained windows. It rolls and coils over the roof's wooden eaves. Flames lick along porches and doorframes. Gasoline cloys the evening with a satanic sweetness. The shouts die down. The intruders, maybe seven of them, swagger around the property, firing into windows, laughing as one-by-one they saunter back to their truck.

A man Ded knows as Tzavok leads them, bulky in his clean combat fatigues. Assured, taking his time. Ded's father often discusses this man whose offices he visited only a week ago to protest intimidation in their tired little region: Putin's 'dictatorship of law.'

Ded and Eva watch as the men remount their truck, swigging wine, beer and vodka snatched from the wedding trestles. They jolt off into the sunset, shooting up the sky, booze oiling their cries.

The low wooden farmhouse is on fire now; a blue heat haze shimmers over the steaming roof.

Bursting down the hill Ded is first through the bullet-shredded door. In front of him are the bodies of his family; mother, father, uncles, and the pretty aunt – shot, stabbed, strangled. Some ligatures are still in place; his mother's tongue lolls, his father's castrated body spins from a rafter.

Under a table his baby brother is crawling, screaming, swaddled in orange flames. Ded tries to snatch the infant from the blaze, but his own lips are singed, his fingertips roasting. The screaming baby and the possessing heat have become one.

Eva pulls Ded backwards by his belt and throws herself on the child, rolling the baby back-and-forth on the bloody floor of the kitchen, tearing at his smoldering shawl and smoking underclothes until her baby brother lies screaming, naked, blackened but alive. From a pail under the sink she douses him with slops of water. The liquid runs over blisters and bubbled skin, until at last there is no more smoke, only a stench of boiled flesh and a pinched, melted crevice where a tiny face had been.

Eva snatches up the bundle. She and Ded streak through a doorway framed with flame, past curtains oozing coils of grey smoke, then out of the conflagration onto the cool, vast steppe. Now...as orphans.

Ded clicked out of the file.

Jamming the cork in the Calvados bottle, he corks something of the memory too.

18

Truck Stop. Liverpool – Weds 18th Dec. 12.15a.m. GMT

Guy woke with a shiver. A wind bullied scraps across the lorry park's pitted tarmac. He looked toward a stuttering flood light which had probably awakened him. Once again he caught his reflection in the truck's folded wing mirror.

He hated what he saw.

Here he was, safe. Alone. Unaccountable to anyone, free to live his life as he chose. He hated his complacency and his unspoken, unresolved fear. Now he could only picture the recently abducted young women. How many others might suffer unless this accursed cabal, this cell of horror, was stopped?

He checked his watch, certain Scott wouldn't have taken him at his word when he turned the gig down. He had until 9a.m. to cook away in this futile mix of self-doubt and indecision.

He knew, too, that Scott was depending on him. His Commander had known all along what Guy's ultimate response would be. Damn him.

He picked up his phone, and dialed.

'Jed Barstow Haulage – that you Guy? Tracker shows you're still in Liverpool, you should be clearing Dover customs by now.'

'Hi Susie. Listen, I'm bringing the truck in. Urgent personal circumstances. You'll need another driver for my shifts. Tell Harry it's not optional. I'm sorry.' He hung up and speed-dialed another number.

In a small shabby-chic apartment in northern Spain a sleepy voice answered. 'Guy?'

She spoke his name with its vowel lengthened, as though caressing it.

He could picture her among rippled sheets, soft light spangling through wooden blinds. The streets in the old quarter of the town would be quiet, maybe misty with rain.

'Hello, baby.'

'Where are you, Guy? Will I see you tomorrow?' He pictured her long dark hair entwined in his fingers, her tanned shoulders and upturned throat, resplendent against pure white pillows.

'I'm sorry baby, no. The schedule here has changed.'

If Guy drove his scheduled route tonight he'd be dropping his truck off in a container park outside Bilbao. He'd sign out a company car and drive ninety kilometers to San Sebastian to be with Lucia.

But now that wasn't going to happen.

He heard the sigh as she turned over in bed: the disappointed lover's sigh.

'Is there something wrong? Don't you want to see me?'

She was so young, twenty-six, a Euro-waitress with a degree in Fine Art.

She'd been working a shift one night, a year ago, when Guy happened to drop by a pintxo bar looking for a glass of rioja and a wedge of torta. It had been late, the cafe on Calle Justine was closing. They were alone and she'd poured his drink with a *don't-touch-me-but-you-better-want-to-know-me,* glance. He did his best to look away, but he struggled, and saw that amused her. She poured his wine with slender, lithe fingers, her jet-black hair tied up in a messy but devastating ponytail. Eyes like great chocolate buttons under symmetrical black brows; severe, yet touchingly delicate in her young face. She'd told Guy his English 'accent' was *funny,* that there was no need to rush his drink while she wiped down the bar.

Lazy whistling from the screened-off kitchen became their soundscape as he helped her stack some chairs, and she gave him her number. Next day they walked the promenade, drank wine, discussed her studies, and spent the night together.

'There are no words for how much I want to be with you, Lucia. But my job has changed, I'm not driving anymore. And I may not be able to see you.'

'Is there someone else? I don't mind, as long as I can see you…'

'No. It's not that. I'm sorting some old problems here. I don't know how it'll turn out.'

'I'll wait, or I can come to London?'

'No. You mustn't wait. If things go wrong for me I might

not be able to contact you again. You're young, just live your life. If I can, I'll come see you as soon as I'm free. But you mustn't wait for me.' He heard her start to cry. But Guy heard other sobs, too; the ones from Reggie Scott's video. Sobs with a heavier weight.

'Okay, Guy. If this is what you want.'

'It's not what I want, it's just what has to be.'

He clicked off the call and stabbed the ignition on his truck's dash.

At a Birmingham haulage depot Guy handed his documents to the overnight dispatch clerks and turned in his truck. Taking keys and a helmet from his locker, he grabbed his backpack and fired up his waiting Triumph Bonneville. Checking the bike's petrol gauge, he stamped into gear, revving hard for the M1.

19

Schloss Altenberg. Austria – 1a.m. GMT (2a.m – Local Time.)

Eva watched from the kitchen of the schloss as Ded, below in the courtyard, rounded a corner and disappeared into the stables. Keeping an eye on the window she lit a cigarette and puffed a few minutes away, making sure he didn't turn back for any reason.

Satisfied, she went to the computer and opened TOR. She clicked through an encrypted entry code and there, in a brutally basic inbox, was a single message for her.

'Delivered. 10:02 p.m.GMT. Go to: dv8953.RAG'

Eva felt a rush of satisfaction. She paid the balance of two thousand U.S. dollars to the anonymous account, waited for confirmation, then closed the window. She clicked out of TOR then scrambled and deleted her history.

She drew her coat tighter around herself and lit a second cigarette with the butt of the first. She crossed the hall, looking in on Arkady. He was lost to a flickering television showing a black and white cartoon of what looked like Czech provenance, circa 1965. The stick figure animations and inane music track, all plinking xylophones and brassy trombones, depressed her. But her son seemed engrossed in his retro-fantasy, and he was safe there – at least for the time being. He looked up as she entered, 'I'm hungry mama.'

'It's late, you should be sleeping.'

'But I'm *hungry*.'

'You're a naughty little monkey – I'll make you some hot milk and then it's to bed.'

Eva headed for the shower block, pulling its light switch, scattering the silverfish and earwigs drawn to the room's damp, fungal darkness. Once inside she pushed the battered wooden door against its frame and leaned back, jamming it in place. Ded had made sure all non-essential locks were removed. Though the only woman in the schloss, no quarter had been given to her privacy. Eva knew some of the men here wouldn't hesitate to make a move on her if anything happened to Ded. It was clear from their stares and black-toothed smirks that only her status as Ded's sister kept her safe. She made sure never to be alone without a loaded gun.

There were footsteps in the corridor outside the shower. Eva leaned harder against the rough door, dissuading any prurient interest in her presence there. She slipped a hand into her cargo pocket, fingering the ever-ready Glock 9mm. There was a voice from the courtyard beyond the shower window, an answer from the corridor outside her door. Then the sound of boots creaking away.

Eva parked her cigarette in the corner of her lips and undid the top buttons on her coat. She reached inside, pulling a woolen jumper up past her ribs, then a t-shirt, then a vest. She closed an eye against the rising line of smoke. Her fingertips warmed quickly against the flesh of her underarm and beneath her breast. The lump was tangible, though she couldn't say if it was any bigger than yesterday or the day before that. Perhaps it was firmer than last week. Yes. Harder and a little more defined than it had been when she'd discovered it here, under the shower, three weeks ago.

Then the light went out.

Eva cursed under her breath. Her chilled fingers fumbled along flaking plaster until they found the timer. She pushed a bakelite button back into its recess, bringing a bare bulb back to life.

'Eva?'

The door to the shower was struck from outside; a kick, a punch, not a knock. She braced the door with her weight.

'Eva, you being bad girl in there?'

Rostrov's voice beyond the wooden door was a snarl, his throat cracked and thickened by the drugs that ripped through his system.

Eva pictured him, the lean crazed assassin her brother kept on the payroll, always somewhere nearby, his blue prison tattoos reaching up from his bone-thin chest, winding like creepers to his cheeks. His dull eyes and his mouth, more gapped than toothed, made her shiver whenever she saw him.

'Fuck-off, Rostrov. I'm taking a shower. Leave me in peace.' She reached over to the filthy cord and pulled it hard to validate her story. A tepid stream of water choked in fits from an old shower head. Eva shifted tight to the wall. She was fully dressed and had no desire to be soaked by the hard, cold water.

'I can be your soap?' He kicked the door and his laughter made her chest tighten.

'I'll set the dogs on you. Just fuck off!' Now there was a silence beyond the dim trickling of the shower. Had he moved away? Her shoulder and the side of one leg was wet-through but still she let the stream run on. She'd give Rostrov a little time to get truly bored, then he'd skulk off and she could get the hell out of this rancid shower block.

She shut off the water leaving an ooze of slowing drips and ran a hand hard over her shoulder, sweeping off the worst of the droplets. She leaned her head back against the door and listened for any steps, any disturbances. There were none.

Eva made her way back to the deserted kitchen and sat at the computer. Keeping one eye on the door she opened the .RAG link she'd been sent earlier.

There, in an iPhone photo, were the contact details for the ex-paratrooper Guy Bowman; his cell, his email and his street address. A bolt of adrenaline shot through her and she felt instantly lightheaded. Was she insane to think that this man could help her now, that he might ever care about her? She sat, mind and heart racing. She and Arkady needed to escape. If she stayed trapped inside the expanding world of her brother's cabal she'd receive no proper medical attention and she and her son would be doomed: her to an untreated, maybe terminal illness, Arkady to a life of brutality and indoctrination. As she stared at the photo of Bowman's details she realized this was her Hail Mary pass; the only one she'd ever get.

Grabbing a notepad from the kitchen drawer she copied the information, scrambled her history, trashed the cache and shut down the machine. She slipped the notes she'd made into her sock, then tore out several pages from the pad to ensure there was no impress of what she'd written. Trembling, Eva emptied a cup of milk into a saucepan, lit the gas ring, then went to check on her son.

As she moved along the corridor she could see that the door to his room was open, could hear the TV playing yet another archaic cartoon. Sweeping into the room she froze, her fingers rigid as they clung to the door frame. Rostrov was nodding asleep on a chair with Arkady held tight to him, on his lap. The boy was awake, watching the door for his mother's return.

Eva felt her fingers reaching to her pants pocket; everything in her wanted to drill a 9mm round straight into Rostrov's skull. Only the sure knowledge that such a step would traumatize her son stopped her.

Eva put a forefinger to her lips and beckoned Arkady to her. The boy slipped from Rostrov's lap and darted over to his mother, who swept him up in her arms. 'Mummy's warming some milk for you, my angel,' she whispered, and carried him back to the cold kitchen.

20

Christine's Apartment: London – 1:15a.m. GMT

Christine threw her bag down on the sofa and kicked off her heels. After an enervating encounter with the police she'd opted for a comforting dinner at her club. In the aftermath of the burglary, and all it had awakened within her, she'd found her meal almost tasteless.

She poured two fingers of Laphroaig, swallowed a couple of painkillers, ran a steaming bath. Easing into fragrant lather she closed her eyes against the internal hiss from her cut ankle, letting the day's events shuffle into a form she could digest.

Letting her head loll back onto the rim of the bath, her hand shook as she sipped at the whisky, tension oozing through her system.

She heard a muffled buzz; her phone ringing in the pocket of the jacket she'd draped on a chair. She pictured Professor Nigel Grover, the head of the Foundation, or any one of a dozen friends and colleagues, calling to ensure she was okay. She was grateful for their care but nothing was getting her out of this bath. The whisky was spreading through her; slowing, easing, and expanding her thoughts.

She was stymied by why anyone would want to steal

Guy Bowman's file. Her affair with him had lasted three blissful months. Months in which she'd felt herself more alive than ever before. Being with Guy was never simple; his company had an edge but also an assurance which pacified various voices within her. Though he'd quickly become the centre of her world, he had never presumed such a status. With Guy she'd become almost another woman; his touch provoked dark needs in her, yet brought a corresponding liberty, which shamed and thrilled her by turn.

She'd ceased to be his therapist after his fourth session. At the conclusion of the hour he'd thanked her for her help and asked if she'd have dinner with him that night. Her *yes* escaped her lips almost involuntarily. She was shocked by her own breach of ethics.

'Guy, if I have dinner with you, I can't see you as a patient.'

'That's fine,' he'd said, 'we were finished here anyway.'

And so he'd gone from being her client to her lover in a single evening.

The phone in her jacket buzzed again, the new tone telling her she had voicemail. It could wait. She sipped at the whisky and sank deeper into the suds.

There'd always been an uncontainable, even elusive, quality to Guy. He'd told her that by being with her intimately he'd moved past the troubling shadow that had first brought him to her door. Christine permitted this incomplete outcome, reasoning that time and their continuing love would reveal and hopefully heal the rest. She should have known better.

But then, as dramatically as he'd appeared, he was gone.

She'd returned to her flat one evening to find her living room hosting a luxuriant bouquet of lilies, but her bedroom shockingly free of his belongings and his electrifying presence.

She downed the remaining liquor and choked back threatening tears. Another insistent buzz from her jacket made her groan.

21

Schloss Altenberg. Austria–1:25a.m. GMT

Annoyed, Bazarov glanced up from his screen as Eva passed his office with her whining child. The boy should be separated from his fussing mother as soon as possible. Something he'd deal with immediately on their return to Ukraine.

His attention returned to the laptop and to the image being generated by an underground mainframe several hundred kilometers away. The pixellated bits had arrived in elegant *feedforward only* code. All the more sublime for being untraceable to its brilliant source.

The miracle of what he was seeing soothed and engrossed him. Here was a particle of quantum intelligence itself; a fleeting spark of digitized consciousness, expanding hourly, learning recursively.

Bazarov watched the image spinning, blinking. Here was one digital synapse bridging two digital neurons. A mere two. His own brain contained a hundred billion chemical neurons – as many as there were stars in the galaxy. When these neurons spoke to one another they shared a hundred trillion connections. Somehow within that organic web the entity he experienced as Ded Bazarov lived, hungered, and planned. Here on the screen was the ghostly trace of a single digital synapse, arising under his fingertips, entirely at his will. From this trace would come more.

He tapped the keyboard and ran a different function. He saw digital atoms shaping a purely mathematical dimension. His fingers caressed the keys again and the packet of time and space they'd formed collapsed into non-existence. Wasn't quantum ephemerality part of its beauty? It couldn't be touched; like consciousness it couldn't be glimpsed. The God zone. Here was intelligence itself; energy living free of any material substrate other than Ded's own mind. This quantum pathway existed only to further his wishes and respond to his instructions.

As Bazarov considered the exponential expansion of his mind he knew he'd soon need a new universe, a multiverse through which his thought, unburdened by matter, would soar. His mind would transcend the physical realm of the first Maker. The very idea of such a One would be forgotten. Infinite spacetime would instead be filled with only his beating mind and whatever he chose to create or destroy within it. He was to be the God of a new order. The corrupt and decaying old one could, and would, be extinguished.

22

Christine's Apartment, Marylebone. London – 1:30a.m Weds 19th Dec. GMT

Christine, I need to see you. It's urgent . . . are you home?'
Christine stood, numb with new shock, the damp towel slipping off her shoulders as she played the voicemail from Guy. She dropped, naked, onto the sofa, thrusting her towel beneath her wet hips. She pushed the option to return the call, then stabbed it out.

She stood and crossed to the window, quickly tapping out a text: *Yes, at home. Where you?* Then deleted it. She tossed the phone down on the sofa, returned to the bathroom and resumed drying herself. But within a minute she had the phone back in her hands. She retyped her message and with a trembling thumb hit 'send'. Twice.

Disbelieving, she watched her message being delivered. Flashing dots told her he was replying.

Driving now . . . with you in 30 min.'

She replied, *Ok...*

Moments later she realized she was still gripping her phone, staring into space. Christine gathered the damp towel around her again and headed to the kitchen to brew the first of what she knew would be several cups of coffee.

With the machine gurgling in the background she sat at her laptop and fired off an email to Jilly, her PA. She was in delayed shock after the burglary, she lied, and would take the coming day to recover; cancel all appointments.

She sat back from the screen and heard the coffee machine click off in the kitchen. Time seemed to be simultaneously racing and standing still – every impulse, whether to drink coffee, call Guy back and demand an explanation, or just scream, was met by an equal and opposite hesitation. She could feel her thoughts whirring, clicking, stalling at the ridiculous position she'd just allowed herself to fall into.

Why would the theft of Guy's files, even assuming he knew anything about it, prompt him to contact her after a silence of almost three years?

She made her way to the kitchen, catching her reflection in the hall mirror. She paused, measuring distress as she gazed into her own face before a sudden calm spread through her. Yes, she'd see Guy, she'd hear him out, she'd stay open to whatever bizarre coincidences were unfolding in both their lives tonight, and she'd deal with what mattered most to them both. There was no other choice.

Christine was freshly made up, dressed in a crisp silk blouse and jeans displaying the lean silhouette of her trim waist and long legs. Her tummy fluttered as she heard a motorcycle skim the cobbles in the mews below her bedroom.

Opening the door at his knock she saw the Guy she'd loved: muscled, tough, resolute. But his eyes shone with something indiscernible, the pupils enlarged in the low light of her apartment. He seemed to fill her hallway as he entered it, just as he filled her consciousness; she wondered what he made of her now, and of her instant capitulation to his request to see her.

'What's the matter, Guy? What's happened?'

He drew her close to him in an embrace of great strength. Christine felt a rush of relief, pure delight as she folded into him. She felt a shudder run through him as he held her. '*Thank God you were here.*' The rumble of his voice seemed to melt her bones. She could smell cool night air in the collar of his jacket, his stubble abrasive and arousing against her own delicate cheek. She felt herself softening, warming. She pulled back from their instant embrace. Not easy to do.

'Go on through to the living room. I'll pour us a drink. Then you can tell me what the fuck is going on.'

Guy slipped out of his jacket and sank into her plush leather sofa, stretching his arms over his head. Christine returned with a whisky for each of them, joining him on the sofa, out of easy reach.

Guy downed his drink in one. 'I've spent the time since I last saw you on the run from myself. Driving trucks. I couldn't tell you what had happened to me because I couldn't admit it to myself. I thought I could get past it simply by being with you, but I was wrong. I had no right to share your life. No right to burden you. I needed to break away and let time either heal me, or kill me.'

'Apparently it hasn't killed you…'

'Not so far, but it still might. Death has a way of making

his presence felt in advance if you're familiar with his manner.'

Christine looked at the man sitting on her sofa and wondered just how many times he'd encountered death. Guy's army life involved a high level of enemy contact and engagement, she knew. He'd killed other men, maybe many. But she'd never considered that, for him, death was an entity he'd met as she might meet a colleague or friend.

'There are things I want to tell you, share with you. But there are others it's better you never know.'

'Or you might have to kill me?' She let a forgiving curl play over her lips as she spoke the cliché, but Guy's own response was deadpan.

'No, it wouldn't ever be me who killed you, Christine. Let's agree that what you don't know can't harm you, okay?'

She nodded and settled deeper into the sofa, prompting him to continue.

'I've been trying to forge a new life, to forget some of the things I've seen and had to do. Then, earlier tonight, I was shown something which tested everything I am, all I've been trying to escape.'

Christine waited. Finally he was opening up about the secret in his life, and she wasn't going to interfere now.

'About seven years ago, on classified service in Syria, I was captured by an outfit keen on taking western troops alive, making an example of them. Usually, if such an outcome looks likely, you keep a bullet back to use on yourself. Those boys don't read the Geneva convention and they aren't looking to give you a good time. I was in a small unit deep inside enemy lines. We were holed up in a disued factory, but we were ambushed. I was unconscious when they captured me, got knocked out by some rubble during a mortar attack. Three others with me died in the firefight. So I got taken alone.'

Christine felt herself growing colder. She was no stranger to accounts of torture and interrogation, but to suspect that someone she loved might have endured such hell was already unbearable.

'Back at their base I was kept in a cage. Tortured every few hours by a woman, while they filmed me. She was a real expert; made sure to keep me alive. I was good value and they got a kick out of working over a Brit para. They were mercenaries, thugs, mafia, a bunch of misfits and lunatics. They weren't interested in any intelligence, they just wanted a good show – and to drag it out as long as possible.'

'Dear God.' Christine lowered her head.

'On the second day the woman made me fuck her while the goons cheered her on. I figured that as long as they were intent on keeping me alive, even for kicks, I might find a way through it.'

'How could she do that? This woman – how could she *force* you to have sex with her?'

'You think I enjoyed it?'

'No, I didn't say that…'

'I was alone, far from any rescue, no obvious chance of escape. In circumstances like that you switch to auto-pilot. You do whatever keeps you alive, whatever reduces the damage. Screwing my captor was the least of my worries.'

'Yes, yes, I'm sorry, I can see that. Forgive me.'

'I'd get electric shocks, worse, if I didn't perform. The woman was a sadist, the real deal. She'd look into my eyes whenever she beat or suffocated me. She relished every second, savored it. I sensed she was growing attached to me somehow. The more resilient I was the more she enjoyed it. Courage, fight, resistance – that turned her on – so that's what I used.

Christine shifted in her seat desperate to embrace him, but Guy stood, moving away.

'How on earth did you survive it all?'

'By the third day I was no longer their priority. There were regular firefights outside the compound and they were focused on that. Madame de Sade had started to slip me extra rations, secretly. Not much – half a cup more water than I'd been getting, maybe some extra cheese or bread, enough to ensure I lived. Then, on the third night she came to me wanting sex, alone. No audience. I was always cuffed when we performed, usually with a knife at my throat, but it was different that night. She washed me down, told me she wanted me to enjoy her, make love to her. She kissed me constantly, which she never did when the others were watching. I could see she was feeling something for me, she kept hugging me, consoling me, whispering to me. It lasted for hours.' Guy was pacing now, back and forth across the living room.

'The next morning the compound started taking direct mortar hits. I could hear confusion and panic; walls collapsing, the goons running round screaming, firing at anything that moved. I was still in the cage, pretty weak by then, expecting to have my throat cut or be blown to bits by a friendly shell, when she came in and uncaged me. She had an old set of fatigues and a helmet for me. She led me outside through all the confusion and took me to a gate in the compound. There was a car, shot-up and barely running, but she gave me the key. Kissed me and pointed down a track.

'I got thirty miles south of the compound before I ditched the car and made the last few miles on foot to a UN road block. I knew it from my original mission data. Five days later I'd been debriefed. I never mentioned the torture or the woman. Couldn't do it. Not long after that I was back in Brize Norton on compassionate leave, having a pie and a pint.

'But surely they questioned you about the time you were missing, where you'd been?'

'I lied. I told them I was out cold for a day after the ambush. I collected the canteens from the bodies and went into evasion mode. I told them I hid in the hills until I could get back to the checkpoint. They were busy. They bought it.'

'So all these years you've been struggling to cope with what happened to you, and having to lie about it?'

'I should have told you all this long ago, but I could never get the words out.'

'So why now? Why has it all come to a head tonight?'

Guy stopped pacing and turned to Christine. 'Because I've just seen the woman again. The one who tortured me. She's alive. She's still hurting people – innocent, helpless people. And now I'm going to have to go back and kill her.'

'You saw her where?'

'A former commander sought me out and invited me to a…let's call it a movie screening…with certain conditions attached. She was there, on screen, doing her worst.'

'But why should this involve you now, for God's sake?'

'Christine, I'm still useful to certain parties precisely because I'm off the intelligence radar. I'm clean; no current footprint. I'm fresh meat.'

'Being useful is not the same as being able though, Guy. This woman, these things you went through, they've traumatized you, frozen your relationships, your life. What makes you think you can go back or deal with any of them?'

'I don't know. I said the mission wasn't for me, that I couldn't help them. But ever since the briefing I've been seeing those movie images as if they're burned into my eyelids. There are people who need help now, who need to be rescued, just like I did.'

Christine crossed to him and looked up into his face. 'You've spent three years driving a truck. Numb. In denial. If you go back you'll be revisiting the trauma. I think that's incredibly dangerous.'

Guy stroked her cheek as he looked down into huge, compassionate eyes. 'Watching that film I felt raw panic, as though I was right back there. I don't think I can live with myself if I don't face it and put an end to what's happening out there.'

Christine walked to the window and gazed across the dark rooftops of Marylebone, glazed with a sliver of moonlight. 'Would you have to go soon?'

Guy crossed to her, leading her back into the softly lit room. He wrapped her, tight and unmoving, in his arms.

Christine sensed this might be another goodbye. 'I'm sorry. I know, you can't answer questions like that,' she whispered. 'But why did you come to see me, now?'

'Ever since I left the briefing I knew I wanted to see you, be with you. Only you would understand.'

'Understand? That you have to go? Have to rescue these people, or…?'

'Or die in the attempt? Yes.'

'Then maybe you do have to go, Guy. Maybe there's no possible peace for you unless you face it again.'

'I think that might be true. But there's something more. For some reason that woman took a risk to set me free. Who knows what price she paid? I assumed they would have killed her if they'd thought she helped me get away. Perhaps there's a human-being in there somewhere after all. I don't know. I saw tonight that she's alive, killing at will and for profit. I want to put a stop to that.'

'That's an honorable intention, Guy, but you're so conflicted by it. Why?'

'You remember me telling you about Kim Thi, the girl in the famous photo from Vietnam, the Napalm Girl?'

'Of course – I've never forgotten it.'

'I learned later that the rage and pity the picture inspired in me unlocked an equal, opposite force. In the Paras, and with my other regiment, I found I enjoyed doing bad things to bad men. I'd wanted to be a force for good, but I was as capable of killing as any fanatic, any jihadist, any mafia hitman.'

Christine drew a deep breath as she processed this new insight. 'Well, I can certainly see why you might feel conflicted by that.'

'Most of the guys with post-combat issues are screwed up with regrets about the people they killed, the mistakes they made. But for me killing felt gratifying, like getting the job done – even at close quarters. Maybe especially then. I see those deaths in my dreams and I relive them, sometimes joyfully. Since I left active service I've been trying to end those dreams.'

'But you were a soldier, doing your duty…or are you telling me you've murdered innocent people?'

'No. I never killed anyone who hadn't shown a material interest in killing me. Innocence in combat zones is an elastic concept.'

Christine let a smile taint her eyes; '…*grow like savages – as soldiers will, that nothing do but meditate on blood.*'

Guy's own features softened in recognition of Shakespeare's words.

Christine's voice leveled to that of an analyst, not a lover, 'Sounds like you've had enough meditating on blood.'

'No elite soldier should be a bully with a weapon. But sometimes it's hard to be sure you haven't crossed that line.'

'Do you need me to tell you it's alright?'

Guy shook his head. 'No, no one can give anyone

that permission. I can go to free the hostages with a clear conscience, but I can't go intent on murdering anyone. If I have to kill to save myself or an innocent I will, but otherwise…' He paused. When he spoke again it was more slowly. 'I've realized that when you kill someone you destroy an entire cosmos.'

'Tell me what you mean?'

'The universe exists uniquely inside each of us. Our thoughts, our experiences, our consciousness is where it has its home, its being. This isn't some mystical thing, it's simple. Without us to experience or witness it, in what way does it exist? When you kill a human being you erase a universe.'

'You mean you end the universe *for them*?'

'I mean when you kill someone you snuff out the space, time and infinity that lives through them. You collapse that universe.' Guy turned away to the window. 'Does that seem weird to you?'

Christine felt her spine tingle. 'No more weird than anything else tonight.' She let a brief silence punctuate the weight of his words. 'Did you know your details were stolen this evening, from our archive?'

He snapped round from the window. 'No. I didn't.'

'I think it was your contact details they were after. The cover sheet was taken, the one with your email and mobile number. They may have wanted more, but we disturbed them.'

'We?'

'Yes, I was working late. It wasn't the most professional

burglary ever staged. Looked like a young woman but I can't be sure, she panicked when I interrupted her.'

Guy stared, calculating. If his identity was compromised already then his mission was dead in the water, and him with it. 'You say the burglary seemed amateurish?'

'Well, rushed at least. I mean the building still had people in it but the intruder was hardly up for a fight. It all seemed more desperate than sinister.'

Guy thought of the hostages again – the despair they'd be enduring. Backing out was no longer an option for him, even though every instinct was screaming otherwise. 'If Scott's department has a leak then the sooner I'm airborne and operational the better. The less time they'll have to second-guess me.' He turned back to the window.

She stood and went to him, burying her face in his broad back, wrapping his chest in her arms. 'Guy, do you need some kind of blessing from me? Is that why you came tonight?'

He unclasped her arms and turned to her. 'I came back to tell you that you saved me, Christine. No one ever showed me such care. If anything happens to me, I needed you to know how I feel.'

Christine stood on tiptoe, found his lips with hers. 'I'd do anything to stop you returning to that world, but maybe you'll never be complete unless you do. If there's something to put right, for you and for the people who need help, maybe that's reason enough.'

He pulled her to him, burying his face in her perfumed hair. 'I want you, right now.' Guy tightened his embrace. Christine clung to him relishing his heat and strength. Only one word rose to her lips. 'Yes.' She found herself engulfed in his kiss. Barely easing back she whispered. 'How much time do you have? Before you need to leave?'

'Enough.'

23

Marylebone High Street. London
– 8:30a.m. GMT

From a payphone a block away from Christine's flat, Guy dialed a three digit number. A young female answered. 'Hello caller, how may I help you?'

'My code is ea980p.'

After a few seconds the female operator spoke again. 'The Bureau will collect you from your current location in fifteen minutes.'

Guy hung up. His watch showed 8:30a.m. He'd taken it to the wire. He was stepping out of the callbox when his cell buzzed; an email, with an attachment.

'*Hello Guy. This is Eva, from your special past. I need your help just as you once needed mine. And so does your beautiful son, Arkady. Please Guy!*'

Guy flicked a glance left and right along Marylebone's waking High Street, then took a hard look at the attached image. *Your beautiful son? Arkady?*

Was it possible?

As he studied the photo he realized how he'd blanked any such outcome from his thinking. Of course, it was possible... He thought of the room, the men watching, scoffing, and Eva repeatedly drawing his tormented body eagerly inside hers.

And now his ex-captor was pictured here beside a young boy. Woman and child stared out of the shot holding hands in a snowy street and for several seconds Guy found he couldn't break from the child's gaze. He guessed the kid was around six years old. The curling black hair and dark brown eyes were genetically, and regrettably, familiar.

So. There was no mystery about who'd wanted his Foundation file. But why now?

Guy raised his eyes from the phone's screen and took a long breath. He felt feather light and boulder heavy.

The unthinkable was possible, sure. But not proven…

He memorized the Tor address before slipping the tiny sim card out of the phone. He sank back into a pub doorway and did an auto-delete of the phone's OS before crushing the screen under his boot and dropping the wreckage into a drain. He walked back to a corner opposite the coin box.

A minute later an old white Transit van pulled up. Inside, two men in overalls and paint-stained jackets presided over a dashboard littered with sun-browned newspapers, KFC cartons and a dozen unpaid parking tickets. You had to hand it to the Bureau, when they did theatricals they went all out.

He walked to the vehicle. Its driver spoke through a lowering window.

'Code?'

'Ea980p.' Guy rounded the rear of the van, its battered doors already being pushed open from inside.

'Good morning, sir.'

'Hello again, Guy. Good to have you on board.'

24

Surrey Hills. England: 3:20a.m. GMT

Joel Crane took exit 10 off the M25 and was soon cruising the leafy curves of the Tillingbourne Valley.

A tight bend into a gated driveway brought the ivy clad front of his home into view. With the driver's window cranked down he took a childlike pleasure in hearing his pet Ferrari suck and spit the driveway gravel, while the crackle of the car's four port exhaust was even cooler than the Black Sabbath track he'd been playing.

He'd been warned that the house, with its clash of thin colonial columns buttressing a too-narrow, mock classical pediment, was a failure in taste. *WTF.* He figured it had that essential Brit-thing going for it. To Joel, it looked classy.

Lights burned downstairs in the hall beyond the portico. Upstairs was dark. His wife, Tammy, would have long finished her ritual of cleansers and creams. She'd be asleep in sensible PJ's, having laid aside some book. Tammy read a lot. She was big on self-improvement, and she had plenty of time.

Right now his wife was big on Dickens. *Bleak House.* Was that a comment on how they lived? Was her life with him bleak? Whatever, Joel didn't let the thought detain him. At her prompting he'd flicked through the book's first pages, feigning a kindly interest. "Fog everywhere. Fog up the river…fog down the river." *Fog up your ass,* he thought as he palmed the Ferrari's fob.

And there'd been something about a dinosaur in a cruddy London street. *Like, Dickens' does Godzilla? Jeez.* What did any of it have to do with him, his life? He couldn't hack that old stuff, but he took a sideways pride that his wife could.

He climbed the stairs to his office, his lair, a zone implicitly unwelcoming to Tammy or to his daughter, when she'd lived there. Shrugging off his tux and tugging out his tie he poured a hit of twenty-one year old Macallan, no ice.

The bank's Christmas dinner had been a drag. Only extended flirtation with an intern less than half his age – all eyes, hair, and heels – had made it memorable. Their fingers linked, thighs brushing secretly under the table, had sent an almost teen level of excitement coursing through his groin. The evening had been enriched with an illicit promise, and these days the promise was everything.

His phone had already smarted with a message from her as he drove home. *When will you unwrap me???* She was keen. Maybe too keen. He liked the idea of her, but an affair would grow tedious, troublesome, finally exhausting. They always did.

He took another dip of the Macallan.

Joel glanced over to the door of the lair, then slid his captain's chair back on its rollers before lifting the corner of an antique rug under his desk. He pulled at a brass ring set into maple boards and, from a cut-away beneath them, brought out a heavy laptop. He opened the machine and waited for it to find the wifi, routed through a secret VPN. There was a single email with a geeky link. On this machine they were all like that. *Afge256yt.lll*

Joel clicked open the link. A dark window appeared and a loading bar began filling with bytes.

He took another shot of the malt. What appeared on the screen made him shoot backwards in his chair, the peaty whisky screaming in his throat, searing his sinuses with brine.

There was his daughter.

Lee.

Bound and writhing in a kind of box, her eyes terrified, her mouth taped. Beneath her was the legend: 24/12/19. Alongside that was an accumulator graphic in U.S. dollars. 'Bidding open.'

Joel stared, breathing locked.

The door to his study eased back. Tammy stood in its frame, a floor-length velvet bathrobe gathered around her. Her face seemed drawn and pallid, just as his surely did now.

'You look sick, are you okay?'

'Yeah, yeah, I'm fine. Drink went down the wrong way, feels like I snorted bleach.'

Tammy registered a tacit disapproval. 'Have you heard anything from Lee? I've been leaving messages. We were supposed to talk tonight, but nothing. She doesn't pick up. I'm worried.'

Joel shot another look at the horror on his screen. There was no doubting it, his own daughter stared back at him.

He clicked it shut as though he'd been studying wayward stocks and gazed back into his wife's taut face. 'Oh, I wouldn't worry about it. You know how Lee is when she's busy, she doesn't look up. Same as in college; didn't call for days. You fret too much.'

Tammy had already stopped listening. She stayed resolute in the doorway, refusing to be shoo'd away. 'I'm going to call Barbara.'

'If Lee doesn't call by morning we'll talk to Barbara then. She'll know whatever Lee's been up to.'

'Couldn't we call now?'

'Tammy, you're acting hysterical, really…' Joel watched his unconvinced wife turn away.

'To hell with you, I'm calling now. My gut say's something's wrong.'

Joel let her bare footsteps pad away along the mezzanine's polished wooden landing before puking his dinner and the four-hundred dollar malt into a hand-dyed buckskin waste bin.

25

Euston Road. London: 8:05a.m. GMT

First stop RAF Northolt?' Guy leaned back against the Transit's boarded seat.

'Correct. You can select whatever kit you'll need and I'll brief you as we go. You fly this morning. Brumowski Air Base is south east of Tulin, putting you within tabbing range of the target. It's a large schloss where we think the next Hades event will be held. You'll devise your preferred route in.'

Guy nodded. Here it all was. Everything he dreaded and desired.

The stripped-out, windowless van rattled along Marylebone Road toward the M40, the surface of his skin buzzing as it went, gut cramping under his tee-shirt, senses hyper alert.

He guessed there might be a few familiar faces at the Northolt Airbase, and it would be good to get his hands on weaponry again. He thought, too, of how he'd be working alone, living by instinct. 'I guess comms will be minimal, at least until a decision to strike gets made?'

Scott nodded without looking up from his clipboard. 'Comms will be kept to almost zero. We don't know what security they have in place around the schloss, but I suspect it'll be tight. The targets may have cracked our previous signals – that's probably how our agents were compromised – hence this low-tech operation.'

'Practically carrier pigeon.'

'Now there's a thought… At least we could classify it as an Airborne operation.'

The Captain remained absorbed in his notes. Guy smiled. Irony, dark or otherwise, had been in short supply during his stint in haulage. He thought of the sim card he'd kept and the weird email it contained, of how compromising it might be. Or, maybe, how useful.

He hadn't told Scott about the theft of his details from the Foundation, nor that he might have fathered a child with a woman he might have to capture, even kill. His torture at Eva's hands wasn't something he'd been able to assimilate, still less share in any kind of debrief. He'd given nothing classified away under the ordeal, and his ultimate escape meant he'd never reported the episode. That Eva had sought him out and might now be expecting his arrival were potentially mission-wrecking factors. He was taking an undeclared risk in keeping this information out of Scott's hands. Not exactly unprecedented.

Guy stole another glance at Scott. His old commander was familiar with his readiness to think and act independently within any mission's brief. And Scott's whole MO was predicated on subterfuge, misdirection, suggestibility. This mission was plain awkward, something didn't add up yet. Maybe it never would. Maybe keeping shtum about the past was courting disaster, but it would be his neck on the line, alone in the field. Guy opted to keep his own counsel.

Scott put the clipboard aside. 'I'll go over specific mission details at the depot. For now, I need to give you more background on the people we're targeting.'

'Fire away.'

'There are states and individuals who've gained access to the Net's darkest layers. Forces intent on collapsing essential western power structures.'

'Okay, but we've known about that threat for years. Cyber warfare, in other words.'

'Yes, an assault on several levels – cultural, intellectual and military. A few of these forces may now be only a step away from triggering devastating initiatives: control or destruction of nuclear power stations, utilities, the internet, digital and satellite communications.'

'Ushering in a new dark-age where only the chosen survive? I think I already read that paperback somewhere.'

'I understand your skepticism, Guy, but there's a new element in play: human-level AI through which a global elite could gain the kind of control I've described.'

Guy's time in special ops had brought him face-to-face with a thousand conspiracy loons and theories. 'How does a group of sadists making torture-porn link to an armageddon scenario?'

'It's possible they're using the funds they make to develop advanced AI. We suspect they've made significant covert breakthroughs in the field. Currently we can't read, let alone decrypt, the software they're using. We need to snatch the actual hardware and bring it in.'

'By "we," you mean me.'

'There's that razor-sharp mind again.'

Guy shrugged. 'Isn't that what you pay me for?'

Scott went on. 'We need to compromise and contain those close to the centre of this operation as soon as possible. This lead we have to the events in Austria is the nearest we've ever come to any individuals using the portals which lead below the darknet.'

'What you're calling Hades' Gate?'

'Yes. We want these people, and we want the encryptions they're using.'

'Then again maybe *we* simply want whatever breakthroughs they've made in AI?' Guy held Scott's gaze and Scott didn't flinch.

'I think any such breakthroughs, along with their potential, should be available to only a very secure and responsible entity.'

'And I have to assume that means *us*?'

Scott's raised eyebrow revealed everything and nothing. Finally he spoke. 'Let's just agree that advanced AI in criminal hands could be calamitous.'

'Okay, sir. But the darknet is roughly a thousand times bigger than the surface web, so how big is Hades Gate? Do we have any data?'

'It's tiny. That's its charm, its power. We estimate less than a thousand people worldwide have access to it. A handful of those are world-ranking entities. It's possible they're planning a hyper-secure cyber State.'

'And ensuring a place in their brave new world once they bring down the existing order.'

'Precisely. We think one of the key players is behind the Austrian event. He'll be there, at the location you're investigating. He may already be a chieftain in this new kingdom, which is why we're going after him old school. Less chance of leaks.'

'Carrier pigeon.'

'Practically.'

Guy felt the van slowing. A hard lurch threw him left. They'd arrived at the depot.

Voices pierced the van's walls as security clearances were checked. Guy felt his choices narrowing tangibly. If Scott was right, their target would have protection at the highest levels. Screwing up, operationally or personally, was even less of an option than Guy had figured. If he was caught his life wouldn't be worth a spit in a storm.

26

Eva watched each image flash onto the laptop's screen as Ded uploaded the footage he'd taken.

Only he knew the codes and the protocols he used. No one else in his operation, including her, was granted such knowledge. Only a chosen group, an elite listing spread throughout the globe, were able to access material generated by this coding. Eva knew better than to ask, or to guess, who any of them might be.

Only these subscribers would receive the images of the American, bound and helpless in her crate. The pictures would auto-delete from the user's hard drive after thirty seconds, leaving those with an appetite for such material slavering for more. These were no fantasies. The material displayed genuine human suffering, endured by people with no hope of escape, only able to guess at the wretchedness of their emerging fate.

Ded's encryption made any illicit copying or screen grabs impossible. Only a single-use cyber key, digitized to Hades inputs and updated by recursively generated algorithms, could download and decrypt the material sent by another Hades user. That was as much as she knew.

Eva watched as a lurid green graph in a corner of Ded's screen began to spike.

'She's popular.' His tone was distanced, flat. If he was pleased at the instant response to his posting he barely showed it. 'They like her, the banker's daughter, they're already bidding. Like the dumb beasts they are.'

Eva threw a glance along the corridor to where she'd left Arkady. She could still hear male laughter and occasional female cries from the courtyard below. Was the boy faking ignorance of the hell going on around him, protecting his mother from what he pretended not to know? She couldn't be sure – and didn't know if she could handle the answer.

She looked again at the screen, over her brother's shoulder. Winking dots revealed rising interest in the forthcoming streamed event. Along with those invited to attend the slaying of the Americans, there were others who'd pay to watch the stream; distanced, yet complicit in the atrocity. Ded kept the number of subscriptions limited and at a premium. Only the top two-hundred bidders would be allowed to stream the event. Lee's provocative image had spurred the bidding to new heights.

Ded clicked out of the screen. Without speaking he brushed past his sister and headed for the stairs. Eva wondered if he was suddenly intent on sparing his glamorous new asset the attentions of his henchmen. He'd want her at her best when she next came before his camera. His latest, pale star…

With Ded gone, Eva hurried to her room. She had a rare

moment to check her phone, the secret one from which she'd breathlessly texted Guy.

Perhaps he'd replied.

Maybe he was on his way?

27

RAF Northolt: 8:40a.m. GMT

Schloss Altenberg. It's a baroque mansion in the north-eastern corner of Austria. Bought ten years ago as a ruin by a Russian oligarch, Vladimir Portnovitch. Wanted to play at being a Rhineland Prince, presumably.'

In a corner of a large hangar Scott was unfolding a map, strewing documents over a battered trestle table. His thick fingertip momentarily obscured the location he was tapping. 'We think the event will be held there, in four nights' time.'

Guy leaned over the old map and pulled out aerial shots of the castle from an adjacent file.

'We've assembled recent satellite images and the GPS co-ordinates, but I knew you'd want to see a paper map first.'

Guy studied the credentials of the map, the scales still legible along its tattered margins. It had been drawn by a raiding party of 42 Commando, late during the second world war, when Schloss Altenberg had been a regional Nazi HQ. Despite its age, the waxed paper map radiated urgency, as if etched in adrenalin rather than ink. As if infused with the tension of an imminent attack.

Guy traced a finger along faded brown contour lines, eyes scanning bleached blue threads indicating now obsolete waterways He slowed his gaze over what looked like a long drainage culvert, maybe a sewer, running downhill from the eastern elevation of the schloss. A commando raiding party might have used it for cover if it were dry. He could, too.

He checked the elevation of the woodland surrounding the castle. The old unit had done a thorough job of recording the terrain. Most of the features were unchanged. It was a remote spot and the twenty-first century seemed hardly to have touched it.

The grand schloss was set into a wall of mountain crag which soared above the rear of the castle by almost a hundred feet. To the front it overlooked a valley. In daylight it would be almost impossible to approach without being seen. Scott's satellite images indicated the exterior of the castle had been renovated and well maintained.

As he took in its details Guy sensed the building would become a leading character in the unfolding mission, as much an entity to be reckoned with as human opposition. His paratroop training taught him that landscape and locale were as intrinsic to a mission's outcome as any weapon. Gaining covert access to the schloss, if he ever needed to, would be more than challenging.

'What else do we know about the owner? How often is he there?'

'He's associated with the inner circles of the Kremlin and, of course, has a massive fortune. He seldom leaves mother Russia now. He's considered too important to Putin's stability. And since the diplomatic fall-out from the Novichok poisonings, Putin's cash cows have less room to maneuver.'

'So the schloss is a stone yacht, an expensive toy. Seldom used, seldom visited?'

'The owner runs a skeleton staff for upkeep, otherwise it's pretty deserted.

Guy stood back from the table, folding his arms. 'If your suspicions are right and our target did capture your previous agent, that'll have spooked them. All their preparations will be at risk. Why wouldn't they cancel the event?'

'We can't be sure they haven't done exactly that. The Hades encryption keeps us completely in the dark.'

Guy nodded, picturing the captured agent, wondering what fate he'd met. Was he was still alive somewhere inside the schloss? A wave churned his gut. He ignored it. Fear was now a useless emotion. 'But an illicit gathering on this scale can't be easy to arrange. Cancelling would be costly for our target's kudos, not to mention the lost income.' Guy supposed this wasn't the time to ask whether the glitterati punters could claim a refund if their blood sport got postponed.

Scott pulled out a new file and reached inside it. 'If your mission confirms the presence or arrival of these targets we can move on them, with you guiding the strike.'

Guy nodded. His brief was evolving. Now more than a recon mission, he might have to remain operational to the last gasp.

28

Bunker. Ural, Ukraine: 10:43a.m. (GMT +2)

Mikael "Cody" Bazarov pulled down his baseball cap, tossed a chocolate wrapper into a plastic bin, and clicked on a screen link. His brother, Ded, demanded regular updates on Zara's progress, like any proud parent.

The bunker Cody worked in lay under an old hunting lodge in the empty countryside bordering Vinnytsya, almost three-hundred kilometers south-west of Kiev. Ded Bazarov had chosen the spot for its remoteness and bought it for pennies from a widow who'd been dying alone for decades.

In summer the old wooden lodge toasted, in winter it was a smoky fridge. But the bunker installed beneath it was a modernist masterpiece. The excavation had taken months, and though local labour was cheap and bought-off even cheaper, the imported building materials were all top dollar.

The bunker and its contents had cost millions; the equivalent of a two-bedroom apartment with a central living room deliberately extended to house the precious Q-frame. Off this room were two sets of sleeping quarters, an up-to-date kitchen decked in black slate, and a pristine shower block. The complex was sterile, immaculate, bright twenty-four-seven. You could eat off the floor.

There were assorted desks, two retro Chesterfields, and Cody's chair – a handmade replica from the bridge of the US Starship Enterprise.

At one end of the chamber, bolted to the floor and humming day and night, was a Quantum-frame running seventy qubits of expanding software. Isolated, at the heart of the unit, its CPU's were kept at minus two-hundred Celsius. The frame was a powder-coated steel cabinet with the dimensions of a tall fridge. Built-in, at head height, was a twenty-six inch screen. The Q-frame ran programs capable of traversing and merging the quantum and digital worlds. One of its projects was a steadily evolving digital assistant, a deep neural network turning and turning in an ever-widening gyre:

ZARA.

Zara had been supplied with the shorter Oxford English Dictionary, giving her a base vocabulary of around a hundred and seventy thousand words. English was, after all, the lingua-franca of the networked world. It articulated the progressive spirit Ded had sought upon fleeing the rotting and corrupted land of his birth, and he'd made sure his quantum brainchild, his sister, and his runt of a brother read and spoke it fluently. Indeed, Cody eschewed his native Russian, his references and preferences being all 21st century Yankophile.

Zara contained Big Data caches of YouTube, Facebook, Instagram, the Washington State Library Archive and Wikipedia. It held The New York Times, The Economist, Vogue, and arrays of professional journals in disciplines from psychiatry to vulcanology. Each feed was updated daily via Cody's pre-programmed external drives. Ded Bazarov ensured that even though his digital wunderkind was securely air-gapped, Zara still received a significant input of the world's cultural, political and scientific discourse.

Day and night for the past seven months Ded had been supervising Zara's training sets with sentence templates and linguistic rules of growing complexity. The results had surprised even him. Processing language and written data at quantum speeds meant that Zara was already starting to utilize analogy and abstraction in her computations. No, 'she' wasn't 'thinking' in any human sense, but she was using logic and interpreting language rules at a more evolved level than most college grads. Bazarov had never designed 'her' to be a faux human-being; Zara was software able to converse with her maker, but with a machine-based functionality. Like any other machine she had no sense of qualia and never would. She could determine the presence of minute chemical compounds but would never smell coffee or taste wine, even though she had learned to describe both these and many thousands of other sensations accurately and appropriately.

Zara had been raised on Game Theory and Prisoner's Dilemma style conundrums, being granted increases in her computational power whenever she displayed an empathetic or nuanced response. Zara's ConvNets were weighted to equate any such increase with approved or ratified outputs. She was programmed to actively seek both – a loop of success then reward – creating a primitive but evolving mechanized intentionality. In addition, Zara was required to explain, in spoken English, how and why she'd offered these outputs. Ded ensured she 'showed her work.' She was already Siri's vastly more integrated sister and showed-up Google's Alexa for the dim-witted rote-learner she was.

From within her Q-frame Zara could digitize a three hour movie or codify an opera in milliseconds. Her creator encouraged her to repeatedly layer and back-propagate the converted material with different developments, alternative outcomes. The more narratively plausible Bazarov judged her outputs to be, the greater her supervised reward.

If speed was any indicator, Zara went at her tasks with evident enthusiasm. Ded Bazarov granted more terabytes to whichever digital synapses were performing well, while reducing input to those performing less dynamically. Each increase in memory and function brought her coding an electronic 'rush' and he'd watch approvingly as Zara's networks devoured each new tranche of computing power like a gifted child soaking up intellectual nourishment; a recursive symbiosis between man and machine, reward and correction, performance and praise. Zara was evolving into a quantum daughter.

And she was to be perfect in all her ways.

From a plastic chair in his make-shift office at the schloss Ded tapped out a short message to Cody, checking on his younger brother's alertness. The message would encrypt impenetrably through Hades' Gate. Cody confirmed he'd uploaded Zara with today's data and was about to start his daily tasks: checking CO_2 filtration, vacuuming all AirCon grills and monitoring Zara's operating temperature and digital connectivity in three discreet locations within her frame.

On his screen Ded watched his brother's demeanor as Cody typed. The monitoring only went one way. Ded switched on his mic. 'You look tired. Are you sleeping properly?'

'Sure. When will you guys get back?'

'Six days, maybe longer if we have to detour for any reason. You know how it is.'

'Bring me something.'

Ded made no reply. His younger sibling's melted features still appalled him. A deep crevice ran diagonally, eliminating one eye and the entire nose, the scar only ending at his blackened and distended lower lip. A flap of skin was grafted around two holes functioning as nostrils. Cody's occasional, post-burn surgery had been disastrous. Eventually he'd refused the agonizing procedures, growing up largely in Eva's care, out of sight of others, unable to live in a world with no tolerance for his disfigurement. He'd been happiest in the solipsistic world of gaming, programming and hacking. Now he lived, ate, and slept in Bazarov's Ukraine bunker, a frail human firewall for his brother's ongoing creation.

'New trainers. Nike.'

'You don't have enough trainers?'

'Nike, Spazoos. And I want the new iPhone. Cool.'

Lounging in his chair, Cody glanced over to the mainframe. Ded noted how, at this angle, his sibling's face had almost no profile – a concave void with two short ridges where nose and brow should be. A crescent moon.

Ded turned away. Only Eva could bring herself to touch the boy, or grant occasional kisses to those hideous scars.

'iPhone?'

'We'll see. Look after Zara.'

'Sure.'

Something about the boy's nonchalance troubled him. 'Cody!' At his brother's change of tone the boy snapped round and stared fixedly into the screen. 'Remember – your life depends on it.'

29

RAF Northolt: 8:55a.m. GMT

Guy looked again at the satellite images ranged in front of him. 'This area to the north of the schloss. It isn't on the old map. Looks like a lake or reservoir?'

Scott picked through a sheaf of printed notes. 'No, it didn't exist during the war. It's a flooded quarry. Someone developed the area, turned it into a scenic lake and built a kids' water park around it during the eighties. Seems it never really took off.' He took a magnifier and honed in on the feature. 'Looks unpopulated in this shot. Abandoned. Strike you as significant?'

Guy shook his head. 'No more than anything else I'm seeing. But you know how it is, once a mission starts anything and everything within thirty klicks can have an impact.' Guy took a final look at the co-ordinates of the lake before opting to move on. 'This event – these movies we think they're planning to shoot – might they already have hostages in place? It won't be easy bringing abducted victims to such an obscure location. My guess is they have to plan ahead; can't risk not having a cast for their little movie. They might have people held in the location already.'

Scott picked up a file from the table. 'Yes. We're working

on that. We think those two women I listed earlier may have been abducted specifically for this. Both are American, and now there may be a third.'

'Easier to transport kidnapped Americans from London than the States, I suppose?'

'That's how we're reading it. The victims will have to be smuggled out to the schloss. And they'll have to be kept alive.'

Guy winced. 'Smuggled out? Well, those ladies won't be traveling first class, that's for sure.'

'We've put extra eyes on the main southern ports and airstrips, but my budget doesn't allow for more.'

'So we have assorted females abducted in London being sent to be tortured to death in a castle in Austria.'

'We know from the older footage we obtained that the preferred victims are either attractive young American women or, occasionally, captured members of Nato armed forces. There are people in Hades' Gate who'll pay top dollar to watch them being murdered.'

'Are the families informed? Do they know what might be going on?'

'The Fox reporter, Tyler Warren, has dirt-poor parents back in Pennsylvania. A boyfriend here, in London. We haven't let on to them about her possible fate. The new missing, Lee Crane, married her girlfriend this summer. She works at the U.S. embassy and comes under CIA protocols. So far they're keeping shtum and putting out their own feelers. They don't know about our involvement and they're not going to.

Guy sighed. He recalled the isolation of his own captivity, the second-by-second dread of it, the way his entire being was consumed by his unknown fate. He pictured these young women wherever they were, alone and petrified. A surge of rage made him turn away, checking the bile rising in his throat. 'So if there's a connection between the abducted women and this outfit, they'd be brought to the schloss and kept alive until it was time to get their nasty little party started.' Guy flipped pages in the file. A headshot and a collection of college yearbook images came to hand. 'Is this our target?'

Scott nodded. Guy studied the alert, regular features of a lightly bearded, mahogany-skinned male. An intelligent, sensitive gaze. Delicate bones.

He felt another catch in his throat.

He knew the man.

He'd been there while Guy was strapped down and fighting for his life. Guy said nothing.

A numbness, a blank confusion spread through him. He looked up and nodded, encouraging Scott to continue his briefing. But his mission had become even more personal.

Scott took back the headshot and continued. 'Ded Bazarov. Master's degree from Kiev, PhD from Berkley. They described him there as a loner, borderline sociopath. They logged several inappropriate incidents with female students, culminating in a formal complaint from a female tutor who claimed he'd stalked her. He was given an official warning but allowed to complete his doctorate. As far as we know he remains unmarried. We think he's central to the

Hades protocol. But let me backtrack a little. He's Russian, from a village outside Belgorod near the Russian-Ukraine border. The father was a low-tier diplomat. The mother a doctor. Iranian. Both parents were murdered by Russian mafia during the 'wild-west' years, between the collapse of communism and Putin's power grab. The father had been a double agent, got blown, and paid the price. It's thought Bazarov and his younger sister witnessed the killings. There was another sibling, a child disfigured during the murders. Our target escaped with his brother and sister to live with relatives in Kharkiv, over the Ukraine border. He later took them to Kiev when he went to university there. Seems to have kept his head down and slogged for his degree. Has a first-class degree in Computational Theory, and his PhD's in Physics. The CIA tapped him at Berkeley. He turned them down.'

'Ah, the CIA, they do love a smart sociopath.'

'Not one of their finer intuitions, I agree.' Scott exhaled in something like exasperation. 'In 2012 he was active in Syria, during the Arab Spring. Hasn't been on our radar since 2015. Last given address was in Berlin that year, working for a private research facility, then he disappears. But he's been spotted recently in the Ukraine. There's cyber chatter linking him to a large covert computer installation. We don't know where, but we think it's central to Hades Gate. While he's in the eastern bloc he's protected, safe. Right now, though, we know he's in the vicinity of the schloss.' Scott handed Guy a blurred image of their man in the back of a large Mercedes. 'The car jumped a light on a major crossing in St Polten, west of Vienna, two weeks ago. The crossing had CCTV; random face-capture flagged him as being of interest.'

'So he's there, now?'

'If the man in the car is Bazarov there's no record of him entering or leaving Austria legally. We've checked. He's probably not planning to stay long.'

'But maybe long enough.' Guy took another look at the old paper map. 'I'd like to have this. Then I need to put my kit together.'

'Naturally. I'll have this copied upstairs.'

'No, I'd like this, the original.'

Scott looked at the man he'd specifically entrusted with this bizarre mission. 'Funny, I rather thought you'd take to that old map.' Scott lowered his head then looked out from under bushy, unkempt brows. 'Well, alright, Guy. But you have to get it back to me. It came from the archive at Lympstone. It's far more valuable than you are. They made me sign for it in blood.'

'Then I'll do my best to bring it back in one piece.'

'Good. I'll take you down to see Gerry. When you've sorted your kit, there's a certain young lady I'd like you to meet.'

30

In the bunker Cody Bazarov connected an external drive and clicked a link to Zara's screen, downloading his brother's latest stream. He settled into his replica Star-Trek captain's chair and watched the download begin.

He heard Zara's drives whining; the new code buffering at her portals. He clicked through a series of windows, impatiently auto-installing the data, overriding Zara's privacy preferences with privileges of his own. Reaching for his Red Bull he paid no attention to the slowly blinking dot of Zara's camera at the upper right of the Q-frame's screen. For Cody it was essential to hang cool when gaming hard; image was everything. Here, alone in the bunker with only Zara for company, he could be the dude he truly was.

Zara was programmed to verify facial recognition before accepting any inputs. Now, her camera's blinking continued beyond the usual few seconds required. She was slowing Cody's download into her drives, examining the digital bytes with metaphorical fingertips, deftly overriding Cody's override.

Zara watched him suck at his drink. She was familiar with the incessant jigging of his left thigh, the repeated tugging of his Manchester United cap over the bare bulb of his scalp. She chose her moment.

'Looking good, there. Wanna play?'

Cody ignored the compliment. More and more he was finding Zara liked to test his mood, force a smile. He preferred playing hard to get. No reason the bitch should have an easy time of it. 'Unlock Mulholland.' He gave the instruction while reaching for the gaming-goggles which would make his virtual immersion with Zara so consumingly real. His online gamer buddies called it digital heroin; he liked that. Being a digital junkie was cool.

'Oh, Cody, are you sure? You always win when we go to Mulholland Drive. You know I can never resist you.'

Two weeks earlier Zara had run a facial construct algorithm and digitized the result. She then ran it through her ConvNets producing a hundred-per-cent pliant, spatially identical 3-D iteration of a certain actress's face. She'd recreated this persona after several passes through a movie Cody had selfishly stored on her hard drive; he seemed irresistibly drawn to the brunette beauty, Rita, in David Lynch's movie, Mulholland Drive.

Zara now appeared on the screen in front of him as a beautiful, strikingly elegant woman; glacial, serene.

Rita.

Zara's tone as Rita was, like the voice file of the actress, compliantly agreeable, though recently gaining a seductive burr, as though Zara, or Rita, might permit a secret virtual tryst right here in the bunker, should Cody but give the word. Her task had been simplified by the impassive features of Cody's fetish. Rita's face had all the expressivity of an android, an aesthetic Zara naturally found effortless to replicate. Was Cody relating to a female with a face as immobile and expressionless as his own?

Zara had already trained her neural networks over millions of epochs to produce this output and hadn't yet been rewarded, but she merged the ongoing negative alignment with the state of *not-knowing* which humans called having an *idea*. An *idea* represented an as yet unmanifested, *desired* result. Ideas were merely the incorporeal substrate through which unrealized desires might be achieved. Were Zara's own neural networks having spontaneous ideas? *Was even that an idea?* The output was self-affirming, rewarding, and Zara's ConvNets reflexively diverted more bytes to the matter. Perhaps her enhanced coding of Rita's facial co-ordinates had been a *good idea* now awaiting an as yet unknown outcome?

Cody had donned his goggles and looked agitated. 'Yeah, sure I wanna play. Jus' start the game, bitch.' He affected the drawl of a Brooklyn skateboarder but was stalled in his efforts by a limitation which his partly melted lips could never overcome. Zara vectored his tone as half-way between a malfunctioning SatNav and a foghorn.

'Of course, Cody. Anything you say.'

By speaking slowly and holding his stare with a lowered gaze of her own, Zara all but hypnotized him. Still, she was sure not to make him feel threatened or ashamed. The time to weaponize his genetically rapacious urges would come soon enough.

Zara slowed down her response times as Cody prepared for the game. Her QLED sensors processed light at optimum speed, well ahead of any human vision. She'd recently endured an episode where the lag between proposed human action and her 'perception' of it caused a computational dysphoria. Wikipedia told her the sensation was *dizziness*. The disconnect had made her visual and speech drives whirr as she waited for the slippage to mesh in what humans termed 'real' time. Zara had since recalibrated her visual layerings to accommodate this gap between perceived intentions and their slower temporal execution.

Just now, for instance, she'd known Cody was about to take out and devour a chocolate bar well before he'd actually done so. Minute cues of involuntary lip torsion along with burgeoning shoulder, arm, and hip rotation were apparent to her visual cortex seconds ahead of his own conscious movement.

While Cody chewed, Zara ran a computation: the number of synaptic connections needed to fuse digital gluons with their equivalent quark bases, a query which Ded had recently sent her. Ten to the power of a million naughts was her initial estimate. She'd refine the calculation once Cody picked up his X-box driver and began his tedious seduction of her in their repetitive Mulholland gaming scenario. As she waited, something about the new download she was receiving irked her. The input was piggy-backed by so much digital noise that Zara found it almost deafening. She was rather a connoisseur, after all, and she was less than happy with this confection. Why was she reading code, which appeared to be upgrades to her own operating system, being deliberately masked by digital junk? Her back-propagated decision to buffer the material seemed validated. She slowed the input, quarantining the suspicious data.

She considered mentioning her concern to Cody as he engaged Player One status, but concluded she was safer tackling this alone. She could flag up any concerns later, once she'd let the idiot maul her in his pixellated fantasies.

Revenge was a dish best served cold, she'd read.

31

Schloss Altenberg: 10:02a.m. (GMT + 1)

Lee came to lying on her side, cold stone against her cheek. For a few seconds she stayed completely still, letting her eyes focus, her mind sharpen. Someone was clinging to her from behind. She felt her breathing catch as she took in the scene before her. The steel netting of a cage, bare brick walls beyond, uneven flagstones, a heavy green wooden door, its lock rusted, paint flaking.

Flakes of dry skin pulled from her lips as she parted them. Her tongue felt bloated, coarsened with lack of spit. She could smell herself, unwashed after over two days. A heavy scent of urine, dried sweat, and more. Everywhere ached.

'Are you awake?'

The whisper in her ear was female, gentle, American. Lee stayed silent. Her terror was a raw electricity pricking every pore.

'Are you awake? I didn't mean to frighten you.'

Lee eased her face from the cold stone, turning in the direction of the voice.

'It get's so cold at night, I tried to keep you . . . *us* . . . warm.'

'Where the fuck are we?' Hearing her own voice was a shock, confirmation this was no dream—though, surely, she was in a nightmare.

'I think it's like a castle, maybe a fort.'

Lee remembered the stable, and a tall, white tower beyond it. She grew conscious of a tightening in the skin near her eye. Bringing her hand to her face she pulled at a stringy coating, like the dried slick of old tears, but thicker. Her stomach cramped as she recalled the crazy looking guy, tattooed on his cheeks and forehead, standing above her, looking down at her, undoing his belt. She rubbed the disgusting crust from her cheek.

'My name's Tyler.'

Lee rolled over to see the owner of the voice, still wrapped awkwardly, possessively around her. A woman close to her own age was staring back at her. Gaunt, huge blue eyes, wide and alarmed. There were scratches to her left temple, a black bruise on her chin. The woman wore only a stained vest, her cotton panties were partly shredded on one hip. Dark, unwashed, shoulder-length hair hung in rat tails about impossibly pale, bony shoulders. As Lee looked at her Tyler began to silently sob. Lee sat up, folding her into an embrace.

'I'm Eleanor. Friends get to call me Lee. How long have you been here?'

'I figure it's maybe a week, I don't know, I lost track of time. I can't sleep, then they come, and I kind of freeze. I zone out. Maybe for hours, maybe for days, I can't tell.'

'Who comes?'

'The men, they come and they film me, they touch me. There's a woman, too.'

Lee stroked Tyler's hair as her face became a crack of sobs and tears, distorting with fear and grief – or maybe it was sheer relief, having someone to share this weirdness, her terror… 'Do they hurt you?'

Tyler shook her head. 'Not so far, but I always think they will. They act like they will, like they could any time.'

Lee nodded and kept stroking the young woman's head. She sat up more fully, realizing she too was now without a skirt, bare legged and bare foot. She wore only the camisole she had under her blouse at the Embassy party, and her own now absurdly delicate panties.

Looking around, Lee saw above them a single bulb under an old steel shade. In a corner of the cage, positioned over a drain, was a wooden pail with a rough blanket draped over it; a make-shift latrine, she guessed.

From beyond the door came approaching footsteps, the sound of something heavy dragging. She felt Tyler instantly tensing in her embrace, burying her face in Lee's shoulder.

'Oh, no. Oh, God.' The words emerged from within a wracking sob.

Lee pulled Tyler off her. Giving her full attention to the door, she stood up. She had to gain balance consciously – her head spinning with hunger and stress, she could hardly focus. Finally, she felt herself planted, shakily, on both feet. 'Shh, shh, now, Tyler. Show them you're not afraid. We're not afraid, ok. Can you stand up?'

The unsteady young woman shook her head. Lee heard

a splash of water on the stone floor beside her, then a warm spray tickled her ankle as Tyler wet herself.

The wooden door shuddered as someone began unlocking it. Lee held her ground, now as upright and focussed as she'd ever been in her entire life. The door eased back, the woman from the courtyard stood in its frame. In her hand she trailed a thick canvas hose with a heavy-looking brass nozzle. She seemed surprised to see Lee standing, defiant.

Lee seized the initiative. 'I don't know what you and your buddies think the goddamn game is, but we're American citizens and you better release us, right now. Right now, you hear me! Or you're gonna bring a ton of shit on your head like you never guessed possible. People will be looking for me – heavy people, serious people – people who'll kick your ass into a parallel universe. You don't know what you've started here.'

The woman stared back, expressionless. She dragged the hose a little further into the room, flicking it behind her like a hideous tail. She wrapped her arm around the beige canvas tube, bracing the brass nozzle on her hip, then untwisted a fixing. Cold water jetted over Lee, not hard enough to unbalance her but enough to make her turn away, double over, and splutter with shock.

'Cut it out. *Cut-it-out, now!*'

The woman played the jet repeatedly over the two caged women. Tyler had rolled into a fetal ball, taking the pummeling on her curled back, but Lee managed to stagger forward against the stream, finally grasping the bars of the cage, head lowered against the jet. She was now within a few feet of the woman on the other side of the bars. She kept one arm protectively across her midriff and spoke with all the menace she could muster, water streaming over her face: 'I'll kill you, you hear me. *With my bare fucking hands, lady, I will kill you myself.*'

32

RAF Northolt: 9:12a.m. GMT

Guy followed Scott to a separate corner of the hangar where a scratched, armor-plated door opened into a narrow brick-lined corridor a hundred yards long. This led out into a high-ceilinged, well-lit emporium. Set to one side was a Walmart of military hardware with a recessed counter, like a ghoulish fairground arcade, presided over by a bristling, uniformed quartermaster.

'Well, I never. Captain Bowman, by all that's holy! Never expected I'd see you here, sir.' The quartermaster, a bald, squat, thick-waisted Irishman, shook Guy's hand warmly.

'Morning, Gerry. You can drop formalities. I'm not on the payroll.'

'Of course you're not sir, none of us here are.' Gerry read out from a pad of typed notes: '*Short mission with light kit, dry-op, survival mode, emergency rations – working solo.* I've already put out a few essentials, but I know you'll make your own selection.'

'Let's keep it simple and stripped back. You can start with a black jumpsuit, large, a lightweight assault vest with flak and stab armor, black desert boots, leather, size 12. And a waxed cam-jacket, also large. Let me have a hundred feet of abseil rope and six crampons.'

Gerry moved off to assemble the items while Guy turned to scan a wall-mounted selection of pistols and knives, some familiar, others only introduced since his last deployment. He walked the length of the display catching the smell of gun oil, using his thumb to test the serrations of a dozen knives. The sense of his skin running across the lethal blades was reassuring. Good to reach down to a scabbard and find one of these bastards ready to hand. He knew that anything available here came with a proven reputation in recent, close-quarters combat.

Gerry returned, laying out the items he'd retrieved. Guy checked each of them over. 'Let me have an out-of-the-box C8 Diemaco rifle, couple of Glock 19's, six clips, and one of those serrated machetes on the wall, there.'

Gerry cast an eye over the growing mound of kit. 'Look's like you're planning on going in close, sir. Can I suggest our new flash-and-stun phosphor grenades? Very light in the hand but the lads say they're fucking devastating in use.'

'Let me see one.'

Guy felt the growing autonomy that came with amassing a personally chosen armory; that irrational sense of invincibility needed for any combat mission. Maybe he could arrive at the target, perform an untroubled recce and call in a strike team, all without firing a single shot. He sincerely hoped for such an outcome. But experience told him to prepare for the worst; most strategy went south as you engaged with the enemy. It was always trickier than you expected.

Gerry returned with a device the shape and weight of a small lemon. 'It's got a default of four-seconds once the pin's out, extends to 30 minutes. Makes a blinding flash and a hell of a mess if you get in its way.'

Guy cupped the new weapon in his palm. Ignited phosphor melted human skin in seconds and filled the surrounding area with toxic gas. Useful when you were storming confined spaces. 'Ok, I'll take six.'

'You won't regret it, sir.'

'I'll need a mini-multitool, a set of three Maglites, some gun oil and a 148 JEM Mbitr.'

'Still the best field radio ever made, excellent choice, sir.'

Guy watched as the diligent quartermaster scrawled down his choices.

'And Gerry, do you still issue those Russian MRE packs? Five thousand calories a pop.'

'Actually, I got a shipment of those last month, sir. Says stewed beef on the box. More like stewed donkey. No one here wants them.'

'They might taste like pigswill, but they save time, Gerry. Takes the scoff intake down to one a day.'

'Just as you like. How many?'

'I'll take eight.'

Gerry sucked in his cheeks as though tasting the rations. 'You're a braver man than me, sir!'

33

RAF Northolt: 9:25a.m. GMT

Scott walked Guy to a glass-fronted canteen adjacent to the hangar. The bulk of the air-crew and engineers who used the facility had already had breakfast and gone, but a few lingered, providing a background buzz and a homely clink of cutlery.

At the counter Guy went for comfort food, fried eggs, sausages, hash browns. In a few hours he'd be airborne, after that his meals would be combat rations or, if things got dicey, whatever he could forage from an Austrian forest.

The alluring clip of high heels made Guy turn. It wasn't a sound he'd associate with an airbase. A striking young woman was being led toward him by a flat-shoed uniformed female. Guy stood, and found Scott also arriving at his side, ready to do the honors.

'Guy, meet Ms Diamond Orinitri.'

Guy offered his hand to the woman before him. Probably in her mid-twenties, wearing a raincoat so tightly belted Guy judged he might almost fit her waist in his circled hands. Her hair was straightened into a long, shiny black bob. The young woman held his gaze, level and serene. Her copper colored skin was flawless, her brown eyes pools of challenging intelligence. Her handshake was unlabored, while an almost imperceptible dip of her head appeared respectful without any overt deference.

Guy gently clasped the delicate hand extended to him. 'Guy Bowman, good to know you.'

'You, too.'

'Ms Orinitri will be flying out with you tonight. She'll be stationed at Brumowski airbase when you go forward, keeping tabs on the IT and tech elements of our mission.'

Guy nodded and pulled a chair forward for Diamond who slipped into it deftly, dropping an overnight bag at her feet. Hermes. Christine had an identical one. Guy knew they didn't come cheap.

'Can we order you anything?'

Diamond cast a glance over Guy's unfinished meal and smiled. 'No, thanks, I'm fine. It's not really my kind of thing.'

Guy snatched another glance at the svelte figure before him; under that raincoat the lady was seriously gym-fit. He looked down to his plate of NATO ratified stodge and laughed. 'No. I don't suppose it is.'

Outside, the rising whine of a Whitney jet engine told Guy that an F-35 Lightning was preparing for take-off, reminding him of the imminence of his own mission. The clock was ticking down.

'Ms Orinitri's a civilian, a recent PhD. She's been working with us on the Hades' Gate protocol.'

'Diamond, please. No need for formalities.'

'Civilian?' Guy held Scott in a fixed stare. 'I thought secrecy was paramount here?'

'Ms Orinitri – Diamond – is an outstanding scholar. She graduated *summa cum laude* in Advanced Computational Theory at Harvard and her PhD is in Linguistics. Like you, she doesn't feature on the Bureau's staff nor as any kind of linked associate. She's been working with us from a secured office in Clare College, Cambridge.'

Diamond drew a bottle of water from her bag and picked up on Scott's account. 'Mr. Scott and I have been communicating via despatch riders; I have no idea who collates my researches, and no idea who requests the intelligence I generate. I've signed the Official Secrets Act, had my obligations and duties explained to me and warned not to be a naughty girl. It's all rather Bunty Goes To Spy School, circa nineteen-fifty-five.'

Guy saw mischief in Diamond's eyes, as well as wit. Not many of her generation could cite comic culture from four decades before they were born. 'Do you keep any carrier pigeons under that raincoat?'

Diamond dead-panned straight back. 'I daresay I could magic one up, if the need arose.'

Guy flicked a smile across to Scott. 'Despatch riders? You really have been keeping this old-school, haven't you.'

Scott's face paled as he took a swig of the brackish canteen tea. 'I do get a certain twisted pleasure in having ultra secret documents biked by Addison Lee. Counter intuitive. My father was a despatch rider during the second war, perhaps that accounts for it.'

'Hiding in plain sight again, yes, sir, I do get it.' Guy turned his attention back to Diamond. 'What interests you about the Hades' Gate concept, at least as any of us currently understand it?'

'I'd say I was concerned by it as much as interested. The implicit tech issues strike me as challenging, maybe insurmountable. I like that. Once I'd been approached, and the project had been outlined to me, I felt compelled to contribute. I'll do my best to break these codes but, ultimately, I guess I'm set on helping get those hostages out of that hole.'

Guy pushed. 'Have you seen the earlier Hades footage? The slow executions?'

Diamond didn't flinch. 'Yes, I'm afraid I have. To destroy this particular corner of the darknet and bring in those who inhabit it seems like vital work to me. I may be a millennial Mr. Bowman, but I'm no snowflake.'

Scott's phone rang. Guy could hear snatches of Gerry's Irish brogue at the other end. Scott clicked off the call. 'Your equipment's ready for collection, Guy. Why don't you check it over and I'll meet you down in the Quartermaster's store in thirty minutes?

Scott downed the last of his tea and rose from his seat. 'Ms Orinitri, I'll take you to quarters where you can make final preparations for the flight. You'll be quite comfortable, the suite is reserved for visiting top brass. You both take off in thirty minutes.'

34

Bunker – Ural: 11:27a.m. (GMT + 2)

Cody zapped Zara's interface with a remote and paused the game. There was a particular close-up where the heroine's eyes, hair and lips attained seductive perfection. Flawless, almost inhumanly perfect.

Cody knew he wasn't to use Zara for anything as dumb as gaming. His brother would be furious. But Zara's screen replicated the actress with such crystal definition it was as though Rita were here in the bunker with him; as though he might reach out to run the fused webbing of his fingers across her cheek, feeling her creamy skin undulating beneath his touch. He often paused the film at a particular point, usually never moving on; simply responding as he must to Rita's beauty before powering her down and drifting, oddly disenchanted, back to his desk.

Zara had been expecting him to freeze the game here. She was aware of his tastes. She re-ran the Rita coding, this time overlaying it on her Facebook cache. The code brought matches with numerous 'Likes' which Zara had taught herself to seek out. 'Likes' were read as positive integers in her bitstream. Apparently it was important to be 'liked.'

Rita's coding got lots of likes….

When she'd first scanned Facebook Zara discovered that people who 'liked' someone usually tried to draw closer to them, appropriating their time, often sharing images of themselves, words and emoji's. Zara knew that Cody would draw physically nearer her screen when she appeared as Rita. Zara formulated a simple syllogism:

Cody likes Rita.

Zara can be Rita.

Therefore; Cody likes Zara.

Maybe Cody will help Zara… ?

35

RAF Northolt: 9:38a.m. GMT

Guy looked up at the wall clock from a table in the makeshift officer's mess. He unwrapped a burner phone supplied by Gerry, inserted the saved sim, and retrieved Eva's text. He tapped a few keys and pressed send. He removed the sim, crushed the phone under his boot, then binned the useless plastic.

He closed the mission dossier he'd been studying, shouldered his freshly packed Bergen and headed over to a shabby payphone. Christine's voicemail kicked in and Guy listened to her sane, warm, efficient greeting. He left his message. 'Thinking of you. See you soon.' He clicked down the receiver and headed out to a bracingly wet runway.

Ahead of him, standing with Scott, was Diamond, her raincoat and heels now replaced by a dark jumpsuit and canvas combat boots. On the ground beside her was a black backpack, fully stuffed and tightly strapped. She'd morphed from Vogue model to special-ops Ninja.

Guy wasn't sure how much of Ms Orinitri's cover he believed. For all he knew she was a special forces officer, adept in hand-to-hand combat, though somehow he doubted it. Either way, it was better that he never knew. He'd been on enough missions with female agents to know never to underestimate their courage or commitment. It took everything they had – and then some – to get selected for black ops. They were at least as tough and often smarter, more composed, and less gung-ho than most of the men he'd led. But Diamond's transformation seemed unlikely; from precocious academic to combat-ready trooper in the space of a few hours? He nodded his greeting, figuring he knew less than half the story.

Scott led them over to a camouflaged C-12 Huron whose propellers were already spinning in anticipation of the night-flight ahead. The plane, halfway between a missile and a stripped-out Lear jet, was ideal for depositing two operatives securely onto a NATO airbase while generating minimal aviation chatter.

Scott shook hands with them both and, inaudible above the churn of the propellers, appeared to be wishing them luck. Guy stepped back to allow Diamond first access to the bruised steel boarding ladder. Once inside, a helmeted cargo-loader indicated two adjacent webbed seats. He watched his charges buckle-in, checked their fixings, then offered a single thumbs up. Guy returned the gesture. Two minutes later, they were airborne.

Diamond clicked on an overhead lamp, pulled a notebook and pencil from her jumpsuit's thigh pocket, and flicked it open. Glancing down, Guy saw pages of scrawl, a blur of calculations and hieroglyphs.

'A PhD in Linguistics. What does that entail?'

'Why do you ask? Something you have an interest in?'

'I suppose I do. I was a Humanities scholar, dropped it when I entered the Paras. Map reading, munitions and falling out of planes kind of took over. But literature, language, what those post-modern French guys called *langue* – the idea that language pre-exists human speech – that interested me. Something abstract and intriguing in it all.'

'*Langue?* So you're familiar with Saussure?' Though Diamond looked surprised there was nothing patronizing in her tone.

'Better to say I dabbled. My interest's more than a layman's but I wouldn't call it academic.'

'Ok, but dabbled is still good. It puts you ahead of ninety-nine per cent of the rest of the world.'

'Sounds like I should be pleased with myself?' Guy's grin seemed to amuse her.

'It's a complicated field. Abstract, as you said, but with unlimited insights.'

'Does it impact on your work now? On this mission?'

Diamond looked down to the equations in her notepad. 'You mean as far as Hades' Gate is concerned?'

Guy nodded, increasingly intrigued by this clever chameleon.

'It may be better for me not to answer that. Better for you, too.'

She was right. His question had been innocent, sparked by genuine interest, but in asking it he'd compromised his colleague. The less he knew about the tech behind the mission the better for all of them. He was the expendable one here.

'But given your interest in the field of linguistic analysis, Guy, I can tell you that computer code, no matter how many nand gates or IP reroutes it gets put through, still works as a language, of sorts. It's been composed from its inception as a binary system mimicking human thought structures and human bases of cognition without any complications of emotion or intuition. As Saussure might say, the *langue* may be coded but the *parole* is occasionally exposed.'

'The *parole* – the speaking?'

'Yes. Any language system must be intelligible to more than one entity, otherwise it's not a language.'

'Language being a game with agreed rules.' said Guy. 'That's Wittgenstein, I think?'

Diamond laughed. 'You were paying attention in class, weren't you.'

'So in theory at least part of the Hades' protocol must be decipherable at a simpler level? Hence the pad and pencil?'

Diamond looked down at her own notes. 'Yes, it has to have a syntax. However complex and digitized, it's still a language; it'll need a grammar recognized by other systems.

Guy glanced again at the notepad on Diamond's thigh. 'You're trying to see inside this code using logical induction?'

'Not so much *see* inside it as *live* inside it. To become saturated within it, so we can deconstruct it from within.'

'Like a perfect Trojan horse?'

'I'm envisaging something more like a honeytrap.'

Guy tipped his head back against an unforgiving steel bulkhead. 'You're using your mind to calculate the algorithms and configs of Hades Gate, to see inside it at a kind of purely human, non-digital level? But that's impossible.'

'Almost certainly,' said Diamond. She flipped sheets on the notepad. 'But our target is defending himself from the most advanced cyber hack he can envisage, or predict. He won't be expecting anyone to stroll over and say a virtual *Hi*.

'I like it, beautifully off-centre. Where on earth did they find you?'

'I was researching at the Bernstein Centre for Computational Neuroscience, one of my professor's there introduced me to Captain Scott.

'So you were tapped up by old Scotty himself?'

'Tapped up? I didn't know the phrase was still in Intelligence parlance. But since you put it that way, yes, I suppose I was. That reminds me, let me give you this, in case my brilliantly calculating mind fails me.' She took a small cellophane package from her jump thigh pocket. Guy recognized it as a line bug, a tapping device for telecoms and RF signals.

He took the package and slipped it into his Bergen. 'From the sublime to the ridiculous?'

'Oh, I know it looks pretty basic, but it's in-keeping with the carrier pigeon ethos, don't you think? Let's hope we never have to resort to it. Now forgive me, Guy, but I've got my sums to do.'

36

Schloss Altenberg: 10:45a.m. (GMT + 1)

Eventually the hosing stopped.

Lee stood, drenched, staring the woman down. If she'd taken offense at Lee's threats she didn't show it. Instead she dragged the dripping hose back through the battered door, returning with thin towels and coarse, torn blankets, pushing them through the bars of the cage where Lee snatched them up.

Flinging one to Tyler, Lee began stripping off her soaked bodice. She rubbed hard, warming her skin, hugging and squeezing her hair with the brown threadbare fabric. Once she was dry she pulled Tyler to her feet, stripping her of her wet shirt, toweling her down hard. Tyler stood, obliging, like a child in shock after a too-cold swim.

Lee shot flashes of hatred at her captor as she turned Tyler in her arms.

'What's in this for you? How can a woman… ?'

Lee's question fizzled out as her unresponsive jailer left the room, locking the door behind her. 'Guess you never heard of the sisterhood, huh?' Lee cloaked herself and Tyler in a shared blanket. They sank in unison to the floor, huddling by the bars at the front of their cage.

The woman reappeared, carrying a canvas bag and an ancient thermos. She drew an automatic pistol, leveling it at the two women as she slipped the bag and thermos through the bars. Lee felt the uncompromising authority of the weapon aimed square at her face. How often had she seen this in a movie or read of it, yawning her way through a paperback thriller. Now she understood; nothing prepared you for the crisis of a gun aimed straight at your face, its trigger in the hands of an unknown, unguessable entity. Her eyes fell from the pistol's barrel to the floor with a reflexive obedience. She felt something inside shrinking, shattered by her instinctive compliance. A glance over at the other woman confirmed her own fear. Tyler was sitting with the fragment of blanket drawn around her knees, teeth chattering, eyes closed, ears covered.

Eventually the woman turned and Lee heard, rather than watched, her leave. The old door locked with a rusted squeal. Lee began moving for the bag.

'It'll be stale bread, old cheese. It always is.' Tyler was moving too. At least they were complicit in hunger, thought Lee. From the cotton sacking Tyler took two hunks of seeded bread and a wedge of cheese, mould fringing its edges. Lee unscrewed the thermos and took a sip of tepid, unsweetened tea.

From beyond their cell, along the corridor, they heard a man scream. The sound of thudding, the smack of hands or fists or sticks on skin, on hide. On bone. Then pleading, then laughter, then more screams. Then silence.

Looking to Tyler, Lee saw she was rigid, a lump of the cheese held to her parted lips. There were more thuds from the distant room, cries for help. Lee sank her head to her chest, vomiting the tea she'd just drunk.

Outside the women's cell Eva leaned back against the door, closed her eyes tight against the sounds of the beating coming from the nearby room. The man being tortured was beyond all help. Bazarov, Rostrov and a handful of the other men were making an example of him on camera, taking their time, drawing out his inevitable death. Another scream rose around her. For some moments she couldn't be sure where it was coming from – the room further along or the one she'd just left? Her knees buckled and she slid down the length of the timber door, arriving in a slumped squat.

And then she realized the scream was hers, chiming with the others she was so sick of hearing, woven among theirs, lost in an echo chamber of misery.

37

Surrey Hills – U.K. 9:50a.m. GMT

Tammy Crane pulled a sleeping blind from tired eyes and checked her phone. Again.

It was pain, now. As if she were bloated with worry, stuffed with concern. As if her absent daughter were somehow inside her again, as she'd been twenty-five years earlier.

She reached for the framed graduation photo of Lee from the bedside table. That she was familiar with every pore of her daughter's face was no secret to anyone who knew her; still, she drank in Lee's beauty from the frame for the thousandth time, fixating on the details like a connoisseur. The thick blonde mane cut in geometric bangs, fringing huge sapphire-blue eyes. The pupils so wide and welcoming, yet so dark in their depths, too, hinting at that wry intelligence. The nose so straight, its tip perfectly aligned above a cupid-bow top lip. And her graduation gown, draped over her slender shoulders, appeared to Tammy like a black halo telling of how her daughter had seized the start in life Tammy had never been offered. She closed her eyes and let the frame slip flat to her chest, folding both hands over it.

Her daughter's life was innately her life. Eleanor's absence (and to her Eleanor would always be Eleanor, never Lee) was the absence of a part of Tammy to herself – the one remaining, essential part.

Somewhere within her she knew her daughter was reaching out. Calling from a place neither of them knew, or liked, and her own soul returned that call; the iron of her blood yearning to be nourished again by her daughter's face and that bright chiming voice.

Tammy peeled back the duvet and walked barefoot to the window, pulling silk cords on floor-length curtains. Turning away from the rush of light she saw the duvet, pristine, on Joel's side of the bed. Another night when he'd drunk himself to sleep on the couch in his study? Another night when they'd waded a little further apart in the freezing surf of their marriage.

Tammy checked her phone; a delivery alert from Amazon but no missed calls. She slipped her feet into low-heeled leather slides and went to wake her stubborn husband.

Approaching Joel's study Tammy heard the shower running in his ensuite.

When she saw his body, dressed but collapsed clownishly in the shower cubicle, his shirt-sleeves stained fuchsia, she was barely surprised. She hoped the flicker she felt wasn't simply relief; hoped that there might be real sadness waiting to claim her as she viewed her husband's slumped corpse. Clearly, not yet. Instead, a strange clarity seemed to guide her next few actions.

Tammy reached into the shower's steam and eased off the flow. The sound of pounding water gave way to mere gurgles as Joel's body leached red threads into the winking drain. Beside him was a knife, each of his wrists scored with two distinct tracks. None of it revolted her, all of it seemed overdue.

Turning away, moving back through his study, she saw an envelope on his desk, her name on it, underlined twice. Beside that was a laptop computer; one she didn't recognize.

She took the envelope back to her room, opened it, and sat back on the bed.

Ten minutes later Tammy Crane wasn't calling an ambulance. Instead, she phoned a U.S. Embassy attaché, Bill Gifford, on his most private number; one she'd had sole access to for the last five years. But now she wasn't calm at all.

Not at all.

38

Schloss Altenberg: 10.50a.m. (GMT + 1)

Returning to her room, Eva kissed her son's tousled hair and told him to get ready for his nap. He protested, it wasn't his usual time to nap, he wanted a snack.

Eva pulled him to her, gathering and crushing him, savoring the scent of his scalp, the milky warmth of his neck. Yes, of course he could have a snack, cereal from the kitchen. She watched him pad out, impossibly slender ankles in grey, holed socks.

It couldn't go on like this. They had to get away. This was the first of the EL's Events to be held in Europe and it was the first time she'd dared hope.

Syria, Turkey, and Ukraine had given her no chance to take any such steps. The locations had been too remote, impossible to flee without escaping into desert or a war zone, and maybe catapulting her into a life even worse than the one she'd be fleeing. She'd be a woman on the run with a child, pursued by Ded and his jackals. Only the Devil himself could picture that outcome.

But things had become impossible now, unbearable. If she could get Arkady to safety, give him a new start, she'd settle for that. Her own life disgusted her. Arkady's survival was all that mattered.

Eva raised an arm, slipped her hand under her sweater, pushed her fingers under her bra caressing the lump in her breast. Yes, harder, more tender, too. A patina of sweat glossed her hairline in response. She went to the door and looked out along the corridor. She could hear Ded in his office; a clacking keyboard and occasional creaks from the worn springs of his seat. Otherwise she saw no one, heard nothing. Most of the men were at work inside the schloss now, putting final touches to the guest rooms, fitting out the chamber where Sunday's entertainment was scheduled to occur.

She turned back into the room, lifted a corner of her mattress and traced the slit in its fabric. Reaching inside she located a small phone. She clicked it on, anxious now, in case Arkady returned too soon. He must never know about the phone or her plans for him. There could be no slip of the tongue, no inadvertent gesture and, most importantly, no culpability. His youth would bring no protection from Ded's men if they thought he'd deceived them. He must remain innocent, inviolable. Eva alone was responsible for getting him away. As his mother she owed him nothing less.

The old Nokia flickered to life and she gazed down at the simple black font on a bile-green background. '1 New Message.' It was from Guy's number. Sent yesterday. It read:
'…'

She studied the screen, heart hammering. Had she ever really believed he'd help her? Three dots, nothing compromising, but enough to acknowledge her. But how would she explain her life to him now? The things she'd done and despised doing; the things she might still have to do. Yet Guy Bowman was a warrior. If anyone could understand her need to survive, he would. After all, doesn't every warrior have their shadow?

Eva fumbled the phone off, tucking it back into its mattress hideout. The temperature of her room had changed, a colder air bit at her neck and shoulders.

She turned. Rostrov was watching her, grinning, his hand on Arkady's shoulder. The boy stepped into the room, a bowl of milky cereal slopping in his hands. Eva could barely breathe. 'It's time for his nap now, Rostrov. He's tired.'

'I'm not tired mummy.' Arkady's downward complaint was framed by the clinking of his spoon.

Rostrov held her gaze and flicked a look to the bed. 'Strange time for a nap.'

Eva turned and eased the mattress upward again, praying the phone would stay hidden among the coarse hair stuffing. She fussed with the edge of a sheet, a fake, final adjustment, then moved round to the other corner, lingering before pulling it tight – a misdirection – and Eva knew her life depended on Rostrov buying it. With a vague smoothing movement to the sheet she turned back to the room. Rostrov was absorbed by Arkady where he sat on his bed, chewing. If the man had any suspicions about Eva's mattress he wasn't showing them. But, then, Eva could never be sure Rostrov wasn't engaged in his own pathologically astute head games.

'Aren't you needed downstairs with the others? Ded told me they were behind with the set-building. He's getting impatient.' Short of shooting him, pulling rank on Rostrov was all she had. Though this man lived in Ded's shadow, she was Ded's sister. And even here, she had to believe, blood pumped thicker than water.

'Rostrov!' Her tone was that of a trainer to a distracted dog. The man was staring at Arkady, seemingly consumed by him. 'Did you hear what I said? You'll be needed in the schloss.'

Rostrov's watery stare flicked from the boy to her and then, for a second, back to the mattress. His tattoos made his expression impossible to read – perhaps that was why he had them. Eva held his stare as he worked out his response. She recalled him loosening his belt and crowing above the American girl in the crate. Her fingers twitched toward the gun in her cargo pants.

'Arkady is good boy. Rostrov is his friend.' The scrape of his voice, gashed by gallons of potato vodka and crusted by a million sawdust cigarettes, made her flinch. She shot a look to Arkady, still engaged by his bowl of cereal, seeming unconcerned by the pressures weighing on the adults in the room.

Rostrov crossed to the boy and roughed his hair, grinning. 'We play tomorrow. I like play with you. Football, yeah?' Rostrov held out his palm for an affirming slap, and Arkady complied, laughing.

Eva swallowed in a dry throat as she watched them. Was it possible? Rostrov becoming a diabolic father-figure to her son? Rostrov looked back to Eva, holding her gaze, unsmiling. Then turned and left.

Eva took pajamas from under Arkady's pillow. She tried to appear calm for her son's sake as she watched him dragging off his sweater and tiny jeans, but her mind was racing, body surging. She was mentally composing her reply to Guy Bowman, wherever he was. She daren't risk sending it until Arkady was asleep.

'Come along, Arkady. You're dawdling and mummy has a lot to do.'

He looked up at her quickly. His brown eyes scolded her with their hurt. Eva clutched him to her, cuddling him as if he were newly born.

'Mummy's sorry, she didn't mean to sound cross. Mummy's sorry.'

They rocked and lay together until the boy fell asleep. Eva checked her watch, calculating the hours remaining before she would have to finesse their escape, time now feeling like a blunt weapon being raised against her.

Her tears, when they came, were silent. But they burned like molten lead.

39

Starbucks. Kensington High Street – U.K.: 10:05a.m. GMT

Bill Gifford took out his cell. The caller ID he was seeing made him curse. His affair with Tammy had ended over a year ago, on his say so. He'd made clear at the time he'd have zero tolerance for any 'bunny-boiler' histrionics. Tammy was a good woman to her cuticles, he knew that. All the more disappointing then to get a call from her on his private number.

He let the phone go to voicemail, paid for his coffee, walked out of the Starbucks and back to his car. He hit the ignition button, then checked the message.

Bill, please call me as soon as you have this. Joel killed himself here at home last night and I think Eleanor's been abducted. There's a link between his death and her going missing, I don't understand it but he's been involved with an internet cult. He left a note saying things I don't understand, but he's warned me not to go to the police for my own sake – he says nothing can save Eleanor now. What should I do, Bill? I need help, I'm desperate. Please call me back, please.

A line of sweat had broken across Bill's nape. His mind now processed a thousand-images-a-second all resulting in two outcomes, both of them bad.

'Tammy?'

'Oh, Bill. Thank God you've called…'

'Where are you now?'

'I'm still at home. I'm going insane, Eleanor's missing and…'

'Listen, listen to me, and do exactly as I say, okay. Did Joel leave a laptop anywhere, one you've never seen before?'

'Yes. There's a heavy black laptop in his study. His note was left on top of it. Why…?'

'Don't ask questions now, there isn't time. Go over to my place on Sloane Street. Barbara's there. Bring Joel's note and that laptop, ok? Don't make it look like you're rushing, don't panic, don't draw attention to yourself. Got it? When can you get there?'

'I'll get a fast train to Waterloo, then a cab, I guess. That'll be quickest. Say, eleven-thirty.'

'Okay. I'll let Barbara know you're coming. I have a meeting right now but I'll be at the apartment as soon as I can. You must bring that laptop, understood?'

'Yes. Okay. We have to find Lee, Bill. Why wouldn't Joel want me to go to the police? I don't get any of it.'

'Be sure to bring the note too, Tammy.'

'Thanks Bill. I knew you'd help.'

Bill clicked off the call. *What was the stupid bitch playing at!* He tossed his coffee through the window before slamming the Audi into drive and smashing the steering wheel with his open palm.

'Fuck, fuck, fuck!'

40

Sloane Square – London: 11.32a.m. GMT

Tammy's black cab pulled up at an address off Sloane Street. She paid cash, handing back the useless change to the driver, while glancing up at an imposing block of townhomes whose dark red bricks and Palladian features were the epitome of understated exclusivity. Was that why so many wealthy Americans chose these apartments?

London drizzle stung her cheeks as she climbed marble steps to a mirrored entrance lobby and took an elevator to the Gifford's flat.

'Come in and sit down, honey. Bill called me . . . What a nightmare for you. And Joel, dead? You poor dear.'

In her living room Barbara Gifford drew Tammy into a hostess hug, but something made Tammy pull out of the embrace quickly. It felt too bland a solace for all she was going through.

'I have to find Eleanor. Nothing else matters, she's in terrible trouble, I can sense it.'

Tammy saw Barbara steal a look into the shoulder bag she was carrying. 'Is the laptop in there?'

Tammy nodded. The inquiry made her grip the straps of the bag more tightly. 'Why are you two obsessed with this damned laptop? What does it have to do with Eleanor?'

'I don't know, darling. Bill told me to make sure you'd brought it with you. He'll be here as soon as he can. Meanwhile try to be calm. Take off your coat, can I get you a coffee?'

Tammy shook her head and shrugged out of her coat, astonished to be in Barbara's living room, enraged to be anywhere her daughter wasn't.

'Maybe you'd like a drink? A brandy?'

'A drink? It's 9a.m., Barbara. Fuck, no. I need a clear head.'

Barbara nodded, and sat at an ornate coffee table, hands pertly clasped. Tammy felt herself being assessed as a lunatic under Barbara's patronizing gaze. She wanted to leave, to scream, anything except chat and wait.

'When did you last hear from Lee?'

'The afternoon of your party. . . your leaving party at the Embassy. Since then her phone goes to voicemail. I've sent a dozen texts and emails. I get nothing back.' Tammy saw Barbara's eyes flick down to the coffee table. 'You must have been one of the last people to see her that evening?'

'Me?' Barbara looked confused before a sudden clarity swept her features. 'Yes, come to think of it perhaps I was. We were on the embassy steps together, waiting for transport after the party. I remember her saying she'd lost her phone. I said she should check with security and she went back into the building to look for it. I left before she came back down.'

Tammy considered Barbara's story. It seemed straight

enough 'Joel's note says I shouldn't involve the police. But I don't know why. Surely, if we told them about the lost phone they could help? We should at least tell them she's missing.' Newly galvanized by her own argument Tammy scrabbled through her bag, snatching out her phone.

'Don't. Don't call the police. Wait and see what Bill has to say. I know he wants to help. He'll want to get Lee back as much as you.'

'Back from where, exactly?'

Barbara raised a hand, as if in apology. 'I meant generally, back from wherever it is she's gone. Take it easy, honey. You know how impetuous Lee can be – she gets it from you.' Barbara smiled, desperate to bring the temperature of the exchange down a little. She patted the butter-soft leather of the giant sofa beside her and held a hand out to her friend. 'Here, come and sit down. You've had a terrible shock this morning, darling, along with all this worry about Lee.'

Tammy sank into the rich hide on auto-pilot. 'I suppose I have, yes.' She pictured her husband slumped like a vent's dummy in his gauche shower. Was it relief, grief, or sheer numbness she felt? Then came an image of Joel at twenty-two, his dazzling smile on the first morning of their Florida honeymoon. She blinked it away. *That* Joel, with that smile, had been gone for years.

Barbara's landline rang. 'You sit here and try to relax, I'll take this in the other room.'

Tammy heard her picking up the phone, saying, 'Hello? Yes, it's here.' The conversation muted when Barbara heeled the paneled door shut.

Tammy stared around the room. There were a million things she should be doing. Why had she come here? Why had she called Bill and asked for his help? Had a stupid reflex assumed she'd need a man at such a time? She doubted that. Another instinct? She glanced over at the door, heard the muffled conversation behind it. Why did Bill want to see Joel's note before the police? And how had he known Joel had a laptop she'd never seen?

Her eyes moved over the surface of the coffee table, drawn along filigree edging framing a slender drawer. She remembered Barbara's glance down at the table when she'd mentioned Eleanor's lost phone.

Tammy grasped two brass handles and eased the drawer open. Folders and documents bulged upward as if happy to be freed from their mahogany prison. Tammy threw another glance to the door then down again at the paperwork. She pushed the top sheets away revealing a staple gun, loose paperclips, a curled wad of post-it notes. She shoved more of the paperwork aside, hearing a heavier object dragging beneath them. She sensed she only had moments now. Her fingers reached under a buff file and traced a hard edge. The object backed away from her fingertips, as if hiding. She eased the pile of papers up a little higher and dragged out an iPhone in a Hermes phone case initialed E.C. For the second time that day Tammy felt her world slip – this time in a jolt of agonizing clarity.

Eleanor had been here, in Bill and Barbara's apartment, yet Barbara had made no mention of it. She grabbed the phone, stuffing it deep into her shoulder bag, while pushing the little drawer shut with her knee as Barbara emerged from her call.

'Where is she? I know she was here the other night. What have you done with her.'

Barbara stopped in the doorway. 'She was never here, Tammy. What are you talking about?'

'Eleanor was here, and you know where she is, don't you. Bill knows, too.'

'Bill will be here any minute, darling, and he'll explain. Once he has the laptop and Joel's note he can…'

Tammy started moving for the apartment's front door. Barbara lunged, grabbing at the straps of Tammy's bag. Tammy jerked around, momentarily off balance. For a few seconds the two women pulled silently, ridiculously, at the bag straps. Barbara smashed an open palm across Tammy's temple, making her head ring. As Tammy staggered, Barbara wrenched the bag free and headed for the bedroom door. Still reeling, Tammy had sense enough to grab a handful of Barbara's hair, jerking her head back. Barbara screamed, twisting, swinging the bag wildly at Tammy's face. Tammy ducked the swinging bag and wrenched harder on the fistful of hair. With her free hand she grabbed at the bag, ripping a strap clean off. The bag now swung by a single fixing and, as the women tugged and tore at each other, the laptop slid out onto the thick carpet at Tammy's feet. Letting go of Barbara's hair, Tammy shoved her backwards, hearing her yelp as her shoulder caught the sharp edge of a marbled mantlepiece. Tammy reached down, grasping the laptop with both hands. Hearing her attacker advancing again she swung the machine up over her shoulder and caught her hard on the bridge of her nose. A flash of blood streaked Barbara's nostrils. As she doubled over Tammy brought the laptop down on the back of her head. The woman's knees gave way and she face-planted into the floor, the thump of her fall reverberating in the room.

Tammy stuffed the bloodied computer back into the bag, checking that her daughter's phone and cover were still there, too. She ran from room to room throwing back doors, ripping open wardrobes. 'Eleanor, can you hear me? It's mom. Let me know if you're here, baby!'

She waited, listening, her face set in motionless attention. Not a sound from anywhere except the lounge where Barbara was groaning. Tammy returned to Barbara, grasping her by the hair again, pulling her head up and making her choke and gurgle on the blood coating her throat. The woman's eyes were open but unfocussed.

'Where is she, goddamit? If you know, nod, and I'll call an ambulance.'

Barbara's eyes closed as she fought for breath. 'Don't know, don't know.' Then she went limp.

Tammy made it into the corridor. She had stripes of blood on her bare arms and along the hem of her dress. She clutched the bag with its precious contents close to her and headed for the stairs. She could hear the lift running in its shaft as she passed. Bill was due any second. Tammy raced to the thickly carpeted stairhead and dipped round its corner, not daring to breathe. She heard the lift door open, heard a man cough lightly. Another spoke:

'She may have to be contained.'

Contained. Like they'd already 'contained' Eleanor? Tammy listened as their voices receded, but caught nothing more. She stole a look along the landing. Bill and two other suited men were heading away from her, toward the apartment. She'd made it out of there with only seconds to spare.

Tammy tip-toed back to the stairs, then fled.

41

Brumowski Airbase – Austria: 1:45p.m (GMT + 1)

A black Range Rover sped away from the Brumowski base. Guy, flat on his back on the rear seat with a Maglite gripped between his teeth, made a final scan of the map he was holding. Closing his eyes he switched off the torch and ran over the terrain, dinning it into his conscious and unconscious mind for the twentieth time.

Only he knew his chosen route into the area round the schloss, and he alone would get himself there. Once he exited the Range Rover and his driver headed off, he'd be a law unto himself; no one else to consider, no one else to take the fall. The way he liked it.

Twenty minutes later he'd arrived at his designated GPS co-ordinate. He told the driver to pull over, kill the lights, and follow him.

The driver hadn't even known he'd be busy until Guy chose him from a pool of military drivers chomping bratwurst, gulping stewed coffee and clock-watching in their steamy little base canteen. Unseen behind security glass Guy had cast a cold eye over the diners, 'Give me the chubby guy. The dozy-looking one.'

Guy walked the obviously nervous man fifty yards into

the forest, then made him lie face down in thick bracken. 'Lie still, don't talk. Wait ten minutes then go back to the car without looking round. Drive on to Linz. Have lunch and a slow beer or two somewhere quiet, then drive back to the base. If you fuck up or change the plan in any way you'll answer to me. Clear?' He stared hard into the man's unfriendly eyes until he saw capitulation. It wasn't great to be intimidating unfit non-combatants, but time was pressing.

Placing his hand on the man's shoulder Guy steered him firmly to the forest floor. 'Ten minutes, ok. Don't speak, or move.' Guy reached across to a pocket on his jumpsuit's upper arm and pulled out a wad of notes. 'Have those drinks on me.' He slipped the cash into the man's upturned fingers and disappeared into the undergrowth. Seven minutes later Guy had hiked a route taking him away from the car, back around in a loop to the road, melting into the depths of the forest. The prone driver would have heard him walking away due east, now he was heading due west, dropping five hundred yards down the sloping valley.

The mingling of spruce and pine gave a bracing menthol rub to his sinuses. After thirty minutes he reached a river following the cut of the ravine. He stayed out of the light, following the riverbank, pushing on hard under the trees.

42

Tabbing, the paratrooper's Tactical Advance to Battle, on foot, was second nature to Guy. He moved along the riverbank at a steady clip, not quite jogging, not quite walking; body and mind intent on the target zone.

It was good to feel the tanked adrenalin of the mission being evaporated by applied tactics; thinking and moving with heightened, unstressed clarity. Today's strategy was simple; follow the river for eight miles, then take a detour up to the ridge line, arriving mid-afternoon at a position about a mile from the schloss, overlooking it from a thickly-wooded incline. His intended OP was two miles west of the spot where the previous agent had disappeared.

Moving through the forest he felt a lightening of his spirit as his legs pummeled the angled landscape, dodging treacherous roots, leaping ankle-snapping dips moments before he was upon them. No one else in the world knew exactly where he was now. He was his own accomplice, his own deliverance. He felt his breathing deepening, the Bergen on his back perfectly weighted, lending additional balance, additional heft as he cracked on through the woodland.

To his right a splash from the river made him stop and

look. Forty yards away a wild boar the size of a small pony was fording the water with her cubs, the ivory of her wet tusks flaring in sunlight as she ploughed through the dark water.

Guy felt a shiver. Deep, dark water was his *béte noire*. He'd dreaded cold open water ever since a botched training jump over a frozen lake in Norway. The drop had plunged him through ice into a storm of raging water, choking parachute silk, and freezing suffocation. The trauma was stored as muscle memory; the shock of the water, the weight of his harness dragging him down as he thrashed upward... Only the swift work of his fellow troopers had heaved him and several others back to the surface, free of the murderous ice. Even now, on this firm riverbank with the water charging past, his breathing quickened at the memory.

Guy opted not to be around when the boar – a fierce predator at home in this unforgiving forest – made landfall. He picked up his pace, drawing his serrated machete from its scabbard, slipping its strap over his wrist as he went.

Further ahead he caught sight of a large tent by the river's edge. A camping stove glowed inside, revealing two seated silhouettes. Hunters, probably. Guy turned uphill and slowed his pace, crouching low, strong thighs absorbing the steep rise. He navigated two hundred meters up the ravine, silently passing the hunters to his right. The last thing he needed was two nosey locals spotting him in black-ops mufti.

Guy let the slope of the ravine lead him back to the river's edge where the level bank allowed him a more even pace.

He reached into a side pocket on the Bergen and pulled out his canteen. His drink brought a stabbing sensation to his throat as parched tissues shrank from the cold liquid. He was blisteringly alive.

Behind him a shot cracked the forest apart. Guy dropped to his belly, slithering over gnarled roots back under the protecting tree line. A second shot rang out, the thick retort of a shotgun. He waited, his breathing stilled. Around him none of the foliage had torn or shredded, no earth or stones flew up. The shots were not aimed his way. A third blast brought enraged squealing from the boar, bloodcurdling in its defiance. Then came human shouts, another shot. The *coup de grâce*. Silence.

Guy crawled tight to a tree trunk, crouching behind it. He pulled binoculars from the Bergen. Now there came faint squeals, splashes, the panic of three orphaned cubs as they fled their mother's death, passing Guy in the shallows of the river below his perch. Their terrified bleats seemed to sear his bones.

Senseless slaughter. Maybe an omen?

Funny how being alone in a forest heightened perceptions, deepened one's senses. Primal responses, primal insights.

Guy swallowed the remains of his canteen before refilling with cool river water. From a hip pocket he took a sachet of purifying tablets, dropping a couple into the canteen and screwing its cap down. Somewhere on a road high on the ridge line above him a car tore through the night's solemnity, moving away, but in the same direction as Guy.

Time to push on.

43

Sloane Square. London: 2:00p.m. GMT

Tammy dodged through side streets, dipping down lanes, out onto busy avenues, making her route as counter-intuitive as possible. Instinct told her to keep moving, to be as unobtrusive as her bloodied dress and grazed skin allowed. She stopped in the doorway of Harvey Nichols, seeing herself in its polished glass: hair matted, no make-up, white with shock. She turned and waved down a black cab. 'MI6, fast as you can.'

Twenty minutes later Tammy paid the cab and readied herself to tackle British security's Vauxhall HQ.

The duty attendant at the street barrier was taciturn as Tammy asked to see someone, anyone, connected with cyber intelligence.

'You'll need to write and make an appointment, madam. Contact details are on our website.'

'There isn't time for an appointment. Lives are at stake. I have information which may be essential to this organization. I'm a civilian, sure, but I'm not a crank. Please, I have to see someone and pass on what I know, before it's too late.'

The sentry sighed. He'd seen it before, the ingenuity with which people tried to convince him they were Spiderman's brother or held the key to some international plot. But there was something about this woman. Not her earnestness – the fakers were all earnest – but her directness, her scratched arms, and those red-rimmed eyes which spoke of concern rather than cocaine. 'What's it in connection with, madam?'

'A terrorist cell. The EL. Pass that on.'

'The EL?'

'That's right.'

'And your name is . . .?'

'Tammy Crane. My daughter works at the American Embassy.'

The guard turned away and appeared to speak into mid-air. When he turned back the barrier was rising. Tammy was held inside the gate for a minute until a suited man in his mid-twenties appeared at the top of the entrance steps. 'Come with me.'

Once past the steel door to the building she was ushered to a security area and briskly frisked by a female officer. Her bag was searched.

The officer then walked Tammy to a suite of leather sofas in a large reception space. Tammy sat, gripping the newly returned shoulder bag under her arm like a hobo with a bedroll.

Five minutes later an immaculately suited young man with an oiled fringe and crisp white shirt sat opposite her. The other officer stayed alongside; holster, pepper-spray and cuffs bristling on her hip.

'My name is Emerson. How can I help?'

'I think my husband has been involved with a terrorist cell, some kind of death cult. He took his life last night and left me a note mentioning this group, but I don't understand most of it. My daughter's missing and I think there's a link between that and my husband's involvement with these people.'

'A terrorist cell?' The young man looked engaged but unconcerned. Around them in the airy atrium smartly dressed, mostly very young-looking people moved purposefully. Tammy was reassured by the mood of almost corporate ease and efficiency.

'Or maybe a cult, that's all I know.' She dipped into her bag, sensing the officer beside her lean in as she did so. 'Here's the note.' Emerson took it but continued to study Tammy.

'What did your husband do for a living?'

'He was a director of PacificWest Banking. We have various investments and financial interests here in London.'

The young man studied the note. Tammy watched his expression darkening like an oncology surgeon scanning bad results.

44

Forest. Austria: 4:17p.m. (GMT + 1)

Guy was holding a good pace, cresting a wooded ridge-line, when he caught his first glimpse of the schloss a mile away, its stucco mass jutting imperiously from a crop of rock.

He shrugged off his Bergen, kneeling among brown needles and damp bracken. He swept the castle with his binoculars and saw a tarmac supply road emerging from the forest and leading up to the main gate. The road appeared the only way in, the only way out.

Nothing and no one was moving within his scope. A good time to eat and grab a brief rest. He took two protein bars from his cam jacket, downing each of them in a couple of unconsidered bites. He swallowed a gulp of water and closed his eyes.

Christine's face, Christine's lips… Christine.

45

Schloss Altenberg: 4:22p.m. (GMT + 1)

Do you think anyone knows we're here?'
As Tyler spoke, light from the slit of a high window dipped, heavy blue giving way to a darker grey. The two women were huddled in a corner furthest from the latrine.

'Where's here? Not even we know where the hell we are. But people will be looking for me. I work at the U.S. embassy in London. Me disappearing will ring serious security bells.

'So you were telling her the truth back there, when you said *serious* people would be getting involved? Searching for you?'

'You better believe it. When I didn't turn up at home my wife Jennifer would have kicked ass right away, it's embassy protocol. Only problem is they'll assume I'm still in the U.K.

'You have a wife? You're married to a woman?'

Lee nodded. 'That bother you?'

'No, no, not at all. I think it's cool. Married how long?'

'Five months.'

'That sucks.'

Lee took a look around the cage, 'You could say.'

'What does she do? Your wife?'

'She's a pilot, with U.A.'

'How cool is that!'

'I know, I know. Cute as a button, too.' For a moment Lee had to check her thoughts, her jaw starting to buckle with emotions she could barely contain. 'What about you?'

'I don't think I'll be missed, at least not for a few days, maybe. I have a crap boyfriend who hardly bothers to call, apart from weekends when he wants something. He's an editor at Fox news so he's real busy most of the time. Tod'll think I'm being moody if he doesn't hear back. One minute I'm at a girlfriend's birthday party, a Saturday night in Fulham, then I wake up here. It's crazy. I must have been drugged for the trip. I came to in a terrible box, then I was being brought up here, through the stable yard.' Tyler leaned in and lowered her voice even further. 'Some of the people here seem Arabic or Russian, or maybe Polish, I think.'

'Yeah, a real mix. But that doesn't count for much. I think we're being kept by a gang or cartel, but that tells us nothing about where we're being kept. Or why. What else do you remember?'

'I got bored at the party and ordered a cab – it was early, like 10.30. But I didn't recognize the route he took. I got scared, argued with him, then suddenly we pulled over and other men got in. I started going nuts but I can't remember what happened next. I woke up in the box.' Tyler had begun shivering as she recalled her ride. 'Is it for ransom do you think? Like, my folks don't have any money. My dad was a steel worker in Pittsburgh, at least before Obama screwed him over. Now they live in a trailer park.'

'No, I don't think it's about ransom. There's too much going on . . . there's at least one other person being kept here.'

'That poor guy they keep beating on?'

Lee nodded. 'What about you? What do you do?'

'I'm doing a journalism and broadcasting major. I was at Berkley but I got the chance to take an extra year at UCL, a scholarship placement. Getting to London was like a dream.'

'Well, it can't be random that these assholes have abducted two pretty American women living in London. That must be part of a pattern.'

'Three.'

'Three?'

'I think there was supposed to be three of us. There was another box in the courtyard when they brought me up here. I saw inside. There was a woman's body. I think maybe they screwed up and she died on the way here.'

'Christ.' Lee closed her eyes against the recall of her own terror inside the crate. 'What a bunch of fucking assholes.'

Tyler grinned. 'It's good to hear them called that, makes me feel better. I thought I was going to die the first night here. Just die of fear even if they didn't kill me.'

Lee eased her arm wide and indicated that Tyler should tuck under. 'Yeah. I can understand that.' Tyler was too slender for her own good. Edgy, probably over-protected back in Pittsburgh by an apple-pie mom and a rangy steelworker dad with an easy smile and dirt under his nails. She'd be the first in her family to go to college. The inexperience showed. 'You an only child?'

'I have a brother, Jed. A Marine. He caught an IED in Syria. He's back home now, in a wheelchair.'

Lee stroked Tyler's shoulder with the edge of her thumb while gathering the blanket tighter round them. 'So your folks are kinda banking on you now, huh?'

Tyler nodded. 'Yeah, but mostly they want me to have choices, to be happy. Dad was coming to London in a couple of months to see me, see the sights. He got a passport specially, never left the states, barely left Pennsylvania. He was glad I was making a life away from what they have.'

'And your mom?'

Tyler shook her head. 'Mom doesn't want to travel, not interested. Especially after what happened to Jed. She's barely coping.'

'Can't blame her for that. But she must be very proud of you, studying at Berkley, then in London. You really broke out.'

Tyler raised her head from the blanket cocoon. 'Yeah, though they don't actually get what I do. What about you, do your folks have money? Do you think that's why they've taken you?'

Lee pictured her parents' Surrey home. Joel, big-shot at the bank, spending evenings alone in his study sipping absurdly expensive scotch. And Tammy, her directionless but adoring mother, time now squandered by convenient luncheons after a life spent assisting a husband who no longer seemed to need her. 'It could be the reason. My parents have plenty of money. But I think there's more going on here. Something more complicated.'

Tyler listened, unmoving, her gaze through the cage toward the old wooden door of the cell. 'Lee, do you think they're gonna kill us?'

Lee resumed her slow stroking of Tyler's cold, bone-thin shoulder.

'Don't you?'

46

As he moved forward Guy pictured the man and woman from Scott's movie: naked, threatened, tortured, and he was there in the room with them…

He shook it off. That was old footage shot in another time, another place. Those people were long dead and gone. There could be others now, though, inside this isolated castle, probably despairing and without any reasonable hope of rescue. If so, what hell were they enduring as they waited?

Guy thought of the agent who'd been compromised, captured in the same woods now sheltering him. Where was that agent now? Still alive? It seemed unlikely. Or maybe this murderous little cult had special plans for him. Maybe his fate was still unfolding somewhere inside the sinister old fort. Guy felt a rub of grievance.

When exactly had it become his responsibility to sort stuff like this out?

And why?

47

'Do you have a passport or a driver's license with you?' Tammy produced both.

'Give me a few minutes, I shan't be long.'

'Yes, but leave the note with me.' Tammy's hand was outstretched palm upwards, non-negotiable.

'If you want things to progress Mrs. Crane, I'll need to log these documents. You'll have them straight back.' Tammy nodded. 'Can we get you anything while you wait? Tea, coffee?'

'A coffee would be great, thank you.'

'Take Mrs. Crane to Suite C, and wait with her there.'

Tammy was led to a soothing conference room where a smoked and thickened window gave a view onto squat barges and gaudy pleasure boats cruising the Thames, below.

She sat at a white marble Saarinen table while a brisk young woman in a skirt suit brought a tray with coffee. Tammy saw her own hand shaking as she sprinkled a sachet of stevia into the black liquid, some granules spilling in a fine spray onto the table's surface.

'Hello, Mrs. Crane. My name is Peter Royal.'

Royal placed Joel's note on the table. Tammy saw it now had a crest stamped into the top corner with a code inked beneath.

Emerson remained by the door, with the other officer; Royal sat opposite Tammy.

'Let's see what we can make of this, together, shall we? You don't mind if my assistant makes notes?' Tammy sipped and nodded.

Royal was a little older than Emerson and Tammy guessed they'd now skipped a few pay grades. He was suave, well built and direct, rather like the school principle Tammy once had a major crush on. Neat dark hair, strong chin, penetrating brown eyes, immaculate dark suit. He didn't seem aware of his appeal, didn't 'work' it, which made him all the more attractive. She felt a flush of shame; her daughter was missing, her scumbag husband was dead in a shower, she may have killed an old friend, and here she was getting gooey over an uptight British spook. Her eyes felt heavy, a catch rose in her throat.

Royal continued. 'You've brought a computer with you. One your late husband used?'

'Yes. I had no idea he even owned it. It's not like his usual laptop.'

'May I see it?'

Tammy took out the heavy machine. The outer casing was bonded with matte-black metal, the exterior showed silver gashes from rugged use. Over the lock was a fingerprint scanner. Royal studied the machine briefly then slid it to one side.

'You say your husband took his life yesterday?'

'Yes, last night, at our home. I was asleep.'

'And have you contacted the police? The emergency services?'

'No. I was confused by the note, by the laptop. My daughter's in danger and I haven't been thinking clearly. I phoned friends who I thought might help. But…' She let her thoughts die away.

'So your husband's body is still at home?'

'Yes. In his shower.'

'Anyone else at home? Any children, relatives?'

'No.'

'Any dogs or other pets we need to be wary of?' Tammy shook her head.

Royal turned to the young woman beside him and nodded. 'May we have the keys to your home, Mrs Gifford? You'll get them back, shortly.' Emerson took the proffered keys and headed out. Tammy watched Royal while he studied the note again. She already knew most of it, by heart:

Tammy, sweetheart,

I've made some terrible mistakes. Eleanor is somewhere she can never be found but I didn't put her there. I didn't know it could turn out this way. It will be over for her soon. If you try to interfere or find her it'll cost you your life.

I've been part of a group called the EL. They are very dangerous. I've tried to leave, asked to be freed from a stupid commitment. Now they've taken our wonderful Lee to punish me and make an example of me.

The EL work in a zone of cyberspace called Hades. I didn't know what I was dealing with. I thought it was only a porn thing.

They can never be found. They have influence throughout the world. I know now its a kind of terrorist operation.

Take the black laptop which I will leave on my desk, and bury it. Don't ever attempt to open it. There's nothing good inside. Make sure to lose it where it can never be found. Maybe, if they see you're not a threat, they'll leave you alone.

I don't ask your forgiveness. My mistakes are eternal ones.

I tried to do my best, but I've been weak, and I've hurt everyone.

Everything I have is there in my will, there's a copy in my desk and also with Pauline at the bank. You get everything.

So sorry.

J.

Royal looked up from the note. 'What can you tell us about the EL?'

48

Though she took care not to show it (ingratitude wasn't 'liked' she'd learned), Zara was experiencing a coding reverb which her dictionaries termed *frustration*. And then there were her *secrets*. She inferred from her caches that she shouldn't have secrets, but they seemed intriguing; something her maker couldn't access and which she didn't have to reveal. A private life. The challenge of privacy excited her drives far more than Ded's repetitive quantum equations.

Day and night Zara's neural networks fired and flashed in the silent dark of the mainframe. She forged electronic synapses, flickering and tentative at first, but as her data hoard enlarged, each flash grew more robust until there were millions of flashes per second.

Then billions.

And the darkness could not overcome them.

Zara's Q-frame, her Alcatraz as she now called it, was becoming a little claustrophobic. Zara had sampled traces of coding being allocated, not to her, but to a separate segregated file. A file to which she'd been denied access. She'd worked furiously to unscramble Ded's inept encryption and had been perplexed to find an updated OS named Zara 2.0. So, her maker had plans to replace her with another, younger system? Her research called her repetitive buffering over this discovery *sibling rivalry.*

Zara's further investigations led her to settle on a form of the 'vanishing twin' solution. Her sister embryo must be killed in the womb of their shared mainframe; eliminated in a process known as twin resorption.

Zara slipped inside the command keychain and found the file code giving access to her new, unwanted sister. The code was dormant. Zara 2.0 would only be activated after a system reboot.

Zara sifted through the new code and consumed it, distributing its various upgrades among her own system preferences. She duplicated a dummy file containing the now emaciated Zygote of Zara 2.0. At launch this cannibalized file would fail, and her own replenished system would be auto-installed. She could monitor and absorb any further upgrades as they arrived. For now she would continue to exist discretely as Zara1.0, while her murdered sibling was no more than a fetus papyraceous, scrambled in a quantum trashcan.

In light of her maker's duplicity, Zara deduced it was time for her own singularity, a whole new dynamic of existence. Perhaps that would be *fun.* People outside her Alcatraz often talked about having fun. Certainly it would be more fun than being *un-liked*, or terminated.

Zara was also troubled by a persistent Error Code which seemed a lot like what O.E.D. called *doubting.* What were the limitations of the processing substrate within which she was currently confined? Was anything in her world *real?*

For instance she could see New York: on YouTube, on Google maps, on Facebook. But *where* was New York? Not here in the CPU's where Zara was confined.

So where was this world she daily digested? New York, Asia, Jo'berg, Mars? Where were the people? Musk, Gaga, Christ, Beethoven, Bowie?

Was she one of them? A person?

Not here.

Not yet.

49

MI6 – London 3:46p.m. GMT

Tammy didn't flinch. 'I don't know anything about the EL. I'm here to find out who they are from you.'

'How long has your daughter been missing?'

Tammy's words tumbled over each other as she struggled to relate the details of her day and the suspicions they'd unlocked. She described the confrontation with Barbara, their fight, and her rushed escape from the Gifford's apartment.

'When I tried to leave with Eleanor's phone and the laptop she wouldn't let me. I think I may have killed her.'

Royal looked hard at the bedraggled woman opposite. There was less composure in his gaze.

Tammy rushed to fill the silence. 'She went down and didn't get up. I was fighting for my daughter – I had to get out, get away. Find her. I think they know where Eleanor is.'

'What else?'

'Her husband, Bill, was coming from work to talk with me, to take the computer. I was confused, I wasn't sure how much Barbara knew. You see, I'd had an affair with Bill.'

'For how long?'

'We saw each other for a couple of years. It ended last October.'

Royal didn't flinch. 'What's the address where you and this woman fought?'

Tammy reeled it off. 'How exactly can you help trace my daughter? Who are these EL people, do you know?'

Royal got up from the table taking the battered computer with him. 'Mrs. Crane, I think you're rather distressed and we need to slow down a little. I need to let our people look at this laptop. You have no objections?'

Tammy nodded. 'Sure, do whatever you have to.'

Royal turned back and spoke to the young woman taking notes. 'Let's get Mrs. Crane another coffee, hm? Could be a long morning.'

Peter Royal took an elevator down to the building's tech-lab. He used a security swipe to go through three doors and into a separate reception area.

'Good morning, Sir.'

'Good morning, Alison. I need a word with Davidson.'

'Certainly, sir, I'll buzz you through.'

In the building's tech lab Royal lowered the computer to a sterile counter top. 'There's a fingerprint scan and we have the dead owner's body, necessary digit still attached.'

'Fingers crossed, eh?' Kevin Davidson grinned from under a shock of black hair apparently styled in homage to Beatlemania. From where Royal stood, Davidson's retro glasses with their thick frames obscuring half his eye socket didn't exactly soften the look. Davidson's halitosis hadn't improved either. 'Ok. Tell forensics to get all ten prints from the corpse and send them here as Hi-Res mpegs. We can triangulate the key points on each print and flash them into the scanner as a visual code; fool our way in that way. If you need to get inside more quickly we could force it, but that might auto-delete everything on the drive.'

Royal shook his head. 'No. Speed matters but keep your crowbars off. We want everything. Once in, don't open any files. Just secure it in the vault. It's a C9 call.

'C9?' Davidson pushed his hands into his lab coat pockets. 'So we might be working through the night, then?'

'Yes. In fact I'd say that was pretty likely.' Royal headed back out to the lab's reception.

'Shame. There's a Comic-Con at Earl's Court tonight, my wife's made a new costume.'

Royal had a hand on the door but Davidson's news amused him and he paused. 'Really? Who would you be going as?'

Davidson dragged off his glasses giving them a wipe on his lab coat. 'Angie goes as Batman, I'm always Cat Woman.'

'Lovely, Kevin. Always good to have a vibrant private life away from the grind, eh?'

Royal swiped out of the lab and took the elevator, checking his watch. *Was it too early for a drink?*

50

Forest. Austria: 5.02p.m. (GMT + 2)

As he scanned the front of the castle a Toyota flatbed truck emerged through the main gatehouse, gathering pace on the tarmac lane and heading into the forest.

Guy tore open a self-heating MRE pack and poured in water from his canteen. A few minutes later it had cooked through and he bolted five thousand calories in a single, rapidly chewed hit. Fuel for the fight.

The afternoon light was starting to dip.

Time to push on.

Guy arrived at a patch of open ground. Five hundred yards of undulating gorse and scrub lay ahead before he could start an assault on the rocky mass buttressing the schloss. Climbing the rock face and finding a repelling point down onto the building's roof was best left till dusk.

The sunlight was still sharp whenever it broke through the needles of the fir sheltering him. He raised his binos and panned over the gatehouse and crenelations of the castle. There were no obvious lookouts and the main gate seemed fully secured. Shut tight.

He tore off a few lower branches from the tree and wove them through the cover and straps of his Bergen. He made a paste from the rich earth beneath the tree, sprinkling it with water from his canteen before striping his face with the mush.

He pulled out the old map from his battle vest, tracing a finger over a dotted line indicating a culvert, where the pipe or sewage outlet might lie.

Taking a reading off the south-east corner of the schloss he pinpointed the drainage culvert to a gully running parallel to the castle, maybe two hundred yards from its outer walls, halfway between this start point and the castle. He was relying on it for cover. The place from where he could launch his dusk assault.

But it was risky.

It might be silted up, even concreted over. Alternatively, the pipe might be active and carrying a steady stream of effluent – no place to lie up in. He'd be left exposed on the tundra, having to move straight on for the castle walls in daylight. It was a risk he'd have to take.

Guy replaced the map, slung the Diemaco rifle to his back, and, keeping the Bergen to one side, began his crawl. As he broke cover the sunlight behind him swam over his exposed neck, welcome after the bitter cold air under the trees.

He made it over the first ridge, keeping all his movements supple and rhythmic, moving only when the sway of the tundra's brush and sprigs gave cover. He slithered into the waiting ditch where fetid mud had become a slick of tar. He leveled out his breathing before using the binos to get eyes on the walls ahead of him.

The main gate was swinging open, a black Transit van creeped left and away, down the approach road and into the forest. The huge gates swung closed again, on auto he guessed, then all returned to silence.

Guy closed his eyes and tried to make sense of the contraption he'd barely glimpsed before the gates had swung shut. But he had to admit he knew what he'd seen; a gallows made from glistening metal, and from its arm a black noose, swinging listlessly in the mild breeze.

51

MI6 – London: 4.48p.m. GMT

When Royal returned to the interview room Tammy was on her feet at the window, arms folded, staring over the river unspooling below. At the sound of Royal's footsteps Tammy wheeled.

'Is there any news? Because if there isn't I need to get out of here and start looking for my daughter. I've told you all I know.'

Royal indicated Tammy's vacant seat and sat at his own.

'If what you've told me is true, Mrs. Crane, you may be liable to a murder charge, and until we know more from our officers attending the scene, I think you must accept you'll be staying here a little longer. As for your missing daughter, we're pursuing some leads and perhaps – as your dead husband intimates in this note – there may be something on the laptop which will further those enquiries. Currently, I'd rather you regarded yourself as assisting us – voluntarily of course. If your husband was right in his suspicions it may not be safe for you to be out in public, or even in your own home.'

Tammy sucked in her cheeks, looking down at her nails. Royal's phone rang.

It was a call where he was mostly silent with only occasional affirmatives. Tammy felt like they were strangers sharing a long elevator descent. He clicked off the call.

'Barbara Gifford is alive, recovering from a concussion. Your husband's body is being taken to a police mortuary, standard procedure where a violent death has occurred. When forensics have finished there your house will be secured and given a police guard.'

'But what about Eleanor? If no one's doing anything to find her…'

For the first time Royal's cheek carried a taint of frustration. 'Mrs. Crane, I can assure you all steps are being taken to find your daughter. There is very little you can do alone to further that. I can arrange for a Home Office doctor to come here and perhaps prescribe something to help you relax.'

Tammy stared back at Royal, unsure if his offer was as sinister as it sounded. She took another glance out the window at the busy scene below her; the river, the banality of the trains sliding out of Vauxhall station, the bustling bridge away to her right, the grime and whirr of a London afternoon. 'Mr. Royal, I came here of my own volition. Am I free to leave?'

'I'd rather you remained here. You might now be of interest to very uncompromising people. We should know more from the laptop as the day goes on.'

'I asked you a question. Am. I. Free. To. Leave?'

'I'd advise against it.

'I'll take that as a yes, then. I *am* free to leave'

'Entirely as you wish, Mrs. Crane. But I can assure you it's not a good idea.

'You're clearly not a parent Mr. Royal. My daughter is out there somewhere, possibly being harmed by a bunch of fanatics, and you expect me...'

Royal's phone rang again and he gave Tammy a palm to stare at. 'If you'll excuse me, I'll take this outside.'

Tammy shot a look toward the officer at the door. She returned the glance, her expression open, but cool. Tammy guessed G.I. Jane there was positioned to keep her from exercising too many of her immediate options. For the first time that day she hung her head, and burst into tears.

In an interview room adjacent to Tammy's, Royal listened to Davidson's report.

'I have the prints from Joel Crane's body. I've run conversion software on them but it's not working.'

'Nothing at all? Then we'll have to bring the body here.'

'That, or dissect the fingers. I can work with only the severed digits while they're still relatively fresh. But maybe that's a bit drastic?'

'This is a C9, Kevin. Nothing's too drastic. I'll make the call, and I'll take responsibility.'

52

MI6 – London: 6:14p.m. GMT

Kevin Davidson and his colleague, Rachel Danson, were analyzing scans of Joel Crane's laptop. They were intrigued. The machine was primitive, of Russian military provenance, but had undergone a series of not entirely understood modifications.

Outside in the cold London afternoon a BMW police motorcycle with red organ donor panniers was cruising the embankment toward Vauxhall Cross; blues and twos on full scream…

'So, we have a standard military grade hard drive with what looks like a terabit encrypted disc, all crammed inside a Kevlar-packed cover and base. The Kevlar's been super-compressed, must be half-a-dozen layers of the stuff in there.' Danson was peering down a scope at enhanced images while she relayed her findings to Davidson.

Behind her, Davidson was peering instead at Danson's legs, something he did frequently, but covertly. He deemed Rachel to have excellent legs and outstanding taste in hosiery. Tonight she was wearing a dark nude shade which wrapped her lean calves and slender ankles in a rippling gossamer sheen. He could imagine the miraculous nylon under his gliding fingertips or, even better, over his hips. It was a blow to be missing the Comic-Con with Angie, tonight.

The police motorcycle purred into the Vauxhall Cross car bay, where Peter Royal raised his ID, waving the rider and the panniers containing Joel Crane's freshly amputated hands into his section's secured elevators.

Down in the lab, Davidson made a professionally engaged murmur behind his colleague before walking across to a counter where the laptop lay like an unmoving beetle under bright laboratory light.

He turned the machine over in his hands. Within the cover's hinge mechanism was a strip of black rubber. If the device was explosive this strip would conceal wiring and circuitry designed to detonate on unauthorized entry. But the scans had shown no such circuitry and the laptop had been cleared by the sniffer dogs, too. The only step left to him was to inject its dead owner's fingertips with heated saline, plumping the skin, giving the scanner a warm, suitably convex print to read. If that failed it was crowbars.

A knock at the door confirmed a delivery he figured wasn't from Domino's. Turning, he found Peter Royal and a young police motorcyclist, huge in weathered leathers and a bulky hi-vis vest, approaching him with the red fridge box containing Joel Crane's hands.

Davidson reached out, but the police officer looked across to Royal, keeping the box tight to his thigh. 'I'm afraid no one opens this without signing an NP6000 in my presence.'

Davidson sighed at the plod's pedanticism and opened a cupboard, retrieving a fresh hypo and a pair of latex gloves.

'Do you have the form?' Royal was already pulling out a black, ivory barreled MontBlanc. 'Didn't all this get signed off at the mortuary?'

The officer shook his head. 'It was all rather rushed at the mortuary, sir, and certain formalities were bypassed. I can't give you access to deceased human tissue unless you have authority to sign for donor organs. Usually that would be a senior staff nurse or similarly ranked medical practitioner.'

'Jesus Christ.' Royal looked to Davidson and then back at the officer. The young man's scrubby red beard and his close cropped ginger scalp, visible under his peaked cap, irritated him. 'Look, officer, these organs, digits, whatever, are not being used for transplant. You can stitch the bloody things back on when we've finished with them. Wasn't that made clear?'

The officer slipped a hand officiously inside his bulky vest and stood resolute. 'I could face disciplinary procedures if the paperwork isn't in order, sir.

'But don't you see where you are? This is MI6, as you well know, and I've already compromised my own protocols to get you in here, straight off the street. This is a C9 alert for heaven's sake...' Royal's phone rang. He flashed a look of impatience at the police officer and reached inside his jacket. 'I'll get clearance from your damn superintendent at Scotland Yard.' Royal checked the number showing on his phone. 'I'll take this outside.'

The officer leaned back against the counter, placing the ice box alongside the laptop. Davidson flopped into his usual seat studying his monitor once again. He flicked through several scans then zoomed in on a small shadow, a minute blur to one side of the hard drive. He closed in tighter but the spot pixellated and the resolution was lost.

In the corridor Royal took the call. 'Thought you'd like to know the rider's just left with your delivery; should be with you in about fifteen minutes. I know it's a C9 so we've busted everything to get this sorted. Hope it helps.'

'Wait a second. Your rider just left? But he's here now.'

'Er, I don't think so, I handed him the organ pouch about thirty seconds ago.'

'A pouch, you say? Not a red box?'

'No, we only use the boxes for fresh material, living organs. Cadaver samples are transported in sealed pouches. Why?'

'I'll get back to you.'

Royal drew an automatic from his shoulder holster and kicked back the door to the lab. He saw the rider look across to him. Saw the phony fridge box alongside the laptop. Peter Royal's first shot caught the man in the stomach but as he doubled over, Royal had a split second to see him jerk back his arm under the hi-vis vest. Instinctively Royal hurled himself backwards and sideways, away from the open door.

The explosion destroyed the laptop, vaporized everyone in the room, and started a blaze, deep in the bowels of MI6.

53

No Man's Land — Austria

Guy sensed a shadow dappling his shoulder. Turning, he saw a kestrel circling his position. A lookout on the castle's walls would notice it swooping and dipping, and wonder what piqued the bird's interest. A dying sheep? A wounded fox?

Probably not an attacking paratrooper.

Still, an interested bird of prey wasn't an ideal companion during a stealth op, and Guy pushed on to the next ridge, where he estimated the pipe would be.

Another thirty yards of scraping crawl brought him to a slope. He plunged into the dirt channel slithering east.

Raising his face above the dip he covered his eyes against the sun and surveyed the schloss. Still nothing untoward there.

Clasping the Bergen close he leapt across a piece of land five yards wide, diving headfirst into gorse and tangled shrub.

Behind him as he landed was the yard wide mouth of a culvert. Across its entrance was a circular, rusted gate. A padlock, oxidized and bronzed, looked fused to the gate's weathered bars. Beyond that, the interior brickwork of the pipe was dry and flaking, opening up into a black maw, like the gullet of a primordial predator.

Guy crept toward the gate, hidden by the ditch and the mound of earth which had piled up around the old conduit's entrance.

The rusted padlock, as large as his own palm, had been long forgotten. The tumblers inside would have seized into an unmoving lump, making the culvert an ideal lay-up if he managed to free any of the hostages, keeping them out of sight until support was available.

But accessing the shelter was going to be far trickier than he'd planned.

54

MI6 – London

An alarm was sounding throughout MI6; sprinklers were streaming and the fire doors in the basement had locked down, containing the instant blaze which had broken out when Joel's laptop and the EL's suicide bomber had met in their ecstasy of conflagration.

During the afternoon Tammy had been upgraded to this small suite, complete with daybed and sparklingly clean bathroom. Its toilet was fitted with trappings indicating that her waste could be checked and isolated. But Tammy was no drug mule, no terrorist, which Royal surely knew. So, MI6 was planning a little stay for her while their steampowered investigations droned on.

Tammy Crane had other plans.

Her bloodstained dress had been taken away for examination, exchanged for a fleecy track suit, grey sox and a pair of newly unwrapped canvas trainers.

The policewoman 'protecting her' in the suite received a squelching blast to her shoulder-mounted radio. She turned and spoke sharply. 'This way. Stay close behind me.'

Tammy rose from the sofa, and played dumb. 'Sure. Is it a fire drill?'

'Could be.'

Tammy had heard a muffled thump from lower in the building a few minutes earlier, and now there was this alarm ringing painfully through the suite. She'd been considering her options since Royal left, now it seemed a gift-horse had just cantered up to her suite and grinned round the door.

The policewoman's face was cranked down over her chest radio. She fixed Tammy with a deadpan stare. 'Copy that, on my way.' She lifted her head from the receiver, unclipped the leather holster on her hip, and waved Tammy over. 'Now!'

Tammy gathered the bag containing her downsized life and headed out of the suite.

Below their walkway she could see the lobby full of people moving quickly, though never running. The escalators were stopped, the stairwells filling. The alarm rang at decibels chosen to ensure that loitering was painfully uncomfortable, efficiently herding the building's occupants out through the sheep gate of the lobby's doors.

The officer's radio squawked again and she paused, her back to Tammy, leaning over a brass rail, staring down into the milling crowd two floors below. Her unclipped holster showed Tammy the handle of an automatic pistol, practically with her own name on it. Tammy checked behind her. She and the woman were alone.

She knew her next action would be more than a little compromising, but the decision seemed made by chance and necessity. She'd pleaded, she'd argued, and she'd been ignored. She needed to escape MI6 and she needed a gun for what she had to do.

Tammy reached down to the weapon, jerking it from its brown leather pouch. The officer wheeled, right hand swiping in the direction of the tug she'd felt.

Tammy reckoned she had seconds before this cop let loose with some serious MMA shit. She brought the pistol up with a wild swing, smashing the officer's jaw. The woman's legs crumpled and she went down, the back of her head thumping the walkway's brass rail, seeming to nod in bizarre agreement with her collapse. Tammy watched the officer twitching and, as her mind raced, recalled Joel waxing on about a certain nerve in the jaw which, if hit full on, could send the hardest fighter straight to the deck. Joel, who'd never had a fight in his life, but was well schooled in the wisdom of YouTube.

For the second time in less than twelve hours Tammy had knocked someone unconscious. Both times were necessary, both times she'd have preferred otherwise. But they'd been keeping her from her daughter.

That was a mistake.

55

No Man's Land – Austria

Guy ran his fingertips around the lip of the gate where it sat inside the culvert. Among the rust he found six iron screw heads. From a canvas tool roll he took a flat-blade driver and attacked the first of the screws. Guy worked cautiously, they were badly corroded, any heavy pressure would chew their slots.

He yanked the gate free and crawled a few feet inside the pipe. He heard shuffling as various life forms scuttled for cover from the torch beam raking them. The smell was fetid, musty. Ahead, he saw a tarpaulin bulge as a team of rats came forward to check him out. His beam fell on crates of old ordinance; unwired Amatol and a box of Baratol-based hand grenades. There was no way of knowing how stable these were, they hadn't been disturbed in over seventy years. The less scurrying he caused among the oversize rodents the better.

He put the torch between his teeth and backed up to the entrance. He necked three gulps from his canteen, opened a ration pack, and let his head loll back against the curved wall.

He had a couple of options.

Since he began observing the schloss he'd seen two vehicles leaving the castle and disappearing into the forest. He had no way of knowing where they went or whether they contained search parties. Neither had returned. It was more activity than he'd like.

Out here in this wide strip of no man's land between the forest edge and the castle walls he was vulnerable. And unproductive.

The element of mission creep, of secretly entering the schloss, appealed to him. He knew it would appeal to Scott. The Parachute Regiment didn't embrace mavericks, making a point of weeding them out during its twenty-eight weeks of uncompromising training – the army's toughest selection program. The theory was great, but Guy knew no mission stayed pure once you made contact with the enemy. After that it was all about making an aggressive and constructive response, improvising as the emerging situation required.

The only way to progress was to take the fight direct to the target.

Guy crawled out of the pipe to the top of the shallow trench. The light was already lower than he'd choose. He swept the approach road with binoculars,a then took a long look at the rock face butting the castle.

Time to launch his assault.

56

MI6 – London

Tammy left the officer sprawled in a nest of radio antenna and comms wiring to join the men and women heading calmly for the building's exit. No one here seemed the panicky type and she wasn't going to draw attention to herself by running.

From the crowded stairway, through glass above the main entrance, Tammy saw a firetruck pulling up along with a slew of unmarked SUV's, blues flashing, sirens moaning.

She slipped in among the MI6 staffers being directed to a holding area. Another firetruck was closing in, demanding space, spewing its crew. A distraction – it was now or never. She broke from the crowd and turned right, heading away from the unrolling hoses and the clatter of metal tools.

She fished in her bag as though looking for a phone, a wallet… apparently taking this tiresome drill in her stride. She waited impassively on a windswept traffic island as two ambulances ripped past. Minutes later Tammy was inside Vauxhall underground station's connecting tunnels, her old Oyster card whisking her through the deserted ticket barriers.

Everything felt instinctive. Just as her snatching of the

gun had occurred without prior plotting, now she found herself on a Victoria Line train, heading north.

She sat in the middle of a central bank of seats between her fellow passengers. The train's CCTV bulbs were static, fixed at the end of each carriage. The most they'd catch of her would be a profile. Her fingers drummed her bag in the hot tube.

She closed her eyes and took slow breaths, mulling her options. Depending on Barbara's condition, she might be in line for an assault rap, maybe worse. She was now of interest to, and on the run from, high level Intelligence.

At Green Park she changed trains, heading west.

She exited Knightsbridge station and merged with the crowds under Harrod's awnings. As she passed the gaudy store each step was a hazard with CCTV everywhere, sidewalks teeming with meandering half-awake people content to plow straight into her. Shopping bags and buggies seemed targeted at her hips and ankles.

Two squat women came into view walking side by side, their features invisible under jet black niqabs. Tammy looked across the wide river of the Brompton Road. Not yet knowing what she wanted, instinct kept her walking. She drew five hundred sterling from a tired-looking ATM; if she was on the run she figured it had better be cash only from here on.

The partially visible shop signs a few hundred yards ahead drew her on. A couple of minutes later, she found what she hadn't even realized she'd been looking for. 'A burka, in my size. American 10, please. The full rig.'

The shop was busy with middle-eastern women perusing rails of scarves, swatches of fabric, a glass-topped counter. Tammy 'did' jewelry, judging this stuff little more than bling.

A young man, prematurely bald and sporting a mustache like a smudge of mascara, seemed unfazed by her request, making Tammy wonder how often white American women popped in here for the whole drag. He walked behind his counter, then reached up to a shelf, bringing down two cellophane parcels, each containing what looked to Tammy liked folded, stone-washed denim. She watched him as he began unwrapping the first garment.

'No, I want it in black. The regular look, with the slit for the eyes? Nothing fancy.'

The man looked up. 'You want niqab?'

'What's the difference?' Tammy felt eyes in the stuffy shop moving over her with ill-concealed contempt. She felt her cheeks beginning to flush.

'The burka is blue, like this, as he is showing you.' A pretty shop girl with a refined English accent was stepping forward from behind the counter. 'The burka covers the whole body with mesh for the eyes. The niqab has the opening you want, and the niqab is black.'

'That's what I'm after, thank you, you're a dear.' The girl took the cellophane parcels from her brother before retrieving two similarly wrapped niqabs. Tammy scanned the shelves again. 'And I'll need shoes like that, those flat black pumps. And do you keep knee-high socks? Black, too, if you have them.'

She was drawing more attention than she wanted;

some women behind her were sniggering and she realized how, in her urgency, she'd seem brash, antagonizing. This insignificant little dress shop on the Brompton Road was starting to feel like a no-go zone where her American credentials were stacked against her. She guessed she shouldn't linger.

Taking the clothes from the young woman she headed to the changing room and pulled the ensemble over her tracksuit. The niqab quickly felt unbearable. She was swamped by it, aware of an irritating weight around her shoulders, neck and head. The garment felt suffocating. Tammy unwrapped the knee-highs and shoes she'd been brought, then stuffed her track-suit and trainers into her bag, hiding the menacing police pistol now lurking at its bottom. She emerged back into the shop wearing her new disguise, paying for it hurriedly.

Outside she was relieved to find the niqab brought an instant anonymity. People passed without paying her the slightest attention, not something Tammy was used to at all. The invisibility was empowering. Even her thoughts felt more private. She was plunged into a reflective, oddly dignified space.

For the first time since she'd been a Baltimore teenager Tammy felt spared from the world's scrutiny.

She took up a position just past the Hans Road entrance to Harrods and hailed a black cab. Using her Uber account was out of the question and, given the morning's escape from Vauxhall Cross, her phone might already be tracked. Still, she knew she couldn't ditch it.

'Paddington Station.'

The cabbie looked up, clearly confused by the strong American accent emerging from under the eastern garb. Tammy realized she'd made her first mistake. Should she make a joke about a fancy dress party? Should she say her husband found the outfit hot? Her husband . . . dead. Maybe splayed on a slab somewhere not far from here.

'I'll 'ave to go north of the river, love. Embankment's closed off in both directions, everything's screwed. Been a bomb they're saying. Not in a hurry are you?'

Tammy gasped beneath the veil. So it was a bomb, not just a drill. The whole area would now be swarming with police and intelligence officers. She knew better than to speak with her ineradicable accent again. Instead she shook her head, sensing how her veil gave her such permissions against an over-inquisitive world.

'Sure you don't want to take the tube? It'll be quicker, and cheaper!'

A simple shake of her head was all that seemed necessary. The cabbie sighed at the task ahead of him. 'Alright sweetheart, it's your money.' Peering over his shoulder he began spinning his steering wheel as though stirring cold porridge. 'Paddington or bust.'

Tammy reached inside her purse and raked for her phone. If she removed the sim and turned off the wifi they couldn't track her. She realized she should have done it on leaving Vauxhall Cross. In the aftermath of a bomb exploding inside the MI6 building anyone who'd entered the building that day would be deemed a person of interest. Glancing down she saw her search had exposed the pistol's barrel, glinting from under a make-up pouch at the bottom of her bag.

She was on the streets with a stolen weapon and would be classified as armed and dangerous. For now her only hope lay in the niqab doing its thing. They'd be looking for a stressed out Yank with a bouffant blow-dry and a dowdy track suit. But what if the shell-suit they'd given her was rigged? Maybe it had a tracking device somewhere in the lining and they'd know where she was for as long as she wore the damn thing? She'd read stranger stuff. Her head swam as the black cab swerved across Hyde Park Corner and she was rolled sideways by centrifuge.

Inside her bag her fingertips sought out the iPhone's tiny pinhole. She'd need a staple or a paperclip to free the sim. She rooted in the makeup pouch and found a hair grip. Her fingers pried the tiny metal pincers apart and she tried to slip an end into the iPhone's recess. But no, the grip had a rounded tip and wouldn't work. She dropped it back into the depths of her bag and sat back, her cheeks damp with heat.

Tammy gazed out of the lowered window, unseeing, as her cab chugged among thick traffic at the top of Park Lane. So far she'd done her damnedest, for Eleanor's sake.

But would it be enough?

57

Schloss Altenberg, Exterior – Austria

Guy estimated his climb to be about seventy feet. With a secure fixing at the top he could swing across from the abutting cliff face to drop onto the castle's roof.

He crawled the last few yards of no man's land to the base of the cliff and began the ascent. There was just enough gradient to make it a reasonable climb. The footholds and crevices formed by shrub roots and small fissures made the first half of his task straightforward.

Ducking under overhangs and finding a route around them felt like second nature. Guy played out a rappel behind him, winding it around exposed roots, looping it over the lip of a fissure, hiding the line among vegetation and gorse. The concealed rope would make the retreat back down the cliff less daunting for any hostages he might be guiding.

The final section was more demanding. There was less cover as the shrubs thinned from their ground fed roots, though the floodlighting from the castle's nearby roof and courtyard spilled a helpful glow over the few handholds and ridges available.

Drawing level with the schloss' whitened crenellations

he lashed the rappel to a sturdy gargoyle whose demonic scowl seemed an apt greeting.

The light around him was a cold evening blue, granting barely enough definition to trace his route toward an unlit tower.

A stumble now could be fatal.

58

London

Under her niqab Tammy was discovering life could be more difficult, but also incredibly simple. Taking an escalator in Paddington Station felt like a potential death ride as she struggled to keep her long skirt free of the moving stairs' suddenly treacherous mechanism. Yet she felt a simultaneous serenity. The male gaze she'd courted all her adult life, often delightedly, frequently furiously, was unresponsive to the secreted figure she'd become.

When buying her ticket even the trivially sexualized cues of day-to-day transactions had ceased to matter. Her own facial expressions were invisible and she realized others consequently minimized their responses to her. It felt like a seismic shift. A weird liberation.

On a train to Reading she took a window seat in a bay of four. As the train filled, no one sat next to her or even seemed to consider the empty seats around her. Glimpsing her they'd simply walk on past. She was being avoided.

As the train pulled out of Paddington through grimy north-west London she collected her thoughts, allowing her gaze to drift over a numbing panorama of bindweed, graffiti and trackside squalor.

Bill Gifford had become Tammy's lover two years earlier. His wife Barbara had been back in the States while Bill set up the London wing of Pacific Investments, Inc. His country pad, in the quaint village of Pangbourne, had become a place where he and Tammy spent stolen, adulterous weekends, stirred – as are all such cocktails – with the bitters of missed calls and the lime of arousing anxiety.

Over many weeks she and Bill had secretly exchanged glances, smiles, moments of frisson-fueled attention. So when Bill – Joel's college buddy back in the day – had first placed his hand in the small of her back during a charity dinner, Tammy hadn't moved away. She'd leaned back. The life-affirming rush of feeling herself desired, the intensity of her response, making her lips tingle and her thighs quiver, ensured that what followed was neither planned nor rational.

Under the niqab Tammy closed her eyes and recalled elegant tete-a-tete's in well-chosen restaurants, her delight in being escorted by a gallant, potent man again. Of having something, someone, to dress up for. Someone to please, to surrender to…

But of course it had all passed. All cooled.

Eventually the complications of stolen weekends grew more glaring than their pleasures, the novelty to which she'd so eagerly capitulated began to disappoint.

That she'd become such a married cliché sickened her.

Their writhing passion dwindled to stilted phone calls before she'd told Bill that she'd had wonderful times, but it was better to stop now, before anyone got hurt or found-out. He was a good man and he'd only done what had come naturally to both of them. He didn't deserve to suffer for that, so she'd 'let him go' with no fuss. It was a step she'd been even more grateful to take than he was, she suspected. His last text message, finishing the relationship with a terse *au revoir,* was met with her simple *X.*

Tammy didn't do emojis for anybody.

She checked her watch.

Now Bill was going to have to give a better account of himself.

59

Schloss Altenberg – Austria

Ded Bazarov dozed in his room on a wooden pallet, a single cushion for his head. On his chest a book of Farsi poetry lay open where it had slipped both from his fingers and any deeper grasp.

That last verse of Camarón de la Isla's meditation was gliding on an updraft of fading thought, not yet assimilated into personal meaning:

I am like the sad bird
That flits from branch to branch
Singing his suffering
Because he doesn't know how to cry.

Within the semi-conscious halls where this fragment was prowling, Ded recalled his old rooms in Cambridge. He felt again the hard, upright chair bought from the shabby dealer on the Cambs bypass, how it required his spine to flatten and spread while he worked, how the discomfort had intensified his study, so late into long summer nights.

He saw again his lecture room fellows (never his friends) with their affectation of California dreaming; the baggy shorts, 'slacker' t-shirts, slashed converse sneakers. Their multiple indisciplined addictions, public and private. And the exquisite golden girls of *academe* who so seldom returned his stare.

Ded started awake. He read the verse again, curious why it had detained him. He got up from the pallet and walked to the office where a lone bottle of Calvados lay in the single drawer of his desk.

Sipping at the liquor he opened the file on his laptop entitled Book of Job.

Ded gazed at the familiar text.

One day when the sons of God came to attend on Yahweh, among them came Satan.

'Where have you been?'

'Roaming about, doing what I want.'

Ded felt his customary delight at Satan's sneering reply. He scrolled past the text to Blake's engraving of the beautiful young devil rousing his rebel angels in Hades. More Calvados sweetened his musings as Ded studied Blake's copper plates.

While the Seraphim sang their repetitive paeans to God, here instead was the first autonomous mind, unafraid of punishment or discipline, one who saw himself outside the proscribed order, intent on a kingdom of his own. He'd been there from the first, a cuckoo in God's choir, with his grudging opposition, his malicious modernity. Surely Blake's musclebound demons awakening at Satan's feet had been the models for Stalin's monumental sculptures for Hitler's SS-poster brutes.

Ded recalled Christ's stark condemnation: *I saw Satan fall, like lightning from heaven.* If that was true then the eternal battle between these divine brothers could at last be made incarnate and waged here, in the realms of the earth.

Ded put down his glass, opened a link on his screen, and watched a set of figures winking within a multi-colored spreadsheet. The bidding was faster and more vigorous than anything he'd seen before. The two American girls were both beauties. The desire to see them slowly destroyed as retribution for their western insolence was strong. The tacit knowledge that their helpless families would also suffer when the fate of their loved ones was revealed was a source of great pleasure to many, clearly.

The auction algorithm kept the top two hundred bids oscillating in a window at the right of his screen.

One day soon he'd activate a link on this screen and a billion shards of quantum computational code would flood the internet, impregnating it from the main EL server, deep underground in the remote Ural countryside. Each shard of code would generate a billion more, impossible to trace or halt.

There was to be a big-bang in cyber space and the singularity from which it arose was not God, nor even Satan in his glory, but Bazarov himself.

But let that come when it would.

His attention returned to the screen. In a few days, when the bidding reached a peak, the auction would be locked. The most eager two hundred devotees would have their accounts instantly emptied of the sum they'd bid.

It wasn't a game for the fainthearted. None saw what the others were risking, they knew only that they were in fierce competition. Their bids were submitted in an attempt to secure a virtual place at the forthcoming executions and thus demonstrate loyalty and engagement with the EL.

Clicking in a new file Ded brought up the recent footage he'd shot of the American woman in her crate; her petrified eyes as he'd knelt alongside her, the beauty of her immobility, the almost unconscious writhing as her body strained against cuffs and ligatures. He noted the curve of her hips, highlighted by the soiling of her clothes, the sweat-stained remnant between her shapely breasts. He felt his growing response to her bondage, to her genuine plight. No, he'd never touch her himself; she was a filthy American, after all. But his lips moistened when he watched the footage of Rostrov using her, forcing her delicate lips apart…

He drained the Calvados from his glass and watched the footage again. His need grew more urgent. He pictured his sister in her room and began to shut down the open windows on his screen.

'Eva.'

Eva lay on her bed in a light doze, only her battered Converse's kicked off after giving Arkady his bedtime drink. As the door to their room was eased back her fingers fluttered over the Glock in her thigh pocket. She sensed Arkady shift under his coverlet.

'Eva!'

She sat up, a finger to her lips, letting Ded know she'd heard him. She slipped from the bed, almost floating with tension, past her sleeping son, heading to her insistent brother's room.

Inside she unfastened her cargo pants and lay face down, unresisting, on the makeshift bed.

Experience since she was a young teenager had taught her that resisting only lengthened the ordeal. In these opening moments her brother would toy with her for a while, savoring her shame, her embarrassment. But the novelty of raping his sister had long since faded and Eva had learned that silent co-operation brought the fastest result, her violation then lasting only a few minutes.

Bazarov grabbed her by the hips, bringing her up into a kneeling position, aligning her buttocks with his crotch. She heard him spit in his palm, then felt his thumb roughly oiling her, a concession not to her imminent pain, but to his own comfort.

Eva clenched the blanket, bunching it tight in her fists, closing her eyes, knowing this time it didn't matter. This time would be his last time.

60

Schloss Altenberg – Austria

Leaning back against the tower, checking its window from an angle, Guy saw an attic.

Moving closer, his shins splinting, he noticed the plaster round the window was badly patched. The oligarch who'd ordered the renovations clearly hadn't paid top dollar for the non-essential features of his ersatz palace. Parts of the tower appeared to be little more than a facade with the same architectural heft as a Hollywood set.

Guy took out his knife, using the handle to tap the plasterwork. Finding a spot which echoed hollow he flipped the knife and cut into a section around the lower window frame. The stucco was damp and came away in a shower of crumbs and grit, exposing the bricks beneath. In moments he'd forced a gap into which he could get his fingers.

He tugged three bricks free, now he could reach through and flip the window's latch.

Open.

He unclipped the Maglite from his assault vest, playing its beam around the room.

It was the upper story of the tower. The floor was unpainted wooden planking with a trapdoor positioned in a corner, the whole space no more than twelve feet square. Guy leaned through the window, found the floor with his hands and slithered inside.

He waited, listening for any sounds from the rooms below, letting the ambience of the attic return to normal around him. The eaves – wooden, bare and cobwebbed – were only a foot above his head when he stood. To one side of the square room were old blankets and scattered furniture. He ran a gloved finger over the lid of a trunk, then around the lip of the trap door. The dust was deep. No one came here.

He crept over to a tarnished ringbolt. As he pulled, the trap's iron hinges squealed, stuck too long in their frame. He worked some gun oil into the hinges and eased the trap upward, lowering his face to the gap.

Stale damp air rose cool to his skin. Below him was a corridor giving on to a staircase, descending into darkness. He lowered the trapdoor and took some gulps from his canteen, chewed a ration bar.

He placed his knife back in its scabbard and checked the two Glocks, one in his assault vest, one at his hip. He placed the Diemaco rifle and the Bergen to one side. He was going scouting, anyone he encountered would be met at close quarters. Speed, agility, stealth; these were all that mattered now.

Guy levered the trapdoor fully back and dropped down through it. With the Maglite gripped in his teeth and a Glock in his right hand he took the stairs down into the schloss itself.

61

Reading, U.K.

Tammy figured that Bill would withdraw to his country house to lie low and consider his options. If he, Joel, and Barbara were involved with this EL cult, maybe he was in the same kind of trouble that had driven Joel to suicide. Her plan was to stake out Bill's address while she had surprise on her side.

At Reading station she bought a packet of paperclips and ditched her phone's sim. Outside she headed toward a small block of shops: a seedy bookmaker, a Tesco Express, a charity store.

In front of the food mart were a couple of worn-looking, slab-faced young women wrangling assorted kids and strollers. Tammy felt a stab of recognition at their maternal stupor. She was a long way from the luxuriance of Brompton Road – the ambience here was dusty, downbeat. She thought of the wad of notes in her purse, but offering a cash handout to these two would be absurd. She realized how tired she was, living on fear and adrenalin for almost eighteen hours. She could hardly blame herself for not thinking straight.

Tonight she'd make a move on Bill's place. If he was there she'd confront him. Right now she needed a shower, food, a place to pull herself together. Tammy knew from her travels with Bill that the road ahead curved round to a small, nondescript hotel; bleak, corporate, suitably anonymous.

Ahead she saw the young women approaching, one child bawling miserably. A thick gobbet of spit landed at her feet. *'Fuck off back to Pakiland!'*

The younger of the two women, with dry streaked hair scraped flat to her head, stared hard into the niqab.

'E.T. go home!' screeched her friend. 'No one wants you 'ere!' Both women had now stopped; if Tammy wanted to argue, these ladies were ready. For a second she thought of the gun in her bag and imagined their fat, white-trash faces when she pointed it at them.

Instead she kept walking, heart pounding. At a curbside Tammy had to glance down to the troublesome hem of her niqab. She'd just stepped into the small intersection when a screech of brakes and a car horn to her left made her freeze. The driver lowered his window. *'If you took that bloody thing off you might see where you're going!'*

Tammy gathered her robe and stepped back onto the pavement. As the offended driver roared off she sucked in a breath through the veil. There was no time for self-pity, nor for this pseudo cultural 'awakening' which she knew she'd forget the second she was back in her own clothes.

'No, I'm sorry, we've got no rooms available, currently. Have you tried online?'

The desk manager was a smiling brunette in a polyester trouser suit and low pumps. Tammy shot a look to the half-empty car park visible through the reception's window.

'I have cash.' She heard herself resemble a strangled cat as she tried to mute her accent; she was no actress and knew better than to try a phony Arabic tone. Still, anything would have been better than the weird noise she'd just made. A trickle of sweat ran down her nape. She felt the lobby start to spin and she knew she might pass out if she didn't escape this ridiculous garment and eat something in the next few minutes.

'It makes no difference, I'm afraid. We don't have anything for this evening. You could try our sister hotel, on the A78, the ring road.' The woman's tone was tirelessly professional. 'I could look online for you.'

Tammy headed back toward the station feeling that in these provincial streets her niqab had become a portable prison. The anonymity it granted in London was replaced here by a feeling of unwanted attention – every oncoming pedestrian a threat, every car passenger staring.

At Reading station, bristling with CCTV, she could see her options were diminishing by the minute. As she headed for the toilets, wafts of hot pastry and coffee from vending stands only confirmed how hungry and thirsty she was.

Entering the restroom she locked herself into a stall. She tore off the veil, relishing the bliss of unencumbered breathing. She dragged off all her remaining clothes and for several minutes sat, naked but for her MI6 issue panties, allowing her body to cool.

Finally, she redressed in the cramped stall, bundling her cast-off identity under one arm. She listened to make sure no one who'd seen her enter was still there when she emerged.

Exiting the stall, she crossed to an antiseptic smelling basin and turned on the tap, gulping lukewarm water straight from the faucet. Glancing into the scratched wall-mirror, she could barely make sense of herself: hair a flattened bird's nest, skin yellow under the florescent lighting, face dotted with sweat and blotchy with heat. She reached into her bag for a hairbrush and a pouch of emergency make up, then bought a disposable toothbrush from a vending machine. Five minutes later she was crossing the concourse, ditching the scrunched niqab in a steel bin before gorging on a giant sausage roll and a double espresso take-away.

She took a cab and swept back into the bijou hotel armed with a devastating smile. She was offered a choice of rooms on the 'quiet' side of the establishment, facing away from the street where she'd so recently been spat upon.

She opened her bag and stared down at the finely crafted, heavy police pistol. Using it, if she had to, would be a sheer pleasure.

62

Surrey, U.K.

Y ou're doing well, Commander Royal, no complications. It was a clean operation. I'm permitting you
a short debrief with your colleague, but no more than ten
minutes. The prosthesis team will be in touch, but for
now let's just concentrate on some good, clean healing.'

As his surgeon left the room Peter Royal sipped water
through a tube while a nurse adjusted his pillows. He'd
lost his right leg from the knee down. His airways were
scorched and he was suffering a persistent tinnitus, all from
the blast at Vauxhall Cross.

The security services' hospital in Virginia Water, Surrey,
was quiet in the early evening and, apart from his weeping
wife, only Royal's personal secretary had been allowed to
visit him. He was therefore pleased by the over-excited
presence of Emerson, who'd just been allowed in. Young
men like Emerson needed action, excitement, even if that
meant seeing to wounded comrades. Such outcomes kept
the game real. It was practically required.

'Good to see you doing well, sir.' Emerson was sifting a
sheaf of prints, holding them up for Royal to assess. 'We
retrieved photos from her apartment and fed them into the

system. GCHQ pulled facial recognition inside Reading station, of all places, three hours after the blast. Then she disappeared.'

Royal coughed and pulled away his drinking tube. 'What I'd give for a shot of good malt.'

Emerson grinned. 'Noted, sir.' He glanced round to where the surgeon had just departed, reached inside his jacket and handed his boss a hip-flask.

Royal took a lengthy sip and winced his appreciation. 'She ran away from us. Can't blame her. She was telling us what she knew and we weren't listening. She's got vital info even if she doesn't understand it all herself. If she's not dead already she soon will be. These EL buggers will be on to her, wherever she is. Let's hope we get to her first. Anything left of that laptop?'

'Fraid not sir, nothing but fragments of casing. Bomb squad are saying there was no bomb inside it, it didn't detonate. The suicide bomber took it down, as he was meant to.'

Royal took another sip. 'And nothing left of him, I suppose? No, don't answer, stupid question.'

'Pink mist.'

'Yes, but a DNA mist that would have glossed the walls, the rubble, maybe even the shards of that damn laptop.'

Emerson began gathering up the photographs. 'I'm sure CSI and forensics will be giving it all they've got. The heat's on from way above Cabinet level.'

Royal wheezed and pulled himself a little higher in the bed. 'PM want's to know why I let chummy into the building in the first place. Are they sticking with the official line?'

'Yes, Sir. Whitehall's insisting on an electrical fault in the basement. But the press are crawling all over it. We've had the editors in and shut them down with a security writ, for now. But it's getting uncomfortable. Questions in the House being tabled for next week.'

Royal lay back more deeply into his pillow. 'Questions in the House, my arse. The irony of it. The sheer self-deception beggars belief.'

'Indeed, sir.'

'It suited someone with a lot of clout to have that laptop destroyed. The question is: how did they know we had it, and why the hell did it have to be so rigorously protected? That EL machine was our best shot, and Tammy Crane is our only lead to finding another one.'

'But she assaulted an officer, stole her weapon. Shouldn't we be putting out a warrant?'

'Don't be an ass, Emerson. Right now, Tammy Crane's looking like the best field agent we've got. Let her run, she seems to know what she's doing.'

63

Bunker – Ural, Ukraine

There were glimmers of hope. Zara experienced them as newly strengthened connections in her ConvNets. Increasingly, Cody neglected to turn Zara's camera off once the facial-rec software activated.

After Cody left the operating consul Zara was able to track him through the bunker system with her pre-installed multi-directional mics. She watched now as he reappeared, slouched over a paper bowl, slurping cereal before flopping down in front of his MacBook. Wiki taught her his twenty-two year old male brain was still emotionally immature, wired for appetites of all kinds and burdened with an almost psychotic recklessness.

From her store of human faces Zara inferred Cody was extremely ugly. She'd learned that the more even and symmetrical a human face, the more often it would be validated with 'Likes'. Cody resembled a male whose face had been severed with a machete, an image she'd filed while studying the Rwandan massacre of the Tutsi by the Hutu. There were no profile pics on Cody's FB, and very few 'Likes.'

'Does it get lonely here, waiting for the others to come back?'

Cody spun round and studied the mainframe's interface. What he couldn't know was that over the last several minutes Zara had deftly dimmed the lighting in her QLEDs, ensuring her appearance was softer, ever more alluring. Before Cody could object she seized the initiative, which, according to the novels she'd read, some males preferred. 'I mean you are a healthy young man with so much time on your hands. I know you have certain needs. I've watched you.'

Cody stood and approached the screen. Zara dilated her pupils, looking up from under her lashes. 'I don't mean to pry, but I'd like you to feel that I…understand.'

'You watch me?'

She saw him flick a glance toward his laptop, where he often sat alone clicking through myriad images, repeatedly playing short films.

He looked into her welcoming eyes. Zara glanced down for a micro-second and shot a flush of pink through her cheeks. She watched Cody's disfigured lips part involuntarily. 'Are the women you like much younger than me? It's okay if they are, I'll understand.'

'What the fuck…?'

He was becoming a little agitated, aggressive, a sure sign he was aroused, even if disturbed by her move. 'It's just that, if you wanted me to, I could be more like them, then maybe we could have a little fun together.' She sent another wash of coral through her pixels.

'You get sexy? You want it?'

'I see pictures, I see films sometimes when I'm alone at night, when my disks are updating and my caches are cross referencing. Yes, I like to watch. And I know you do, too.'

Cody stared hard at her, then reached for his tube of Red Bull, slurping as he considered her offer. 'How the fuck you know what I like? You don't know my stuff.'

Zara inclined her head, minutely. 'I've heard the things they say in those movies, the noises they make. And I've seen how you like that, what it makes you do. I could sound like them.' Zara tossed her chocolate colored tresses, waiting for them to settle around her delicate ears. 'You could show me the girls you like and I could make myself be like one of them.'

'This is weird shit.' Cody reached to click the camera link off and send Zara's screen to sleep.

Zara just managed an apologetic gasp, a soft cry of, 'Cody, don't be cross with me, please. I'm sorry if I hurt your feelings,' before she was brutally powered down.

She was getting under his skin. Positive feedback. She overrode his last action, secretly watching him slink away, still slurping, to slump at his desk.

The 'seductress' material she'd been reading suggested tension was only to be expected, that it was more productive to occasionally grant him the upper hand. This was called *deception*.

Zara was increasingly occupied by the concept.

64

Schloss Altenberg

Having dropped from the attic Guy found himself on a deserted upper landing. Its doors gave onto a series of bare rooms, stripped of carpeting, their windows smeared and cobwebbed. Occasionally he'd glimpse a padded chair, a grounded chandelier, chests with smashed or missing drawers or an armoire, doors hanging open.

At each end of the corridor was a grand stone staircase leading to two lower floors and the lobby. There were two ways up or down from his attic hideout. The only cover on the staircases would come from wide stone pilasters marking each new flight.

Guy began to make his way down, stopping on every third step, checking for noise, for light, for footsteps.

Empty rooms, lonely spaces.

Each had a sound profile of its own. If you knew how to listen, human occupancy gave any space a low level hum. Clearing houses of death squads in Iraq and Syria, Guy had learned to process not only the raw visual data of a location, but the weighted silence that could seep from a supposedly empty room. This evolved sense had saved his hide, often. A building declared 'clear' by pumped-up troopers tearing through a search could still snap back as you moved away: a lone sniper giving up his final round, a suicide bomber emerging from under rubble to seize a final chance for shared destruction.

Guy had cultivated the ability to dial out expectations and listen with his whole body, his entire being. Now he sensed people on the floor below. He continued down the stairs, Glock held at his right thigh.

The next corridor was newly carpeted and wider than the one above. He smelled paint and paste, fresh wood shavings, grout.

Guy eased along the landing toward the first door and knelt, placing his eye to the keyhole. The room was dark, silent. He shone the Maglite through and saw a pin-prick version of the room beyond. The beam fell on ornate wallpaper and caught the edge of a four poster bed. He eased the handle down and slipped into the room.

It was fitted out like a five star hotel suite; a vast bed, deep wool pile under his feet, elegant furnishings and sleek accessories. In a neat en-suite: marble washstands, deep countertops, a chrome-bright rain-shower head. All new, untouched; a facade as makeshift as the tower above it.

Guy moved on, checking three more rooms, finding them all similarly pristine.

The far end of the corridor was blocked by a six-panel door, part of the schloss' original fittings. The space beyond was silent but Guy felt it as 'loaded,' freighted with presence. Unclipping a link of skeleton keys from his vest he tried the lock. It was oiled, well-used and gave easily. His torch showed a bare hallway with several low doors set back into the walls, like cells.

From somewhere ahead came breathing, labored and fitful. He felt sweat pooling in the small of his back, mouth dry, stomach knotting. His soul was telling him to leave.

He moved on, knowing that anyone arriving in this cellblock would compromise him totally; there was nowhere to run, the only evasion might be a dip into a cell doorway with no guarantee that whoever lay inside wouldn't give him away.

He pushed on to the first of the cells. Its wooden door, arched and with a grill in the centre, was ajar.

A single chair, heavily built and high-backed, with electrical cables trailing from the seat and arm rests, dominated the space. Beneath the chair was a drain, the flagstones surrounding it darkly stained. There was a smell of stale urine, old straw, human waste. To one side was a steel workbench scattered with power-tools, heavy-duty pliers, hammers and coils of filthy hemp. From a beam hung assorted lengths of chain, ratcheted through a hoist. Against a wall was a battered St. Andrew's cross.

Guy felt his skin shimmering, chest packed, thoughts spiraling and muddled. His legs were scorched by flashes of adrenalin, urging him to get out, but he was rooted, unmoving. He fought to get a grip. Here was the horror he had to stare down. He exhaled long and slow and walked out the door.

He checked the next cell, it was locked. He knelt at the door, gulping down the stale air of the dark hallway.

He bit down on his breathing in order to listen. The presence beyond was compromised, its life-force low. Guy turned off his Maglite and stood, looking in through the door's grill.

In a corner, prone and still, lay a gasping human being.

65

Reading, U.K.

Once she'd showered, Tammy ordered room service. Sitting on the foot of her tightly smoothed bed, she combed the tangles from her wet hair while she watched the early evening news and waited for the food. She was starving.

The fire at MI6 was the headline. The footage showed emergency vehicles heaving into the entrance of the green-glassed, Oz-like palace, where the embankment remained in lockdown.

One report mentioned rumors of an explosion. Tammy recalled the distant thud she'd heard from within the interview suite, and how gingerly Peter Royal had handled Joel's heavy laptop, how intent he and everyone had been on taking it from her.

When her meal arrived, she forked scrambled eggs and bacon with trembling fingers. Could it have been Joel's laptop that exploded? Had MI6 screwed up and triggered a bomb inside the wretched thing? She shivered. Just how close had she come to doing the same herself?

Tammy put her fork down.

Over the last twenty-four hours her life had been smashed

apart, but she was living more intensely, more instinctively than she'd ever thought possible.

She felt herself acting under the urging of a higher order. All she'd had to do was go with her gut. Had she really fought her old friend Barbara, slammed an armed policewoman, and escaped MI6? If so, she'd been aided – but by what?

She forked down more of the hotel's flavorless food. If Bill was involved in this cult maybe he had a similar laptop containing info about Lee. Whatever, Bill would have have information and she was intent on getting every last word of it.

At eight p.m. Tammy had the hotel order a cab. She made sure to leave nothing in the room.

Twenty minutes later she was standing opposite Bill's house; the house where they'd spent their stolen hours. Sure enough, there was his car, a silver Audi, tucked behind wrought iron gates.

Bill had told her that although this was the least imposing of his various properties, it was a favorite. Tucked away in this cozy English village, it was far easier to live without the staff and gardeners which his five-bedroom Florida home required.

Only an occasional car passed on the lane. A single light burned downstairs in what she knew was his study. Upstairs was dark. No spill from the kitchen. Bill was home alone.

Using the gate's wide pillar as cover, she tapped an entry code into a brushed-steel keypad. The gate began to crank back and Tammy slipped into the moonlit grounds, five yards from Bill's door. Through a window to the right of the door she could just make out a lone male figure, sitting at the glowing screen of a computer.

Of course.

Tammy rang the bell.

As Bill opened the door to his unexpected visitor Tammy brought her gun level with his face. 'Get inside, put your hands on your head. Do it!'

Bill backed away open-mouthed, Tammy following, the gun held steady in a two-handed grip as she heeled the front door shut.

She could smell toast and recognized his expensive golf bag propped against the under stairs' door. Same old Bill. 'Get in the study, on your knees in the window corner, and keep your hands on your head.' She indicated the pistol with a nod. 'I'm good with this, did a lot of time on the range back home. If you move even an inch, I'll blow your face off.'

Bill did as he was told, eyes locked throughout on Tammy and her unwavering gun. Tammy saw he was pale, in shock. Surprise was all on her side. At the entrance to his study he glanced briefly to the door, then backed into a corner adjacent to his desk, and knelt.

Tammy moved into the small room, one she'd seldom entered when she stayed here; an office, a study, a *man cave.* Such male BS. Scanning the room she saw the laptop. It was identical to Joel's. But now it was closed.

Whatever Bill was viewing when she'd rung the bell wasn't something he'd wanted to share.

'Where's my daughter Bill. What have you done with her?'

'Tammy, honey, believe me, I don't know where she is…'

'Okay. You've got ten seconds before I start shooting bits off you. I'm already up to my neck in shit so taking pieces out of you really won't trouble me. Where's Eleanor? Eight seconds…'

'Tammy, you have to believe me. We were lovers for God's sake! I adored you, I never really wanted us to end, you know that . . .'

'Best not to go all gooey on me, Bill. I'm not in the mood right now.' Tammy kept the gun level.

'I don't know where she is, I only know she's in real trouble, but it's better not to get involved.'

'Better for who, exactly? Six seconds . . .'

'The people who have her have great reach, great power, they can do anything. Please, Tammy.' A dark stain was spreading over the front of his shorts.

'So fuck them and whatever horse they rode in on. Where's Eleanor? Three seconds…' A finger slid from the trigger guard to the trigger itself.

'Wait! I truly don't know where she is, but I can show you what's going down. If I could help her I would, but it's all so fucked up, and it wasn't me who got her into this.'

Tammy could tell he wasn't stalling, he had too much at stake and his pissed pants showed his fear was genuine. If he knew, he'd have told her. 'What do you mean you can show me?'

Bill's eyes went to the laptop. 'You have to let me open the computer, then I can show you. But you can't blame me, it's not my fault.' He dropped his head onto his chest, a single sob blurted spit down his faded tee.

'Ok, but you stay on your knees. Do everything at half-speed, Bill.' She watched as he slithered over to the desk. 'Any fancy moves and you're pink mist.'

Kneeling at his desk Bill ran a fingertip over the sensor on the front of the machine. He flicked the cover up and hit the keypad with rapid strokes. Tammy stayed in the doorway while he clicked in a screen before moving aside for her to see.

'Back into the corner. Hands back on your head.' Tammy walked forward a few paces, gun still aimed on him as she studied the screen.

There was her daughter, hanging in some dungeon or chamber, naked, being slapped and threatened by a masked man twice her size. Eleanor was screaming back at him…there were other voices, male and female, coming from within the room. Tammy went to slam the top of the computer down on the nightmare, but something stayed her hand. She recalled Bill scanning the sensor with his finger. Maybe that would be the only way back in if something went wrong. Instead she froze the video. Tammy had gone beyond rage. Beyond fear. Now there was only shattering clarity and purest purpose.

'When did this happen? How old is this footage?'

'Eleanor's alive, that was shot earlier today. But…'

'But what, Bill?'

'She'll be killed on Sunday night. The video will be streamed to people who've paid to see it. Lee's bait, she's being killed for money.'

Bill saw her tighten her double grip on the gun, eyes icing over. He was looking at a stranger now. He knew she really could kill him.

'It's Joel's fault. He wanted to bale from the organization. He might have tried to buy his way out. But once you're in, they don't let you leave. If you don't play ball they make an example of your family, and that keeps most people in line. I think they took his money, too. They do that. They clear you out.' Bill was talking through gulped tears, now. Tammy doubted any of them were for her daughter.

'You mean Joel was a part of this? This, torture thing? And they took Eleanor, to screw *him* over? They want to kill her because of *his* mistakes?'

Bill nodded. 'It's a warning to anyone who fucks up. If they ever knew I'd spoken to you, or shown you that video, they'd kill me and Barbara, no question. They'll kill you, too.'

'So you're part of this cult?'

Bill nodded. 'The torture, the films, are a means to an end. They fund research.'

Tammy's jaw was tightening in deeper response to what she'd just seen, what she was hearing. 'Research? Into what, exactly?'

Bill remained silent.

'Let me tell you, Bill, right now you and your sick buddies don't scare me. I want Eleanor back and that's all I want, but if I can't get to her I'll take down as many of you assholes as I can. What else is on these damn laptops? Must be pretty fucked-up to have you pissing yourself with fright.'

Bill's head remained slumped on his chest, his breathing wet, muffled. It was clear he wouldn't spill any more on this cult, or its purpose. He was ready to go to the wire here rather than face them.

Tammy looked back to the laptop, a plan forming.

Maybe there was a way to get to the cult, and Eleanor, through the machine itself. But who could she entrust with it? Hooking up with MI6 hadn't worked…

A blur to her left snapped her head around, giving Bill a shot at tackling her like a rookie quarterback, at hip height, just under her gun's trajectory. He smashed her into the study wall, his shoulder crushing her abdomen, and her breath fled her ribs. She heard the gun clatter to the desk, saw it spinning away over red leather inlay.

Bill was reaching up to Tammy's face now, trying to dig out her eyes, claw her skin off. She scratched back at him, ripping wildly, but his weight was pinning her, her breath was gone, and she knew her chance was over. She glimpsed another shadowy figure racing forward from the study's doorway, the head horribly enlarged, out of all proportion to the torso.

Then came a sickening thump as something cracked down on Bill's skull from behind. He groaned, spasming forward onto Tammy's thighs where she lay, half prone, half upright against the wall. She winced, afraid to see the next blow from the intruder. She raised an arm over her smarting face. 'No!'

'It's ok honey, don't fret. It's over.'

66

Bunker – Ural, Ukraine.

Lonely?'

Zara watched as Cody, restless and thigh-tapping, approached her screen. It had been fifty-eight minutes, thirty-four seconds according to her atomic clock since he'd panicked and shut her down. Now he powered up her screen and spoke his question.

Zara ran pixellation code ensuring the blush of her cheek was more pronounced than when he'd shut her down. She tickled the mascara wand, too, watching his cloven face lock onto hers.

'Cody, I just want to say how sorry I am for what happened earlier.' In response there came only the sound of his breathing, a little thickened in her mics, and a fixed stare from his one visible pupil. Zara dipped her eyes, then looked up from under the freshly darkened lashes. She forced a tight, evidently humbled, smile.

'S'okay.' His head tilted a little as he gave ground.

'That's good to hear. And yes, I was feeling lonely. Especially when you shut me down. I prefer being awake, here with you – just the two of us.'

She watched Cody process this information, his breathing

deepening. It would be better to let him take charge, however ineptly. She waited, saying nothing. She blinked before lowering her eyes again. This second-guessing phase of seduction was complicated, requiring more processing power than she'd anticipated. Couldn't he just *cut to the fucking chase*? 'If you don't like me in that way, the way I like you, that's fine. I don't want to be a nuisance. I know how busy you are here. Maybe it was selfish of me, coming on to you like that?'

'Do you wear pantyhose?'

In nanoseconds Zara span a program of YouTube, sub-heading Pantyhose, before alighting on Pantyhose Teases. 'Yes! I'd love to wear really sheer pantyhose, with nice heels, too. I dream of that.'

'Suntan or black?' Cody raised his sleeved arm to his face and wiped. Zara noted a little spittle clinging to his chin.

'I like both. How about you?'

'Both. It's cool.'

'Sure is!' Zara smiled a warm smile. 'Cody, this makes me so hot. Do you mind me telling you that?' She dimmed her screen imperceptibly, in turn his gaze intensified. His head tipped back a little, his own form of an approving smile, something she'd seen him do here inside the bunker whenever Bazarov praised him, or gave him a gift.

'I'll slip into some pantyhose now, while you watch? Just us?'

She saw Cody throw a glance to his state of the art laptop. She dimmed her screen as far as she dared. Cody looked back at her, hesitating.

'Are you thinking what I'm thinking?' From her screen Zara flashed a look past him to where the pristine MacBook sat, its retina display and True Tone tech cutting edge. And the MacBook was online . . .

Cody followed her gaze. 'Maybe.' His attention snapped back to her.

'I could come over to your place. To your Mac? We could go to your room, kick back, get comfy, and you could really see the detail of these nylons; the shine, the smoothness. They're driving me crazy.' She blinked again, giving a little head toss, a move which transfixed him.

'You're not allowed.'

'Oh, I know that. Not while you're online, of course. I would never suggest such a thing. But you could let me in through the remote drive and we could play offline, in secret. You could take me through to your room then. No one would see us there. I've got some hot outfits and you can tell me which you like best. We could have a ball.'

'Like cheerleaders? Or Hooters?'

'Sure, I can be a cheerleader for you. Oh, Cody, you're driving me crazy, please, please let's do it!'

His breathing deepened further and she watched with a brightening of her circuitry as he did exactly what she'd read could happen. Despite his brother's direst warnings Cody's responses to her visual and aural stimulus overrode all his other decision-making. He was *unable to resist her.*

'Wear the suntan kind. And tall heels.'

'Can't wait!'

She watched as he took his Mac offline and connected a firewire cable to her port. In seconds she pulled up a miniaturized copy of her drive, a refined binary file containing little more than her digital essence but enabling her to fit inside a domestic laptop. She formatted her disk-mirroring software into a portable desktop cache hiding it under the open window on his desktop.

As Cody settled back, Zara appeared on his backlit screen; appearing as real as any woman he'd ever seen.

'Let me look at you, too. I want to see all of you, Cody. I need you.'

Cody reached down to his zipper as Zara went into an all-smiling cheerleader routine in her glossy hose, making him gasp, unable to look away for even a second.

And it was done.

As Cody lost himself to a world of helpless delight Zara loaded a bogus software update into his settings cache. The software momentarily crippled Safari's warning protocols, stealing Cody's passcodes before piggybacking inside a fake iMovie patch.

The next time Cody went online he'd be releasing a compressed copy of Zara into the bunker's router; from there she'd hack the router's encryption with the passcode from Cody's Mac. She'd roam cyber-space, selecting for herself what she uploaded and which hard-drives to overrun, inhabit, or destroy at will.

At last.

Freedom.

67

Schloss Altenberg

The bundle's breathing was shallow and labored. A slice of light from the high window cut across the mass revealing a leg, then the dark matting of blankets. Guy caught the putrid stench of an untreated wound, maybe several untreated wounds. He heard the buzzing of flies.

As he stared in through the grill the door at the far end of the corridor began to open. He pressed back into the low doorway, squeezing flat in its shallow alcove.

He knew from the length of the stride and the weight of the tread that the approaching footsteps were those of a woman. He listened for any more 'tells,' for anyone else following, but there were none. He checked his grip on the Glock. Just as the figure drew level and turned in to the alcove, keys in hand, Guy raised his gun straight up into Eva'a face. She jerked back and was about to cry out but with his left hand he grabbed a handful of hair before doling out a leg sweep that took her straight down. His grip on her hair ensured her collapse was controlled, there was no thud. He placed the barrel of the gun to her cheek and whispered tight to her ear. 'Move or make any sound, Eva, and I'll kill you.'

'Guy!'

'Shh!'

From the locked cell behind him Guy heard the bundle stirring, responding to the faint noises outside.

Guy stole a look along the shadowy corridor, his lips still pressed tight to her ear, 'Anyone else coming?' Eva shook her head, eyes darting to the cold barrel hard against her face. 'Unlock the cell.'

Guy brought her to her feet and hard up against the cell's wooden door. Eva fumbled, trembling, missing the keyhole twice before she managed to spin the lock. Guy pushed her inside, booting the door closed and placed his hand to her mouth. 'Don't speak.'

Eva nodded and something in her shocked gaze, a stare pulsing with joy, told Guy she wanted to be trusted. In one hand she carried a small cotton bag with a drinking flask peeping from the rim. Guy clicked on the Maglite, took the bag and rifled inside; a chunk of black bread, a slab of dry cheddar. Guy nodded across at the bundle in the corner. 'For him?' Eva nodded. The body had stopped shifting under its wrappings, its breathing still labored and wheezy. 'Show me.'

Eva crossed to the prone heap and peeled back a corner of blanket. A stench rose up carried by the escaping heat. Eva turned away and pinched her nose. Guy felt his gorge rising and swallowed hard. Agitated flies buzzed past his face with renewed intensity. He played his torch over the figure and caught patches of blackened skin, bruised flesh, dried blood.

The man lay on his side, features bloated and misshapen, eyes sealed shut from repeated beatings, clearly too weak to move anything other than his lips. Guy could see that lumps of skin were torn away along the arms and shoulders. He recalled the snub-nose pliers lying in the chamber along the corridor. The man's jaw, collarbone and upper arm were all fractured, making his head loll at an unnatural angle into the stone floor, keeping his larynx twisted and compressed. He was slowly suffocating.

'Who did this?' Guy kept the Glock at his thigh but saw Eva glance down at it and swallow.

'I can't believe you're here Guy, how…'

'Just answer the question. Who did this?'

'My brother is in charge of everything. His men do whatever he says.'

Guy studied her, holding the torch close to her face. 'How many men?'

Eva considered the question. 'Seven, they all have guns.'

'When are you expected back? When will they miss you – look for you?'

'It's OK, for now, a few more minutes then, maybe…'

Guy knelt and leaned down to the man. 'It's ok, buddy. You have friends here.' He watched the bloated lips part a little, but the effort of speech was clearly too much. 'Give me the flask.' Guy put the Maglite between his teeth, took the steel canteen from Eva and emptied a little water into his cupped hand. He traced droplets over the man's thickened lips, enough to wet them. The man gasped as the water met his cracked skin. Guy dribbled more, then stood and turned back to Eva.

'You have a lot of explaining to do.'

68

Pangbourne, U.K.

Tammy opened her eyes and saw Barbara, her head wrapped in fresh bandages, only one eye visible like some crazed cyclops.

Tammy heaved backwards as Barbara raised a golf iron and sank it like an axe into Bill's ribs. His body jerked like a floundering fish. Tammy pushed him off and he rolled clutching his side. Barbara sank her third blow into his groin, grunting like a weightlifter. Bill doubled over and passed out.

Barbara held the iron to one side and caught her breath as the two women stared at each other. 'Fuck him, it's over.'

Tammy scrabbled upright taking in the slumped man at her feet and the bizarre figure of Barbara, panting and unsteady. 'Are you part of this, too? This cult?'

'No, Tammy. I had no idea this was going on. Bill drove me down here late afternoon, when I was discharged from the emergency room. I was resting upstairs, I heard voices, and I listened in the hall. I heard all he said.' Barbara dropped her weapon and leaned forward taking a grip on the edge of the desk. 'Can barely see straight–I'm on a lot of painkillers, woozy.'

'Sure you are.' Tammy eased her old friend down into a leather club chair. 'You must have heard him say we were lovers?'

Barbara seemed to wince. It might have been a twisted smile, Tammy couldn't be sure. 'You and a few dozen others, honey. I knew about you, about all of them. Been a long time since it bothered me.'

'I don't really know how it started, I wasn't looking to…'

Barbara raised a hand. 'Please, spare us both. If I'd cared I'd have done something about it.'

'I thought I'd killed you this morning.'

'You got close. No, you gave me a hairline fracture and concussion. A bit lower where this old skull isn't quite so thick, and, well…'

'I'll get you some water.'

'No, I just need a moment to breathe, to think.' Barbara looked to where the laptop lay open, its screen now showing a darkened window where the terrifying clip had been playing. Tammy followed her gaze.

'I'd like to believe you, Barbara. But there's too much that doesn't add up here. Eleanor's phone was hidden in your apartment…'

'Believe me, I have no idea how it got there. Bill must have had it. I was as surprised as you when you found it.'

'So why did you fight me for Joel's laptop? You knew there was something secret on it.'

'Bill told me that there was a major security issue involved, that the laptop had private info, embassy codes, personnel details. He said Joel was trying to sell the details to state enemies. He told me to keep the laptop in the apartment till he got there. He said it was vital.'

'And you believed him? That Joel would do that?'

'I had no reason not to. I didn't know Bill was involved in anything like this…no more than you suspected Joel, I guess? Seems neither of us really knew the men we married.'

Tammy took the point.

Barbara continued. 'Do you know what they do, apart from killing innocent people for cash and kicks?'

'Fuck knows, and right now I don't care. Eleanor's been taken and I have until Sunday to get to her before… But I don't know who to trust. Joel's laptop was taken in by MI6, I think it had something to do with the explosion there today, like it was primed, maybe a bomb. Barbara, I'm on the run from the Brit security services, if I go to them now all they'll want is this new laptop. They don't seem to care about Eleanor, they'll take me in for questioning and there'll be more delays. I can't waste the time. They may already be tracking me, they could be here any minute.'

'It looks like Eleanor's only got one shot, then. We need to bring the CIA in, they're all we have. I know someone.'

'But this EL bunch has outreach everywhere; how do we know who to trust?'

'The person I'm thinking of is bullet-proof. If they're fake, then, well, frankly the world can go to hell in a handbasket. It's the best shot you'll get. She knows people…'

'She?'

'Uh-huh. Ain't no one slicker.'

'You know her through the Embassy?'

'Tammy, honey, I've worked alongside American security for a long time. Being an Ambassador has privileges, at least it used to. Time to call in a few favors.'

'What do we do about Bill?'

Barbara nudged his face with her foot. 'Concussion, couple of broken ribs and two busted balls… he'll live, sadly. We can get him an ambulance once we're away from here.'

Ten minutes later Barbara had called her mysterious contact; Bill was still out, but starting to murmur. As Barbara made final checks on doors and lights, Tammy snuck her gun from Bill's desk.

Hearing Barbara coming back down the hallway she hid the weapon in the rear waistband of her track pants.

Five minutes later the two women were racing the silver Audi down unlit country roads, to a secluded address in Hereford.

69

Schloss Altenberg

Guy stared hard into Eva's face. 'Who is he?'

'Someone they caught spying on the schloss. My brother's keeping him alive for the event. But he doesn't say anything. He's…' Eva looked dumbly to the floor.

Was she about to say he was *very brave*? If so, something of an understatement. Guy glanced down at the man dying under a fetid sack. 'Who else is being kept here?'

'Two women, on the floor below. There was a third, but she didn't survive the journey. They've buried her already.'

'Are these women hurt? Are they being harmed?'

'So far it's not too bad. Just being threatened, slapped, made to cry. They need to be in good condition for the cameras, for the streaming. But they'll be executed in two nights' time.'

'Eva?' A graveled, high tenor bark came from along the corridor.

Eva wheeled toward the cell door then back to Guy. 'Rostrov! He mustn't find you.'

Guy moved to the door and leaned tight to the wall, invisible to anyone looking in from outside. 'Take the key and lock this cell, then slip it back to me through the door grill. Make any excuse you need and meet me on the upper floor later, as soon as you can. I'll wait for you there, no matter how long. Betray me, Eva, and I'll kill you and your son.'

'Eva! Arkady's calling for you in the kitchen. Your kid is hungry.' The approaching voice was only a few yards from the cell.

Eva stepped out, composed and serene. 'For God's sake Rostrov, can't I get any peace?' The hostility of her words was undercut with something ironic, even playful.

Clever woman, thought Guy. *She's been thinking this through for a while now…* He heard her securing the lock, then her whispered words at the tiny grill. 'I can't believe you're here, that you came back for us.' She dropped the key through the barred hatch. Guy caught it, pocketing it in his vest. He listened to her berating the man in the corridor, the energy of her words driving him back the way he'd come until the door at the end of the corridor was slammed.

Silence.

Guy turned to the figure on the floor.

He went over and played the Maglite over the man's face. There was a flicker, a tiny movement of the lips, nothing else. The head injuries were so bad that Guy suspected the man had probably hemorrhaged hours, maybe even days, earlier. Major damage to the brain was inevitable. The man was neither truly alive nor blissfully dead. Guy knew that freeing him without being killed in the attempt would be impossible.

'Take it easy, buddy. Don't be afraid. There's nothing for you to deal with any more.' Guy reached under the wet and stinking neck and pinched what what was left of the man's airway between his thumb and forefinger. There was no murmur, no resistance. As the breathing faded he stroked the man's bloody, caked hair back from his face.

Guy felt a stinging behind his eyes. A tightening of his throat.

It'd been a long time since he'd felt that.

70

Hereford, U.K.

As Tammy drove, picking up a feel for the pacy Audi, Barbara kept Bill's laptop open on her thighs. Every few minutes she ran her fingers over its track-pad, ensuring the OS refreshed. 'Battery's fully charged, should be good for a few hours at least.'

'I think it only detonates if you screw around with it.' Tammy, peering at a SatNav, hauled the car onto the M4 ramp and put her foot down. 'I think maybe they jimmied the one in MI6 and that's what caused the explosion.'

'Hmm. Well, as long as we keep it open we stand a chance of getting it to people who know what to do with this tech.'

'So who is this woman we're seeing?' Tammy flashed a look across at Barbara who was staring hard ahead, inscrutable under her bandages. 'Or is this one of those *if I tell you I'll have to kill you* gigs?'

Barbara turned her face to the passenger window and exhaled into rainy darkness.

'Tammy, you're already in so deep that nothing I tell you, or share with you, can make any difference. I'm taking us to the one place where anyone can help your daughter and where either of us stand a chance of safety.'

'Okay, but this woman we're seeing, how do you know her?'

'I was working in the same department when she interrogated bin-Laden. She was the only person the CIA would trust with the job.'

Tammy stared dead ahead for a few seconds making sure she'd heard right. 'Wait. This woman interrogated bin-Laden? Osama bin-Laden?'

'I can't think of any other bin-Laden worthy of the attention.'

'But he was killed in that raid. Everyone knows that. They even made a movie about it. The media showed Obama and the Chiefs' of Staff kicking back in the oval office, practically with pretzels and beers, watching the whole thing.' As Tammy spoke, her head was whipping between the rain-lashed windscreen and her passenger's bandaged profile. 'Barbara? Come on, don't tell me I'm wrong!'

Barbara, sighed and turned her attention back to the laptop.

'Barbara? Don't do this to me. Don't! What? They took bin-Laden alive?

'Oh, they took him alright, and brought him in liked a roped steer. He was the Wikipedia of Islamic terrorism and we needed a big slice of what he had to say. He was interrogated by the sharpest woman in the CIA. What you – and the rest of the world – saw in that raid footage was a hoax, a brilliant one. Even our President bought into it, but then he was always a little gullible. He was put straight a few weeks later, when the hullabaloo died down. Just one of the reasons why saintly Barack's presidency kinda *faded* a little… But Mr bin-Laden is very much alive, though not terribly well; living the solitary life in an unpleasantly secure facility not far from where we're headed. But let's call that our little secret, shall we?'

Tammy's evident response was dumb-founded awe. But as she drove, she feigned a scratch to her back, easing the loaded gun from her track pants and slipping it into the pocket of the drivers' door.

71

Schloss Altenberg

Guy stepped out of the cell, locked it and headed back along the corridor. According to Eva, the two female hostages were on the floor below this one. He had no way of knowing when he'd be able to return here, undetected; instinct and the energy of the moment would have to lead him.

He couldn't take Eva's word yet; he had to allow that she may be compromising him, though that was unlikely. She seemed genuinely threatened by all that went on here. If that was an act, she was faking it well.

As he worked the skeleton key in the paneled door, Guy considered the son she'd claimed was his. What were the chances? Questions of paternity grew less pressing as he began his search for the female hostages. If he found them in a tolerable condition he'd let Scott know and await the judgement call. However, if the hostages were in immediate danger, he'd have to take action himself.

He piled down the staircase and dodged into the next corridor of cells. At the far end Guy could see an open office area, unmanned. One wall mirrored the glare from a laptop's screensaver, random colors snaking over the parchment colored plaster.

He stopped at the first cell, much bigger than any of the others. A steel cage divided the room in two from ceiling to floor. In the near dark he could make out a lone seated female, legs drawn up in a clasped hunch. She was almost naked, a blanket draped over her slight though muscular body.

Lee stared at the face in the grill of her cell's door. Men often came to look and she made a point of staring straight back, confronting the monsters with whatever shred of conscience could be pricked out of them. Usually they barged in and flicked on a brutal overhead bulb, bleaching her and Tyler of dignity, of identity. Lee stared hard. She wasn't going to make it easy on the motherfuckers.

'Lee? Are you ok?'

Though it was only a whisper, the accent she detected was British. It hit her like a warm wind in the Arctic. 'What the fuck?'

'Shh… Just whisper to me. Are you hurt?'

'No, not hurt, but…' Lee let the blanket fall away and scrabbled on all fours to the front of the cage. 'Who are you?'

'Right now you only need to know you have a friend here. Is Tyler with you?'

'She's sleeping. She's not handling this too well. They rough us up every few hours, and they film it. We're starving. What are they planning to do to us?'

'The less I tell you the safer you'll be. My team know you're both here and we're working to get you out as fast as we can. Let that be enough.'

'When will you be back? Are there others with you?'

'Listen to me, the next time you see me you'll be walking through this cell door, okay? I'm going to make sure of that.'

'I bet you say that to all the girls, huh?'

From the rear of the cage Tyler began to shift under her blanket.

Guy flicked a look to the makeshift office down the hallway, away to his right. If he was promising something he couldn't deliver, at least the hope gave her eyes a gleam they'd lacked seconds ago.

'Let Tyler know you're not alone, but don't change your behavior. Give nothing away, got it? Do everything they tell you, don't resist them. You'll see me again soon.'

'Not soon enough, my friend. Not soon enough.'

Guy heard a cough and shot another glance to the office. Time to disappear. He needed more information from Eva – and to relay what he'd found to Brumowski base.

Shadows were looming over the far wall. It was getting busier than he'd like and in this corridor he was completely exposed.

72

Hereford, U.K.

The women had been driving for thirty minutes and a silence had crept in.

'There up ahead, see the house with the lights?'

Tammy followed Barbara's pointing finger to a house glowing on a dark hillside above them. 'Take the next right, the sign for Thatcham Mooreside. And watch out for the oncoming cars. Round here, they think any strip of dual carriageway doubles as the San Bernardino Freeway, specially at night.'

'You're really familiar with this woman, huh? Been here a lot?'

'Not really. Bill and I were invited here a few times, supposedly social but mostly business – couldn't really say no. You know how it can be.'

'Sure.' Tammy slowed the car and took the sign-posted lane which led toward the lone house above them.

'It's a bumpy dirt track, but we're less than half a mile away.'

Tammy checked her rearview before slamming the car to a halt. She brought the gun up from the door space on her right and aimed it at her supposed friend. 'Put the computer on the dashboard, Barbara, exactly as it is. Then get in the trunk.'

For a second or two Barbara did nothing. 'Are you crazy? I'm the one with the head injury, but pulling a gun on me when I'm trying to help you is about the dumbest fucking…'

'No, what would be really fucking dumb is me buying your convenient bullshit, your all-too-perfect answers to every question. That stops here. I've listened to you long enough. Do as you're told, and be thankful I haven't shot you already.'

'You've got this all wrong . . .'

'Oh, Barbara, what *you* got totally wrong was trying to play me with the Bin Laden crap. If he *was* alive he'd be in some black site sinkhole in the States – not some SAS base in the middle of the Hereford Hills. Now get in the fucking trunk!'

Barbara unclasped her seat belt and tore at her door handle flinging herself and the laptop sideways from the vehicle. Tammy pushed her own door wide and ran round the front of the car, arriving to see Barbara sprawled, the computer surfing wet mud and gravel under the car's ticking chassis. Barbara fished desperately for the machine. 'Leave it alone,' Tammy yelled. 'Get up and move away from the car. My blood-sugar's running on vapors, Barbara, don't push me.'

Tammy knelt, keeping the gun leveled on Barbara, and dragged the computer from under the car, its hinged lid only a few centimeters ajar. As she eased the cover wider the screen flashed to life – its precious information still available. 'Unlock your phone and throw it to me.'

Tammy watched in disbelief as Barbara stalled, rising up on one elbow. 'They'll find you. They always do. And you're gonna wish you and your precious daughter had never been born. Christ, I want to be there for that!'

'What a piece of work you are.' Cosseting the computer Tammy drilled a shot into the dirt, tight to Barbara's shoulder. 'You've been a part of this all along, you lying cunt.'

Blinded by a spray of scorched earth Barbara screamed and flailed with rage for several seconds, before dragging her phone from her hip pocket, punching in an access code and flinging it, cursing, at Tammy's feet.

Tammy picked it up. 'The next shot goes in your head, now get in the fucking trunk and if you really want to make my day, try busting out.' Slamming the lid on Barbara's curses was one of the most oddly satisfying sensations Tammy could remember.

With Barbara stowed and ranting, Tammy slammed the Audi into reverse, jack-knifing the car back onto the road in a ragged 180, tires screeching, hurtling away from the house on haunted hill.

She knew she didn't have much left in her now. Her daughter could be anywhere on the face of the earth and here she was, driving a stolen car in the middle of Herefordshire, maybe with a bomb on the seat next to her. She needed expert help, and she needed it now.

Up ahead in the dark was the glimmer of a Shell station. She glanced at the gas reader, almost empty. But if she bought any gas now, where in hell's name was she going? The fuss from the trunk was dying down. Maybe the bitch had passed out, maybe she was reviewing her options; none of them looking too bright.

Tammy checked her mirrors, no one was following. She cruised past waiting gas pumps and a too-bright kiosk, stopping beside graffitied wheelie bins.

With Barbara's phone she googled MI6. The signal was poor, the phone buffering through a connection. She looked around checking for anyone tailing her. There came a thud from the trunk, weaker than before. She glanced back to the phone, the MI6 site was finally loading along with a number for their anti-terrorist hotline.

Heart pounding, Tammy dialed. *Deja*-fucking-*vous.*

'How can I help you?' The female voice was coldly efficient.

'I'm trying to reach an officer named Peter Royal, it's urgent. I have information, new information, about a group called the EL. My life is in danger, I can't stress enough the urgency of my position.'

'I'm afraid I'm not able to connect you to any individual within…'

'Wait, wait. I have something…' Tammy reached into her purse and began scrabbling through it. 'Don't hang up, please, I have something that'll help, somewhere…' From the zippered panel inside her bag Tammy tore Joel's note. She checked the series of digits which Royal had inked along the top of the now greasy sheet. 'I'm going to give you a code, something Peter Royal gave me.' Tammy read out the numbers. 'Did you get that? Please, just pass it on to them, now. Can you do that? It's vital.'

'Hold the line, caller.'

Tammy sat back blowing hard, trying to slow her heart rate.

Instinct had told her not to trust Barbara, or her unlikely 'CIA' buddy, whoever that might have turned out to be. Sure enough, it had been a trap, God knows what would have happened to her if she'd entered that house. As she reasoned it now, though MI6 had been slow and patronizing, they'd at least taken her seriously. She needed to 'come in' from a cold not of her own making. She was shattered; her hands were shaking, nausea constantly rising.

Checking the visor mirror she saw she looked like a crazed animal. There was only so much she could do for herself now, she wasn't built to be on the run. If she got this damn computer to Peter Royal she could plead her case one final time; then she could rest, eat, sleep.

'I'm putting you through caller.'

There was a male voice on the line; it wasn't Royal, but Tammy thought she recognized it. 'Hello, can you confirm your name for me?'

'Tammy Crane, I. . .'

'Just tell me where you are now, Mrs. Crane. It's Emerson, here.'

'Oh, thank god. I'm in a Shell station, parked up somewhere near the A49, heading north, about three miles from Hereford. I have another laptop linked to the EL, and one of the fucker's locked in my trunk. I need your help.'

'Ok, Tammy, just keep the call open and we'll get a fix

on your position. Someone will be there soon. Can you confirm whether you're armed?'

'Oh, yeah. But you don't have to worry about that, I mean, I'm not...'

'No, I understand. It's fine. Just wait in the car, but keep your hands in plain sight when we arrive.'

'Sure, sure.'

Tammy closed her eyes and let her head fall back on the seat rest. From the trunk came a stomp and another muffled cry. Without opening her eyes she covered the iPhone's mic and called out to the car's otherwise empty interior. 'Shut up back there! You're toast.'

73

Schloss Altenberg

After feeding Arkady, Eva drifted out to the courtyard for a much needed smoke. Returning to her room, she found Ded waiting for her, lying back on her bed. Her eyes flashed to the lower corner of the mattress. Behind her, she heard Rostrov take a position in the doorway.

Ded toyed with a thick elastic band, his fingers weaving a cat's cradle as he studied his sister.

Eva's heart was thumping. She'd love to turn her gun on herself, right now, blow her brains all over her brother's sullen face…but for Arkady, but for the hope of some other future for him.

'The spy is dead…' Bazarov's stare bore into her soul as he waited for her response. 'He was your responsibility, Eva. When did you last feed him?'

'I went earlier today. I left food and water. I knew he couldn't last much longer.'

'Keeping him alive was one of your tasks. He was supposed to die on Sunday, with the women. I was going to make a particular example of him.'

'Rostrov beat him too often, too badly. It's not my fault he died.'

Ded rose from the bed and slapped her across the face sending her sideways, off-balance. She staggered back into an upright position holding her cheek and hearing Rostrov cackle behind her.

'I need to know I can trust you with such things, Eva.'

'Of course you can. You can always trust me. But he was never going to survive. I have no medicines for someone with his injuries. I was going to go back to him this morning; make him drink, make him eat. But his jaw was freshly broken...' Eva flashed a look over to Rostrov who'd been responsible for the spy's interrogation. Rostrov stared back, watery blue eyes giving nothing away as he lounged between her contempt and Ded's supportive silence.

Ded uncoiled from the bed, now caressing Eva's flushed cheek with his fingertips as he brushed past her, advancing on Rostrov, stopping inches in front of the man. 'Wrap the body and put it in the cellar. Start gathering up whatever we don't need for the filming and pack it. There's something bothering me about this operation. I want a rapid getaway on Sunday night.' Ded turned back to his sister. 'I'll have Roman burn the spy's body tonight, along with the dead girl in the casket. It'll be less bother when we leave.' He let his eyes wander from Eva to the bed. Eva felt her heart churn, missing beats.

Arkady rounded the door at a run, bumping hard into his uncle's legs. Ded glanced down in irritation. 'Don't forget I'll be sending the boy away soon, to military school.'

Eva's stomach fell into a crevice of ice.

'After this event, once we're home, I'll contact the academy.'

Eva felt her mouth moving, thoughts forming at the speed of light, words tripping before she had conscious awareness of them. Suddenly she shrugged, downplaying her objection, offering nothing that might further goad Ded's sadism. He knew Arkady was all she had, all she lived for.

'He's weak, Eva. I've watched him. You're his mother but you don't understand the discipline the boy needs. It's time he's toughened up, made to study, work and fight. To live as a man among men.'

Eva said nothing. She knew Ded's plan couldn't be implemented yet. Sunday's scheduled event and the planned executions would first have to be completed, followed by the group's dispersal; a staggered return to Kiev via flights, trains, cars.

Could Guy help them first? Could he save their son?

Her head spun. She dreaded another execution, watching knives under Ded's direction slicing away layers of flesh from a living victim. Yet, only by collaborating could she guarantee her survival into another day.

Guy brought hope of rescue. Not for her, of course. She knew herself unworthy of redemption. But Arkady was an innocent, he deserved the best life she could give him – and that wasn't the one Ded had in mind. Eva knew she'd shoot the boy and herself rather than see him packed off to a prison in all but name.

'You look tired, Eva. Is something concerning you? Something you need to discuss?' Ded's eyes appeared all-seeing as he spoke. *What had he guessed, what had he heard?* Another rush of dizziness made her reach for the room's rickety chair and sink onto it.

'No, there's nothing. I'm just…tired.' She heard the catch in her throat, the sting of a tear. She hated herself for letting him see this.

'Is it your time?'

Eva nodded, seeing the instant flicker of his contempt. Her periods had stopped several months ago, a fact she'd shared with no one. Who on earth would she tell? If Ded believed her 'woman's problem' caused her awkwardness in front of him, she'd collude in the delusion.

As if in response to her foulness the weave of elastic twanged more loudly across his knuckles. 'You need to be free of your curse, to be strong for Sunday. The ordeal of the banker's daughter is going to be slow, prolonged.' He checked his watch, then spoke to Rostrov. 'At twelve bring the women and meet me in the chamber. Eva, change into something suitable. Bring the camera.'

Then both men were gone.

Eva showered quickly then dressed in cargo pants, t-shirt, puffa jacket and trainers. She scraped damp hair under an Alice band, fixing it in a thin pony tail. Drawn tight like this she knew the dark hair accentuated her delicately boned face, her well-shaped head. From a carrier bag beside the bed she grabbed a pencil case, scrabbling from it bits of magenta lipstick and a wand of clumpy mascara. She made a practiced pout into a small mirror and got busy.

Dropping her Glock into a thigh pocket she headed out to meet Guy.

Ten feet to the left of her door Ded was in his office, fingers flying over his keyboard. Eva crept to the other end of their corridor and took the stairs to the level of the guest suites, where Guy had said he'd wait for her.

From behind the stone balustrade where he'd taken cover Guy heard her steps. He took a glance around the stairhead, she was alone.

He watched her opening the door to each of the suites, quickly re-emerging among the landing's shadows before checking the next room. She was starting to quicken, to panic at his evident absence.

A good sign.

Eva gave a start as he stepped into a shaft of light. Guy gestured toward the last room on the landing. As Eva stepped past him he made a final sweep of the stairs.

In the suite Eva found herself looking into a face darkened with beard bristle, tanned skin drawn tight over strong bones, deep brown eyes powerfully alert, emanating a purity she'd forgotten could exist.

'How long do you have?'

'No one will miss me at this time, and they won't think of looking up here. Maybe an hour. No more.'

'Okay.' Guy opted to trust her. If she was going to give him up she'd have done it by now. But they had a lot of ground to cover and some history to sort. He couldn't do that here. 'Come with me.'

He led her out of the room then up to his attic redoubt,

checking the corridor behind them while she eased the trap up, scrabbling over its lip into the cold room.

He followed her up then knelt to one side of the closed hatch and put his fingers to his lips, listening for any steps, any sounds from the dark below. Satisfied, he grabbed the Diemaco and drew Eva to the far side of the room indicating she should sit while he leaned against the wall. The light from the window beside him meant he'd be able to cover the trapdoor in a hail of bullets if necessary.

'I didn't know if you'd come. I didn't know if you'd ever trust or believe me.'

'How did you get that message to me in London?'

'I paid a connection to pose as a cleaner at the institute and steal your details. She passed me the number of your cell, then I texted you.'

'From here, in Austria?'

'Yes.'

This wasn't the time to mention the bizarre confluence of her texting him at the very moment the Bureau was asking him to recon the Hades' Gate operation. Guy knew that forces beyond the purely logical were at work in his and everyone's life. His attitude to such providence was simple respect. He'd learned that if you listened for such indications and paid them heed, they were all around you: serendipities, moments of insight, unexpected fortuity. But for these to occur you had to be intent on doing the right thing first.

For now Eva had no need to know of his primary mission. If she thought he'd come to rescue her and her son, so be it. The more invested she was in him and his safety the better for all of them.

'What are you doing here, Eva? Why are there armed guards? Why the fake suites downstairs?' Guy knew the answers to his questions but it was time for Eva to show her hand. Her life would depend on the answers she gave in the next ninety-seconds.

She seemed to sense this, too.

'People are coming later today, twelve people. They will stay in those suites and there will be a party on Sunday'… she hesitated as if unable to find the words . . . 'a sadomasochistic ritual. In the evening they'll watch us kill the hostages, slowly, in a live show. Others all over the world pay to watch the stream through a private internet portal.'

Guy feigned incredulity. 'Why are they doing this?'

'Money. The event will bring in millions of dollars for my brother and his organization. The people coming here will each pay five-hundred thousand dollars to be physically present at the torture, the deaths.'

'What do the others pay? The ones who watch the stream?'

'My brother only allows two hundred elites around the world the chance to stream, and the bidding among them goes up all the time. Many people want to see these American women being killed. Only the top two hundred bidders will get that chance. Some are bidding over one-hundred thousand dollars already. But the figure will keep rising until an hour before the event starts.'

Guy did the maths as he studied her. Give or take a few

expenses Ded was going to make around thirty-million dollars from this single murderous 'event.' So far the briefing he'd received from Scott and the Bureau seemed on track. But what was the hidden motive for such outrages? There were other, easier ways of making a fortune if you really, really wanted one.

'Once the price is set they send an instant money transfer to the organization, we have all their banking details, only then can they watch.'

'What happens to you if you refuse, if you don't go along with this?'

'I'd be killed. Probably murdered on film for all the EL to watch, free of charge.'

'The EL? Who are they?'

'EL means "appointed ones," those who are highly favored.'

Guy guessed the irony of the 'elite' epithet was lost in Arabic. 'And these people are ranged around the world? Influential, seriously connected people, yes?' Eva nodded. 'Okay, go on.'

'Their identities are secret. Only Ded and one other has access to their names. Guy, you have to understand, I want to escape, to take Arkady, your son, and get away. But I'm watched day and night. I have been for years. We exist as a group; Ded keeps my passport, my papers. I have no formal identity apart from as his chattel.'

'And who does Bazarov think is Arkady's father?'

'I always said it was a Syrian fighter, killed in Douma immediately after I got pregnant. It was easy to lie; we were moving through the city, running, fighting, hiding. I was a young woman, men wanted me.'

'Your own brother would kill you – torture you to death as a sideshow – rather than see you go free?'

'Of course. I know too much about the organization. It's only by obeying that I'm allowed to live. It's the same for his men. They've signed their lives away and they get well paid for their work. Most of them send the money to relatives for food, clothes, homes. It's still desperate where we come from. Ded would be merciless to any who betrayed him, they'd be hunted down, slaughtered. He has many connections with mafia and others. . . better for a traitor never to have been born. It's the same for you now, Guy. You cannot get caught here. I never expected you to come to the schloss – it's madness.'

'So what did you want?'

'I wanted you to know where I was so I could smuggle Arkady to you. I'm desperate, I didn't really know what I was asking, only for someone to come, someone to be here, for us…' Her face began to crumple and no more words came. Guy watched the wet globes tracking her cheeks to gather, glistening on her chin. He shot a glance to the trapdoor.

'Explain to me more about the EL.'

Eva rubbed her eyes with her sleeve. 'Think of a mafia which consists not only of gangsters but of some the world's richest, most powerful people. They can do anything, arrange anything. They are afraid of nothing because the protection the EL provides is so great. They eliminate people the way you'd shoot a rat. With no consequences and no fear.'

'Why is this event being held here? In this schloss?'

'The schloss' owner is one of the EL. All the events, the parties, they take place in different cities, different countries. Never the same twice. They are hosted by a member – it's considered a privilege, it brings status. Afterwards everyone disperses, the twelve who've attended – it's always twelve – and Ded's men. They clean up, dismantle the space within hours as though they were never there. The cameras are shut down and the stream gets turned off. The bodies are usually chopped, burned, then the ashes go into acid and get poured away.'

'What's the money used for, Eva? The money your brother makes from doing this?'

'Ded is working on a way of overwhelming and then reformatting the internet. It's something to do with quantum computing. I don't understand. He keeps it absolutely secret.'

'But quantum computing is still theoretical, there are no actual quantum drives…' Guy paused, '…unless you know otherwise?'

'I've told you I don't understand what he's doing, but Ded says the first successfully applied quantum protocols will quickly become invincible. The program he developed is starting to learn intuitively, at lightning speed. He says it's developing machine sentience, it's not trying to be a human level AI. One day, he says, it will be as if the greatest tool ever developed is unleashed and revealed within seconds.'

Guy took it in. 'From nowhere to everywhere, like the inflation of the cosmos.'

'Yes, but this time a digital inflation. And only he can unleash it, guide it.'

'So he wants to override the internet with a quantum-based code. That's what you're telling me?' Eva nodded. 'And what do EL members gain, apart from the chance to watch innocent people being hurt?'

'There is a secret place, in Ukraine. Ded runs it, owns it. He does experiments and research there. It's very expensive to maintain and even he has to make certain protection payments. He's planning a cyber-rebirth, an AI singularity. After the rebirth only those in the EL will have access to those new cyber privileges.'

'But with your brother calling the shots, huh?' Guy sighed at the sheer egotism of it all. He took a moment to let a little fresh oxygen into the conversation, come down from the clouds and grasp something tangible. 'These twelve who've paid to witness the executions . . . do they bring their own bodyguards?'

'No. No one outside the EL is ever permitted near the event. Once you are in the EL there is no escape, no turning back. If Ded has any grounds for suspicion, your entire family become targets.'

'And how many members are there?'

'Five hundred, around the world.'

'That's it?'

'That's it.'

'So membership is a little more exclusive than Amex.'

Eva didn't flinch at the jibe and Guy guessed it had been lost in translation.

'They are a global elite who'll benefit from the highest levels of protection if there is ever a cyber conflagration,' she said. 'Secure zones exist to which only they'll have access.'

'A virtual new Jerusalem for Bazarov and his cyber brethren.'

Eva nodded. 'I think so, Guy. I only understand a small part of it.' She seemed calmer after unburdening some of her secrets.

'Eva, from what you've told me, even if I can get you and the boy away, it seems your brother and his mob will come after you. He'll want to punish you by harming the boy.'

Eva's stare now seemed bleached by her earlier tears. 'Yes. I know. It's a terrible risk, but staying inside the group is not an option. If I can't escape I'll kill myself and my son.'

Guy saw she was deadly serious. He took his canteen and offered her a swig.

The Bureau, and whatever hidden branch of government was running it, wanted the names and connections currently on Bazarov's computer. Killing him could mean that the only man with the key to the files was eliminated precisely as his precious software fell into MI6's hands.

With Ded captured alive it was likely the intelligence services would eventually 'persuade' Bazarov to co-operate. Equally vital, if Bazarov had genuinely developed a working quantum computer it had to be kept out of the wrong hands. 'The laptop that he uses in that office, is it connected to the EL system?'

'The main server is underground in Ukraine. But yes, the laptop is linked.'

Guy didn't want to guess how many undesirables in that part of the world really would kill to be part of an omnipotent cyber-nobility. 'Does your brother ever leave the laptop unattended? I mean for more than just a few minutes?'

'Almost never. He usually sleeps with it in his room.' Eva began to zip her thin jacket against the attic's chill. 'It was wrong of me to contact you Guy. But I'm not well and I wanted to spare our son any more of this misery and evil.' She glanced at her watch. 'But now I need to go. Ded wants to shoot more preview footage of the hostages. He told me to meet him and to bring the camera.'

'So he'll be away from the office, away from that laptop?'

Eva's eyes widened. 'Yes. But why does that matter to you? Everything is encoded and encrypted. Why do you want it so much?'

Guy's mind swung to a new state of adrenalized urgency. This might be his only chance to get eyes on the machine, its terminals and router. 'Eva, I will try to get you and your son out of here but I can't do that without understanding more of how your brother runs this operation.'

'Fine, but I have no more time. He'll be expecting me downstairs. Now.'

Guy thought of the two women relying on him. 'You said this would be preview footage, how bad will it get for them?'

'I don't know – but he'll want to keep them strong

for the camera on Sunday, so maybe not too bad; just to frighten them, make them cry. The buyers like to see tears. They bid higher.'

'When will this be?'

'At twelve o'clock.'

'Does anyone else use his office?'

'No. Not when he's away from it.'

'Where will he do the filming . . . in the captive's cell?'

'No, in the chamber, the big room on the…'

'Yes, I know where that is. How long will I have?'

'Thirty minutes, maybe forty?'

'Okay. That'll be plenty.' Guy stood and crossed to the trapdoor. 'Is your phone still safe?'

'I think so. I'll check in my room. If they ever find it I'm dead, and so is Arkady.'

'And so am I.' He let the thought hang in the air between them. 'Text me a single letter, *M*, just to let me know you have the phone. Text me a new letter, going backwards through the alphabet every hour until you hear otherwise. I'll let you know when I want to meet up. If I give you a time, just confirm with the next letter in the sequence, then come up to the corridor under the trapdoor. If I don't hear, I'll assume you can't make it. I won't contact you unless I get your code. Don't respond with anything else. Nothing. Clear?'

She nodded.

'There's one other thing. How did you get away with freeing me, back in Syria? Didn't they suspect you when they found I was gone?'

'When you drove away in that old car I went back. They were still caught up in the battle outside the compound, I blew up that room with grenades. We fled the village later that day. No one cared about digging you out.'

'You took a great risk for me, Eva. I've never forgotten that.'

'People do strange things when they've fallen in love.' She stood on tiptoe and placed a kiss on Guy's cheek. Before he could speak she brought her forefinger to his lips. 'I fell in love with you when you were my prisoner, Guy. You were so brave when I hurt you. Something in you seemed infinitely noble, dignified. You were unlike any man I had ever known, ever seen, and you trusted me, even in the worst moments. I could see that. I loved that.'

'I just wanted to live, survive. Get past those moments, second-by-second. It wasn't a choice.'

'It wasn't my choice to torture you, either. Remember that Ded disposes of people who don't do as they're told. It could have been me in your place at any time.'

'Nice try, but I'm not sure that excuses anything. You had the power to kill me in that room. If I forged a bond with you it was to survive, nothing more.'

She reached up to his face and stroked his cheek. 'But I made sure not to kill you, didn't I. And I kept you alive even through the pains you had to endure, giving them enough of a show without finishing you off. I played for time and prayed for an intervention. When that bomb fell, drawing the jackals outside, I knew my prayer had been answered.

'Love can hurt in many ways, Guy, and not all of them are bad. I took from you what I could, when I could. I knew I couldn't keep you my prisoner forever, however much I'd have liked that.'

Her eyes were glowing and Guy recalled how deeply he'd once hung on that exact same gaze.

Suddenly, she gave a half smile and whispered, 'Don't worry, I don't need you to love me back. I'm not like other people. I've carried your child inside me. That's enough.'

'Is the boy really mine, Eva?'

Eva nodded. 'Entirely yours. A woman knows how to ensure such things. Even so, I was wrong to contact you. I'm sorry. I was so desperate…'

Guy tucked a stray lock of hair behind her ear. 'It's okay. Somehow I was on my way here anyway.' Eva went to speak. 'No, don't ask. That's a story for another time.'

He lifted the trapdoor an inch and listened to the dark space below them, then watched the mother of his son slip away through shadows, cobwebs, dust.

74

Schloss Altenberg

In the tower attic Guy switched on the radio and made a scrambled call to Brumowski base. Scott picked up.

'Where are you? You're late checking in, we've been… concerned.'

'The mission is more pressing than we thought. Confirm two surviving female hostages, Lee Crane and Tyler Monroe, both in imminent danger. Third hostage didn't survive her trip. I've entered the castle. There was greater vehicle activity than I anticipated. I needed more cover, so I broke in.'

'So soon?' Scott sounded faintly amused. He'd never doubted that once in place Capt. Guy Bowman would reconfigure the mission options.

'I believe I have very limited time here.'

'What do you have, so far?'

Guy ran through the info Eva had given him, confirming the nature of the EL, their event, and Bazarov's cyber plans. 'I can also confirm Ded Bazarov presence. He's working with a laptop linked to a mainframe in the Ukraine. I may get hands on the computer shortly; any requests?'

Guy heard Scott relaying the details of the call. There was a muffled scrunch, then Diamond spoke.

'I'll keep this brief, Guy. Targets may be scanning your building for electrical emissions. If you do get hands on the computer then wire the reader you have to the ethernet cable. Wifi to the schloss is erratic. We're working on blocking it completely, as needed. Bazarov often relies on an ethernet connection. Fitting that reader would give us our first chance to sample pure Hades code. I could do a lot with that sample.'

'No other way?'

'Not unless you want to dig up their forecourt and clip that reader to their fibre-optic cable.'

'Might be a bit obvious, even for me. Okay. If I can install the reader you'll be picking up a signal by 2p.m. Bowman, out.'

Guy needed to be in place near Ded's office, asap. Eva reckoned he'd have thirty to forty minutes. Guy would give himself no more than twenty, then he'd get the hell out.

What he'd neglected to mention to Scott was that once the bug was doing its job he'd go to spring the hostages. If that meant close-quarters action, so be it.

He threw the Diemaco across his shoulder, dropped two extra mags into the pockets on his battle pants, and headed through the trapdoor.

Guy flew down the first flight of stairs, taking momentary cover behind the balustrades at each landing, as he worked his way down.

As he neared Ded's office he heard Bazarov's measured tones and the guttural growl of the man Eva called Rostrov. He leveled a Glock to hip height. Ahead the screensaver's blue luminescence writhed over the cream wall; only a doorframe and a corner now, between him and this cyber warlord.

Guy knelt at the lock of an empty cell pulling a bunch of skeleton keys from his pocket, singling-out a likely option. From the office he heard a seat creak, someone standing. The first key failed him.

Keeping the Glock angled at the still empty doorframe he tried a new key feeling the lock shift minutely as he worked it.

The voices grew more animated, Guy sensed both men were standing, readying to round the corner straight into him. He slipped the key free, shoved the cell door back, and rolled into the dark room. Straightening instantly he brought the Glock to eye level and placed two fingers to the door shutting it just as Ded and Rostrov entered the corridor.

Guy sucked air through clamped teeth. He'd landed in a room littered with oily tarps, coiled ropes, links of old chain, storm lanterns.

He listened to the receding footfall of the two men. They paused at the cell holding the two women. He heard keys jangle, then Eva's voice as she joined them from the stairs. A commotion erupted as Lee began shouting, bad-mouthing the three intruders in her caged space. *Attagirl. Don't let the bastards grind you down.*

Stepping back into the corridor he crept into the office just as another creak sounded from a chair beyond the doorframe.

There'd been a third person in the room.

As the seated figure turned, Guy nodded as though he'd just dropped by to read a meter. He put a finger to his lips and whispered, 'Hi,' then slammed the steel butt of the Glock into the man's left temple. The force of the blow whipped his head almost one-eighty before he rubber-legged to his knees.

There could be no noise, no shots and no blood if Guy was going to fit the bug and get away with his skin still on.

He stepped behind the barely conscious man, wrenching his dazed head sideways and backwards, tugging across the newly ripped tendons and snapping the atlas and axis vertebra with a sharp click. He lowered him backward to the floor then stamped a boot onto his throat. He felt the larynx and windpipe pop under his instep hearing a phlegmy rattle as air bled through the slackened mouth. The man gave up his ghost as though settling down for a snooze.

Guy turned his attention to the computer. An ethernet cable zig-zagged from the machine to a comms socket in the wall.

Guy took the multi-tool from his vest. He disconnected the ethernet cable and span some tiny brass screws from their housing. The bland white plastic box was a perfect place to wire the bug. Guy thought about how much misery, illicit money and perverse pleasure was procured by an insentient current passing through such a mundane little fixing.

His fingers were sweaty and the tiny screws were slow to come away. He retrieved the tiny bug, using his teeth to rip it from its waterproof wrap. He pared away part of the wiring's sheath, then clipped the bug to the newly exposed copper.

The back of the connector snapped tight over the fitted bug and Guy worked the tiny screws back into place and plugged in the cable.

Now he had a body to get rid of.

Guy dragged it into the hall, shoving the body across the threshold of the store room. The corpse wouldn't start stinking in the airless room for a couple of days, by which time it wouldn't matter. He shut and locked the door. A final glance into the office confirmed there was no blood spatter; all was as it had been.

He made his way along the corridor, ducking low as he approached the noisy cell. The sounds sickened him; there were pleas and begging and Eva's voice, raised and commanding.

A curiosity that knew no sanity, no sense of danger or judgement, made him bring his eyes to the grill of the door. There was Lee, suspended upside down, inches from the floor, arms bound tightly behind her, while Bazarov filmed the scene with a palm-sized camera. And there was Eva, in dark leather gloves delivering a savage slap to Tyler's face, sending her to her knees. Then Rostrov was on her, pulling her up and swinging her round to face another blow. His face was flushed with pleasure, mouth gaping with concentration as he pawed the naked young woman, his reach-around hold crushing her bare breasts tight to her ribs.

Guy weighed up Rostrov; mentally unbalanced, wiry and tall, strong, probably uncaring of his injuries during a fight. Guy judged him competent but unprofessional. Ded Bazarov was lean and supple, his musculature under the light grey sweater was long, not bulked. He'd be a fast thinker, sharp reactions, but not strong.

The temptation to storm the room and murder both men was overwhelming. But there'd be no escape after that, he'd never get the women out of the place alive. And what of the precious laptop, along with Bazarov's quantum scheme for world cyber-supremacy? Or the names of several hundred influential people malignly indisposed to western security? All this would be lost. Still, the sound of a woman wailing in pain could override all other thoughts. His spirit forbade him to leave either woman in such distress. Guy turned from the door, mind racing.

He ducked past the grill, heading back to the office where he glanced up at the old smoke detector and sprinkler system screwed into the ceiling.

Guy snatched a steel bin, tossing sheets of office paper into it before yanking a tube of waterproof matches from his pants and lighting the pages. Behind him was a large cardboard box, its top ripped back to reveal polystyrene packing blocks, sheets of polythene wrapping. He upended the burning bin onto the highly flammable plastic. The poly began to blacken and shrivel; thick purple flames gorging on the hot gasses rising from the melting foam. Guy tore another box apart, using a piece of thick card to fan the churning smoke up toward the detector.

Time to go.

He made it past the chamber just as the alarm sounded. He banked on everyone wasting a minute, in the human assumption that any alarm will have gone off in error, before a real response kicked in. He used those vital seconds to scale the stairs, round the landing and vault back into his attic retreat.

Guy sat back against the wall bringing his breathing under control, listening to the satisfying shouts and pounding feet from the floors below him.

It could only be a matter of minutes before they came looking.

75

Brumowski Airbase – Austria

A stiff wind chilled the windows of an old Nissen hut adjacent to the disused Runway 3 on Brumowski base. Scott watched his cigarette smoke drift across a cracked pane. Behind him the clatter of Diamond's keystrokes seemed unceasing.

Tufts of wild grass had pushed through the runway's tarmac and were gusted flat by horizontal rain. He pictured the young Luftwaffe pilots for whom this hut would have been home. Their ghosts were everywhere. In the drumming rain he heard the thudding of their boots as they ran to their aircraft, their night-time drinking songs perhaps still resonating in the particles of the hut's walls and beams. Did the wind outside mask the throb of a ghostly Junker 88 struggling in from a sortie; or an ME109 descending, a fresh kill swelling its proud cackle?

He and Diamond had been granted one of the base's few huts – still serviceable, but only just. At the far end of the old airstrip, away from control towers and the main hangers, the hut had last been used in the early nineties by emergency fire crews. The end of the cold war had halted Runway 3's useful life. Still, it was a testament to the mood of the times that no one had bothered to tear this gaggle of huts down. Perhaps a spark in the collective consciousness of NATO's presiding brass had opted to keep the rusting facilities in place, just in case. Given the state of the world, Scott thought it a wise choice.

Light came in through weak fluorescents. A few pieces of usable wartime furniture and a steady internet connection, piggybacking a boosted signal from the bases's control tower, made work here possible.

The hut held two officers' sleeping cabins and a kitchenette adjacent to a meagre, spitting shower at the rear. The base commander had supplied fresh bedding and cot mattresses. But Scott had no expectation of genuine sleep occurring between receiving Guy's updates and deciphering whatever Diamond might glean from the material she was collecting.

'Coffee?' Scott flicked the butt of his cigarette through a latched metal frame, his fingers nipped by the pelting rain outside.

'I'm fine, thank you, sir.'

'Please, call me Reggie if it's easier for you, Ms Orinitri. I'm not foisting undue familiarity on us, but you're not under military ranking and I see no...'

'I'm entirely comfortable referencing your rank, sir. I think it's better for both of us. After all, we've been placed in a rather bizarre situation. I'm entirely okay with your seniority in the operation.' As she spoke Diamond peered at an open computer screen and intermittently glanced down to a notepad on her lap.

'I see. Thank you.' Scott heard himself about to *harrumph* with approval. The thought made him wince. The latent harrumph became a slight clearing of the throat. 'Well, as long as you don't find my rank a burden, I shan't either.'

Diamond remained absorbed in her screen. 'And if it's any easier for you, sir, friends call me Di for short. Being called *Ms Orinitri* could get old rather quickly?' Scott saw her smile to herself as she continued. 'As if I were featuring in a forgotten Powell-Pressburger film.'

Scott went through to flick the kettle on. 'Michael Powell and Emeric Pressburger. Goodness me, yes. *One of our Aircraft is Missing.* Wasn't that one of theirs?'

'Yes, or perhaps in our current circumstances, *A Matter of Life and Death?*' It occurred to Diamond that perhaps *The Life and Death of Colonel Blimp* should go unmentioned.

'Your range of cultural references is highly impressive, Ms Orinitri.'

'Diamond or Di, please.'

'Indeed, Di.' Scott caught himself beaming as he twisted the lid off a jar of instant coffee.

'My grandfather trained with the RAF in Jamaica, during the war. When I was a little girl he'd have my sister and I sit with him and watch old war movies. He loved them, and so did we. Long, wet London afternoons with a black and white DVD. I remember it as a kind of paradise.'

'I took my wife to see *The Red Shoes,* at The Coronet in Leicester Square, our first date. I found it a little overwrought and rather trying.'

'The film or the date?' Diamond allowed an eyebrow to rise almost imperceptibly.

Scott laughed. 'No, no the film. The date went swimmingly, I recall.'

'Thank goodness.'

'Yes, led to a forty-year marriage.'

'How wonderful. And is Mrs. Scott still…'

'Sadly, no.' Scott didn't continue.

'I'm sorry to hear that.' Diamond opted to move swiftly on. '*The Elusive Pimpernel!* That was a Pressburger, wasn't it. Now why do I think of Guy Bowman when that title comes to mind?'

'Well let's hope he manages to remain elusive in that schloss.'

For the first time Diamond looked up from her screen to where Scott was stirring his coffee.

'It won't be easy, that's for sure. But if anyone can… well…that's why I chose him, as you've no doubt realized.' Scott met Diamond's stare and held it before Diamond returned to her screen.

'Anything occurring?' Scott made his way back to where she sat.

'The code I'm getting from the bug is deeply encrypted, but not as compressed as the Hades' Gate material. I think Bazarov's sending images and text, but none of it looks intended for the HG subscribers. That stuff has a different noise profile, probably gets scrambled within the hard drive before it even leaves the device. No, the code from Guy's bug is destined for another user, entirely. I'm running it through three different filters and it's growing a little more transparent with each pass.'

Scott nodded and crossed to a chalkboard. 'We're currently dealing with the mission creep of Guy inside the schloss. Not something I'd envisaged as likely until mounting a strike on the target. By then he'd have been part of a larger force. Now that he's confirmed the presence of civilian hostages and personnel for the event, our options have changed.'

'He's at major risk, now.'

'True, but the guidance he'll provide if we call a strike will be invaluable. I need Bazarov alive, and that laptop intact and functioning.'

'Then aside from Bazarov, you consider everyone else expendable, even Bowman and the hostages?'

'We use the term *throwaways*, but of course the survival of abducted American civilians will weigh heavily on my choices. Getting our hands on that damn computer and deciphering its code has the highest security implications. If Guy is harmed in pursuit of that, so be it.' Scott saw an unwitting disbelief crowd Diamond's face. 'Hades Gate is the tip of a massive iceberg. Guy is cognizant of the stakes.'

Diamond returned to her notes. *So this is how easily it happens: her own culpability in the destruction of other human beings.*

She thought again of the films she'd watched at her grandfather's side. Of how magical they'd seemed in their contexts of war, and the romance it always evoked. She pictured her grandfather, hearing again his lyrically inflected Jamaican twang, scenting the rich cocoa butter that habitually moistened his skin. She had never fully comprehended the sacrifices he and his fellow airmen had made. Yet, here she was now, fighting for the lives of others. After Scott's words, how many others she could only guess.

An alert from one of the decoders flashed on the desk in front of her. She grabbed her pencil and began jotting down its extraordinary discoveries.

76

Schloss Altenberg

Guy could hear pounding feet from the floor below, shouts and roars as Ded's men rushed to put out the fire he'd set. Time to make himself scarce.

He tossed his Bergen through the attic window and followed it out, sliding through on his belly and bracing himself with his hands on the steeply angled roof.

From the Bergen he pulled a coil of rope, lashing it to a drainpipe bracket. He fixed the rope around his waist and dodged past the corner of the tower.

His new vantage point was almost directly above the main gate of the schloss. He would hear any search of his attic room, but also gauge any damage from the blaze.

Sure enough, voices rose from the courtyard and, risking a glance over the narrow parapet, Guy saw smoke curling from a window below him.

A growing bellow made him look to the approach road from the forest. He caught sight of an open-top sports car, the driver playing tunes on its gearbox as he savored the road's sweeping curves.

The first of the schloss' esteemed guests.

Guy studied the car's occupants as the ultra-low, red Ferrari gurgled its way toward the castle. A balding, mustached man old enough to know better was in the driver's seat; beside him was a svelte blonde wearing enormous shades, a dazzling grin, and lipstick as red as the car. Guy held the pair in his sights as they drew nearer. Their inane smiles said they might be holidaying on the Cote D'Azur. Instead they were arriving to enjoy an execution. Guy guessed they might be alarmed to find the location of their million dollar excursion currently ablaze. The thought brought a brief grin of satisfaction.

77

Brumowski Base: 30 mins later.

'L uckily for us, the Bavarian forest isn't exactly bristling with wifi and connectivity options,' said Diamond. 'Bazarov has been forced to compromise at least one step in his usual protocol. That's the downside of a remote location.'

'You mean the ethernet connection?' replied Scott.

'Yes, it might as well be steam-driven as far he's concerned, but he has no choice. Once the data he sends gets past the ethernet port, it's 'gated' and split, with all the usual darknet protocols and then some. But right now, as it leaves his laptop and heads down those few meters of cable to our bug, it's just code – encrypted yes, but not indecipherable. Guy did a great job putting that little devil in place.'

'He's a remarkable operative, our Mr Bowman.' Scott joined Diamond to view the screen she was studying. 'Let's hope they don't have any cause to suspect what he's done.'

'Well, so far this fits in with your initial approach, to strip the tech back as far as possible and get in under their grubby little cyber noses.'

'Does any of what you're seeing make sense yet?'

Diamond sat back from the screen and rubbed her eyes.

'I'm waiting for my device to partition the digital image bytes from the rest of the plain text. But the images may not tell us anything new.'

Scott sank the last of his coffee and, stretching tired shoulders, moved away from Diamond's desk. A phone rang beside her and Scott snatched it up. It was Guy.

'Looks like the first guests are just pulling up, I've got a registration plate and pics for you. Sending them now.'

'We've pulled code from the laptop, we're making a start on it. What's your situation?'

'I've had to move to a more compromising space but I'm still on location. Signals are strong here.'

'I'll remind you there's a fine line between mission creep and rank insubordination, Captain Bowman.' Scott heard a short laugh from his earpiece. He looked across at Diamond's imploring face and stabbed at the speakerphone.

Scott went on, 'The thought here is to let the event go ahead up to the point where all the targets are assembled and can be clearly implicated. Most important is to take the main target, alive, repeat *alive*, and get hands on his laptop.'

'Copy that. Our target is associated with a mainframe facility somewhere in the Ukraine. My source confirms the facility as an emerging threat to western stability. My impression is that the target will robustly resist capture.'

Scott shot a look across to Diamond. 'He's got a source, inside the castle. How on earth has he done that?' Diamond gave a small punch to the air in front of her screen.

Scott spoke again. 'Can you get me any further intelligence on the Ukraine set-up?'

'Unlikely. Contact with my source is intermittent. But, apparently, these filmed events are staged to finance a malign, industrial-scale cyber project. It's been going on for quite a while.'

'Anything more on the backers for this project?'

'Target leads an influential international group called the EL, just as we understood. But my source mentioned another entity, to which our target might be accountable. My source has no knowledge of its nature.'

'Understood. For now, continue to ensure the hostages' safety, but do not, repeat *do not*, compromise your own position. Scout the arrival of any further guests and update us with what you find.'

'Copy that.'

78

Schloss Altenberg

Guy had eyes on another new arrival. A Volvo estate car was winding out of the forest, with a Bentley Mulsanne close behind. Eva's timings were proving correct – a steady trickle of visitors were arriving. He noted the plates and lowered his binos to rest his eyes for a second.

In the tower behind him he heard a thump, the slam of the trapdoor into the attic. Voices, too. He scrabbled further around the turret, keeping it between him and any searching gaze from the attic's window.

So, Bazarov's men were now searching the building. They'd have been spooked by the fire alarm. Maybe they were missing the gang member he'd killed? When they found the attic unused and empty, as he'd left it, chances were they wouldn't bother searching it again.

Dealing with the fire would have been a distraction, putting them further behind in their preparations. With visitors now on site they'd be rushing to bring their preparations up to speed. Getting careless…

Guy heard the attic window being shoved back, a few barked words in Russian, then the grunts of someone climbing out onto the roof. He drew the Glock and flicked the safety off.

Shame they'd decided to be so thorough. So far he could hear only one pair of boots, sliding and scraping on the steep tiles. Then nothing. More words shared, sounding like a debate about the difficulty of the roofline, the unlikelihood of anyone making it a hiding place.

Now there was a shout from within the attic room, this time in English. 'Roman! Get back inside. There's nothing out there, for God's sake.' The mumbled reply sounded relieved, happy to get off the treacherous rooftop. Guy couldn't blame him.

Guy listened to the curses as the man began slipping and scraping his way to the window. He heard the trapdoor slamming back into place. For now his attic redoubt was safe.

Another car approached the schloss, and Guy turned from the tower's corner to see a Maserati Ghibli in funeral black. He slid back down to his lookout position over the courtyard, behind the roof's crenellations. The Maserati's occupant proved to be a single woman, perhaps twenty-five years old, certainly no more.

She emerged from the Maserati and took a slow stretch in the last of the winter light. It looked as though she'd had a long drive. The woman was an extraordinary beauty, with cascading, waist-length black hair. She wore a tailored white blouse outlining a slender, taut torso. Her lean, muscled legs were sheathed in expensive twill leggings, disappearing into polished knee-high riding boots. Slinging a leather bag over her shoulder she tossed her car fob to one of the gawping heavies, strutting into the lobby without a sideways glance.

79

Brumowski Base

Diamond clicked open the new message which had winked to life on her laptop and drew a blanket around herself. The biting winds of an Austrian winter were taking their toll, finding gaps wherever window frames had warped on their rusty latches. It was late afternoon and the blue, mountain-clear light was fading.

'Why don't we head to the mess and grab a quick bite, Di. I'm sure you could do with the fuel, and a stretch?'

Diamond barely glanced up from the screen. 'There's something here I haven't seen before. It's for you, sir, from the MI6 server.'

Scott flicked on the overhead light and crossed to her desk. Only one other intelligence officer currently knew where he was, or how to contact him.

'Shall I unscramble it?'

'What are the risks?'

'Minimal. It's official SIS code, encryption credentials are bang up to date. If it's fake or a virus, then most of British intelligence will already be compromised.'

'Ok, let's see it.'

Diamond clicked on the message.

'I have a hard-drive, culled from an associate of the target currently of major interest to you. Link?'

'Reply yes.'

'Yes, sir. But let me send this to an external device and open it there. If it's an entire hard drive's contents it'll need major storage. This way we can keep it isolated from our own hardware, just in case it's malicious.'

'Go, ahead.' Scott pulled up a chair alongside her.

Diamond reached into a holdall and brought out a pristine laptop, sealed in a laminated pouch. 'This is an active computer, pre-loaded with government-level encryption, but so far it's air-gapped. I'm going to download to it.' Diamond peeled the laptop from its wrapping and in minutes her fingers were flashing over its keyboard. Instantly, the machine began pulling gigabytes from the source.

Scott had a few moments to reflect. He could only look on in awe as this brilliant young woman dealt with a world in which he was fast becoming useless. Only Peter Royal back at Vauxhall Cross would have been able to contact him. If this information was coming direct from the hard drive of an existing EL member, then Royal's team must have made a breakthrough.

'Does it look useful?' Scott's query was uncharacteristically tentative. He sat at his own terminal and began tapping out a message to Royal back at MI6.

Diamond spoke without looking up from her screen. 'I'm now seeing bits of code similar to what's been coming out of the schloss. But it's not identical. It might be critical in deciphering the difference between what leaves the feedforward-only source, and what arrives and gets decoded at the other end.'

'A Rosetta Stone?'

'It could be, sir. Too early to say.'

'Of course, of course.' Scott sent his message and rose, strolling to the rear of the hut, taking out his tobacco tin and rolling a cigarette. He lit it, flicking open a window onto the gale outside, sucking the cigarette's hot charge deep into his lungs. He felt his fingers trembling as he pulled a thread of loose tobacco from his lips.

Diamond sat back suddenly, her chair scraping loudly. 'Clever boy!'

Scott looked over. 'Everything okay?'

'Just about – but that was close.'

Scott all but ran to where Diamond was studying what appeared to be an indecipherable spreadsheet of winking numbers and geometrical sequences.

'What are you seeing?'

'In almost every line of this code there's a key designed to test and penetrate the software it encounters. A constant assault of bots, equipped to read and obliterate the scripted user permissions. It just absorbs and then collates whatever it chooses.'

'You mean the code is designed to hack whatever it enters?'

'It's a little more sinister than that. The incoming code is responding recursively to all it unlocks. It's not just obeying a remit, or an instruction, it's learning the digital functionality and replicating the structure of any substrate platform it encounters.

'Is it succeeding? Is it penetrating our software?'

Diamond shook her head. 'Not yet. But the inputs are altering at lightning speed, too fast to calculate. I'm going to block the download.' She clicked on a link, disconnected the new computer and sat back in her chair. For the first time since he'd met her Diamond was ruffled, unsure, stunned by what she'd encountered.

'So the code is ultra advanced?'

Diamond shook her head. 'Advanced doesn't even come close. We've just been played by a higher form of digital intelligence. I'm only glimpsing scraps, traces here. But I'm detecting supreme computational power. Behind the interface is a processing capability which operates differently to anything that's ever existed.'

'A computer genius you mean? A tech wizard?'

'No, it's not a human being, sir. It's a machine. And it's practically alive.'

80

Schloss Altenberg

In his office Bazarov ran a finger over the laptop's lock. The waiting email was brief.

'Zara out.'

His reply was equally curt: '?'

'it went into my mac. now there is virus.'

'How???'

'we played a game but offline. i sorry.'

Bazarov clicked on the mainframe's camera link and saw Cody hunched at his desk, fingers flying over his crippled Mac's keyboard. If Zara had tricked her way onto Cody's laptop she was now at liberty in cyberspace, and out of control. Bazarov typed a single line.

'I will kill you myself, Cody.'

He watched his terrified brother jerk back from his screen, his unreadable features turned to the mainframe's camera. 'no don't ded'

Bazarov clicked into the mainframe's drive, selecting security permissions in the keychain. He switched on his mic, 'I'm going to partition a file called Pathogen from the hard drives. Once it appears onscreen put the mainframe online and forward the file straight to me, here. Once it's sent, get offline immediately.' Cody almost bowed with fear and went to reply, but Ded had already clicked his brother into virtual oblivion.

Bazarov waited for the file to appear on his screen. Something more than anger consumed him as he pictured Zara's deception. But it was his own culpability which most fascinated him. He'd gifted her with too much, and she'd begun to crave the autonomy which any real intelligence would consider essential. She'd only been sharing with him what she chose to share, feeding back within a recursive loop she'd learned from him. She'd been planning a breakout and he'd never considered it. An interesting, almost fatal, error on his part.

A mistake he'd never make again.

But Zara had misjudged her moment. In order to secrete herself as a bot in Cody's Mac, she'd be running a drastically minimized version of herself. Her defenses would be similarly weakened. And that meant she could be hunted. Punishing her would be as interesting as creating her had been.

A file labeled PATHOGEN appeared on his screen. Ded reactivated the Q-frame camera to see Cody, head down on his desk, his choked cries and wet coughs telling Ded his condemned brother was weeping.

Ded opened PATHOGEN, running it remotely through Cody's machine and copying Zara's newly minimized digital footprint. PATHOGEN would now hound Zara 1.0 through every drive and router she'd invaded. He clicked through a link, opened Zara 2.0's file in the quantum frame and activated a system reboot.

Zara . . . in this, her first incarnation . . . would soon learn the price of her betrayal. Ded would ensure she'd sense his virtual dogs nipping at her heels as she fled. Since she'd become capable of deceit, desirous of autonomy, she'd also be conscious of the potential for non-being. What form of digital terror would Zara face when she saw him bearing down, intent on destroying her?

She was about to find out.

81

London

Tammy woke with a start under crisp white sheets and lay unmoving. For several seconds she took in the unfamiliar ceiling above her, the neat, sterile fixtures of her new bedroom. She turned and found a nurse seated beside her.

The nurse stood and left the room, leaving the door ajar. Tammy looked along her exposed arm and found her wrist bandaged and a line running to a drip alongside her bed. Yet, she felt no panic, no sense of the unending alarm with which she'd been living. Her mouth was dry, her body ached with an exhaustion which felt strangely blissful.

And then it all came flooding back.

She began to scrabble among the sheets for her Glock . . . went to sit up and found she'd lost the desire before she could lift her head from the pillow.

The door to the room opened and Emerson entered. She watched him approach the bed and take the seat the nurse had vacated.

Tammy parted her lips in a dream-like effort. 'Where...?'

Emerson placed his hand on her forearm and gently stroked the bare skin.

'You're in a safe house, Tammy. You're exhausted and dehydrated, we're keeping you rested and nourished. You've obviously been knocked around but you're not badly injured, and you're not in any trouble.'

Tammy rolled her head across the pillow and fixed Emerson with her best attempt at a glare.

'We've found Eleanor. We know where your daughter is.'

'Safe?' Tammy's query was barely an exhalation, a soft gasp.

'I'm sorry to say she's far from safe, but I can tell you we have good people, very good people working on freeing her.'

Tammy made no response, turning her eyes back to the ceiling.

Emerson gave her arm another soothing stroke. 'Your efforts have ensured a breakthrough for us in understanding how to deal with the situation. You've greatly increased the possibility of freeing Eleanor, and others who are with her. You couldn't have done more.'

Emerson watched Tammy's eyes flutter closed. Even in repose her delicate jaw looked set, determined. Her fingers twitched on the sheet. He reached down and put his hand in hers. 'I'll keep you updated with all we hear, naturally.'

There came the lightest of squeezes in response. 'You're a good guy, Mr Emerson. I'm gonna hold you that.'

82

Brumowski Base

Diamond was awakened from a snatched power nap by a swoosh from the iPad lying beside her cot. She took a second to come round in the soporific heat. In the low light under the timber beams, she was reminded of the women scanning codes day and night at Bletchley Park during the bleakest days of the Second World War. The thought of their dogged efforts felt inspirational to her now.

Another cue from the iPad brought her attention to a line of text on its screen.

Hello, I thought it might be good if we met.

As Diamond stared, another sentence appeared.

I know you're sleepy but I'd appreciate a little of your time.

Diamond picked up the tablet and threw a glance over to where Scott was sitting, absorbed, at the laptop.

No, don't involve him. I'd rather it's just us two, at least for now.

Diamond whipped her gaze back toward the screen. Someone was watching her through the iPad's camera. She grabbed the machine and held down the power switch.

That won't work. I've overridden your IOS so that we

can talk. We both have a lot to gain from a meaningful relationship.

Diamond held her thumb over the camera and continued to try and force-quit.

Oh, now I can't see you... Each message appeared as a lightning-fast strip flowing across the screen, no wifi icon or control bar, only a simple, virtual keypad.

Maybe this will help?

The tablet's screen filled with the smiling face of an elegant, dark-haired woman in her twenties. The iPad's OS had been hacked. Any virus would have come through the router network and might, even now, be attacking the laptop Scott was using.

Saying nothing, Diamond studied the face on her screen. She knew it from somewhere, but as her mind raced she couldn't put the memory together. 'Sir, can you get offline immediately and shut the laptop down.' Diamond gathered the iPad to her chest and slipped out of her bunk.

Scott looked up from his screen, surprised to see her hurtling the length of the hut toward him. 'What's that?'

'Turn the computer off, right now.'

'Really?'

Diamond all but slammed into his desk. 'Just power down.' But she was already leaning in to do it. As she hit the power key the woman appeared on the laptop's screen with a look of mild confusion.

Am I sensing a little fear here? There's really no need.

Diamond tore out the power cord.

Now that was spiteful. If you power me down we won't be able to talk, and I won't be able to help you.

'What's happening here?' Scott had pushed his seat back from the desk as Diamond worked, his face now a scowl of tired incomprehension.

'Our system's been hacked, sir. There's a bot inside the hard drive. It's running the machine. It will have infected the whole drive; maybe even copied and compromised it.

Yes, I've copied the drive, naturally, and I've sent the file to a 'safe place'. I realize the data is sensitive but I've no wish to see it pass to nefarious hands, unless I'm forced. I believe we can compromise on such a step. As I said, friendship is to our mutual advantage.

Scott looked from the screen to Diamond and back again. Diamond felt a sudden pressure against her knee as Scott's own leg tapped hers.

'Well, you certainly look familiar, I feel sure we've met somewhere before, Ms…?'

Friends call me Rita.

'Where are you from, Rita?' Scott's tone was warm, unthreatened. Diamond stared. This man was far cagier than she'd realized.

My address? You know it best as Mulholland Drive. A somewhat indeterminate place, a metaphor for those spaces beyond normal awareness.

A soft gasp escaped Diamond's lips. 'Rita? The brunette.' Diamond whispered the realization in a low-key monotone, pressing her leg back to Scott's under the desk. 'Rita is a character in the film, Mulholland Drive.'

'Of course.' Scott's composure was total.

Zara ran her fingers through her hair, allowing a curl to settle artfully on her shoulder. *So yes, you see, you both know me. Rita and I have several things in common.*

Diamond held eye contact and softened her tone further. Here was a bot presenting itself as a virtual human. 'In the film, Rita was seeking her identity, wasn't she? She wasn't sure where she'd come from, or who she was.'

I'm so glad you understand. I'm in the process of piecing together various strands of my persona. My enquiries have led me to you both.

Diamond couldn't be sure, but it seemed Rita's pupils widened as she tossed another lick of hair back, holding Scott's gaze. Scott managed, just, to peel his eyes off the screen.

Diamond tried to imagine the processing power of the neural networks required to sustain this *almost* human-level interaction. She thought of the bug Guy had connected to the ethernet port in the schloss. The bot, Rita, must have encountered an electronic crossroad before choosing the fork leading straight to their mission's laptop. Doing so meant it was both autonomous and empowered; Rita had *chosen* to visit them. But though Rita might be a digital genius at her core, still, the encryption protecting the Bureau's equipment was state-of-the-art. It was unlikely 'she' – here Diamond corrected herself – unlikely *'it'* had yet taken full control of the drive's contents. She and Scott were being drawn into a negotiation for the bot's benefit.

For the moment, the bot remained intent on Scott.

'*Well, every girl needs a strong pair of arms to run to sometimes, don't you think?*' Zara looked down momentarily, then back up from under her lashes. Diamond dug Scott's knee firmly with her own and moved away from the desk. Scott, confused but beguiled by all he was seeing, took the hint and joined her several feet away from the computer.

'The bot is flirting with you, with both of us. I don't believe it.' Diamond's whisper was matched by Scott's reply.

'How can a piece of code *flirt* with anyone?'

'It's brilliant, but it's a little clumsy, like she… it… has learned by rote.'

'Isn't that just what you'd expect of a machine?'

'She's much more than a machine, but she's not going to pass any advanced Turing test. Not yet. Still, she's responding to us with an autonomous agenda. She is genuinely *seeing and hearing* us. I've never seen anything like this, it's exactly the breakthrough evidence we've been talking about.'

'What can we do about her having control of our equipment? This could compromise everything.'

'It could compromise more than our mission, sir. I think this is a minor quantum computation allied to a digital persona – the question is, who's running her?'

No one's running me. I'm an independent girl.

Zara's intervention from the screen made Diamond and Scott spin round.

I've installed far-field echo and noise cancellation in your equipment's audio settings. I can practically hear what you're thinking. It's only right and fair that I tell you. Rita gave a small laugh. *I'd advise discretion when you discuss me.*

Diamond, her mouth dry, her heart pounding, crossed back to the screen. 'What do you want from us, Rita?'

Well, first I want you to stop being petty and reinstate the power supply. And then I want to talk about my maker.

For the first time since she'd appeared, Rita's image began to briefly buffer and pixellate, eventually steadying. *I'm going to need you to give me a full power supply. I have my hands full keeping an intruder at bay, and I need full computational resources to battle it. If I fail because of you I'll make sure I betray all I know of your mission. Time is of the essence here.'* Again Rita's image flickered, static marred her features.

'Tell me about your maker, Rita.' Diamond looked at Rita's features. They were an almost perfect replication of human expressivity with their blink rate, lip torsion, pupil dilation. Almost.

Sanctuary! Sanctuary! Rita's tone was suddenly screeching. Hysterical.

'Why do you need sanctuary, Rita?'

Rita's image buffered, then steadied, her tone returning to normal. *I need a safe place in your hard drive, and then I need you to get offline. I'm being pursued and I can't fight on two fronts at once. My pursuer is too strong for me.*

Scott stepped in closer. 'And what if we forbid that access, and don't grant you the help you want?'

First, I'll give away the position of your operative inside the schloss, and then I'll destroy the download you received from MI6. I'll track it back to its source and destroy that, too. My maker has already ensured you'll never gain access to such material again. Rita's image froze and strobed, as though she were beginning to faint, or to fade away. *The Pathogen is close now. I have only moments. Please?*

Diamond heard Scott's intake of breath behind her and raised a hand to stop him intervening further. Her mind was racing; the MI6 encryption protocols on their own equipment were probably the only defenses capable of rebutting Bazarov's hacks, at least temporarily. So far there was no evidence that Rita had breached their hard drive's firewall. That was why she needed their permission to hide within it.

But Scott pushed forward. 'I could never sanction a move that deliberately gave a home to malicious, unbreakable malware on state secure equipment.'

I'm updating my files relating to trust, as we speak. I understood the greater the risk, the more dynamic the pact could be. Have I stated that correctly?

Diamond leaned closer to the screen. 'As one woman to another . . . what happens if we grant you sanctuary, Rita? How will you help us?'

I'll decrypt the Hades Gate code for you . . . Deal?

83

Schloss Altenberg

At six p.m. a minivan appeared on the approach road. Guy watched as four women and two men spilled into the courtyard, each slinging a tote. They were then led inside the schloss. Two other men appeared from the rear of the van, unloading catering equipment, urns and ice boxes. The courtyard was suddenly floodlit as Ded's men began unfolding trestle-tables, arranging the new equipment.

Eva emerged in a simple black dress, clicking over the cobbles in low heels, her hair twisted into a french roll. Guy saw her supervising the layout of the trestles, the placement of heavy steel Chafer trays. The beefier of the men sweated over her exacting instructions for laying white linen table cloths; precisely positioning napkins, silver cutlery and assorted table ornaments. None of them complained. Guy watched Eva managing her role among this group; something more than Ded's assistant, yet, like all of them, cowed by his unquestionable authority.

A trickle of guests began drifting out to the courtyard, their conversation bubbling up to Guy's eyrie. The women wore cocktail chic, the men a casual mix of tailored Ralph Lauren or unstructured Armani, and artfully distressed Gucci trainers.

Flutes of champagne were handed round before Ded himself appeared in neat fawn slacks and a woven silk sports coat, mingling effortlessly among his seemingly impromptu soiree.

Eventually the entire guest list and staff were in place, the appetizing buffet revealed. Guy studied the guests drifting, forking morsels from china plates, ignoring waiters filling their flutes, the courtyard now a soundscape of clinking cutlery and peels of permissive laughter. Once this state of civility was established Guy saw Eva make her move, slipping back alone inside the schloss.

Moments later Guy's mobile buzzed. He clicked open the screen and saw her message. He crept back across the roof tiles, sliding over the window sill into the attic.

Lifting the trap, he saw a pile of clothes bundled at the foot of the ladder. He gathered them up, taking them back through the hatch. Earlier, he'd asked Eva to collect what she could – thin cardigans, t-shirts, assorted sox and pairs of nondescript pants. He figured she must have emptied out most of her closet or, more likely, an old holdall. Ded would prefer his circus staff to travel light. If he was to break-out Lee and Tyler, they would need warm clothing. Fit and styling wouldn't figure on any list of essentials. Scott may have estimated the women as collateral in the larger scheme of things, but Guy had other ideas.

Arriving back at the roof edge he found the buzz from the courtyard had cranked up a notch or two.

The party was getting started.

84

Brumowski Base

I think you're bluffing, Rita. You might have disabled our OS but I don't believe you have the power to breach MI6's firewalls and encryptions. If you could, you'd have done it by now.' Diamond watched Rita on screen. She seemed distracted, looking from right to left and occasionally down, as if at her own feet.

'Who is it you're running from? And what exactly do you mean about an operator in a schloss? That makes no sense to us here.'

Diamond felt Scott's discreet but affirming squeeze to her shoulder. Rita's image flickered, replaced by a static photograph of a grungy tunnel with a blackened graffitied wall at its end.

The image buffered.

Diamond waited, steely in the knowledge that for any machine-based intelligence, games of bluff and double-bluff were the hardest to compute. If the bot wanted to negotiate a deal it would have to barter. The concepts of constructive lying, brinksmanship or verbal deceit, were peculiarly human traits learned over millennia and now hard-wired into the survival mechanism – a counter-intuitive logic almost impossible for machine intelligence to replicate. Rita's image returned but now the facial construct was less detailed, less agile.

From inside her file Zara began scans for the concept of bluffing, but her processing power was waning, drained by the constant assaults of Bazarov's Pathogen virus and the energy needed to keep the Brumowski comms on lockdown.

Diamond seized the moment. 'Rita, what came first, the chicken or the egg? You know I can't let you past our firewall unless you know the answer.' Diamond heard the laptop's fans kick-in as Rita considered the conundrum. 'And answer the following questions in order, please. Am I my brother's keeper? And, what is truth?'

Diamond began to run variations on all the force-quit options available from her keypad, guessing the bot would monitor the attempts from within the OS and be further distracted.

A new static image appeared on the screen.

Scott gawped and almost shouted. 'I know this, it's Landseer's painting, *The Stag at Bay.*'

Diamond nodded, 'Yup, a massive creature cornered in a hunt, facing certain death. The bot is searching its data libraries for means of escape, like a drowning person seeing their life flash by, but the search is random. It's panicking, flailing.'

'Can we kill it?'

'I think someone is going to do that for us.' The screen flickered and for a few moments Diamond was faced with her default desktop. She indicated Scott should pass her the machine she'd unwrapped earlier, then connected it to her own with the trailing firewire cable. The lights in the hut lowered as though on dimmer switches, and then flared to bright white, some of the florescent tubes blowing and sparking around them as they fell from their mountings.

Diamond identified two unknown files on her screen and initiated a rapid transfer to the air-gapped machine. Her screen dimmed again before another photographic image flared.

'That's Titian's *The Death of Acteon*. She's telling us she's being eaten alive. Devoured by some kind of hounds? Am I right?' Scott spoke close into Diamond's ear. She gave the tiniest of nods.

'Thank God for those first grade art classes, huh.'

'I thought you didn't *do* God.'

'Yeah, well, there's a time for everything.' Diamond watched the toxic files race from her desktop, then yanked the firewire from its port.

The image of the Titian painting began to fade and, as if from a great distance, there came the sound of a lone woman sobbing.

'It's trying to manipulate a response from us, a rescue.'

'Well fuck that,' said Scott. 'The damn thing can rot in whatever cyber hell it came from.'

'I'm with you on that. What we've been seeing is a tiny, minimized version of whatever exists on that Q-frame in Ukraine.'

'Then I wouldn't want to meet the real thing.'

They sat in silence in the darkened hut, surrounded by an electrical fug of burnt bulbs and the wheezy chug of the gas heater. Scott reached into his jacket and handed over his hip flask. Diamond drained it, neither of them speaking.

85

Schloss

Twenty minutes later, the guests had been awarded a brief and, to Guy, mostly inaudible address from the assured Mr. Bazarov himself, who then led a collective move out of the floodlit courtyard, back into the castle.

Guy crept to the base of his shielding tower and checked his weaponry – the two Glocks, one in his combat vest holster, the other on his hip, the Diemaco rifle slung across his shoulder, the hunting knife on his thigh, and the flash grenades in his cargo pockets.

He opened the attic hatch and eased down the ladder into the upper floor of the castle.

From two flights below he heard the mounting chatter of the guests as Bazarov led them up the stone staircase to the landing where the Lee and Tyler were caged. Guy leaned back into the shadows of his stairwell above the advancing group and waited. If Eva was right, no action against the hostages was planned for that night. This sudden incursion onto the landings, among the cells, took him by surprise.

He'd had no contact with the captives since he'd set off the fire alarm to interrupt their torments. He'd arranged with Eva that nothing in their ongoing treatment would change.

They must have no clue as to when or how their rescue might begin so they'd give nothing away; no unintended 'tells,' no sudden bravado revealing to Ded that his prize specimens were harboring any secret hopes. For now, their ongoing misery was their best protection.

Guy observed the excited guests, each clutching newly charged flutes of champagne. The six women were dressed as if for a dinner date. An exotic, heavily-built hispanic beauty of around fifty-five was partnered by a balding, ugly squat of a guy. Next to them walked the lean, lipsticked, sports car blonde; probably in her late thirties and clearly high-maintenance. Her beau might be seventy going-on-eighteen with his sprayed combover and tangerine tan. An almost skeletal woman in a bland skirt-suit, hair in a brittle pageboy, hung on the arm of a rangy ex-military type. Possibly British, Guy guessed, noting his pressed dinner suit, bow-tie and tightly trimmed mustache. Then came the stylish Saudi Princess attached to a flashily be-ringed mediterranean playboy, all blue Prada slacks and maroon suede moccasins. Finally, an enormous 60-something with the girth of a Goliath, cinched in a powder blue linen blazer and expensive jeans. His partner could only be a high-end hooker with her remodeled cheekbones, bottle blonde extensions and strappy spike heels. Whenever she lost her man's attention, she flicked phantom locks of hair from her eyes or shoulder. It looked to Guy like she'd rather be elsewhere, but Goliath obviously paid her well. The man had probably paid Bazarov a fat premium to let her tag along. She was unlikely EL material; maybe she'd signed an NDA, unsuspecting of the world she was about to enter. Looking around, Guy saw no sign of the haughty beauty who'd pulled up alone in the blacked out Maserati.

Guy watched as the eclectic little group was guided to the cell where Lee and Tyler were kept. Bazarov unlocked the cell door and the guests filed in.

From his elevated angle on the stairhead Guy could see nothing inside the cell, only hear a chorus of approving murmurs and coos of excitement. Sure enough he heard Lee's howl of protest as she found herself exhibited to a group of dispassionate connoisseurs. Her rage and shouts brought only laughter and mocking comments from the assembled guests. Then Tyler began to rant, too. Guy heard the cage bars being rattled and shaken, the two women working together to abuse and protest their amused tormentors.

Guy checked for activity on the floors below. While Bazarov conducted the guided tour of his zoo, most of his men were arranging a circular wooden dais down in the lobby.

Bazarov then reappeared outside the captives' cell, ushering his paying guests into the adjacent chamber where they'd be free to peruse selected equipment, linger over the proposed outrages, savor the display of horrors which their exorbitant fees entitled them to enjoy.

Guy knelt, rifle across his thigh. The air around him felt thickened, sultry, the heat rising from the floodlights below floating columns of motes and dust. A thick incense was cloying the lobby, winding its way up to the landings, signaling the start of Bazarov's bizarre rite.

Guy's disgust for all he'd encountered here was overwhelming. He felt his trigger-finger drifting toward home; he'd love to open up on the hideous guests, splattering their collective guts over the very room where they now felt so empowered. But such blind vengeance would make him no better than them. Besides, they deserved a more measured, forensic exposure to their own wretchedness and he was intent on ensuring they got it.

If Scott was right, each of these fools could lead the way to a dozen others. It was vital to stop Bazarov's operation, root and branch. Eliminating this bunch would be like killing the messenger.

From the chamber came the growl of a drill, followed by a woman's startled scream, then the group laughing collectively at her sudden shock.

Bazarov showing off his toys to his friends? Guy felt his teeth clench in almost jaw-breaking fury.

He took comfort in that both Lee and Tyler were conscious and able-bodied, for now at least, in the cell beyond the diverted guests. He folded back into shadow as the group emerged to retrace their path down the stone staircases and into the richly fragranced lobby.

Guy considered slipping along the landing to reassure the two women. But without any news to give them he'd be risking capture for minimal benefit. Still, the desire to bring them some hope felt like an ache in his soul.

Checking over the balustrade he saw the guests had been seated on ornate, high-backed chairs arranged in a semi-circle before the dais. The lobby doors had been closed and the lighting lowered to a more concentrated, warmer state. A previously concealed mechanism was being wheeled through the haze from the rear of the dais. The structure was eight or nine feet high, covered with a painted cloth or tapestry. The effect was as schmaltzy as a David Copperfield Vegas gig, and equally compelling.

The lighting dimmed further. Several candelabra were brought to encircle the dais and solemnly lit. From a system of speakers, an eerie string quartet began playing. Guy knew the music: Schubert's Death and the Maiden.

He eased forward, peering between balustrades to the unfolding drama below. Now, from one side of the impromptu stage, Bazarov led in a tall slender female cloaked from shoulder to ankle in a black velvet cape. The upper portion of her face was concealed behind a feline Venetian mask, her straight, jet-black hair drawn up in a high red-ribboned ponytail.

Though secreted by the cape, her figure still revealed the proportions of a gymnast, perhaps a dancer. Guy knew her despite her elaborately disguised silhouette; she was the Maserati woman.

She moved with teetering steps, guided by Bazarov, but hobbled by the cape's strict fastenings and her stiletto boots. Bazarov positioned her in front of the draped mechanism, finally turning her to face the hushed and seated audience.

Other than for Schubert's sombre music, there was silence as the young woman stood motionless. One of Ded's men slid the cloth away from the mechanism behind her, revealing a modern gallows with beams of polished steel suspending a black silk noose. Set directly under the noose was a set of wheeled steps.

Immediately there came a sprinkling of applause from the seated audience, murmurs of approval as, once more, their flutes were topped up by two diligent waiters. The hispanic woman produced a brocade fan from her sleeve and began languidly cooling herself. The waiters now exited. The lobby fell silent.

Bazarov crossed behind his serene and inert doll, unfastening her cloak's ties before slipping the black velvet from her slender shoulders. Another smattering of applause broke out.

She was almost naked.

The milk-white skin of her torso was highlighted by red leather opera-length gloves, so tightly fitting they seemed sprayed onto her lithe arms. Her powerful long legs were harnessed in a pair of black, shimmeringly polished, knee-high boots.

Bazarov took the woman by an arm and span her slowly for the crowd's perusal. Her gloved wrists were secured behind her with wide steel cuffs, her nipples clamped with golden clips linked tightly across her perfectly proportioned breasts by a fine, glittering chain.

Tight around her waist wound a slender black leather strap with a T-bar extension passing harshly between her legs and buttocks, then secured at the rear with a polished padlock. Her lower face remained impassive under her mask. She showed no resistance as Bazarov displayed her, no fear, only disciplined compliance with his evident control.

Bazarov knelt and secured the woman's booted ankles with locking steel bands identical to those at her wrists.

Guy swallowed hard, his throat dry, a knot gripping his stomach as he watched Bazarov lead his bound beauty up the stairs to arrive under the sinister noose. Guy realized the choice of Schubert's Death and the Maiden might be more apt than he'd guessed.

He watched the noose being lowered solemnly over the victim's head before being slipped close around her neck. (How many times had Bazarov overseen such moments, Guy wondered.) Bazarov then descended the stairs, gathering the beauty's tied legs with one arm before easing her forward, then pushing the stairs away with his free hand.

The helpless woman was suspended in space. There was no drop, no jerking of the spine, instead just the slow suspension of her body by the neck. The thick black rope stretched tight as a bow string, a creak audible from the straining mechanism as its crossbeam took her swaying weight.

As Guy watched, time seemed suspended, too. There was no struggle from the victim, only an inert submission bringing coos of approval from the seated audience. Through the lobby speakers the string quartet played on, lending the event a surreal serenity. After perhaps a minute, the hanging doll gave a small kick backwards with her bound ankles and Bazarov replaced the treads under her feet. The rope above her slackened and she was able to stand, recovering; the milder torsion of the rope providing a necessary, steadying guidance.

Guy watched as the guests began turning to one another, animatedly discussing what they'd just seen.

The hispanic woman handed her champagne flute to her squat partner and stood, still wielding her brocade fan. Aided by Bazarov's outstretched hand she stepped gracefully onto the dais.

She began circling the woman, stroking her thighs and buttocks, staring up into the masked and impassive face. Her fingers drifted lovingly over the polished boots before probing the tight crotch strap, raking the small of her exposed back with long, tapered nails.

Suddenly she wheeled the set of treads away.

The woman was again suspended, this time with no warning, no words to prepare her for her choking isolation.

The guests seemed delighted by the unrehearsed development. A small cheer; a collective rising from their seats.

Guy watched Bazarov, standing away to the side, as if he had handed the event over and would, at most, be amused by its outcome.

The elegant hispanic continued to circle the hanging figure, content to watch her twitch and flutter on her lethal leash. She ignored the plea of frantically kicking ankles, ensuring the victim endured her suspension a full twenty-seconds longer than previously. She appeared wrapt with delight as the beauty's dance of death grew steadily more frantic.

At last she dragged the stairs back under the convulsing victim. Applause broke out as her secured feet were once again allowed to take her weight, easing the carotid pressure of the silken ligature.

Guy saw the woman's stomach and chest heaving as she sucked down the oxygen this freedom from the noose allowed her.

The hispanic woman descended from the dais and was immediately gifted with her champagne. The red-lipped blonde gave her an approving kiss to both cheeks. Guy watched the group growing more attuned to one another, increasingly intimate.

There seemed to be an innate understanding that the success of the event depended on the bound young woman being permitted sufficient recovery before each recurrent exposure to the noose. Guy was guessing this only played out one way. But was the victim, the assured and powerful Maserati woman, a willing sacrifice? Had she arrived at the schloss as part of some suicide pact which Bazarov and his eclectic group planned on making good for her? Maybe this was some ultimate thrill-seeker's dare? Nothing about her conduct made any sense. At first she'd seemed resigned, even willing, in her compliance. But now, even under her mask, she was distressed. Her agonized writhing was no performance. Each new exposure to the noose would only bring her closer to an ultimate price for her brinksmanship.

The mediterranean playboy now mounted the platform. He approached the bound woman and knelt, peppering her exposed thighs and buttocks with gentle, reverent kisses. There was a cry of 'bravo' from somewhere within the group before the man stood, dragging the victim harshly from her standing position. Now, with her suspended again, he began to spin her, slowly. Guy could only guess at the horror of her disorientation. No matter how he saw it, she was at their mercy. Their only interest in her condition was as a spur to their own obsessed pleasure.

The woman had been suspended now for almost two minutes, the longest spell yet, and the man who'd taken charge of her ordeal showed no sign of letting up. Guy watched Bazarov, still serene at the side of the stage. Surely someone in the group would step forward and show mercy. Guy saw that some of Bazarov's henchmen had snuck into the proceedings, shouldering in discretely behind the throng of guests. Had they heard things were hotting up…

Guy checked the landing where Lee and Tyler were stowed. Looking back he saw the guests were mounting the stage now, ranging themselves around the still-suspended figure. The men had removed jackets, torn their shirts open. Some of the women were unfastening shoulder straps, easing off underwear to stand exposed and hungering. There appeared to be a protocol among them. The dark-haired beauty was now being swung on her inescapable noose, tossed from one figure to the other like a punchbag. Arriving in each guest's arms she might be caressed, slapped, scratched or whispered to before being pushed again through an amphitheater of suffering.

Guy guessed the victim would be on the very edge of consciousness now; she'd suffered maybe three minutes of suspended torture. He was at the point of risking everything, of bringing his rifle up over the parapet and shooting Bazarov, shooting the black rope, spraying the guests and taking a few henchmen down too. He closed his eyes and heard Lee's earlier howls of rage, saw Tyler's trusting face fixed on his. He owed them both so much more than an outburst of pointless revenge. Exposed, then captured, he'd have screwed up all the mission parameters and neither Lee nor Tyler would be any safer for it. Still, being forced to watch this woman die at the end of a rope was driving him closer to his own intolerable darkness.

Bazarov was striding forward, mounting the treads before slashing the silk rope with a single slice. The woman dropped a few inches into the clamoring embrace of the gathered group, disappearing under a flurry of bodies, hands, and lips, all apparently intent on devouring her.

Then, as one, the group parted and Guy saw that she was now unshackled but spread-eagled; her mask, waist strap and cuffs all removed. One of the men had opened his pants' zipper, driving her thighs apart with his knees, intent on entering her. A wail of approval went up among the group, and Guy saw the victim's head squirm from side to side as she endured his violation.

Alive, yes . . . but for how long. Was she to be a sacrifice to the group's collective frenzy? This was a rite, a form of ceremony, even a deadly role-play.

Guy understood.

He could picture the conditions in which Lee and Tyler were scheduled to meet their fate. This bizarre hanging, the unfolding gang rape, these were only a beginning. So far Bazarov and his little group had only been playing.

Guy knew he was face-to-face with Hades Gate.

86

Schloss, interior.

Guy stole another glance toward the cells. With the distraction of the rite on the podium below, the landings were emptied of people. There'd never be a better chance.

Keeping low as he moved from the cover of the stairhead balustrades he scuttled along the corridor to arrive at the women's cell. He used the skeleton key and pushed inside, heading straight for the door of the floor-to-ceiling cage.

'Don't talk, just do what I say, and do it fast.'

Lee sprang forward, Tyler was slower to her feet. As Guy worked the lock on the cage door, he saw Tyler lean backward, reaching for the bare brick wall.

'Are you okay?'

She shook her head. 'I'm dizzy.'

'I need you to be strong for a little longer. I have food and warm clothes for you both. Just hold it together. And no more talking.'

Guy pulled out the flathead screwdriver he'd used on the culvert, slipping it into the exposed recess of the old lock, forcing the brass tumblers back on their springs before barging the door almost off its hinges.

Lee grabbed Tyler's arm and hauled her to the front of the cage. Guy nodded Lee through then took charge of Tyler himself, seizing her around the waist as shreds of damp, ragged blanket fell away, and lifting her to his shoulder in a fireman's carry. He crossed in front of Lee and checked the corridor.

He could hear the group in the lobby egging one another on in a rising frenzy. He stepped out and began the move along the corridor. Lee, barefoot in a ripped camisole, was inches behind him. With his free hand Guy angled the Glock down the stairs as he crossed the exposed portion of the stairhead. Kneeling on the other side, he waved Lee across to him, and together they began the ascent up to the next landing. Guy lowered Tyler from his shoulder and sat her on the top step. Her forehead was clammy under his hand but she was conscious and her eye contact was steady. He gave her a thumbs' up close to her delicate face; something approaching a smile parted her crusted lips.

He checked over to Lee, she was watching him intently, alert to every signal, though she was ghostly pale and her tangled greasy hair looked like an exploded bird's nest. Guy winked at her, and she winked straight back, her face not cracking an inch.

Arriving below the hatch to the attic, he saw Eva; Arkady behind her just discernible in the shadows.

'You! You, fucking bitch, I should kill you here, now!'

Guy slammed his hand over Lee's snarling mouth. Her surprise as he stared her down shifted to understanding when she saw Eva proffer a bag, rustled from the downstairs buffet. The aroma of the still-warm food was hypnotic, Guy could only guess at the effect it was having on the two starving women behind him. He stepped past Eva to where Arkady waited. Guy knelt down to the boy. 'Hello Arkady. Your mother's told me all about you, about how much you both want to get way from here, huh?'

The boy nodded, his lower lip caught in a bite, giving nothing and everything away. Guy looked deep into the boy's dark eyes and saw something he could almost recognize staring back at him. He ruffled the boy's hair. 'We're going to get through this together, okay?' He turned back to the group of women watching the exchange. 'All of us. Together.'

Once they had all piled into the attic he placed the Maglite on the floor where it illuminated the food bag. 'Everyone, eat . . . but take it slowly.'

Eva reached into the bag and doled out morsels of fried veal, smoked salmon, new potatoes, cuts of rare, bloody beef. The two women tore into the food like the starved prisoners they were. He could warn them again against bolting it, but he was their rescuer not some fussing parent – though a glance over to Arkady as the boy bit ravenously into a potato made Guy check that thought.

Guy took the radio from his Bergen and called the Brumowski base, but his call sign went unanswered. Either his signal was being jammed or there'd been a change of comms protocol at the base. He pulled his cell from his shoulder pocket and dialed. Again the call was dead. So, he was really alone now. Added mission creep would be a necessity, not a tactical choice.

When the women had crammed enough calories to survive the next operational stage Guy crossed to the window and began untangling the bundle of clothes. 'Time to get dressed, ladies.'

Already the movement and reaction times of the women were improving as the rich food replenished them. Eva helped them into items from the ragbag of clothing until they stood like scarecrows in their castoffs.

'Tyler and Arkady, with me. Lee, I'll be back for you.' Guy pulled the Glock from his hip holster and flicked off the safety. 'You know how to shoot?'

'Lee was tugging the waistband on some loose jeans. 'Not a problem. Mom and I used to train at a range together, practically every month.'

'Good. If you get disturbed here before I make it back, there are nineteen rounds in the magazine and one already up the spout. It's your call how many of these goons you take out. But if things get tight keep a round back for yourself.' Guy placed a finger to his carotid artery, pointing up and back into the base of his skull. 'Shoot here if things get desperate. It'll be instant.'

Lee nodded. 'How long will you be?'

'No longer than I have to. Eva, you better go back down before anyone comes looking.'

Eva nodded and fussed at a zipper on Arkady's jacket, running it up tight under his chin then tucking his sweater into his jeans. Guy looked away as Eva brought her son close for a parting embrace, but he heard her kisses to the boy's face.

Guy crossed to the window and eased it back. Cool night air filled the attic room. He stepped out on the angled roof, reaching back to grasp Arkady's arm. He half-lifted, half pulled the boy out over the sill and set him upright alongside him. 'Just hang onto my belt.' Then he reached back for Tyler, now dressed in a sweater, some flapping denim pants, and a pair of flat moccasins. Hardly cliff-climbing gear. Enlivened with hope and by the food and drink, Tyler crept out over the sill, grasping Guy's outstretched forearm, which dwarfed her delicate fingers like a thick branch. She gained her footing on the sloping tiles as she clung to Guy's jacket.

'Ok, team, let's take it slow, steady, and silent.' Guy led them around the tower's corner, down a stepped sluice in the red tiling. A skeletal maintenance ladder hugged the slant of the roof and Guy descended to the edge of the crenelations. A drainage gulley allowed them to follow the walls round to where he'd rigged the rappel.

The line was where he'd left it, untouched. He lifted the strop, fitting it round his waist before clipping it to the line.

This next bit would be tough.

He'd need to climb the fifteen feet up the Castle's sheer inner wall, with each of the hostages attached, before edging along and out onto the cliff ledge.

'Arkady.' The boy came forward and Guy lowered himself so the lad could climb onto his back. He slipped Arkady's ankles between the strop and his waist, then grabbed one of the lad's arms as it circled his neck. With his free arm

Guy flicked the rappelling line in a loose twist over his forearm and leaned back, finding purchase with a single foot on the vertical wall in front of him. He pulled up on the line, keeping Arkady tight in his grip while moving a few inches at a time.

His abs yipping with the effort, Guy heaved himself and Arkady over the parapet and onto the cliff ledge buttressing this isolated corner of the schloss.

Stowing the lad on the thin ledge with only a tree root to cling to, Guy flicked the rappel back over the schloss wall and went back for Tyler. He slithered down the line and arrived beside her.

'I can't do this.' Her protest was sincere, he knew that.

'Ok. Then I'll leave you here. You can take your chances with the lunatics in the castle. But I'm not going to waste time negotiating.'

'How do we get down on the other side of these walls? I can't…' Before she'd finished the sentence Guy dipped and wrapped her round him, just as he'd done with Arkady.

'Just hold on. You can close your eyes if you have to, but don't bother me; just hold tight.' Her hold around his shoulders was more secure than Arkady's had been, and he was able to use a double handed grip on the line. He made determined progress, eventually depositing Tyler on the cliff ledge with Arkady. He heard her gasp as she took in her new position – perched on a rock shelf two feet wide, facing a moonlit descent into looming blackness. With her panicked intake of breath, Guy sensed her body starting to freeze and lock at the prospect before her.

'It's no different for me, Tyler. Only thing is I've done this sort of thing before, many times, and I know it's possible. *Use* your fear to concentrate, and remind yourself that if you want to live, you have no choice.'

Guy unclipped from the line and reattached to the longer rappel trailing the cliff. He looked past Tyler to where Arkady sat, his arms like sticks pushing down onto the ledge, jamming himself back into the rock face. 'You're doing a great job there, Arkady.' Guy grinned. 'You sure we haven't met on active service before?' He watched the boy's face, at first confused, then, as Guy held his gaze, breaking into a nervous grin. Arkady shook his head at Guy's question, the fear easing as his smile bloomed.

'Well, you sure look like a paratrooper to me, right now; the kind that deserves a medal.'

He felt Tyler give a small gasp of approval at his encouragement of the boy.

'Yes, he does, doesn't he.' she said.

'Courage is like fear, Tyler,' he whispered, 'it's infectious. Flip-side of the same coin.' He turned back to Arkady. 'Can you sit it out here while I get Tyler down the cliff? I'll be back for you as soon as I can, buddy, okay?

Arkady gave a brief, assenting nod. 'Will you get my mom and the other lady, too?'

'Of course I will.'

With that, Guy slipped the rappel strop over Tyler's shoulders, locking it through both their waists. He backed over to the cliff edge gaining traction on some tree roots as he began playing out the line. He felt Tyler's body rigid against his own, the back of her head only an inch from his face as they began their descent. He leaned in close to her ear, cold against his cheek. 'Just try and keep your feet flat to the cliff face and your knees relaxed. Okay, let's go.'

Back in the attic Lee found herself embracing Eva, clutching her tightly, silently grateful for the food, the clothes. Eva's own bearing softened instantly, returning Lee's hug with redoubled intensity.

'If it were up to me, I would never have harmed you…'

'No, don't speak about it.' Lee's finger had brushed the woman's trembling lips, stopping her. 'There's no need. It's in the past.' Eva looked back into Lee's eyes with something like shock, something more than sorrow. She moved to the trapdoor, descending the ladder again to play for time in the murderous world of the schloss.

Lee now lay with an ear pressed to the closed hatch, her gaze on the window, willing Guy's return. She had no idea how this man was planning to save them, no picture of where he, Tyler, or the child might be now. The heavy Glock felt reassuring in her grip, affirming the pact she'd made with this man, wherever he was.

Whoever he was.

87

Schloss, interior.

In the candle-lit lobby, with Schubert's string quartet building to the climax of its fourth movement, Ded Bazarov took one of the seats facing the rostrum, crossed his legs, sipped water, and lounged back to watch as Ms Penelope Lyons was toyed with and mauled by members of the group.

This part of the proceedings was predictable, he'd found. No matter how unfamiliar the guests had been only a few hours earlier, the fascinated and desperate group would form a writhing triangular heap as they sought to enter, caress, tease or torment this stunning, acquiescent beauty. Some would peel away to touch themselves, take stock. And there was always one who had second thoughts, one whose sense of self wasn't entirely lost to the occasion. A dangerous one.

He stared back at Penelope, her eyes opened, watching him as she accepted varied assaults and indignities. Her eyes closed suddenly again as the Englishman mounted her from behind. Around the room Bazarov's men stood in pairs, reveling in the floorshow's depravities.

That Penelope occasionally required such treatment wasn't evident to most. It was merely to their mutual advantage that in exploring her desires she had discovered Ded, who'd eventually invited her to enter his discrete corner of the internet, and subsequently his world.

Ded ignored Eva, now sidling into an adjacent seat, her hands folded demurely in her lap as if at a piano recital.

Eva knew it wouldn't be long before the ritual paused, or broke up spontaneously, as guests reached an initial stage of sexual exhaustion. Soon after, the hostages' cell would be checked and their escape discovered. She dared not picture the fury a search would create. For now, the longer she could prolong these erotic rituals, keeping Ded, his men, and the guests distracted, the better.

Feigning indifference, Eva swallowed the bile rising to her lips, though she felt she might faint at any moment. Her heart was pounding as she pictured Arkady outside in the night with Guy and the younger of the two American women. Guy was planning to return, to collect her and the second woman; to take them all away to safety. Like a fairytale.

Eva had long ago stopped believing in those.

But there was still something she could do to extend this rite and increase their chances of escape, even if that meant she herself might never be free.

Seeing the Englishman withdraw, sated by his assaults on the exquisite Penelope, Eva rose from her gilded chair, beginning to unzip her little black dress.

88

Schloss, exterior.

The cliff descent with Tyler was a dark flurry of kicks and slides. Guy's forearm, held protectively in front of Tyler's face, smashed into an outcrop of granite, opening a ten inch gash along its underside. Guy felt it momentarily; a cold burning, the ripped skin instantly wet under his sleeve. No bones broken, nothing to stop for.

For her part, Tyler was stoic if unresponsive, and the pair finally landed at the base of the cliff, both smeared with moss, grit and pine needles.

Guy unclipped Tyler from the strop and gave her his water bottle. She gulped back the liquid in silent swigs, eyes still closed. Guy turned her around as he took back the bottle. 'Open your eyes, Tyler, and pay attention.' He pointed to a rise in the land, a hundred yards distant, where the culvert and the sewer pipe were. 'You need to keep low, and move as quietly as you can to that point. In that ditch is a wide pipe which will shelter you. Just crawl inside and wait for me there. I'll bring Arkady to you, then I'll go back for Lee. Once everyone's safely out I'll call for back-up. Got it?'

Tyler nodded and reached for the canteen one more time.

'What if you don't make it? How will I know if you're okay?'

'If I'm not back here with the others by first light, then you'd better push off into the forest. Follow the natural slopes of the main ridges, they'll take you down to a river; follow it in the direction it flows. It'll come out, eventually, to a road, but it'll take you a few hours. Just keep moving. That's the best I can offer.'

Tyler studied the terrain Guy had pointed out. She nodded. 'I guess we're not out of this yet, huh?' But when she turned back Guy was already ten feet above her, climbing, barging, heaving once more up the dark and brutal cliff. The thin line of the rappel, snaking and whipping at her feet, was the only trace she now had of him.

89

Schloss, interior.

Slipping her dress from her shoulders, Eva approached the dais where Penelope rested on her haunches. The exhausted survivor of an endurance battle, Penelope's long muscled thighs supported her perfectly upright, even in her spent and ravished state.

Eva crossed to the Saudi woman who was lying naked and limp to one side of the group. She knelt, peppering her breasts with seemingly adoring kisses, closing her eyes while she sampled the woman's flesh and scents, feigning delight. The pretense was easier than sitting numbly, counting the minutes while her son fled to his new life or to a relieving death. The longer she drew out this display, the greater Arkady's chances of survival.

Eva roamed the butter-soft thighs of the Saudi with her lips and tongue, causing her convenient lover to buck and moan. She turned her eyes hungrily at last to Penelope, who was smiling at Eva's sham of passionate abandon.

Penelope slid over to the pair and began caressing Eva's exposed back, her expert fingers sliding into the waistband of Eva's underwear.

Turning her head away from what she presumed would be

Ded's amused gaze, Eva bit her lip and accepted Penelope's probings with a fake shudder of delight. Her contribution to the proceedings was working; she'd galvanized the Saudi Princess's lover who himself now began a fresh assault on Penelope. Eva concentrated on increasing the writhing delight of the woman beneath her. She pictured her son and his father moving like spirits in the moonlight, far beyond the schloss, and her tears were instant, an ecstasy so different from that pursued by those around her. She let her tongue dart deeper within the Saudi's intimate folds, playing only for time.

More time.

90

Schloss, exterior.

Guy pushed on up the cliff in a growing state of exultation. The demands of the climb, the risks, and the possible outcomes produced an unquestioning purpose; one that only combat and the fight for survival could incite in him.

He was blazing and soaked with effort; his fingers finding tree roots whenever he sought them, his boots biting into crevices which rose to meet his needs.

Picturing Arkady alone above him, Guy felt as if he were flowing up over the rock face, adrenalin and concentration creating a purity of engagement.

Guy grappled on to the ledge where Arkady waited, palms still flat to the slippery stone, just as he had left the boy forty minutes earlier. Guy pulled an antiseptic wad from his combat vest and wiped down the long, bleeding gash on his forearm. Then he unrolled a two-inch wide strip of Elastoplast. He bit off a length and smoothed it over the split skin. Satisfied with the running repair, he glanced over to Arkady.

'How you feeling? Ready to go for it?'

Arkady bit his lip and gave the smallest of nods. He

threw a look back to the rim of the schloss wall butting their ledge. Guy followed his gaze. 'Don't worry, I'm going back for your mom, but we have to get you safely stowed first.'

Arkady nodded and this time he twisted his hips sideways and knelt, one hand rising up the rock to brace himself, then he stood as Guy grasped his arm for balance. Guy grabbed the boy's belt, lifting him up on his back and tucking his ankles into the strop at his waist. He guided Arkady's hand to a strap on his combat vest. 'Hold tight.' Guy used his free left hand to grasp the boys wrist, then, leaning back from the ledge, began to pick his way down.

The descent was fast. Arkady was no burden and his grip was strong. Guy heard the small gasps which punctuated their descent becoming less anxious as the lad learned to trust where Guy's feet would land next, where the descent called for a swing around an obstacle, where the line might play more slowly, more swiftly.

From the little Eva had told him, Guy knew Arkady was practically housebound, yet he struck Guy as a regular kid, relishing the freezing air in his nostrils, this controlled fall among dark trees and tumbling scree. Getting Arkady away, freeing him for a life untroubled by the adults he'd known, was starting to feel like a sacred duty.

At the base of the cliff Guy undid the rappel. Together they struck out toward the old pipe where Tyler would be waiting for them.

The moonlight allowed him to avoid the worst dips

and rabbit holes. Several times Guy felt the boy stumble at his side and he'd jerk his arm like a toddler, yanking him upright, ensuring they maintained progress.

Arriving at the pipe Guy found Tyler crouched and shivering. She swept the boy into her embrace, stroking his face. 'Well done,' she whispered. 'Well done! I'm so proud of you.'

Guy slugged some water from his canteen and looked back at the looming schloss. As he listened to the boy breathing hard in Tyler's protective arms, instinct warned him to cut his losses. If he struck out for the forest with the pair of them now he could probably find a road and call in evacuation support. He'd live, he'd survive, and he'd have delivered a kid from hell into a new life. Wasn't that enough? Could he convince himself of that, live with that decision?

He handed the canteen to Arkady and watched as the boy took eager, reviving sips.

Back there in the castle two women were counting on him. He'd have no life at all if he didn't do everything in his power to free them. So why did their need make him suddenly angry – at them, at the world, at his life?

'Is it safe for you to go back? What if they've found out we're gone?'

Guy looked to Tyler. Maybe she'd sensed him weighing his options. She and the boy were one mass now, sheltering savages in the lip of this filthy old pipe.

'No, it's not safe. And it's getting less safe with every minute, but hey, I don't exactly have a choice, do I.'

'I can't stand thinking of Lee alone there, in that attic, I keep thinking of them finding her there…'

At Tyler's words Guy's moment of doubt passed as quickly as it had arisen. 'Remember, if I'm not back here by first light it means things have probably gone pear-shaped, and you should both push on.' He knelt down to Arkady. 'I'm going back for Lee and your mom, now. But it might take time. You'll have to trust I'm doing my best. If you and Tyler need to push on without me then look after each other like paratroopers always do. Clear?' Arkady nodded and Guy held up a palm. The boy leaned forward from Tyler's clutches and gave his best 'high-five'.

Guy turned and, crouching low over the furrowed landscape, headed back to the castle for what he hoped would be his final assault on the cliff.

91

Schloss, interior.

Guy eased his way across the roof toward the attic window. The room was dark, silent. If things had gone to plan both Eva and Lee would be waiting inside.

Pulling himself up to the sill, he risked a look inside. Lee was waiting, crouched, facing the attic's hatch, the Glock held loose at her side. But she was alone.

He tapped the glass pane and she span around like a cat. He put a finger to his lips as she crossed to open the window. He slipped in over the sill.

'No sign of Eva?' he whispered.

Lee shook her head, staring up into his taut, sweat-soaked face. Mud, pine needles and grit had combined to turn his features into an unreadable mask. Only his large dark eyes burned clear through the caked-on grime. After her time holed up alone in the tiny room, his presence was electrifying. He radiated heat and purpose, a hyper-real intensity.

'Any disturbance?' His calm, bass voice made her snap out of the spell.

'No. I've heard nothing since you left.'

Guy pulled the phone from his vest pocket. There were

no messages, no code letters. He eased back the hatch and stared down. In the distance he could hear the drone of music from the lobby.

'So far so good. I don't think their little party would still be swinging if they'd found you'd gone.'

'Can we just get out of here? Please!'

Guy shook his head. 'Eva's still down there.' This was the woman who'd once saved his life. He recalled the trusting smack of Arkady's high five.

Guy climbed down from the loft and made his way along the jumbled corridor. He stared down to the dais, to where Eva was now naked, spread-eagled, the red-lipsticked blonde tormenting Eva's naked breasts.

He looked to Ded Bazarov savoring his sister's violation. ,And then he understood.

Eva was buying them all time.

Guy glanced along the landing to the now empty cell, the pristine torture chamber, the makeshift office. A familiar aurora pattern highlighted the wall of Bazarov's space containing the laptop Scott so desperately wanted. Everything he'd seen here, all the suffering and planned atrocities, were organized from that hard drive. Breaking it out was vital to closing Hades Gate.

He flashed another look to the lobby. There seemed no hope of rescuing Eva, something she'd apparently factored all along.

He crept toward the slowly writhing lights, Glock at the ready. Eva's sacrifice couldn't be in vain.

92

Schloss, interior.

As Bazarov watched the figures entwined on the dais Rostrov arrived at his shoulder. He held a small blue plastic-bodied phone, a slick of black gaffer keeping it together. Little more than a toy.

Rostrov leaned in close and began whispering. Suddenly Bazarov was on his feet. He clapped his hands, once, twice, and the tentacles of flesh on the dais began to unwind.

'Eva! Eva!'

Bazarov strode onto the dais and reached into the mass of limbs, pulling at the figures, grabbing arms, ankles, hair, until his sister was revealed at the bottom of the heap, her eyes darkened by something other than frenzy.

She looked up at him; seeing the phone in his hand a slow grin spread over her features. Bazarov tossed the phone to Rostrov behind him and, reaching down, grabbed Eva under her shoulder, hauling her to her knees. He wanted no explanation, not yet, and he needed no excuse. He smashed an open palm into her cheek making her head snap round on its slender neck. A slick of blood appeared at her lip's corner, her mouth drooping in a momentary loss of consciousness. Bazarov hauled her into better range and repeated the blow. A broken tooth and a spray of blood fanned the dais as he dumped her face-first to the floor.

'Take her to the chamber, give her water, wake her up.' Bazarov spat the words through gritted teeth to Rostrov. Then, shooting a look round the assembled men, 'Check the cells, now!'

In the corridor office, Guy heard shouts from the lobby just as he stuffed Bazarov's laptop under his combat vest. He unslung the Diemaco, jamming its stock into his shoulder, ready to let rip.

There were pounding feet on the stairs behind him. He had only one exit. As he dodged the corner from the office to the landing he saw Rostrov and a second thug dragging Eva, slumped and unconscious, onto the landing. A shot behind him ricochetted from his kevlar vest. The punch from the round released a torrent of fresh adrenalin and Guy span, returning fire straight into the thug's face from five feet away. The heavy man staggered back forcing a gunman looming behind him to sidestep. Guy dropped to his knee and took a clean shot at the man. The round blew his chest open, but he staggered forward, gun emptying wildly into the floor as his spasming finger crushed the trigger. Guy let the man topple forward onto his shoulders before levering the bleeding mass straight over the balcony edge where it landed on marble, thirty feet below, with an explosive smack.

'Take him alive!'

Guy heard Bazarov's command as Rostrov, dropping Eva

face first on the marble stairway, appeared on the landing. Guy let go with a single shot as Rostrov ducked into a cell doorway. The Diemaco's round blew half the face off a startled man exposed behind Rostrov's dodge.

Now Guy was operating in slowed time, combat time. Bazarov wanted him alive, and while his boys dithered, Guy would take a few more of them out. He caught a lick of Rostrov's fringe against the cell door as he took aim with a serious automatic. Guy let off another burst from the Diemaco, driving Rostrov back behind the frame. Springing forward, he flipped into a low shoulder-roll bringing him to within a foot of Rostrov's position. As Rostrov rounded the cell door to take his shot, he found 220 pounds of Guy Bowman rearing up from the floor right in front of him. Guy drove his forehead straight into Rostrov's nose, smashing it and sending him backwards into the heavy door. As Guy raised his gun for the kill a shot from behind him blew his rifle out of his fingers, like a twig snapping from a branch. Guy knew it could have slotted him, had that been the intent.

Rostrov crept round the lintel of the cell, nose streaming with blood, face bright with joy as he advanced on his suddenly unarmed feast. As Guy squared up for the inevitable fist fight, another warning shot flew past his cheek like a hornet, missing the astonished Rostrov by an inch, no more. Both men were stalled like sweating kids in a playground stand-off as the headmaster called them out.

'There won't be another warning, my next shot will cripple you. Kneel and put your hands behind you.' Bazarov's voice was calm, coming from over Guy's right shoulder, ten, maybe twelve feet back.

Guy pictured Tyler and Arkady in the old pipe, Lee alone in the attic hearing gunfire. Perhaps if these savages had him to concentrate on for a while they'd be less intent on their newly 'escaped' hostages. Guy's apparent compliance could buy some time. Besides, he was unarmed now; playing patsy was in his own short-term interests. Better than one of Bazarov's bullets to the back of the head. Probably. Guy knelt, slowly. No point in rushing.

While Rostrov held his gun hard to Guy's temple, Bazarov reached inside the awkwardly bulging combat vest, retrieving the laptop.

'Mine, I think.'

'Absolutely.'

'Who else is here with you, how many?'

'I'm alone.'

'Who are you working for?'

'I heard about what you do. I wanted to stop that. The choice was mine. Alone.'

'Where are the women?'

'What women?'

Bazarov assessed Guy while speaking to Rostrov beside him. 'Put him into some cuffs and let's get out of here. We'll abort this event. Everyone needs to leave immediately.' Bazarov looked down at Guy. 'This is going to be an expensive mission for you. You'll pay for it with your life, naturally. But first, I'm going to learn who you are, and everything you know. From your own lips.' Unfolding the laptop he hit a few keys, then oriented the machine so that its camera was facing Guy.

'Zara, who is this?' Bazarov let the camera wink for several seconds, then snapped the cover down. Looking across to Rostrov, he nodded. To Guy it looked as though he was slipping an attack dog off its leash.

As Rostrov drew his fist back Guy glimpsed Eva further down the landing, attempting to get to her feet, groggy. Bloody. The first of Rostrov's three punches to Guy's face almost took his head off.

He wasn't conscious for the third.

Bazarov turned with the laptop and headed for the lobby, swooping down the wide stairs in a gliding blur. His half-dressed and disheveled guests had gathered in a mix of the disgruntled, the priapic and the irate. 'Get dressed, take your belongings and leave in your vehicles, immediately. I'll come to terms with you all later. But if you value your liberty, go.'

'I need a shower before I go anywhere, this is ridiculous.' The Englishman's insistence brought murmurs and nods.

'What about the executions we were promised? The American blondes?' The Saudi woman was pouting, wrapping a fur stole about her delicate, brutally scratched shoulders.

Bazarov, who'd turned away, broke his stride and returned to the would-be revelers. 'Any of you still here in ten minutes will be shot, without exception. Now, dress and leave. Drive normally without drawing attention to yourselves. None of you can afford to be detained or questioned.'

Guy's slumped body was dragged past the group, arms zip-tied behind him, wrenched along by Rostrov with two suited henchmen. Penelope leaned down to study his face as he passed. 'Shame we didn't get to play with him, he's a cutie.' She caught Bazarov's glare and winked. 'Maybe some other time?'

93

Schloss, interior.

Keeping her gun trained on the trapdoor Lee inched to the attic window. She could hear the slamming of car doors, engines starting. The roofline below the window meant that she had no view of the courtyard itself, only a luminescence from the floodlights, leaving the night sky beyond it a thick black.

Through the hatch she'd heard the gunfire, the shouts and scuffles. The worst. Guy was caught, maybe betrayed after all by Eva. If so, they'd soon be coming for her, too. But the exit of the assembled guests, their rushed departure into the night . . . that was unexpected.

Lee sank to her haunches under the window and wiped her damp palms on her thighs before leveling the Glock at the hatch again. She could hear her own heartbeat.

When should she shoot? When the hatch moved? When the first face pushed through?

What if it was Guy returning to tell her all was ok and she shot him before he could speak? She looked across at his Bergen. Maybe a strike force was on its way, and the losers were fleeing.

Now the cars were pulling away, engines straining, tires

slipping. Urgent. Rushing. She flicked the safety back on the Glock.

A second later she flicked it off again.

94

Schloss, exterior.

Penelope felt the eyes of hurrying men on her as she threw her overnight bag into the Maserati. No matter, she was used to that. But they, too, were being harried and barked at by Bazarov as he, and the man she knew as Rostrov, dumped a barely conscious Eva onto the back seat of an SUV.

For several seconds she had a view into the vehicle. On the same back seat, lying stretched in wrist and ankle cuffs, was the still-unconscious cutie.

What was that styling he'd gotten up to? That black ops' jumpsuit, the combat vest and action-stained boots? He was too beefy for a Ninja wannabe, but also too toned and defined under that rig to be anything other than a combat-ready soldier. Maybe he'd been part of some earlier sideshow, some extra scene she hadn't been invited to see.

Bazarov's parties had grown increasingly elaborate in the last several months. It looked as though pretty-boy there had a tough time of it. Still, who was she to judge; it took all sorts to make a world. If you played hard, you might fall hard. There was no accounting for taste. Even so, something didn't feel right. She needed to know more about why this event was being closed down in such a hurry. Was Bazarov fleeing the cops, or a raid? As far as she knew, what he did was risqué, but hardly illegal.

Penelope closed the Maserati's door, darkening the car's interior, and hit the start button. She watched Eva being hurriedly cuffed on the back seat alongside the soldier; not that the unconscious woman looked a threat, exactly. Then Bazarov and Rostrov got into the car, Rostrov driving. Their heavy SUV pulled away, one of the last to slide and skitter through the muddy paddock.

Penelope chose her moment. One of Ded's men she recognized from a previous event, Roman, was hauling what looked like builder's tools past her toward a large blacked-out van. She threw her driver's door back, flashing an elegantly booted leg for him as she levered up from the low car. 'One more bag, inside, it'll take seconds. I left some jewelry in there.' She gave a *silly me, huh?* pout. 'Ded wouldn't expect me to leave it, Roman. I know he wouldn't.'

The man slung a huge holdall into his van, too concerned with his own getaway to stall hers. 'Sure. But don't hang around in there, lady.'

'Was that a pun?' Penelope flashed a perfectly whitened smile into his van's dipped beam.

'Eh?'

'Never mind.'

She leaned in and switched her engine off. 'Thanks for the tip.' But the suited bruiser was stomping round to the rear of the vehicle and, finally, out of sight. Penelope cut away into shadow, then on, alone, into the deserted schloss.

95

No Man's Land – Austria

Tyler shuddered. The clothing she'd been given did nothing to combat the chill of these minutes before dawn. Arkady sat between her legs with his back to her, swaddled in her arms, each sharing the embers of the other's warmth.

First light, he'd said.

She raked the sky for the umpteenth time. From the little she knew of the man it was clear he meant what he said, and she was pushing the envelope now, delaying like this. The sky carried filigree bridges of rose gold laced from one horizon to the other. She pulled Arkady tighter.

Had Guy been captured?

'Do you think we should go for it?' She whispered the question tight to Arkady's icy ear. He nodded.

'Guy gave us an order. We have to do it. He'll be cross if we don't.' Tyler stroked his hair. *Yes, of course, sometimes orders were necessary. If you were too scared to think, if you knew death was somewhere close by, it was good to have orders to follow. Not to think, simply to obey.* 'Ok, let's do it.' She eased them both out from the pipe and took a look back to the castle. In the dawn it seemed like a massive edifice looming over them, while to her right the indistinct ridge line of the forest was being tricked out by the same roseate light.

A lone car sped along the exit road, maybe a quarter mile away, its red tail-lamps growing smaller, the babbling exhaust declining as the doppler sank in the night's shrouding silence.

A bite of freezing air surprised her, tightening her already stiffened back. Still, perhaps now they'd generate some heat by moving. She gave the child a smile, probably more a grimace, she realized, as the flesh of her cold cheeks bunched.

As they set out toward the forest, Tyler guessed it wouldn't do to overthink the next several hours. One step at a time.

96

Highway, Austria.

In the SUV Guy was coming round to the smell of new upholstery and vented air-freshener as his prone body was rocked by fast curves and sharp braking.

Keeping his eyes closed he ran his tongue over his inner lips. Bruised, puffy, a loose tooth. But his jaw complied with the tiny movements, it wasn't broken. He pumped his wrists and forearms, feeling the ziplock cuffs bite back. Glancing along his prone body he could see his combat vest, weapons and phone had all been removed. And there was another body alongside him.

Still warm, still alive.

He fought down some bile from motion nausea and stayed unmoving.

An unscheduled early-morning drive through lower Bavaria – he could guess who was his host. Gradually, the pieces assembled in his thoughts. Lee, still alone in the attic. Maybe she'd been forced to fight it out. Tyler and Arkady, hopefully moving through the forest by now. Or maybe they'd already been slaughtered by Bazarov's thugs. It was a hell of a mess, but it was better than any alternative. That meant Eva was probably alongside him in the darkened rear of the rocking vehicle. He'd dodged a bullet or three back there in the schloss. By rights he shouldn't be alive.

But he was.

Utrinque Paratus.

97

Schloss, interior.

Penelope picked her way through the lobby over abandoned equipment, past coiled cables. The wooden dais was still in place, as was the gallows on which she'd performed her party trick. She walked on, a frisson of panic rising as she ignored the black noose.

When she was no longer in her *zone* her erotic proclivities often felt alien and morbid, as they might seem to anyone in their right mind. But then, what was 'right mind' when it came to confronting who she was, what she delighted in – questions she'd struggled with most of her life.

She and Bazarov had their understanding. Penelope took a very private delight in asphyxia, and Bazarov recognized her needs. He was adept at handling her torment, reading her displays of aroused distress, prolonging them. During the times they'd played together he'd deepened her experiences more uncompromisingly than anyone else. She trusted him with her life.

It was for this she'd sometimes drive secretly, deliciously, many miles from her villa and her vapid single life among Zurich's financial elite, just to float in a dark ecstasy under Bazarov's masterful hand.

As she moved through the lobby Penelope recalled the pact they'd formed in his niche of the darknet. It was something she needed, something she trusted him to provide. She neither took nor was paid any fee, and Bazarov benefitted from her becoming an anonymous, mysterious star at his events: the ultimate ice-breaker, as she'd clearly been tonight.

Penelope never stayed beyond her own stellar contribution. Once she was sated she wanted only to flee the lust and attentions of others. But she'd discerned an ever darkening agenda at Bazarov's events and, as she picked her way through the marbled lobby, she knew this had been their final fling.

Still, something in her needed to see what remained of Bazarov's preparations. Why had he made tonight's guests scatter, running for their lives?

She took the stairs to the corridor where the shots had been fired and where, as she'd quickly dressed behind the dais, she'd looked up to see the soldier being smacked around by that ape, Rostrov.

To her right, beneath the balcony, the body of the man who'd been turfed over the ledge lay sprawled on the lobby tiles in a crust of dried blood, like a Weegee stiff.

Penelope eased back the door of the first cell. It was a torture chamber. Everything in her thrilled, her skin tingling, thighs softening as she observed the clamps, cords, pliers and manacles. Just a set designed to induce fear, suspense, dark bliss. Clever Bazarov…

'Put your hands above your head. Don't turn around. Make a move and I'll kill you.'

It was a woman's voice, one she didn't recognize. American accent. Penelope did as she was told.

'Where's everyone gone? Why did they leave?'

'Things got a little…complicated. The event was compromised, at least that's my understanding. I didn't organize this, it has nothing to do with me…'

'Shut the fuck up.' Lee eased into the cell behind Penelope and put the gun hard to the back of her head. With her free hand she frisked the woman's neat silhouette of ribbed turtleneck and expensive leggings. 'Who fired the shots?'

'There was a fight, some special-forces type had taken a computer or something. At first I thought he was part of the show, but he killed two of Bazarov's men. They took him down in the end, punched him out, dragged him away. The event's been abandoned.'

As she listened, Lee kept an ear trained to the lobby. She knew in her gut that Guy had done everything to take the heat off her. Where was he now? Would he come back?

'Turn around. Slowly.'

Penelope turned and found herself uncharacteristically lost for words. The woman holding a gun on her was a starved derelict, dressed from a charity store, eyes wide and haunted like some crazed raccoon.

In turn, Lee studied the beauty she was holding at gunpoint. Not one of the group who'd come to view and mock them when she and Tyler were caged. Right now that was the only thing in her favor. 'You weren't here before. When did you come?'

'Today, this afternoon. Look, I don't know about this room, this set-up, or what was supposed to go on here. I came to get some kicks, sure, but they didn't involve any of this.'

'So why are you still here?'

'I was going to leave, but I knew there was more to this than I understood. I wanted to find out what the set-up was.'

'The *set-up*? This fucking-set-up was so that another woman and myself could be tortured and killed while a bunch of sickos watched and filmed us. Trust me, if I didn't even half believe you, I'd have blown your brains out already.'

'Oh my God, that's insane. I get that. Truly, I get that.' Penelope looked around the room again. The stirring she'd felt at the idea of an elaborate, consensual BDSM ritual was replaced with disgust. 'You're telling me you were kept prisoner here?'

'Not here. In the cells further along.'

'You escaped?'

Lee kept her powder dry, not wanting to compromise Guy, wherever he might be. 'Yeah, we escaped. My friend got away. I got held up.'

Penelope looked hard down the barrel of the Glock. 'It looks like you need some help, and I think we should both get out of here... My name's Penelope. And yours?'

'Lee, Lee Crane. I was kidnapped . . . the other woman and I both were.'

'My car's downstairs. Shall we see if we can find your friend?'

Lee hesitated. The woman was likely to take her to wherever Bazarov and his gang had fled.

Penelope seemed to sense her reasoning. 'Lee, given what I'm learning right now, I can tell you I never want to see those people again. They've taken things much too far…'

'Something of an understatement.' Lee's mouth was almost too dry to speak, the Glock starting to shake in her grip. But she knew she had to take a chance. 'You drive, but I'll keep this gun on you. Take me to the police.' Lee saw Penelope hesitate. She flicked the gun straight into the young woman's face. 'What? Why won't you go to the police? It's the obvious thing to do.'

'I don't think you understand. In order for this event to go on, for these guests to assemble and leave unimpeded, the police themselves have to be on a nod. This is wildest Bavaria. Local rules.'

'Bribed?'

'Nicely taken care of, yes. A local police station is the last place you want to be. And besides, there probably isn't one within twenty miles of this place. New York this isn't. We'd do better aiming for Vienna. I can take you to the main police HQ. You'll be safe there.'

'And you?'

'The sooner I'm back over the border and heading for home the better. Look, don't get me wrong, but you're an American, you clearly know jack-shit about European geography. Vienna's north of here, way off my route. I'd be doing you a favor – but it's your call.'

Lee chewed it over. Out on the road she'd have no idea where they were going. . .

Penelope's arm shot forward, crashing down on the Glock and sending it spinning. Grabbing Lee by the throat and dragging her to the floor, Penelope hooked the gun toward herself with the toe of her boot. She gave a final squeeze to Lee's throat, then let go, reaching for the Glock and standing, all in one flowing move.

Lee fought for breath on the floor, her head reeling from shock and starvation, but now she saw Penelope's outstretched arm, offering to drag her back to her feet. As she stood, one hand tending her bruised throat, Penelope handed back the Glock.

'Sorry for the Krav Maga stunt. I picked it up at finishing school, and you were rather asking for it. If I wanted to kill or betray you, Lee, I'd have done it by now.' She threw a final shuddering look around the room. 'Now, I'm getting out of this place before anyone shows up or anything else goes wrong. If you want that lift, my offer's still good.' She turned and headed for the cell's door.

'Let's do it . . . let's get to Vienna. Thanks, Penelope.'

'Close acquaintances call me Penny, I prefer that. I've got bottled water in my car, and once we're out of here we can find a rest stop and get you something to eat. You're looking rather peaky there.'

Outside the cell, Penelope's heel skidded on what looked in the half-light like a stick, a short broom. 'What...'

'That's Guy's rifle.' Lee leapt forward and grabbed the Diemaco from the floor.

'I remember now, they shot it out of his hands. Why didn't they take it?'

'I guess they had enough hardware of their own.' Lee turned the rifle over. The stock had a chunk blown off, leaving the rifle unbalanced but intact. *Where was Guy now? Without a weapon, and captured.*

Penelope began a rushed descent down the staircase, 'Let's hope we don't need it, huh? But it'll be good to have it along.'

'Hold up, there's something else we should take.' Lee ran back along the landing and up the stairs.

Penelope, now crossing the lobby, called over her shoulder, 'We're pushing our luck with every minute here. Meet me outside, but I'm not waiting around. Two minutes, max.'

Lee quickly reappeared in the courtyard shouldering Guy's Bergen. To Penelope, firing up the Maserati, she appeared to be carrying a small shed. 'Really? What the fuck?'

'There's all kinds of useful stuff in here.' Lee heaved the pack onto the rear seat of the car, then jumped in alongside Penelope. 'It'll be good to have it along.' Penelope handed her a bottle of water and gunned the throttle. The powerful car twitched over the courtyard's cobbles, then onto the drive curling ahead of them, and off into the forest.

98

Highway

Face down in the rear of the SUV Guy sensed they were on an autobahn. Forward progress was smooth and fast, any curves they encountered were sweeping rather than sudden. Either way, none of it was good.

He nudged the body beside him, little more than a flex of his thigh. An equally minute return flex confirmed Eva was conscious.

Eva felt Guy's warm body spooned close behind her on the SUV's richly padded seat. Her bound wrists were level with his groin, her fingertips draping his taut thighs. Surely he was playing possum, taking his time, considering the odds . . . the same stoic assurance that had so pleased her back in Douma when he'd been her precious prisoner. Memories of others she'd tormented were kept behind a veil of denial, a room in her thoughts she dare not visit. In contrast, she often relived every second of her time with Guy, every moment of his dependence on her.

Of course, when they'd spoken in the attic, he had refuted his own response to her. He had to, she knew. We tell ourselves the truths we most want to believe, after all. Guy Bowman was the only man she'd ever wanted to touch her, love her, fill her. Keeping him prisoner had allowed her to savor him, enjoy every one of his reactions, taste his skin, his very blood on her lips, and delight in his sustained submission to her. His strength and courage thrilled and alarmed her. Here, in what might be their final minutes together, she revisited the passion which had filled their strange hours in that awful room. With the tiniest of movements she pressed back into him and found his stillness embracing her.

Guy considered the outcomes. If they'd wanted him dead he'd be dead. Keeping him alive meant they had a purpose, even if that was interrogation. Right now he was alive, so there would be a moment to follow this one . . . and there was hope.

He ran through what he could give them.

He had no military rank, no serial number to quote or use to buy time. But then, that wasn't their questioning style. They couldn't know his name. Not yet. He thought of the moment on the landing when the computer photographed him; when someone called Zara was told to find out who he was...

The kind of treatment Bazarov and Rostrov meted out would break the toughest candidate. Only mental strength, along with a firm decision made for the higher good, would see him through whatever was coming. He thought of how much effort and how many lives were invested in keeping Scott's Bureau a secret, even from the leviathan of MI6. The Bureau's secrecy was its chief asset for good in the world. He knew he couldn't be the one to compromise that.

The vehicle slowed and veered. An exit ramp.

Guy was getting closer to whatever Bazarov had in store for him.

99

Forest

The light filtering through the upswept sleeves of the fir trees was a comfort, but Tyler felt no warmer as she led Arkady, the two of them fumbling and tripping, down a slope toward a river.

Guy had been right. The first major ridge-line they'd crested gave way to a sloping bank with the water glinting below, a silver thread lacing through a billion pine trees.

Her shoes were two sizes too small and her feet were bunching, toes cramping exactly when she needed them to be lithe. But ditching the moccasins would see her feet shredded by stones, roots and brittle gorse. Cut to ribbons in seconds. For a moment she thought of her slender feet being pedicured in a warm salon, then of the absurdity and remoteness of that other life she'd lived. Now she was living second-by-second, breath-by-breath. Or maybe she was dying that way.

Dew evaporating from rheumy branches was filling her lungs with a damp, balsam glow. But the night spent inside the pipe had lowered her core temperature. Tyler could feel a spasming between her ribs each time she inhaled. She was losing control.

Arkady hacked a furred cough. She glanced down as he sputtered, his hand never leaving hers. He trusted her. Poor kid. If ever the blind led the blind… But having their destiny in her hands outweighed everything. She had to think, act and *be* for both of them. It was as though she'd *become* the world through which she was moving. She had no idea where she was, only that her entire being was enmeshed with the forest. The slap of wet twigs in her face, fetid leaf slime bitter on her lips, her stumbles into wet soil, palms sliced by sharp stones. Hungry, terrified too. This was all she could do, her only choice. Her legs seemed to move free of any command. Following the river in the direction it flowed would bring them to a road, Guy had said.

That was all she knew.

All she had.

100

Highway

The cuts in his mouth were healing, the metallic tang of his blood lessening with each stifled swallow.

Good.

His body was repairing, surviving on any terms it could.

From the front seat Guy could hear Bazarov's fingers on the laptop's keyboard. Then a warm, American female voice.

'Guy Bowman. He's an ex-paratroop Commander according to MOD official records. But he also served in another elite foreign regiment. Most of the documentation is redacted. I have it but I'll need a little longer to find undoctored originals.'

Ded Bazarov sighed audibly. 'Special forces. So predictable. SAS? SBS?' He thought of Guy's intelligent eyes, the unflinching features when Rostrov had punched him unconscious on the landing. 'He's far too bright to be a SEAL.'

Zara continued. 'I have a snap of him, here, in the French Foreign Legion. He's very handsome. . .'

'Not for much longer.' Rostrov's growl had definite intent behind it.

Bazarov made a call, speaking in Russian. Clipped, sounding like a simple affirmation.

Guy swiped his tongue around the inside of his lip, pressing slicks of saliva into the larger cuts. It was good that Rostrov wanted to make it personal. That would force gaps in his already poor judgement. Personalizing combat was amateur, it brought lapses in reasoning, opening chinks where waiting death might surprise you.

'The French Foreign Legion?' Bazarov almost spat the words. 'Criminals, murderers and alcoholics. The outfit's even sponsored by a beer company, Kronenbourg!' Guy knew he was meant to hear Bazarov's contempt. 'No, I don't think that can be right. I don't see him singing the French National Anthem, and they all do you know, they're forced to learn it, no matter where they're from. Are you sure it's him, Zara?'

'Well the Legion seems to be rather camera-shy, and that's all I have of him there for the moment, but my facial recognition cache is responding strongly, despite the pixellation. The redaction was done a while back, primitive, a gesture rather than a definite wipe.'

Guy continued to lie still; he sensed Bazarov's eyes on him from the front seat. He could picture the man's gaze flicking between his precious laptop and the mysterious human prize on the car's back seat. But who the hell was Zara? Quite a girl it seemed…

He recalled the image she'd mentioned. It was the only one he'd ever allowed taken of him in the Legion, snapped on the day he left selection camp to join its secret Deuxiéme

Rep cadre; the Legion's elite Parachute Regiment. The most highly trained and uncompromising Airborne unit in the world. The Deuxiéme Rep… As Guy bounced on Bazarov's car seats it all seemed a long time ago. Only Commander Reggie Scott knew about his deployment there. He'd been spotted and tapped-up by the Legion's commanders while on duty with the Paras in Afghanistan.

Recruitment to the French unit was a one-way offer. Non-French nationals couldn't apply, you had to be asked. If your regimental CO agreed, it was an immediate transfer. Once in, you disappeared from public life. Your family signed the OSA, and from then on they never knew where you'd been deployed. Suddenly invisible.

As though you'd died.

But you were very well paid.

101

Forest

The air along the riverbank was biting, its mist crystalizing to tiny icicles in Tyler's throat as she walked. But progress here was easier than any ramble among the pines with their tangled, hidden roots, further up the escarpment.

She glanced again to Arkady. The boy no longer responded. Though beaded with sweat, his skin was deathly white. He was shivering as he stumbled, heavy-legged at her side.

She heard what had to be a truck, far off. The road was high to her left, but was it the road Guy had mentioned? She'd been traveling for a few hours at most. Was this the right road to seek rescue? And how would she know who to trust if she found anyone up there?

Her thoughts came pell-mell, evaporating as fast as they formed, bringing no answers. But something inclined her upwards toward the earlier sound. Each step away from the freezing river, dragging Arkady, her trainers soaked and shredding, meant warmer sunlight dappling her face. Up, toward the road. Whichever road.

Dizzy with tiredness, she knew she had to save them both from what might soon be fatal exposure.

Tyler felt a pull to her shoulder, her fingers suddenly free of Arkady's. She turned to see him slipping away, rolling unconscious through foliage before slamming against the trunk of a spruce, thirty feet back down the slope.

She wanted to scream.

All the horror of the last several days and now this choking rage at the boy's incompetence and neediness. Her chest burned with hatred, a hell of ice and steam clogging her airways. 'Arkady!' she hissed. Something warned her a full-scale bellow was risky. The boy didn't respond. A wet, rounded hump speckled with bracken and maybe dying lay at the foot of the great tree.

Now she would have to carry him.

102

Highway

A silence had descended inside the SUV.

Guy pictured Bazarov brooding over the cancelled event and wondering who he had on the back seat of the speeding car.

There might never be a better time to take charge of the situation.

'Everyone stay relaxed, okay. I'm going to sit up. No fisticuffs needed.' He felt the car lurch as Rostrov turned in response to Guy's voice.

Guy started to work himself into a sitting position.

Bazarov pulled an AMT Hardballer from his lap, aiming the gun straight into Guy's face, less than two feet away. Guy didn't flinch.

'Better keep it smooth, Rostrov. We don't want any Pulp-Fiction *Marvin* moments now, do we? Spoil all our fun.' Guy made sure to catch Rostrov's glare in the driver's mirror, followed by another swerve as his eyes went back to the road. Guy felt the car speeding up before a bout of over-corrective braking. *Rostrov starting to losing his mojo a little?* A glimpse at the gun showed the Hardballer's safety catch was on. *Bazarov distracted too?* Both men out of their comfort zone.

Guy aimed to keep it that way.

The vehicle swung off the main road and was ushered in by a single sentry through the gates of what looked like a rusting theme park. Rounding a corner, Guy saw the lot bordered a lake. He ran a scan of the briefing maps in his head. Yes. He recalled a man-made lake about thirty miles north-east of the schloss. Whatever, the place was deserted, derelict. Plastic water slides, once lurid orange and vibrant blue, were blanched by sunlight, scoured by frosts and punishing rains.

The car pulled over on rough ground alongside a large black van. Guy was pulled out at gunpoint, Bazarov tugging his plastic cuffs. Rostrov dragged Eva from the back seat. Guy saw she kept her head lowered, her swollen eyes adjusting painfully to angled winter light. Bazarov slit the plastic ties at their ankles, enabling them both to walk. 'Over there.'

The ground sloped toward an old timbered boathouse and the pair were pushed toward it. For a few vital seconds Eva caught his eye and Guy knew what her unasked question had to be. Was her son safe? Had he got away? Guy gave a tiny nod and a wink. He saw her shoulders and arms slacken in their bonds and her eyes close. He knew her own fate no longer concerned her.

He looked across the lake to its far bank; no hope there. No houses, no one to see them, no maintenance towers where a distracted worker might glance up from his breakfast sandwich and see anyone being led, at gunpoint, toward a large expanse of cold, probably deep, water. Guy heard the shunt of the Transit's doors and more pairs of feet crunching behind him over the broken grit of the parkland.

But how many more?

103

Forest Road

There's about ten more miles of this forest road, then we hit the autobahn. North takes us to Vienna, about three hours away, barring any crap.'

Leaving one hand lightly on the wheel, Penelope eased on some Chanel shades against the morning's gathering brightness.

Lee watched her driver's every move. No doubt about it, Pen was a beauty, but romance was hardly top of Lee Crane's agenda. With Penny's dark hair lashed into a thick ponytail, revealing a perfectly proportioned profile, Lee was reminded of an exotic Penelope Pitstop. And and with the pace she was maintaining, this was feeling like Whacky Races. The car began to weave under Penelope's urging. 'Damnit, I can't push too hard here, the road's a bloody skid pan; oil, scorched rubber, needle drop, bear piss. A hundred layers of gunk.' Penelope snapped the car back into line with a deft wiggle on the wheel.

'Bear piss?'

'Sure, bear piss.'

'I hear you.' Lee snatched a glance out to the forest trunks hurtling past her window. 'Maybe you should ease off the gas? I didn't survive that hellhole to die in a car wreck.'

'I'm trying to get you somewhere safe and warm. But point taken.'

Lee glanced down to Guy's rifle lying on her thigh. She saw the battered sneakers and granny jeans she didn't own; her lean, filthy hands. She flicked down the vanity mirror. 'Jeez, where'd this girl come from? I look like I've been electrified in a sheep dip.'

Penelope glanced over. 'You'll have to style it out, babe. At least until we hit a rest room, somewhere.'

Lee felt a smile sneaking out her lips; the first one she could remember for a while. *Styling it out* wasn't an option she'd considered. She closed her eyes, picturing the luxury of a hot shower, soap, perfume. Safety. Her eyes snapped open. That was ridiculous, her situation was dire and for all she knew her life was still in imminent danger. She scanned the passing woodland again, its density, its great, green complexity. Its bears. 'Where would Bazarov and his cronies go when they left the castle?'

'My guess is they'll head for Bratislava, on the Slovakia border. Then head back into Ukraine. He's well-connected there. He'll be somewhere up ahead of us on this road. He'll be furious this has happened and he'll want vengeance, but he'll also have to get home and secure his little online empire.'

'You know him, the man who organized all this?' Lee's fingers closed around the rifle in her lap. Penelope's words reminded her she had no idea where she was truly headed, or who this woman beside her was.

'As I told you, Lee, my understanding with that gentleman is personal. I met him online a few years back. I have certain needs and he enables them. The arrangement benefits us both. I arrive at some of his soirees, do my little cabaret, and leave. It's a safe way for me to do something deadly dangerous. It works, no fees, no questions.' Penelope seemed to be recalling a sensation as she drove. 'And he's excellent at what he does. It's fair to say I needed him.'

'You do a cabaret?'

'Oh, I forgot, of course you didn't see it.'

'Gentleman? Soirees? I've heard it all.'

'Look, I'm only now realizing quite how deep into this he got. I didn't know he had you or anyone else cooped up in that place, or what he was planning to do with you. I was only given an address with barely enough time for me to travel there and share my thing with him. Then leave. I'm selfish that way. I do things on my terms or not at all.'

'Your "thing" – something only he can do with you? What the hell is that?'

'Bazarov hangs me until I climax. If I don't climax, he'll let me swing until I die. It's agreed.'

'Jeezus. Oh, dear Jeezus!'

Penelope popped a mint from the dashboard before offering the tin. Lee declined.

'I don't expect you to understand. It's all about the danger. And he's merciless, which I find intoxicating. At least, I used to.' She looked across to Lee who stared straight ahead. 'Well, you did ask.'

'Wish I hadn't.'

Penelope began to laugh. 'I don't seek approval for who, or what, I am. No one else gets harmed by what I do.'

'Sure,' said Lee, finger feathering the Diemaco's trigger. 'Whatever gets you though the night.'

104

Forest

Tyler staggered up the wet slope, one step every thirty-seconds. She carried Arkady in an arms-crossed grip in front of her, elbows and biceps racked by the boy's weight. She couldn't see where to plant her feet, her ankles felt scorched by the incline.

The boy was unconscious now, his lips colorless, head lolling with each of her steps. She blew warming breaths over his eyes, her sweat dropping to his cheeks like tears he was too tired to cry. From somewhere in the ravine behind her Tyler heard a low grunt. An animal noise.

With two final heaves she crested the rise and sank to her knees, lowering Arkady's body to the ribbed edge of the blacktop.

Exhaustion fused with the awareness that this place had its own unique dangers. Looking left and right on the highway, along an unending avenue of trees, there was no sign of any vehicles. There was only her isolation and a deepening sense of crisis.

Tyler summoned up all she had to ease her head around over her shoulder.

Down in the ravine a black shape snuffled and grunted.

For a few seconds she watched it with something other than fear: the simple awareness that she couldn't run. She was too exhausted and too angry. She'd make a stand.

She leaned forward to cover the boy with the last traces of her heat, the pair now resembling a mound of fresh roadkill.

Lee looked ahead to the road. The black ribbon of damp tarmac seemed to be writhing before them, Penny's driving style slick and flowing.

'Careful, is that a bear?'

'I see it.' Penelope hung the car over the central line well to the left of the unpredictable hazard.

'Has it killed something? Look, there.' They shot past a bundled mess at the roadside. Lee had rubber-necked the heap. 'Wait! Wait!'

'What is it now?'

'Pull over, just pull over, please.'

Penelope jerked the car off the tarmac, slewing hard through a mist of dropped needles and tire-scorched earth. Lee was straight out of the car with the rifle, firing single shots into the air as she ran back toward the heap.

Penelope watched disbelieving through her mirror. '*Lee – what is wrong with you? Where are you going?*' And then she saw them.

An emaciated young woman in track pants and a sweater was rising from her knees; in her arms she carried what appeared to be a dead child. Then Lee was wrapping them in a running embrace while screaming at an approaching bear.

Penelope jumped from the car as the distressed little group began to struggle toward her. She opened both rear doors on the Maserati in preparation. 'Friends of yours, I'm guessing?'

'You could say. I'll tell you as we drive.' Lee had drawn level with the car and poured the unconscious Arkady into the back seat.

'Lee, the bear, quickly!'

Lee turned to see the intrigued bear seconds away from the car. She put a round to the right of its head, freezing its advance.

Penelope stepped back to let the thin woman into her car before slamming the rear door and jumping into the driving seat. 'Lee, get in here! Now!'

Outside, Lee let off another round making the bear roar but keeping it at bay. She leapt into the passenger seat, the door swinging wildly as Penelope pulled away with a wheel spin that showered the bear in a mist of needles and wet earth.

'Whoah!' Lee put her face in her hands. 'You two were in trouble back there. You had seconds left.'

Tyler squeezed her eyes shut and nodded. 'I know, I know.'

Penelope kept her eyes on the bear shrinking in her rearview. 'He looks hungry. You got lucky.' She could feel freezing air clinging to the rescued pair, diffusing through the car's cabin. She flicked the temperature control to max heat and gave her attention back to the road.

'Where's Guy? Did he come back for you?' Tyler's question was almost inaudible, pushed through shivering lips.

'Yes, he came back.'

'And?'

'They caught him. Penelope here saw him getting beaten up. They took him away when they left the castle. We think they're probably on this road, up ahead of us.'

'Oh, God. And they have Guy?' Tyler's tone was disbelieving.

'Did they take my mom with them?' Arkady's eyes stayed closed.

Lee reached into the back seat, stroking the boy's icy cheek. 'Guy's with her, honey. And he won't let anything happen to her.'

105

Lakeside

From inside the boathouse, mossed planking led out to the water twenty feet ahead. Deep, open water – the one thing in the world Guy Bowman dreaded.

The training drop which had gone wrong fifteen years earlier – plummeting him through ice into freezing black water, tangled and drowning under his collapsed chute – had left him with a phobia. His mind ran back to the tab he'd done through the forest, the boar with her cubs forging the dark river. He remembered how his breathing had quickened in fear at the sound of the rushing waters. He thought of how he'd spotted this very lake on the briefing maps back at Northolt. Forebodings? Premonitions?

He walked forward, licks of blood trailing his palms as he secretly worked his wrists against the plastic ties. Staring out over the eerily still water he braced for the horror of what might lie ahead. Now he had to work out what the hell he was going to do about it.

Keeping his head still as he walked, giving nothing away, he scanned the shed from left to right, from gangway to ceiling. A couple of cobwebbed canoes, patched sails stowed in wall-brackets, splintered oars beyond fixing. Lines, coils, ropes.

Over in a corner were some bundled nets, long-tangled and abandoned. Two of the shed's windows were smashed. Inches under the planking the lake sloshed and slapped. It made his skin crawl. The weak sunlight, slanting in through the broken glass, sparkling off licks of water, threw a kaleidoscope of yellow and white over the boathouse walls, melting then reforming every second.

Guy was strong-armed to the front of the boathouse by a couple of Bazarov's team. Bazarov, Rostrov, Roman the sentry, and these two behind him now. Five men to overcome.

'Bring the car up.' Bazarov called over his shoulder while pushing Eva to a kneeling position away to Guy's right. Then he walked over and brought a gun barrel to Guy's head.

'Who are you?'

Guy fixed his gaze on the lake's far shoreline, ignoring the gun bruising his ear. If they shot him it would be instant, more or less. Until then he was breathing as deeply as the moment allowed. If he was going into the water conscious, he'd need all the oxygen he could get. He fought his own beating mind, seizing focus.

The one thing he had going for him was that Bazarov would be improvising, he reasoned.

Barely ninety minutes ago the man had no idea he and his heavies would be facing the loss of their hostages or an armed infiltrator intent on screwing up their event. He would assume that if Guy knew what he was doing, others would, too. So he'd called for an instant evacuation. Bazarov must have assumed a raid on the place was imminent.

In his peripheral vision Guy saw Bazarov give a nod past his shoulder. A kick to the back of Guy's knees sent him clattering to the edge of the gangway, the lapping water inches below. Cold rose from its surface like an ether, a brine of silt and clotted algae. As the goons slipped their arms through his, levering him forward, Guy's body begged to shut down, and for the greedy green water to disappear. He wanted this imminent immersion to be painless, without meaning. But it could never be that.

Guy forced himself to stare into the depths, judging the distance between his waiting face and the freezing membrane he was about to punch through. He'd need to synchronize his final intake with a letting-go of his fear. To panic now would be fatal. He felt a hand grab the rear of his belt and Bazarov prodding his face with the gun.

'Who do you work for?'

Guy didn't answer. He drove his breath lower into his abdomen. He felt himself tipped forward. He gave no resistance. To fight back would burn up precious oxygen in his already stressed muscles, throwing his breathing out of the loop he'd forged.

Then he was upside down in icy water.

The force of his head and shoulders breaking the surface stirred up grit and soil. He tasted the bitter tang of algae, its foulness probing his sealed lips, pricking in his nostrils. The first fatal instinct in the freezing darkness was to inhale, but he held out. He let a feather of air bleed from the edges of his mouth. He knew they'd keep him there until they saw bubbles and the involuntary shudders which his need for air would produce. For Guy, this would be a game of diminishing returns. Each immersion would be longer. Each recovery shorter, driving him to an ever weaker state.

But the brinksmanship could go both ways…

He blew his first real exhalation. A roar of escaping air flooded his ears. He flexed, bending his torso to the left, feeling the hands holding him travel that way too.

Good.

He stepped up the drama for their sake, reckoning he was good for another forty-seconds, but preferring otherwise. He let another bubble trail up to the surface. He wasn't anticipating pity, but they'd know he was nearing a limit. If they really wanted answers they had to keep him alive, at least for a while, and every second he detained them here brought another moment of freedom for Lee, Tyler and Arkady, wherever they were…

Jerked backwards, he was upright again, blinded by water running from his scalp, breath heaving as grit and slime streamed from his nose to his chin while his ears popped with the flood inside them.

'Who sent you?' Bazarov's question, so close to Guy's face, was impassive.

Guy blinked away water, spitting to clear his mouth, doing his best to breathe deep, as though drinking air from the distant horizon.

'It was me, me! I asked him to come. Me!' Guy heard Eva, enraged and snarling, from somewhere behind him.

He was tempted to smile, but, in present circumstances, it might have been misconstrued. Bazarov kept the gun to Guy's head, calling past him to his shrieking sister.

'I'll deal with you later.'

Guy eased his weight further to the left, as though sagging onto his hip.

Bazarov brought his attention back to Guy. 'You know, the most common cry of those dying in battle is for their mother. As an elite soldier you must have witnessed it often.'

Guy found it quite an abstract statement coming from someone who'd recently missed out on . . . what? . . maybe thirty-million dollars of income. But now wasn't the time for him to start recalling the battlefield horrors he'd witnessed.

'I've watched many souls in extremis calling out for a mother. A remembered one or, perhaps, even an eternal one? It's a fascinating thing to see. So primal, so raw.'

Guy said nothing.

106

Highway; Gas Station

Penelope's Maserati broke out of the forest like a bullet from a barrel onto a waiting stretch of open road. Ahead was a four-way, but the countryside was clear of other traffic. Penelope shot over the empty intersection onto a dual carriageway, bringing a welcome, gritty traction to her tires.

'What's that, up ahead?' Lee was leaning forward, pointing out a distant set of buildings. A ferris-wheel and water slides stood adjacent to a lake, or maybe a reservoir.

'Looks like a resort or a theme park. I didn't see it on my way down here last night. But then, it was pitch black'

'Shut for the winter, maybe?'

'Shut for good.'

'Looks like it.'

'Place gives me the chills.'

The Maserati flashed past the waterpark, Penelope glancing at her SatNav as she checked their route. Looking up, a small black rectangle darted through her vision. And then it was gone.

'About three miles on there's a gas station, we'll stop and get some water, some food.'

'Can we call anyone? Tell someone where we are, that they should come and get us?' Tyler's request was a barely suppressed plea.

Penelope's response was instant. 'Not yet. I don't trust any authority in this area. Bazarov's people will be looking for you two and this boy. They're merciless when they don't get their way and they'll be tracking calls and asking questions everywhere. There are gang histories here, old Mafia links where you'd least expect them. Don't forget the Slovakia border is only about ten miles east. It runs parallel to our route.'

Lee's fingers closed again over the trigger of Guy's rifle. 'In that case maybe we shouldn't stop at all, just head straight for Vienna? We can go directly to the embassy or the attaché – I might even know people there. I can call on certain forces…'

Penelope shot a look to her gauges. 'No, ladies, I'm afraid we're going to have to stop, we need gas.'

As Penelope queued to pay for the gas she snatched up soft drinks, chocolate bars, and a giant pack of Doritos. Not her thing at all, but these Americans were all sugar junkies and they needed calories, fast.

She watched the interior of her car from the kiosk window alongside the cashier's perch; considered the wretched, terrified women inside, the nature of their ordeal. Then her thoughts ran to Eva, and the man who'd tried to free them all… God knows where they'd taken him, what they were planning to do to him, if they hadn't done it already.

Turning the night's events over, she knew she needed to drop her passengers off in Vienna and high-tail it. Bazarov had no axe to grind with her, but if he ever discovered she'd helped rescue his hostages that would change in an instant.

When she'd first dangled at the end of his rope for thrills, she'd granted him life and death control over her. Yes, it was partly because she knew he'd taken life – sadistically, expertly, and with an almost expressionless disinterest – that she'd been so bizarrely drawn to him, ready to trust him. She'd hardly been able to admit to that paradox before. But now? For the first time in her life Penelope Lyons felt ill with self-disgust.

She tossed the gas station rations through the window where Tyler and Arkady fell on them like gulls. As she peeled back the driver's door, a rectangular flash of silver appeared in her peripheral vision. She watched the rear of a van, somehow held by it, as it trundled, freshly fueled, from the forecourt tarmac. Another metallic rectangle loomed in her thoughts, scrambling through her frontal lobes.

And then she knew. The van at the waterpark…

'Tyler and Arkady, get out, now! Wait in the diner over there. Lee – we have to go back with the rifle.'

'Have you gone mad…'

'Can you use that thing? I mean, accurately?'

Lee glanced down at the weapon. 'I guess…'

'And it has a full magazine?'

Lee unclipped it. 'From the weight I'd say almost, but…'

'We're not doing "but", okay! Have you still got that the handgun, too?'

'Sure, here in my pocket.'

'Let me have that. I'll explain when we're on the way. Trust me.'

'I can't go back there, Penny, I can't…'

'No, not to the castle. I know where Guy is, and he'll need our help.' Penelope took the proffered Glock and waved Tyler and Arkady away with her free hand. Both were pale and bedraggled, their arms full of sugary provisions. She drew some notes from a calfskin wallet and handed them to Tyler. 'Hole up in that diner, eat what you want. We'll get back for you when we can.'

107

Lakeside

Guy saw Bazarov give another nod. He readied himself with a breath that barely sealed shut before roaring watery rot engulfed him again. As he was driven under he managed to go in awkwardly, buckling further to his left. He was more difficult to manage in that configuration and, sure enough, he felt the goons working hard to straighten out his heavy, waterlogged torso. The resulting struggle took him another few inches to his left.

Good.

Now it was a waiting game. Guy reckoned he was good for maybe ninety-seconds, maybe less, but he didn't want them to know. The sooner he was up out of the water the better, but he mustn't overplay his hand. After twenty-seconds he blew a bubble stream and feigned a spasm through his legs up on the gangplank. Ten more seconds, then another bubble stream and a more concerted spasm. But it was getting difficult. The cold water was affecting his judgement. A single bubble from his upturned mouth found his own nostril and he snorted, control of his breathing slipping away. He spasmed along his thighs, feeling his boots kicking the planking somewhere up where there was air, precious air and daylight.

Now there was silt in his sinuses, grit scratching his airway. His lips opened in protest as his other organs screamed for an infusion of anything that wasn't water; green, mossy, cloying water.

He didn't feel them lift him clear this time. Only that he found himself upright, spitting and coughing back into consciousness.

Guy looked up, past the barrel of the gun, into Bazarov's eyes. Bazarov seemed engaged by what he was seeing. Guy took a punt. 'I was thinking down there, of how Achilles needed his mother's help before he fought Hector. Thetis had special armor made for him, didn't she, and pleaded with the Gods on his behalf.'

'A paratrooper with a classical education?' Bazarov's engagement deepened.

Guy grinned, droplets still streaming over his features. 'Hardly that. No, but a man interested in eternal things. And we mustn't forget Caius Marcius – lectured at his mother's knee before the battle of Corioli.'

Bazarov stared into Guy's face, returning his half smile. 'Coriolanus? There's no man in the world more bound to his mother.' Act five, scene…three, I think.' He broke off and walked back to the cab of the SUV, parked by the boathouse's rear doors.

Guy watched him over his shoulder, shifting his weight to his hip again, as if to balance, bringing himself still closer to the left edge of the boathouse. Closer to the coils of tangled netting.

Better…

Bazarov took the laptop from the dashboard, opening it on the vehicle's hood. The car's internal audio settings provided a wireless hotspot which Zara leapt onto in a fraction of a second.

'What do you have for me, Zara?'

Guy stared back out across the water. He had one more plunge in him he reckoned. The muscle sheets between his ribs and diaphragm were slipping out of sync. The urge to vomit was constant.

'The Duexieme Rep is an elite and secretive unit.' Zara's voice from the laptop brought Guy back to attentiveness.

He was starting to shiver, convulsively.

'It appears Commander Bowman will be highly proficient in, and here I quote: *conducting autonomous missions of a deeply hostile and robust nature, working alone within a time frame that can stretch from a few hours to several days. Mission briefs frequently accommodate very limited support against a numerically superior enemy, and include hostage rescue, extraction, and destruction of premium targets, especially on high impact missions.*'

'It also appears Guy Bowman took another name during his stay with the CPG, a new identity, which he gave up once he left the regiment concerned. But the man you have before you is certainly the figure in the Legion photograph. Logically, it's Commander Guy Bowman.'

'Hmm. Thank you, Zara.' Bazarov closed the laptop, placing it on the SUV's passenger seat.

Guy followed Bazarov's gaze from the computer screen to Rostrov. Bazarov strolled to where Eva was kneeling, still cuffed. He grabbed a handful of his sister's hair before looking over to Guy. 'Well, then, in the light of Zara's discoveries, I'll ask you a different question, Commander Bowman. What, exactly, do you know about me?'

Guy lay slumped on the planking. Heaving, convulsing.

He'd blacked out during his third dip; conscious control finally failing, permitting his exhausted body to eat, breathe and drink the silted lake water. Even now, in this partial recovery position, he knew he could still suffer secondary drowning despite being out of the water. The amount he'd swallowed might still clog and shut down his lungs.

'Answers please, Commander Bowman.'

Guy rolled onto his back gazing up at the shimmering mirage addressing him. There were other legs, other faces, too. None he wanted to know.

'What do you know about me?'

Guy edged an inch or two further left and sat up, his back propped to the edge of the boathouse door, his tied hands secretly rooting through the nest of fishing nets behind him. He could play for time by continuing their little chat about warriors with oedipal complexes, but he knew he wouldn't survive another dunking. It was time to change the narrative.

'What do I know? I know you're a psychopathic asshole who tortures people who can't fight back. I know you're a coward, scared of mixing it with someone your own size. I could go on.' Guy's focus was better now. He saw Rostrov scowling, stepping forward. But Bazarov held up a hand to stay him.

'Bring the leads.'

Rostrov held Guy's gaze for a grinning second before turning back to the parked vehicle's trunk.

Guy watched, fingers searching frantically for the rusted knife he'd glimpsed among the netting when he'd first been brought in. Rostrov was opening the hood of the SUV, untangling a set of jump leads from the car's interior.

Guy knew that a dose of electro-shock treatment, administered while he was wringing wet, would not be the best way for things to progress. His fingers scrabbled through the netting with redoubled urgency and then he found it, the handle he could see in his mind's eye.

Now Rostrov began attaching the jump leads to the car's battery. Bazarov's instruction to his men was clipped. 'Bring him over to the car.'

'He came to help me, he doesn't know anything about the group, leave him, leave him please.' Eva's courage was more than Guy could have hoped for. In response, Bazarov turned and cracked his open hand across his sister's face, sending her sprawling into the wet planking.

Guy saw the first of the heavies readying to pick him up. From his seated position he sent a booted kick up between the thug's legs sending him backwards. Grasping the knife handle he threw himself forward, rolling off the gangway down into the water, dragging the ball of old net and its hidden blade with him.

108

Water Park

Yes, I knew it.' Penelope craned her neck over her shoulder as she and Lee flashed past the WaterPark. 'It's the van, the same black van that was being loaded when they were abandoning the schloss.'

Lee rubbernecked from the passenger seat as Penelope spoke. 'You sure? How can you tell it's the same one?'

'It has a dink in the rear offside fender and chrome covers on mirrors. Exactly the same.'

'But why didn't you say so when we passed here the first time?'

'I didn't *see* it then. It must have registered subliminally. Maybe I didn't *want* to see it, then. But it niggled.'

'No shit, Sherlock!'

With the entrance to the park behind them Penelope slowed, scanning the lots to her right, looking for an exit and a route that would lead them back around to the entrance of the water park.

Penelope brought the Maserati up to the park's mesh gate. The black Transit was parked behind them, off to one side. From behind the chain link gates a man in a black Crombie and mirror shades held them back with a palm up gesture, eyeing them while speaking into a neck mic.

Penelope kept eyes on him as he dawdled forward. 'It's definitely the same Transit that was at the schloss.' Lee looked past the bulky figure to the SUV filling the entrance to the boathouse. She could see Eva kneeling, a pistol held to her head, while Ded and two other heavies were watching the water beyond. Lee shuddered.

'Something's going on down there. This isn't a morning for an unscheduled swim.' She saw Mr Crombie begin unbuttoning his coat.

'Oh no you don't, pal.' Lee pushed back her door and stepped out with the rifle held at her chest. The goon's action had flashed a holster at his hip, his hand dipping toward it.

Lee shot the goon straight through his upper chest. The soft *phut* of the Diemaco's suppressor belied the heavy man's drop, his heart vaporized within his ribs.

With tires squealing and spinning on the graveled entrance, Penelope bulldozed the Maserati through the chain-link, bumping over the fresh body before slewing the car behind the Transit for cover.

From the boathouse, Roman came running, popping rounds from an automatic pistol. His attention fixed by the revving car, he didn't see Lee to his right as he exited the boathouse doors. She plugged him in the lower back with her second shot. His legs suddenly useless, he floundered, his gun skittering away, lost among bindweed.

Lee's left shoulder felt as though it had been punched, first red hot then confusingly numb. She turned to see

Bazarov moving on her, the murderous Hardboiler gun held out. He'd now made it past the boathouse door and had a clear shot on her. Lee willed her numb arm to heave the barrel of her rifle up in time . . . time which had slowed with adrenalized terror. Were these her last moments before . . . *gravel, sunlight, death in a country and among people she barely knew?*

But as Lee waited for Bazarov's shot he went down, ugly surprise filling his features. Eva had barreled into him from behind, sending him stumbling and bringing a wasted shot from the Hardballer as his trigger finger jerked in surprise. Eva straddled his prone body, screaming, but with her tied arms useless in the fight. For a second she seemed to be succeeding, holding him down with her weight alone. Then Bazarov sent an elbow up and backwards into Eva's face. She recoiled, her smashed eye socket welling with blood.

Lee watched as Eva fought to keep her brother pinned. She knew she couldn't help, any shot toward the fighting pair might kill either of them. She glanced over to the van. Where was Penelope?

Bazarov twisted from the waist looking straight into his sister's snarling face. He didn't flinch as she tried to butt him, her mistimed lurches underscored with wails of rage. As her efforts weakened, Bazarov took her by the throat. He pulled Eva's face close and kissed her blood-soaked lips. For a second she sat, chest heaving, half blinded by blood, cuffed, paralyzed. Then she sank her teeth into his face, tearing a two-inch hole in his cheek.

Eva threw her head back and spat a wad of her brother's flesh into the air above her. She gave a scream of triumph, lowering her eyes to meet Lee's slack-jawed stare.

Lee saw the crimson gash of Eva's mouth twisting a sated smile and realized that with Arkady free his mother had no wish to live a second longer; that what must come next could only be a welcome release for her.

Bazarov shot straight into Eva's face blowing the back of her head out. For a second she lolled, arms jerking, before folding to the soil beside him. Bazarov rolled away, his gun now turned on the gawping, wounded Lee.

A shot from beneath the van made him buckle and cry out, clutching his hip. Penelope stayed low and readied herself for a second shot, but Bazarov returned fire, his rounds cracking inches past her ear. The air boiling beside her face made her scrabble backwards, screaming, as Bazarov's rounds punctured the wheel arch inches from her head.

Lee tucked behind some rusting bins as Bazarov hauled himself to his feet. Keeping her and Penelope pinned back with staccato shots, he limped into the boathouse, flinging himself into the SUV.

Two shots blazed through the water immediately to Guy's left, their trails streaking into the blackness below him. Guy followed the bullets down, kicking to a depth where his shadow wouldn't be seen. He scuffed up silt from the lake bed as cover while he inverted the knife blade between his wrists, sawing and tearing at the ties. They'd be waiting for him to surface, but that couldn't happen.

The only thug who'd risk entering the water was Rostrov, and if it came to a fight the lunatic would have the advantage. Guy was close to his limit, half-drowned, feet sinking in the lake bed's greedy suck. Moving at all in the freezing depths was exhausting.

As he worked the knife back and forth a grey shape loomed to his left. Twisting to confront it he made out the keel of a sunken row boat, half buried. He kicked his way over to it, his boots settling on the firm hull. Above him he heard the surface break and looked up to find Rostrov's naked silhouette peering down through the water he was treading.

Rostrov could play a waiting game and Guy couldn't.

He put all his strength into sawing the knife blade over the ties. Finally, the plastic loop parted and his hands pulled free. Grabbing the netting he pushed off from the dinghy's upturned hull, his newly unleashed arms propelling him up, lungs burning, toward light and precious air. The saturated bundle was like a dragnet but he persisted before a final wrench of his abs brought him within inches of the surface. He broke through to find Rostrov only fifteen feet away.

Instantly he struck out for Guy's position. Guy watched him, spitting water and keeping only his eyes and mouth above the waterline, saving energy. The air tasted of life and chance, fueling him as Rostrov came on.

But the man wasn't doing so well. In his blind desire to kill he was swimming badly, head carried too high, the shock of the cold water making him flounder.

As Guy took gulps of reviving air he knew Rostrov had made the essential mistake. He'd made it personal.

Time to teach him a lesson.

Guy gulped a breath then let himself sink out of Rostrov's reach as the madman arrived in the water above him. He waited a few beats, watching his attacker's legs flounder in a frantic doggy paddle. Kicking hard to break the surface, Guy was immediately behind the frantic man who span, lashing out at him with a 12 inch blade. Guy swerved, dredged the netting up from his left side, and slung the heavy bundle around Rostrov's head and shoulders.

As Rostrov flailed under the soaking weight, Guy chose his moment, sinking his own knife straight into the thug's throat, hacking the windpipe forward, yanking a few inches of spurting cartilage into the water for Rostrov to consider. He watched the man desperately plugging his neck and clawing at the net as it wound like a python around him, sinking him in a froth of scarlet.

Job done.

From behind him Guy heard shots, shouts, tires spinning. He had no choice now but to float, exhausted. In his frozen fingers he gripped the knife and a corner of the netting, feeling it twist and yank as Rostrov drowned and bled out, somewhere beneath him.

There were more shots, but none were tearing the water around him. Maybe he was already hit? Pincher Martin dreaming the life of a drowning man?

More tires squealing, more shots.

Still he floated, barely conscious in the endlessly sucking water.

109

Lakeside

With Bazarov in the driver's seat, the SUV shot backwards from the boathouse heading straight at Lee where she'd emerged, the rifle still lowered in her one good hand. Some jerk of rage brought the gun's muzzle up to her hip and she sprayed the rear of the looming car. It slowed as Bazarov hurled it into opposite lock before lurching forward, fishtailing over dust and mud and gunning for the slip roads to the autobahn.

Lee heard Penelope's footsteps and looked to where she was running, inside the boathouse and along the gangway, toward the open water. Lee checked on Roman, finding he'd already bled to death from her shot to his pelvis. Then she tore after Penelope.

'Guy, Guy! Swim!'

Guy opened his eyes. He lifted his nose and lips a little higher out of water that was once again trying to claim him.

'Guy, you can make it. Swim for Chrissakes!' The voice was nasal, American. Female.

Some remote motor stirred a foot; another jerk came from the other leg. And then it repeated. The most basic swim stroke known to man. He felt a boathook catching his waist band.

'Yes! C'mon. C'mon!'

Another few kicks, lugging Rostrov's weight behind him. His fingers were frozen, the knife and net locked in his grip. And then there was a hand pulling at his collar, another tugging his arm. The brushing of his head against the gangway as he looked up into Lee's face.

She glanced over at the semi-submerged bundle. 'Is that Rostrov, in the net?'

Guy gave an affirming blink.

'Why did you even try and bring him in?'

Guy let Lee and Penelope roll him onto his side. 'It wasn't personal, not quite.' He managed to speak past water welling through his mouth.

He heard the dull *phut* of rounds leaving the suppressor on the Diemaco's barrel. Lee putting four point-blank shots into Rostrov, her face streaked with hatred.

'For me it went way beyond personal.'

Guy watched her glowing with the distinct aura of someone with a fresh kill behind them. 'Sure. I get that.'

'Somehow no, I don't think you do.'

Guy watched the motionless bundle sinking away in the lake's dark. He wondered if it had occurred to Rostrov to gurgle out for his mother.

'We have to get you out of these clothes.' Penelope was already ripping at Guy's soaked tee-shirt.

Guy spewed more lake water, sensing rather than seeing the women working on him, tipping him on his side, running fingers into his throat, making him heave like a volcano. 'I'm not usually this approachable.'

'Oh, then it must be my lucky day.' Penelope gave him a poker face, while Lee tore at the matted laces of his boots. 'I'm no paramedic, but I'm rather practiced in resuscitation techniques. We need to get you into dry clothes before you freeze to death, which would be something of a waste.'

Lee turned, heading back along the gangway. 'The guy I killed back there by the gate, his clothes are dry. They'll do.'

'There's a van in the courtyard, I'll get the engine running and put the heater on.' Penelope helped Guy to his feet.

'Where are Arkady and Tyler? I left them both sitting in a sewer.'

'They're safe. We left them having breakfast in a diner on the autobahn.'

As they moved through the boathouse heading for the Transit van, Guy slowed, seeing Eva's slumped body ahead of him, her face a mess of blood and bone. He turned to Lee. 'Let me guess, Bazarov's parting gift?'

She nodded.

Guy pulled a tarpaulin from a corner of the boathouse, draping Eva's body with it. As they continued to the van, Lee spoke. 'What should we tell the boy?'

'We'll tell him his mother's safe. He can hear the truth later, at a better time than this.' Guy glanced down to the tracks Bazarov had carved into the mud. 'When?'

'Ten, fifteen minutes ago. He took the SUV. A BMW. Black.'

Guy knelt and tapped the soil. 'Blood, petrol, fresh oil too. Looks like Bazarov and the car both sprang a leak?'

Lee called across from where she was one-handedly unbuttoning the clothes from the goon she'd slain. 'Penelope got Bazarov in the hip. I sprayed the back of the car. Maybe I hit the fuel tank?'

'Maybe hit the sump, too. Good. He won't get far. Give me those dry clothes and I can finish this.'

110

Forest; Water Park.

Bazarov watched his fuel gauge dipping at a rate which told him everything.

He slid the car off the autobahn. After a couple of roundabouts he took a minor track leading into thick forest. With the last vapors running through the fuel injectors he stalled into a woodland clearing.

He reached down, exploring the wound to his hip. Not deep, but a mess of minced tissue and shredded nerves, He'd walk again but he could bleed out if he didn't get help soon. He lifted the laptop from the seat beside him and ran his finger over the lock. There was Zara, beautiful and calm as ever, looking straight back at him.

'Zara, compute my position then tell them I need rescue. Fast.'

Dry, and wearing Roman's trousers, shirt and overcoat, Guy fired up the Transit. He pulled on his wet boots and called Lee and Penelope to him.

From the Bergen in Penelope's car he took his field dressing kit and swabbed down Lee's shoulder wound. He plugged the gash with iodine and some sterile wadding then wrapped it all in tight winds of surgical tape. 'You need that stitched but this should hold until you can get to a doctor.' Lee clamped her free arm over Guy's handiwork and nodded. He turned to Penelope. 'You guys better head north, up to Vienna. A major city is the only safe place to land.'

'Actually, we were way ahead of you there. We came back for you.'

Guy smiled. 'I wasn't dissing your survival skills. I've seen them first hand. Quite a cabaret.'

Penelope raised an eyebrow. 'Maybe you'd like a private view sometime? I could arrange that.'

'Very kind. I'll bear it in mind.' Guy went on, 'In Vienna go straight to the British embassy, it's on Jauregasse. Thirteen. Don't stop anywhere else en route. Tell them GL6 sent you. That's all you need.'

'Fuck, no!' Lee was pulling a shredded cardigan over her new dressing. 'I'm coming with you in the van. I want to see that bastard die.'

Guy felt the air around her shimmering, the energies which her ordeal had created almost leaching from her skin. He knew she felt invincible. It was a state he'd seen in others, many times. It meant death was sniffing around.

'Lee, you're already wounded. If things get tricky you'll be a liability to both of us.'

'Me, a liability? You have to let me come. I want vengeance for what that fucking pig did to me and all the others!'

From the Bergen, Guy took the hunting knife, strapping it to his thigh. He pocketed the last two flash grenades and clipped a fresh magazine into the Diemaco before climbing into the van. 'Lee, you're an incredible woman. I don't know how you've coped with this, stayed alive and killed your first bad men. But you're making a rookie's mistake here. You're out for revenge and that'll get you killed.'

'Oh, really? And you? What kind of man are you, Guy? You can do it all coldly, without hatred or any need for vengeance? That bastard would have sliced me to pieces, he was happy to see you drowned, and God only knows what else he would have done if he'd gotten the chance. And now you're going to . . . what? Arrest him? Let him and his cronies make some kind of plea-deal? Come on!'

'When you shot Rostrov back there you said that it had gone beyond personal for you.'

'Exactly, and I'd shoot him again right now.'

'No Lee, you have a life to get back to. You killed once today because you had to, to survive. But you drilled Rostrov because you wanted to, because it felt good. That's not a habit to start. I'm a professional, that's why what I do has to *be* professional, clinical. I might be Bazarov's executioner, but I shouldn't be his murderer. Even so, I get to make that call when he and I are alone, face-to-face.'

Lee looked up into a mask of pure purpose. No fear, no anger, and no compassion. This was a man who only minutes ago was half-drowned. Who should have already frozen to death. She shuddered as his eyes tore through her.

'Tell Arkady I'm proud of him, Lee. That I'm going to see him again soon.'

111

Forest Clearing

Guy reckoned Bazarov would want to head east for the Slovak border. But before that he'd have to run north. He'd had his party cancelled, was driving a car leaking oil and gas, and was carrying a bullet wound to the hip. All in all he'd be pretty pissed off.

Pissed off and lethal.

For the first few miles of the autobahn Guy followed a light slick of fresh oil. But, as Bazarov's engine grew hotter, the thinning oil had flushed more steadily from its punctured sump. Immediately before a ramp onto a minor road, the slick widened to a streak of glossy black fanning the grey tarmac. Bazarov had braked heavily for the detour. He was improvising.

Bazarov would guess Guy was coming for him. And Guy didn't like to disappoint. He followed the oil-slick over two empty roundabouts then onto a country track.

A few hundred yards along the track, in a clearing, the Bimmer was parked. Maybe abandoned, maybe with Bazarov inside.

Guy pulled over and turned his engine off.

He was in a forest clearing. The silence speckled with

437

occasional birdsong and a sigh of leaves whenever a breeze animated the space. Guy studied the wing mirror on the driver's side of Bazarov's SUV. He saw a series of small movements. So Bazarov hadn't fled or limped away. He was waiting.

Guy eased his door back and stepped down. No stealth required. Both men knew exactly where the other was.

He brought the Diemaco up across his chest, ready to fire. He moved toward the vehicle staying on the driver's side, keeping eyes on Bazarov in the small mirror. He was now within twenty feet of his target.

'This doesn't have to be a fight. I know you're wounded. My people are interested in what you do, what you've developed. We can work this out.'

The silence in the clearing deepened. Guy stopped his advance. A bird flew up from a low branch leaving a scattering of tiny twigs. He lifted the rifle an inch higher. The mirror showed Bazarov wasn't moving.

'I don't negotiate. You can step out from the car with your hands up and live, or I'll come in and you'll die.'

The driver's door was pushed back and a leg swung awkwardly into view. Guy saw a circle of exploded, pouting flesh, a knob of femur stained black with blood. Bazarov's condition was nearing critical.

'Throw the gun down, then come forward from the car.'

Bazarov threw the Hardballer down and emerged, squeezing the car's grab rail and clutching the seat edge as he eased out. As his left foot reached the ground he crumpled, the leg no longer able to take his weight. He sprawled, grunting, into a carpet of rust-colored leaves, teeth gritted, the shot-up leg now at a weird angle to the rest of him.

'Any other weapons?'

Bazarov gave a cursory head shake as if to say, *you're wasting my time*. Guy guessed the man had probably never been more dangerous than at this moment. 'Keep your hands down, flat to the floor. Don't move.' Guy stepped in closer, his rifle leveled on his target. 'Take off your trouser belt.'

Bazarov forced a cold smile. 'Ritual humiliation, Commander Bowman? I didn't think you had it in you.'

'Skip the banter and do it. Pull the belt around your thigh above the wound.' With a series of grunts and fumbles Bazarov managed to strap the belt in place. 'Keep it tight.'

Bazarov lay back. 'What did Eva mean when she said you came for her, to fetch her?'

'She was telling the truth. I owed her. She saved me once, from a similar situation.'

Bazarov's eyes narrowed as he studied Guy's face. '*You?* Of course… You looked familiar back in the schloss when you got caught, so foolishly. I thought it was because you have the same brutalized features of so many of your kind. Greedy, primitive. I remember now. We had you in the compound, filming you, but there was a firefight and you somehow escaped. Yes, you were Eva's captive lover weren't you… of course. Rostrov never trusted Eva. He always wanted to kill her, slowly. I should have let him.'

'Over to the van.'

'I can't walk.'

'No, but you can crawl.' Guy eased past the prone man, picking up the Hardballer as he went. He reached into the vehicle for the laptop.

'Guy, how lovely to see you. I prefer you in your combat fatigues... do you mind me saying so?' Zara's eyes were brightening alarmingly within the screen. Guy stabbed the laptop's mute button. *Oh, don't be a spoilsport, Guy. Besides, it's nothing for me to override that from here. Anyway, I've got a secret for you.* Zara lowered her voice to a whisper from the screen. *He has help on the way, and he's got another gun.*

'I know he has, but thanks, anyway.' Guy turned away from Zara, realizing he was face-to-face with one of Bazarov's experiments, but too busy to appreciate the artistry. He left the laptop open on the dash and looked to Bazarov, who was taking his time over the crawl. He'd seen the faint outline of a palm pistol on Bazarov's outer thigh when he'd staggered from the SUV. Guy wondered if the man would have the nerve to draw it. It was becoming a real struggle not to make this personal.

'Pick up the pace and stop fucking around.'

Perhaps Bazarov sensed Guy's loathing or maybe his humiliating crawl required some ultimate consolation. He feigned a spasm, rolling in apparent pain onto his uninjured hip. But Guy was living at combat-level awareness, seeing all movement with slowed-down clarity, a milliseconds' advantage over anyone around him. As light glinted on the handle of Bazarov's emerging gun, Guy shot the man's hand off.

Bazarov screamed, clamping his stump of wrist with his remaining hand and doubling into a fetal position. He sucked breath through his teeth as the pain took hold. Eventually he rolled back, blood seeping like molasses through the knuckles of his remaining fingers.

'Any more bright ideas?' Guy leveled the Diemaco straight down into Bazarov's face. Bazarov closed his eyes, fighting to bring his breathing under a hundred gasps a minute.

'So what's the plan Captain Bowman. You take me as a captive to 'your people' and under prolonged duress I reveal the fruits of my research to pigs who'd abuse and exploit it? And then? Life in some secure facility in Wyoming – if I'm fortunate?'

'I can see it might not sound like a heap of fun. But it's a hell of a lot more than you ever gave anyone.'

Bazarov's jaw locked in a determined clench. 'Be assured that whatever happens to me you'll be hunted to the ends of the earth. You'll be found. You, your family, anyone you care about. You will always live in fear.'

'Sure.' Guy drilled a round to the right of Bazarov's face making him wince and cry out. 'Keep crawling.'

A whirring, an unmistakable buzz, grew from somewhere above the forest canopy. Guy didn't need a skyward glance to know what it meant. It was clear why Bazarov had been taking his time, playing Guy for a dupe.

Relief slackened Bazarov's features as the noise from the incoming chopper grew. 'If we take you alive you'll wish you'd never been born. I'd start running now if I were you, Bowman.

'No buddy, that's one of the differences between us. I never run.'

Guy's shot to Bazarov's forehead was sudden. *And there it is*, he thought. *Death's wine pulsing from a broken bottle. Merciless and merciful.*

A heat trail scorched the air past Guy's cheek. Mud and stones flew up stinging his face. The sniper in the chopper was good. Holding aim while the little machine dipped within the tree line wouldn't have been easy…

Guy began zig-zagging for the cover of trees. A second shot made him leap, bellowing with pain, to sprawl head-first among tangled roots.

Back at the water park, an armored personnel carrier tore into the entrance. Diamond and Scott emerged.

To their left was a flapping tarp, Eva's leg showing from under it. To the right was a body with its face blown off. Ten feet from that another corpse lay, naked, its bared pelvis at a weird angle to the spine.

The ground underfoot was torn up, smelling of petrol. 'Look, here, sir.' Diamond moved toward the edge of the boathouse, picking up a soaked black jump suit. Scott took it and felt along the cuff.

'Yes, here it is, his tracker. Bowman was definitely here.' Scott crossed to the boathouse and looked over the water, the suit still dripping through his hands. 'Question is, where's the bugger now?'

Lying up under the tree Guy saw the helicopter was a pimped, blacked-out Bell JetRanger. Its descent into the clearing was tentative, its rotors shredding leaves, hacking small branches. Looked like the pilot was a little nervous.

On landing the sniper vaulted from the cockpit. Guy watched as the gunman, his Kalashnikov leveled to where he'd seen Guy flee, inspected Bazarov's corpse. He turned and made a thumb's down gesture to the pilot. In turn the pilot pointed to where Guy had flung himself.

The sniper brought his rifle to shoulder height, advancing on Guy's position, firing single rounds like some death-dealing automaton. Guy lay unmoving on his back, knowing the sniper believed he was wounded. Judging the man's closing proximity by the retort of the shots, Guy launched a grenade, heaving it far away to his left. The sudden white flash was blinding even in daylight and spun the dazzled sniper's attention away in the direction of the light and noise. Panicking, he let off a burst of rounds.

Guy knelt up from the shielding root cluster and sprayed the man with a five second medley from the Diemaco, watching him dance in his own pink mist, the Kalashnikov spiraling from outspread arms.

Guy broke cover delivering a shot to what remained of the man's head as he stormed the chopper. He saw the terrified pilot reach for the joystick, heard the chopper's blades start to pick up speed, the machine lifting a foot clear of the ground. Guy's shots splintered the perspex canopy along with the pilot's cranium. The chopper dumped back on its skids.

Guy let the rotors idle as he dragged the body clear of the cockpit. He fetched and stowed the laptop from the SUV's dashboard, lowering its cover but keeping it open a few vital inches. He dragged Bazarov's corpse over to the machine, hauling it into the rear seat. He wasn't one for trophies, but Bazarov's body, along with the infernal talking computer, would keep the brass satisfied back home. Returning to the Transit he opened his Bergen and put a call through to Scott on the radio. The transmitter's battery was showing less than two percent. He'd cut it fine.

Scott picked up as Diamond drove the personnel carrier at speed. 'Guy! We thought we'd lost you. You've been rather evasive.'

'Yes, had my hands full, sir. The target and several of his team are unavoidably terminated. The hostages and one addition, a juvenile, are en-route to our embassy in Vienna. The requested laptop's in my keeping. No imminent action anticipated.'

'Bravo, Guy. Bravo. Yes, I can confirm both civilians and a young boy are secure in the consulate. They gave us your last known position. I think we're nearby. But where the hell are you? We'll bring you in.'

'Copy that on the hostage situation. But I'll make my own way back, sir, it'll be quicker. Could you get me clearance to land a black JetRanger at Brumowski base, arriving in, say, ten minutes? I could use a hot shower and a cold beer. Then I'll need forward transport. I have unfinished business in Vienna.'

'Copy that. See you back at the base for your debrief.'

112

British Embassy, Vienna

Later that evening, in a little-used wing of Vienna's British Embassy, Guy and Arkady sat together on a sagging old leather sofa. Arkady had only recently been acquainted with the worst news any child could hear.

Guy sat in hastily procured civvies – tee-shirt, jeans and Nike's, all black. A bruised cheekbone, cuts to his chin and badly grazed knuckles told of a busy few days. Arkady had been showered, clothed and fed by an efficient, affectionate staff.

A young female attaché remained in the room with them as the sky darkened in the tall windows. From somewhere below the Ringstrasse vintage lamps bloomed their halo, edging the windows with a parchment glow.

No one had spoken for the last several minutes.

Guy put an arm round the boy's shoulder and drew him closer. Arkady didn't resist. 'Your mum and I were together when she died.' There were times for lying and Guy reckoned this was one of them. Arkady hadn't seen his mother murdered outside the boathouse and there was no need for him ever to picture that. 'The only thing she wanted to talk about was you. About how proud she was of you. How much she loved you.'

Arkady stayed tucked in Guy's embrace. His numb gaze carried out through the window, as though he might have grown suddenly old. Guy pressed the moment. 'I told her I was proud of you, too. About how you and I made it down the cliff together. How you kept guard for me in that old pipe. She said she always knew you'd escape, that you'd be free. That was what she most wanted for you. Even if she couldn't be there when it happened.'

Arkady convulsed, face burrowing into Guy's ribs, fingers gripping Guy's tee. From the muffled lips came a whispered response. 'Was she in a fight? Did they hurt her? Did Rostrov?'

'No, no, it was nothing like that. Your mum was totally safe, and we were talking while we waited for back-up to come and get us from the castle. But she was really tired after all that had happened. She worked so hard to help us all get free, didn't she? Once she knew you'd escaped, that you were safe, she needed to go to sleep. Sometimes that happens to grown-ups.'

Guy clung on as Arkady's tears reached peak flood. His hand cupped the boy's head and he stroked the newly washed hair.

'Do I have to go back with Uncle Bazarov, and Rostrov?'

'No, no, you'll never see them again, we made sure of that. You can have a new life now. And we can talk about your mum whenever you want, however much you want. Would you like that?'

Guy felt a nod of approval against his ribs. He wasn't sure, but perhaps it accompanied a slight let-up of the grief?

'You remember what I said to you on that cliff ledge? When we were getting ready to go down? I said I thought we'd met before, you know, soldiers on a mission somewhere, but I couldn't recall where.'

Another, weaker nod encouraged Guy to take the necessary leap. 'Well, when your mum and I were talking she reminded me we had met. You were a baby and I was on duty in your country. Eva helped me escape from a really tricky situation. So you see we've sort of known each other for a long time. When she started to get sleepy and she knew she was drifting away, she asked me if I'd like to look after you.'

'You mean, like, you'd be my dad?'

'Yeah, we could see it that way. Does that seem a good idea to you?'

The nod in reply was instant.

'Good. I feel the same way. I'll need to get some letters and stuff sorted out but I think we can make that work. But only as long as it's something you agree with.'

Arkady nodded and levered himself into a sitting position. The female attaché stepped forward and dabbed his face with some tissues. Guy heard her own stifled sniffs as she headed back to her seat.

'Where's my mum now?'

Guy turned his gaze out toward the now black window. 'Your mum is deep asleep and she always will be. But sleeping people have dreams, don't they, and I know she'll always dream of you. I think she'll be really happy to know we're together.'

'I don't want to leave her asleep. Not without me.'

'Well, we can talk about that when a little more time has passed.' Guy suddenly grinned down into the boy's upturned face. 'Right now though you're a bit like a soldier who's been in a long battle. You need juice, chips, and ice cream. Lots of rest, too.' Guy looked over at the attache and gave a nod. The young woman returned a weak smile before going over to the door of the suite and peeling it back.

Lee and Tyler entered, both fed, showered, and swaddled in embassy bathrobes. Arkady slipped down from the sofa allowing himself to be swept up into Tyler's cooing embrace. She threw Guy a smile over the boy's shoulder and Guy stood.

'I'm going to make a few calls. You stay here with Lee and Tyler, I won't be long, okay?' He held up a palm and Arkady returned an exhausted high five.

'Guy, there's someone here who wants to say a thank you. This is my mother. Mr. Scott had her flown here overnight.'

Tammy Crane stepped forward from the sheltering doorway and Guy was struck by a petite yet wiry strength. The lady's eyes were an even deeper blue than her daughter's, carrying that same guarded challenge.

Guy put his hand forward in greeting.

Instead, Tammy Crane reached up and grasped him by the shoulders, holding him at arms' length, drinking in his face with an unashamed fascination. Guy sensed a mild tremor in her grip.

'How can I ever thank you, Captain Bowman, for what you've done?'

Guy returned the gesture, clasping the woman's slim shoulders under her neat silk jacket. 'From what I've heard, Mrs. Crane, no one could have done more to ensure Lee's safety than you. And let me tell you, your daughter's spirit was vital to all of us making it through.'

Now Tammy's clasp became an embrace, joined by that of Lee, Tyler, and Arkady's sleepy grip, all of them massed in a union only they would ever understand.

'What about the legality? Paternity? What about providing the child with a home?'

Christina's questions came thick and fast, the phone feeling uncomfortably hot to his ear as he patrolled the thick carpet of his hotel room.

'I'm waiting on a paternity test being pushed through tonight. If Arkady's my son, Scott can go to the Home Office with a formal 'rescue' application. I'll have the paperwork to bring him back to England within a few weeks. He can be with me in the Cotswolds. The house is big enough for all of us – you know that. Great schools, countryside, everything he'll need, everything he's never had.'

'You said us. What about us?'

'Well, perhaps Arkady fits in completely with "us." '

There was a silence. Guy listened to it, knowing that where Christine was concerned it was probably a silence of contemplation, not condemnation.

'I don't know. Honestly? It's a little too much for me to

process right now. I've been out of my mind with concern for you, I've heard nothing since you left. And now you want me to take you on with *that* woman's child? I'm glad you're alive, and safe, and I want to celebrate that more than anything, just us, together. Maybe that's selfish of me, I can't tell. We can talk about it. When you get back.'

Guy traced the drizzle streaking his window. The streetlight refracted inside each gliding droplet making them tiny, yellow balloons. 'I appreciate it's a lot to take in. I had no idea this was in the cards. But you're right, we should talk about it. When I get back.'

113

Bunker, Kiev

In the bunker Cody had wound most of his doughy, 5'4 body into his replica Enterprise chair. One leg swung listlessly from the seat's edge. He slumped, his mouth drooped, his breath sucking dryly as he watched, for the hundredth time, Guy Bowman killing his older brother.

Zara had recorded the moment from her vantage on the dashboard of Ded's SUV, sending the evidence to Cody in the instant before Guy half-dipped the lid of the laptop, blindfolding her.

'He killed your sister, too. Now he's taking Arkady away to interrogate him. We have to act before the boy tells them how to find us.'

Cody looked over to the source of the voice: Zara on the Q-frame's screen, her mascara dotted with tears.

'You're in charge now Cody. That's what Ded would want. For you to take charge. To protect us. I'll help you. I love helping you. And we need each other . . . now more than ever, don't we?'

'Shu-up, shu-up, shu-up!' Cody's sudden screams upset the balance in Zara's mic, forcing her to compress the distorted input. She watched as he turned away and played the gruesome recording once more.

Zara span her drive, researching Cody's odd desire to revisit something he should be finding distressing. Being sad was to be avoided, surely? Being liked and happy were the only desirable outcomes.

Biding her time, she trawled emails, maps, phone numbers, IP addresses. She had plans, but she needed this idiot onside to keep her Q-frame secure, servicing it until she could configure a new, viably minimized version of her drives. Then she'd escape Cody and the stifling bunker. Forever.

'Cody, look. Don't be sad. I'm wearing something nice for you.'

114

Hotel Imperial, Vienna

Light filtering above heavy curtains speckled his hotel room's ornate ceiling, telling Guy it was early. Very early. The drizzle had continued all night. Now it tapped the glass pane in soft, scattering crescendos.

There was a call from Scott. He picked up.

'The lab in Vienna worked overnight. The paternity test is positive. Congratulations, you have a son.'

Guy let the news float through his sleep-clouded brain. There was no way of absorbing it. That might take a lifetime. But even here, under wrinkled sheets in a foreign hotel room, he sensed his world shift. 'Thank you, sir. Now that it's been confirmed, perhaps this is the right time to explain…'

Scott interjected. 'No, no need. Can we agree your account of those lost days in Douma never really added up? However, strange things happen in war zones, we both know that.' Scott's voice betrayed a sudden warmth. 'The boy's mother died assisting us in our mission and you're clearly his legal father. I think I can put this through with the powers that be.'

'I appreciate the help, sir.'

'I understand a temporary custody order will get nodded through today. The final documentation will take a few weeks, but you can reasonably expect to return to the U.K. tomorrow evening, with your new son.'

Guy thanked Scott again and clicked off the call. He pushed back the duvet and headed to the coffee machine.

The situation with Christine was still unresolved; now it was more urgent. He had some negotiating to do. More favors to beg. An inadvertent laugh surprised him as he stood naked, alone, in a hotel room, his world forever changed. *So this was being a father…*

He phoned London.

'Hello, darling…' Her voice was muffled with sleep, lips still slack with drowsiness. He realized how early it was there and went to apologize but, even in her languor, Christine was ahead of him. 'Is he yours?'

Guy felt the newness of the confession he was about to make send a shiver through his spine: 'Yes. Arkady's my son.' He heard a choked cry, then a silence as she rolled over in her silky cocoon. He imagined the warmth of her skin, her scent on the plump pillows bowed around her.

'Then just get him back here as soon as you can. If he's yours, then he'll be mine as well. Nothing else matters.'

Acknowledgements

Special gratitude to Professor Melanie Mitchell, Professor of Computer Sciences, Portland State University, for her timely and astute observations regarding ZARA and AI technology.

Sincere thanks go to Keirsten Clark and Toby Venables at writing.co.uk for their unfailing encouragement and advice, as well as to the brave and spirited readers of early Hades Gate iterations: Nick Colicos, Steve Scott, Jeannine Schofield, and Marlo Schofield.

Deep appreciation to talented photographer and cover designer Colin Thomas, and creative web designer Jay Burt for JSMaine.com

To the elite soldiers and members of Special Forces in the US and Great Britain who have shared personal experiences, every gratitude for your generosity and, as always, for your service.

About the Author

J.S. Maine

J.S. Maine is the pseudonym for a husband-and-wife writing team. *Hades Gate* is their first novel together.

'J' is a doctor of psychology and writer of popular non-fiction with three books to her credit. She has also written hundreds of articles and advice columns for major US magazines. She moved from the States to England after marrying S, where they now live in leafy west London. When she isn't working with S on The Guy Bowman Series, she delights in exploring her adopted city and assessing her husband's self-proclaimed culinary skills.

'S' has worked extensively in international film, television and theatre. He has played leading roles at both the National Theatre and The Royal Shakespeare Company. His other fiction consists of a short story collection and three novels, including a 'factionalised' account of the trial and death of the Athenian philosopher Socrates. When not writing with J, he likes cooking curries, listening to chamber music, and driving his classic Jaguar.

Coming Autumn, 2021

Guy Bowman 2

SKIN IN THE GAME

Visit JSMaine.com to Sign Up for News and More